Catherine Banner began writing her debut novel, *The Eyes of a King*, at the age of fourteen, after school and on summer holidays. In 2006 her portrait was displayed in the Exceptional Youth Exhibit at the National Portrait Gallery, which showcased talented and inspiring young Britons. Catherine was also featured in the *Observer's* 2008 'Cool List'. She is currently in her second year at Cambridge University, studying English. *Voices in the Dark* is the second novel in the trilogy, and Catherine is now working on the third title.

VOICES
IN THE
DARK

Catherine Banner

CORGI BOOKS

VOICES IN THE DARK
A CORGI BOOK 978 0 552 55661 3

First published in the USA by Random House Children's Books,
a division of Random House Inc.
First published in Great Britain by Corgi Books,
[an imprint of Random House Children's Books
A Random House Group Company]

This edition published 2010

1 3 5 7 9 10 8 6 4 2

JF

The Random House Group Limited supports the Forest Stewardship Council (FSC),
the leading international forest certification organization. All our titles that
are printed on Greenpeace-approved FSC-certified paper carry the FSC logo.
Our paper procurement policy can be found at www.rbooks.co.uk/environment.

Set in Bembo

Corgi Books are published by Random House Children's Books,
61–63 Uxbridge Road, London W5 5SA

www.**kids**at**randomhouse**.co.uk
www.**rbooks**.co.uk

Addresses for companies within The Random House Group Limited can be found at:
www.randomhouse.co.uk/offices.htm

THE RANDOM HOUSE GROUP Limited Reg. No. 954009

A CIP catalogue record for this book is available from the British Library.

Printed in the UK by CPI Bookmarque, Croydon, CR04TD

NIGHTFALL,
THE TWENTY NINTH
OF DECEMBER

I want more than anything to tell you the truth about my life. I am a criminal, also a liar. But I swear this will be a true account.

That was how I began as the coach drew away from the city, south and then west into the darkness of the moors. The woman opposite me was pretending to sleep, one arm around the shoulders of her little boy. The old man next to me kept sighing and shaking his head. He was saying the rosary; the quiet clicking of the beads was the only sound. We were all avoiding each other's glances. The snow and fire behind us made wild patterns on the glass. Every few seconds, the old man glanced back and sighed again, as though he had left a good life behind him. Fires were blazing on the walls of the castle, throwing black smoke over the stars. I imagined that he had some ordered existence in the city, and this ritual was all that he could carry of it with him into the unknown.

I owned nothing but the clothes I wore and the contents of the pockets. I kept checking them to see that everything was still there. I had given the driver fifty crowns and my christening bracelet as payment; by the time we set off, it was nearly midnight, and the queues at the harbour stretched a mile. But I still had a pencil and a stack of papers and a box of matches and a candle and the medallion Aldebaran had given me.

We did not speak to each other. This would be a long journey, ngers and had nothing to say.

sary beads, but ever since I was

in stories; they came more easily

t out on this journey, I had thought

rything down and explain it. And yet

ly this time. It was nearly impossible to

the coach, and my heart was heavy. I put

pocket and tried to sleep.

the coach!' someone shouted when we had

s. It was only the driver, cursing at a broken

wheel and grumbling about him with his rifle raised. Ahead were the lights of a village. We would have to stop for the night here, the driver told us. If he fixed the wheel now, the horses would be too cold to continue, and besides, this road was dangerous. We would go on to the next inn and stop there. The woman made some protest about this. A cold wind was sweeping over the snow, driving it in gusts against the windows of the carriage. We stepped down, shivering. The little boy clung to his mother's overcoat. I offered to take one of her cases, but she shook her head. The driver unhitched the horses and led them beside him, and we walked in silence towards the lights.

None of us had money for a bed, so we all ended up in the front room of the inn. This was just a windswept village in the middle of nowhere. The little boy and his mother slept in a corner with their heads on the table. The old man got out his rosary again, then put it away and ordered a bottle of spirits and sat there drinking it and watching the snow fall. I listened to the wind growling and thought about what I would write. Then I got out the paper and pencil and began again. But it was no good. I sighed and crossed out the start of it.

The inn sign creaked and rattled in the wind outside. I could not write; every time I tried, it was wrong. When this had gone on *for some time, the old man got up and came towards my table, holding out the bottle of spirits. 'Here,' he said. 'Maybe it will cure your writer's depression.'*

'It's kind of you.'

He poured me a glass, then waited to see if I would let him sit down at the table. I drew out a chair. He settled slowly, flexing each finger so that the joints cracked. I could tell from his face that he had once been handsome, and his eyes were quick and kind. I sipped the spirits and waited for him to say something else.

'Where are you going?' he asked eventually.

I shrugged. 'I don't really know.'

'Neither do I. I am trying to find my family. Maybe they have gone to Holy Island; that's what I am thinking. But there again, they could be somewhere else.'

'I'm supposed to be going to Holy Island too,' I said. 'But . . .'

'But you don't think you will,' he said. 'Now that you have set out.'

'How did you know?'

'Ah,' he said. 'A lifetime of studying human nature. Now, tell me what you are trying to write.'

I thought about this for a long time. 'A letter to my brother,' I said eventually. 'I've done a very bad thing. I don't know if he'll forgive me, but I want to explain. And I want to tell him . . .' I hesitated.

'Go on,' said the old man kindly.

'I want to tell him the truth. He's only a baby now, but I want to record it, for when he grows up. I was never told the truth, you know? And I think if he knows it, he will stand a chance.'

He nodded for me to continue.

'And I want to tell him about our life in the city,' I said. 'Because that's all gone now. He'll never know it.'

'Admirable,' said the old man.

'Not really,' I said. 'Not if you knew.'

'So tell me,' he said. 'Maybe it will make it easier to write if you tell me first.'

'Do you think so?' I said.

He shook his head. 'I can't tell. It depends.'

'It is a long story,' I said. 'It would take a while to explain.'

'This will be a long journey,' said the old man.

I folded the paper and drank the rest of the glass of spirits. It burned in my chest like fire and gave me courage and made me melancholy at the same time. He introduced himself at last as Mr Hardy. I told him my name was Anselm. We sat there talking about nothing at all for a long while, and the wind cried like voices in the dark outside. Then, as the darkness drew on, I started to tell him the story. There was nothing else to do on this bleak night. I told him how it started with our shop and with the graveyard and with the old days on Citadel Street, and there I got confused and fell silent, trying to think where it began. 'With Aldebaran's funeral,' I said eventually.

'Aldebaran is dead?' he said, and started as though he had been struck in the chest.

'Yes,' I said. 'He died in July. Did you not know?'

He shook his head. Everyone in the country knew it, but this man had somehow missed the fact. He went on shaking his head and said, 'Aldebaran is dead,' again, but this time it was not a question. 'Tell me this story,' he said. 'I want to hear.'

JULY

The crowds came from a hundred miles to Aldebaran's funeral. They lined up against the barriers before dawn had yet risen and threw flowers and sang patriotic songs. But a strange hush followed the coffin as it drifted out of the cathedral. We followed it in silence. Leo went first, with his hair cut too short and a cigarette jammed in the corner of his mouth. My mother and Jasmine walked together; my mother kept letting go of Jasmine's hand to brush away her tears. The back of my neck burned under the eyes of the crowd.

Jasmine was pulling away from my mother, trying to get closer to the coffin, but the guards kept her back. The king was just ahead of us. He had insisted on walking beside his chief adviser to the grave. Everyone had argued against it. An assassination, the government believed, was always the start of something. But the king ignored them and went with his hand on the side of the coffin all the way down the main street.

The coffin bore our small wreath, but apart from that, there was nothing of Aldebaran about it. It was mounted on a gun carriage and draped in flags, and soldiers with their bayonets marched on either side of it. Every few yards, someone in the crowd would pitch a flower over the barrier. The blossoms thumped on the wood of the coffin, and the boots of the guards ground them into the dust.

Jasmine was crying; at six years old, the noise and solemnity had got the better of her.

'Here, come here,' said Leo, and tried to pick her up, but she shook her head and shrugged up her coat so that only her eyes showed. Leo reached out helplessly, and his hand found my shoulder instead. Somewhere, a band was playing, and every few seconds, the gun salute in the Royal Gardens shook the foundations of the city. Starlings rose in drifts from the ruined armaments factory. They circled dizzily over us, making endless patterns against the clouds.

Not long after that, a fine drizzle began. 'Oh, have some mercy!' said my mother, struggling with her new black umbrella and swiping at the tears on her face. It sounded like a stupid thing to say – as if the clouds would hear her and keep the rain from falling. But everything this morning had sounded stupid. The river hissed and seethed as the rain fell harder; the raindrops thundered on the wood of the coffin. We stood beside the open grave while the priest, a bishop from the south who none of us recognized, drifted over and opened his prayer book. 'Jesus said, "I am the resurrection and the life,"' read the bishop. '"He who believes in me will live even though he dies; and whoever lives and believes in me will never die."'

I did not know if Aldebaran had believed in God. He had never spoken about it. The bishop had a thin and cracked voice, and the rain made it feebler. He kept stopping to wipe the rain from his spectacles. It came down like arrows. The regimental uniforms of the foreign heads of state were spattered with mud up to the knees. Jasmine broke free and knelt down on the side of the grave. She watched the coffin descend, not caring that the dirt and rain covered her Sunday clothes.

'Jasmine, come back,' murmured my mother.

'Let her,' said Leo. 'It's all right.'

' "We brought nothing into the world, and we take nothing out," ' said the bishop. ' "The Lord gives, and the Lord takes away: blessed be the name of the Lord." '

As the coffin descended into the earth, the drums and the cannons fell silent. We each threw a handful of wet mud into the grave, and the foreign dignitaries and government ministers stepped forward and did the same, staining the sleeves of their uniforms. The king was so close on the other side of the grave that I could make out the tears standing in his eyes. He gave Leo a quick nod. They had met each other once, years ago. But the king was already turning now, and the guards ushered him towards the graveyard gate. The band took up their dirge again.

We listened to the procession fading. Then we could hear only the drum, and afterwards not even that. The rain dripped from the spokes of my mother's umbrella and gusted across the graveyard. Crows flapped, buffeted one way, then the other in the driving wind that howled in the dead branches of the trees. Someone had cut the grass around Aldebaran's grave, but beyond that, the graveyard had lost all appearance of order years ago.

'Come on,' said my mother. 'Let's go. There's no point staying here.'

Leo shook his head. Out of the rain, two figures were appearing: my grandmother, in her neat mourning clothes and with a black scarf over her head, frowning because of the rain, and Father Dunstan, our own priest, after her.

'Will you say another prayer, Father?' asked Jasmine,

sniffing, as he came up beside us. 'Uncle didn't know that old man.'

Father Dunstan stood on the end of the new grave and made the sign of the cross. His prayer book was awash; the pages buckled under the rain's assault. ' "The steadfast love of the Lord never ceases, his compassion never fails," ' Father Dunstan read. ' "Every morning they are renewed." '

'Amen,' said Jasmine, sniffing. 'Say another.'

Father Dunstan went on reading. He read all the funeral prayers in his book. Then the graveyard fell silent, and the rain dwindled, and there was nothing to do but go home.

In several of the houses, Malonian flags were still draped from the windows or clinging wetly to the washing lines. Beggars moved among the listless crowds with their hands outstretched. Two war veterans on the corner of the street called out as we passed, 'Spare a coin, sir! In the Lord's name have mercy on a poor man!' Leo gave them each a shilling. Our own street, Trader's Row, was a mass of flags; they blazed orange from every window. 'Look!' said Jasmine, startled out of her tears.

'Everyone liked Uncle,' I said. 'See? The whole city has come out to pay their respects to him.'

'So why haven't they found the bad man who shot him?'

'I don't know.'

'But I don't understand—'

'Shh,' said my mother, and put a hand on Jasmine's shoulder to quiet her.

Leo had not heard. He was walking ahead of us with his hands in his overcoat pockets.

Our closest neighbours were standing out on their steps:

the pharmacist and her two sons, Mr Pascal the secondhand clothes dealer, and the Barones from next door. Michael caught my glance as we passed. He was my oldest friend, and to see him there was some consolation. We went inside; then my mother shut the door, and the noise of the crowded city vanished. Leo sat down at the table in the back room. My mother put the kettle on the stove. We all stood around and could think of nothing to say.

'It's so unfair,' my mother said eventually.

'I know,' said Leo.

'He would never have wanted to go like that.'

'I know.'

There was another silence. A few raindrops crackled on the window. I added more coals to the stove and tried to turn them over without interrupting the silence that had settled over us.

'I must say,' my grandmother ventured, 'I thought it was a lovely ceremony. And he was old, Maria. He was eighty-six. I'm sure I'd be glad to die at such an age.'

'He was shot,' said Leo. 'No one would be glad—'

'Why haven't they caught the man—' began Jasmine.

'Shh,' said my mother. 'I don't know. They will.'

She went to the stove and took the kettle off it and put it back on again. Still it would not boil.

In a box on the table was all that Aldebaran had bequeathed to us. I took out the things carefully and replaced them again; it was something to do. He had not left much. The chief advisers took a vow of poverty when they were sworn into office, and after they died, all their papers were burned. There was a wooden box for Jasmine, his christening medallion for me, and a ring for my mother. For Leo there was a book in a paper wrapping that still lay unopened. There was also a parcel with *To the baby* written across it in red ink. My mother's baby was not due for several months, but it seemed Aldebaran had thought of everything.

Jasmine lay down under the table and began to cry in earnest. Aldebaran had been her teacher, and his death left her the last in the family with powers. Although they had argued bitterly in all their lessons, she had really been the one he loved the most.

'Hush,' said my mother. She knelt down beside the table and stroked Jasmine's hair. 'Come on, Jas. He wouldn't want you to make yourself so unhappy. And it is not for ever. You know that.'

'Dead is for ever,' said Jasmine. 'Dead means dead, and you can never be not dead again.'

'He will still watch over you.'

'He won't.'

Someone tapped at the door. The neighbours were out in the street waiting to pay their respects. 'Anselm, go and let them in,' said my mother.

The neighbours' chatter drowned out the silence of our house, and by the time they began to leave, darkness was falling. The Barones stayed a while longer than the rest. My grandmother was still here, and Mr Pascal, who could never be made to leave any funeral. We stood around the table in the back room and listened to the guns fire yet another salute from the Royal Gardens. Leo and Mr Pascal lit cigarettes, and the smoke rose and made strange patterns under the ceiling.

'Tell me,' said Mr Pascal when the silence had drawn out for several minutes, 'who succeeds Aldebaran as chief adviser?'

'I believe it is Joseph Marcus Sawyer,' said my grandmother.

'Sawyer?' said Mr Pascal.

Mr Barone shook his head and ran his hands over his thinning hair as though he wanted to fix it in place. 'I don't know why the king has chosen a man like that,' he said.

'He is not so bad,' said Mr Pascal. 'He may be the best we can hope for, under the circumstances. At least they say he has powers, and it has to be someone with powers. In these days, it is a miracle they found anyone at all.'

'As far as I heard, those powers left him when he was a child,' said Mr Barone. 'And all the world knows he was a collaborator.'

'There are worse things.'

'Are there?' said Mr Barone with a sharpness I had never heard in his voice before. 'Are there really worse things?'

Mr Pascal breathed out and held his cheeks there. He was a large man, and it made his face look round and shapeless like a baby's.

'What's a collaborator?' said Jasmine.

'Come on, Jas,' said Michael, ruffling her hair. 'I'll teach you a card game.'

I caught his glance and followed him out of the room, and Jasmine came after us. We sat on the floorboards of the shop, between the counter and a rack of old clothes, and Michael dealt out his stained playing cards and occupied Jasmine with a list of rules. She was still close to tears, but the distraction worked. In the back room, some argument was rising between Mr Pascal and Mr Barone. I tried to listen, but the rain obscured their voices. It was coming down hard again. Trader's Row was deserted, except for the old newspapers that circled in the rising gale.

'Your turn, Anselm,' Michael said, making me start. I had been thinking of other things. He handed me two crumpled cards, and I played my turn without knowing what numbers I put down. The storm rattled the windows and howled in the chimney. It made the side gate crash and shudder against the wall.

'I should go out and lock that,' I said.

I got up and went out. In the yard, the wind was ferocious. I wrestled the gate back into place. Then, as I turned to close it, there was a quick movement in the shadows on the other side of the street. Someone was standing there, in the dead space between the two gas lamps, watching me.

The man's silhouette was strange; there was something unearthly about it. I looked at him, and he stared back at me. Then he turned and walked away. The breeze made the lamps gutter, and in that jumping light, I could not make out his face. But as he vanished, I saw what it was that made his outline strange. Across his back was a rifle. It gleamed as the darkness overtook him. The rain was driving down hard now out of a dull grey sky. I shivered and bolted the gate and went in.

At first I thought I would mention it to the others. But the Barones and Mr Pascal and my grandmother were all getting up to leave. After they had gone, a cold silence fell on the house, and I did not dare to raise the subject. Leo sat down at the table and rested his head against his arms.

'Are you all right?' said my mother.

'I will be all right tomorrow.' She put her hand on his shoulder. 'At least he is buried now,' said Leo. 'That's the worst thing, not knowing. All that ceremony makes things better. I don't know why, but it does.'

None of us answered. He was speaking from experience. His parents, the famous Harold and Amelie North, had been missing for more than two decades. I knew that he still lay awake at night because he did not know where they were. It seemed Leo's family was condemned to suffer every time our country rose and fell.

'Come on,' said my mother, picking up the box of Aldebaran's things. 'Let's go to bed. Nothing is right this evening.'

We followed her upstairs to the living room and watched while she lit the lamps and Leo turned over the fire.

'Here,' she said, setting the box down on the mantelpiece. She put on the ring. I took the medallion and Jasmine the box. 'Are you not even going to open this book, Leo?' my mother asked.

Leo shook his head. 'What's the use?'

'What's the use? Uncle must have meant something by it. Don't you want to know what it is?' He shook his head again and closed the bedroom door behind him. My mother left the book lying on the mantelpiece. It was still there when we put out the lamps.

It was half past eleven, but from the square of light falling below the window next to mine, I could tell Michael was still awake next door. On nights when neither of us could sleep, we opened the windows and leaned out and spoke to each other. We had done that since I was a little boy and our family first came to the shop on Trader's Row. 'Michael?' I said, and pushed the window up. After a few seconds, I heard him raise the window on his side.

'Are you all right?' he said. 'It must have been a long day.'

'Yes.'

'Here. Take this.'

His skinny arm appeared with a bottle of spirits. I took it and drank some, out of politeness more than anything. A gale blew through my room, troubling the pages of the books on the table and making the faded picture on the wall swing wildly. 'What was the service like?' Michael asked.

'Grand. Like you would expect. But it was just us, those foreign heads of state, and a few famous people. He should have had more family there. I could tell it troubled Leo.'

'And I'll tell you someone who wasn't there,' said Michael. 'The Alcyrian president.'

'Wasn't he?'

Michael leaned precariously out of the window and handed me a newspaper. It was tomorrow's edition; Michael's father always walked to the end of the street to get it from the printers' at ten o'clock. The first seven pages were taken up with Aldebaran's funeral. Michael had underlined a single paragraph: 'The new president of Alcyria, the self-styled Commander General Marlan of the New Imperial Order, was conspicuous by his absence. Many saw this as a sign of the new Alcyrian government's growing hostility towards its neighbours.'

'General Marlan?' I said. 'Aldebaran hated him; he wouldn't have wanted him there.'

'But he should have been there. Everyone else was. Even a few of the presidents from the west and the Crown Prince of Marcovy.'

'I know.'

'And now that Aldebaran is gone, what's to stop Marlan

from invading every other country on the continent?' said Michael. 'That's what I want to know.'

'It won't happen,' I said, because Aldebaran had always said it. But the newspaper thought otherwise. Several pages were taken up with a discussion of the chances of war with Alcyria and the chances of civil unrest from the New Imperial Order here. They had groups in every nation on the continent. They marched about in mock uniforms, and held rallies, and stood for government at every election under the banner 'Liberty and Justice'.

'I think it was them,' I said. 'I think the Order were the ones who did it.'

'It's why my father got so angry,' said Michael. 'At least, that's part of it. Joseph Marcus Sawyer has been linked with General Marlan. Everyone knows Sawyer was part of Lucien's government. He's no choice for chief adviser. What was the king thinking?'

'I have never seen your father angry like that,' I said.

'No,' said Michael. 'He was talking tonight about getting out of the country.'

'Does he really mean that?'

'I don't know. He doesn't want to see another war.'

'But what about you? What do you think?'

'Maybe it isn't so crazy to think of going, now that Aldebaran is gone. My father was in the resistance, and everyone knows it. And people are leaving Alcyria.'

'I know,' I said. We had seen them arrive in the city with their belongings piled up in carts and a dazed look in their eyes, as though they hoped they were about to wake up from something. 'I know,' I said again. 'But where would you go if you left? Michael, you are not really serious?'

He did not answer, just sighed and changed the subject.

The wind was growling so fiercely now that I could hardly hear my own voice, and we were both shivering. 'We should go inside,' he said. 'My father is in no mood to catch me leaning out of the window.'

'Listen,' I said. 'I have to know – you are not really serious about leaving?'

He sighed and I saw his shadow on the pavement shrug its shoulders.

'I'll talk to you tomorrow,' I said.

'Goodnight, Anselm.'

'Goodnight.'

I heard him push the window down. The rain began to fall again, but I remained where I was. As I stood there, the lamp came on in the shop below. Leo must be down there. I had known he would not sleep tonight. The light threw the letters from the front window backwards onto the pavement: L. NORTH & SON, DEALERS IN SECONDHAND GOODS. I stared at those words for a while, and thought of Aldebaran in the graveyard in the dark and of his assassin, alive somewhere, awake or sleeping or drinking at some inn. Then I tried not to think about it any more. The rain was falling hard again. I ducked to go inside.

As I pushed the window down, I started. Just for a second, I thought I saw that man in the alley opposite again. But the street was deserted. I must have imagined it. A newspaper was spiralling under the streetlight; that was all. I pulled the curtains closed and turned up the lamp. The bedroom grew close and safe in the yellow glow. The narrow bed, the rickety desk piled with books, the rug worn through in the middle, and the saint's picture that hung on the wall – all of them were so familiar that they drove out the darkness of the city. I kept my eyes on that picture as I undressed. The saint stood at the prow of a ship in the darkness, holding forth a crucifix. We had never been able to work out who he was; even Father Dunstan, when we asked him, could not be sure. But when I was a little boy, I called the figure St Anselm and asked him to protect me from danger. Until I was ten or eleven years old, I had a hopeless fear of the dark. Perhaps it was childish, but when I whispered, 'Defend us from all perils and dangers of this night,' on the evening of Aldebaran's funeral, it was still the saint I was praying to.

The clocks were sounding twelve. The largest bell, in the new cathedral, went on chiming with a steady note. The guns fired a final salute, and the city echoed. Then there was no sound at all, except the wind growling in the alleys and driving the rain hard against the windowpane. After a while, it died away too, and left the city in silence.

I suppose I should go back to the start and tell you the history of our family. I told myself the story that night as I lay in bed listening to the wind fighting in the streets and sleep seemed a thousand miles away.

It started with two families. The Andros family were the richest bankers in Malonia. The North family was famous because the Norths were Aldebaran's descendants. After the revolution, when half the royalists in the country were exiled or missing, the last remaining members of these two families were left stranded in the city. My mother and my grandmother moved from place to place before I was born. From my earliest years, I knew the names of the streets where they had lived: Slaughterhouse Lane, Greyfriars Square, Paradise Way. And the last – the place they finally settled – Citadel Street. That was where my mother and Leo met.

Of course, I had a father. I asked about him sometimes, when I was still very young, but I had my mother and Leo, and my grandparents, and Leo's grandmother Margaret for the first six years of my life, and to wish for anyone else seemed heartless somehow. Even Aldebaran treated me as a relative from the start. After Sunday dinner, he would stand in the light of the fire and show me magic tricks, and I wished I had powers so earnestly that I used to cry sometimes over it. Can you become part of a family by wanting to be? I don't know. You can get so far with lying that you convince yourself that it's true and genuinely feel a kind of outrage when anyone questions it. That is the closest thing that I can think of. And if you could measure, Leo was the one who loved me best from the start.

There is one night I remember more than anything. It was the winter when I was six years old, and all through the dark months, I had been troubled by nightmares. On this night, something woke me suddenly and drove out all hopes of sleep. It was past three o'clock and the building was silent. The last embers of the fire threw strange shadows over the walls. I lay shivering, tracing pictures in the uneven plaster of the ceiling. I imagined the largest mass was the land of England, and the smaller ones were ships sailing round its coast. Sleep seemed as far off as another world. And while I lay there, I began to be afraid that there were spirits in the room around me. I was sure that if I moved or made a sound, they would awaken and get my soul.

I stopped breathing. I thought that if I breathed too loudly, they would find me. I was scaring myself, and I knew it, but I could not help it. I counted as long as I could without taking a breath, and then breathed out carefully so as not to make a sound, and went on like that, minute by minute. I began to pray for Leo to wake up.

The minutes passed, and the clock chimed the hour, and then the quarter. I waited and heard it chime again. 'Leo?' I whispered.

Then, at last, an oil lamp brightened in the next room, and I heard his footsteps. He appeared out of the dark and stood beside me. 'Are you all right, Anselm?' he said.

'I can't sleep.'

He sat down on the edge of my bed and leaned over to build up the fire. The coal caught and started to drive the chill from the room. In the sudden light of the lamp, I could make out every grey strand in his hair. Leo was twenty-two, and his hair was already greying, but at the time I did not think much about it. 'Was it a nightmare?' said Leo. 'I thought I heard you call out.'

'I don't know,' I said. 'Papa, don't go away.'

He brushed the tears from my face with his jacket sleeve. 'No. I'll sit with you for a while until you fall back to sleep.'

Leo could always sense my thoughts without asking, and I could usually tell his. He had not spoken for the first few years of my life, and I had learned to tell what he was thinking from the very air that surrounded him.

'Will you read to me?' I said.

He went to the mantelpiece and took down Harold North's second-to-last book, *The Sins of Judas*. He had read it to me twice already. But tonight he did not open it. He just sat there frowning. 'When I was a boy, I used to dream too,' he said after a while had passed.

'You still do,' I said, thinking of the way he cried out sometimes in the dark and startled us all awake.

'Not nightmares,' he said. 'I used to go away from here.

21

Far away. They were like visions, these dreams. I used to dream about England.'

'England?' I said.

'Yes. All the time.' He said it with an air of surprise, as though he was talking of someone else.

'Tell me about it,' I said.

'All right,' he said. 'All right, I could tell you what I remember.'

He began softly. His outline was very black against the fire. He told me stories of another place, where there lived a girl who wanted more than anything to dance and a boy who would become King Cassius. And Aldebaran was there, just a wanderer on a journey, a man who disguised himself as a servant to hide from the law.

'And then what happened?' I asked when Leo paused.

'I don't know.'

Sleep was dragging me down now like the waves of the ocean. The story had settled my heart. 'Was it all true?' I whispered.

'There is no way of telling.'

'But couldn't you ask Aldebaran about it himself?'

'He doesn't speak about England. Not any more. Sometimes I think he doesn't remember it. Or doesn't even believe it exists.'

'Then how do you know that story?'

Leo answered so calmly that I thought I had heard him wrong: 'Because I used to have powers.'

I sat up. He turned and gave me a quick, sad smile. 'You had powers?' I said.

'Yes.'

'Real powers like Aldebaran? You could make things move and tell the future?'

'Yes. A bit, anyway. I never bothered much with them.'

'Why didn't I ever know?'

Leo shrugged. 'They have gone now. I gave them up the year you were born, and it didn't seem worth telling you.'

'Why did you give them up?'

'All these questions . . .' He shook his head and gave that same sad smile again. 'I decided they weren't any use. I mean, for anything that mattered.'

'Is that true? Powers aren't any use?'

'It's just what I thought at the time. Anyway, I would never have made a great one. And that's all in the past now.'

I lay still, trying to see him as a great one, a man initiated into an ancient line of heroes. I could not do it. He was just Leo, my papa, who stood at a market stall all day and spent the evenings sweeping the floor and carrying up the water and reading me stories. 'Papa?' I whispered. 'Did you ever dream about England again?'

'No,' he said. 'No, I never did.'

'But how could you stop having powers just like that?'

'I didn't. They keep their hold on you, Anselm. But I never dreamed about England again.'

'Are you sure?'

'Yes, I'm sure.'

But there was something very final about the way he said it, something that made me remember it long after that evening, long after he had left me and turned out the light. There was always a kind of darkness about Leo, a cold side to his spirit that none of us could reach. In that, he was exactly like Aldebaran.

I never had nightmares again after that. Instead, I always dreamed about England. I saw it as a green and enchanted place, inhabited by minstrels and poets and wandering outlaws. And after that night, Leo became a kind of hero to me. I did not think about it all the time, but sometimes I would see him waiting at the school gates in his old leather jacket or bending tiredly to dig the cold ash out of the stove, and I would think, My papa was once a man of some importance. In those days, he had a market stall in the coldest corner of the square, and his coughing every winter's night was fierce enough to rattle the windows. But I knew secretly that it would not last. Leo was destined to be a great man. It was written in the stars somewhere, and all we had to do was wait. In my dreams, I saw a shop with our name on the sign and Leo in a new suit of clothes presiding over the counter. Years passed before it came true, but I never lost faith. It would have taken more than years to make me do that.

Our last winter in Citadel Street, the windows were leaking and the pipes were frozen and Leo was coughing worse than ever. My mother circled a shop for rent in the newspaper. The page lay on the table for several weeks, gaining dust and tea stains. Leo considered it in silence. Then I came home one day to find them packing up our things. I was not surprised by it; I had known he would say yes. It was his destiny.

The shop was a dark building full of dust and broken glass. We moved in at Christmas, in the bitterest cold you ever knew, and the landlord left before we could ask him how to turn on the lights. Only Leo's spirits could not be darkened. 'We will fix it up,' he said as he carried our boxes up the stairs by lamplight. 'It will be the best secondhand shop in the whole of Malonia City.'

'In the whole of the continent,' said my mother. She

carried Jasmine up the stairs and set her down on a mattress. Jasmine was two years old and would not sleep. She toddled about the floor, examining the boxes. 'What do you think, Anselm?' said my mother.

'It's all right,' I said quietly. 'It's not how I thought it would be.'

'Listen,' she said. 'Every step forward looks like a step back at the start. It's always a struggle to move on to something better. Did you know that? But things will be better here, for sure. You can help your papa in the shop every evening and have your own room with a desk in it.'

I nodded and followed Leo back down for the last boxes. 'Let's paint our name on the window,' he said, taking hold of my arm. 'What do you say, Anselm?'

The idea caught my imagination in spite of everything. There was an old ladder in the back room, and we had a can of black paint. I held the ladder and Leo wrote.

'What are you two doing?' said my mother, coming out with Jasmine in her arms and laughing up at us. 'Leo, that ladder does not look safe, and it is past midnight.'

'It will not take long.'

'You two!' she said. She hugged Jasmine to her and laughed until tears fell from her eyes. 'It will look terrible in the light of day. You should sketch out lines and draw it properly.'

'We will, one day,' said Leo. 'What shall I write? Help me, Anselm. You are the clever one – give me inspiration.'

'Write "L. North and M. Andros, Dealers in Secondhand Goods".'

'Don't put my name on it,' said my mother, still laughing. 'I want nothing to do with this. I am going out to my own sensible job, and you two can carry on your schemes without me.'

'Mama, what Papa write?' murmured Jasmine. She was falling asleep in my mother's arms.

'I know what,' said Leo.

He climbed up another step on the ladder. From where I was, I could not see what he was writing. He was balanced on the top rung now, in his oldest shirt and faded soldier's boots, his eyes fixed in concentration as the dark got darker. 'Maybe it is too late,' I said. 'Maybe we should finish it tomorrow.'

'No,' he said. 'No, I can see well enough.'

He worked in silence, frowning as he painted in each letter. 'Look at the stars,' whispered my mother. 'You can tell how cold it is.'

I turned without letting go of the ladder. The stars looked as if they were shivering, very low down over the houses. In an inn nearby, music started rustily, a violin and an accordion. It was a song the travelling musicians used to play at the new inn on the corner of Citadel Street. It made this place already a kind of home. The song was by Diamonn and called 'I Would Follow the One I Love'. My mother sang the last verse very quietly in Jasmine's ear:

'Love brings down many captives, and lifts up many
     princes also.
Love is both the cruel cold sea and the mariner's true
     star.
And love is the poison in the blood and in the heart
     the arrow.
I'd follow him, my heart's own soul, and never ask how
     far.'

'There,' said Leo, jumping down from the ladder. 'Look at it, Anselm, and tell me what you think.'

I stepped back and narrowed my eyes against the dark.

'It is not straight, is it?' he said. 'But what do you think of the words?'

'I can't see.'

'Wait a minute,' said Leo. He went inside and lit an oil lamp, then held it up behind the window. His face was ghostlike through the dusty glass, but the letters stood out blackly. They shimmered as the light moved: L. NORTH & SON.

Nearly five years had passed since that night. I was eleven then and still dreamed of England. Jasmine was a two-year-old who had yet to show any sign of powers. But between then and Aldebaran's death, our lives became what we had wanted them to be. I don't think we realized it then. I only knew it afterwards, when nothing was right any more.

After Aldebaran's funeral, the street sweepers came out in the driving rain and cleared away all traces of the crowds. And I kept expecting that life would return to normality. But the days passed and it didn't. My mother and Jasmine were both prone to fits of angry tears. Leo went about quietly with his eyes on the ground. I began to wish school would start again, to give me a reason to leave the shop. And every morning the newspaper was full of reports on the hunt for the assassin.

One night Leo and I sat up late counting the day's takings, and afterwards neither of us had the heart to get up and go to bed. We listened to the rain against the windows instead. Every time I glanced up, I would think I saw someone in the alley opposite. The fourth or fifth time, I got up and went to the front window. But the street was deserted. No one passed in the rain-washed dark except a couple of stray dogs chasing a newspaper. The face of the latest suspect was emblazoned on the front of it – a thin man about Leo's age who was with the New Imperial Order.

'Do you think he did it?' I said.

'Who?' Leo asked me.

'That man from the Imperial Order.'

Leo considered the question, his cigarette halfway to his mouth, then shook his head.

'Why not?' I said.

He sighed. In the half-light he looked very old; the grey hairs on the sides of his head showed unforgivingly.

'Why not?' I said again.

'Because I don't think Aldebaran is dead.'

He spoke so quietly that I thought I had misheard him. 'What?' I said, but he got up and began shifting boxes around without meeting my eyes. A crate of books slipped and went thundering to the floor. We both bent to pick them up.

'This shop!' he said. 'It is getting out of hand.'

'Papa, tell me what you just said.'

He ran his hand over his face. 'I just can't see him as dead. I don't know how, but I can't see it. I did, after the funeral, but I've lost all certainty now. Anselm . . .' He shrugged, and I knew by his carelessness that he was getting to the most important point. 'I have these dreams.'

I tried to see into his face, but he kept his eyes lowered. 'What about?' I said.

'The past or the future – I can't tell. Aldebaran is in some of them.'

'But maybe . . .' I hesitated. 'Maybe he is still living.

I mean, in another place but still watching over you.'

Leo shivered and ran his hands over his arms as though to warm them. 'We had better finish this and get to bed,' he said.

We began shifting the piles of old things, though to-morrow was Sunday and we would not have to open. Upstairs I could hear my mother and Jasmine's voices. 'How was trade this evening?' I said to drive out the silence that lay between us.

'No one came in,' said Leo. 'You saw yourself.'

'What did we take today?'

'About four hundred.'

'It's not so bad.'

'It is not good either,' said Leo. 'Not really. And I had Doctor Keller here again while you were out talking to Michael.'

The doctor was our landlord and fond of making un-expected visits. 'What did he want?' I said.

'Just to look around. What does he ever want?'

'I'm sure Jasmine kept him entertained.'

He smiled. Leo's smiles were hard-won and faint, the more so since Aldebaran was gone. He picked up a box of books and set them down on the counter. 'Mr Pascal gave me these,' he said. 'Maybe they aren't worth anything. Have a look – tell me what you think.'

I turned over the pages of the book on top. It was an adventure story by a John Sebastian Urquhart, printed in fancy type. 'Jasmine might like it,' I said.

'Yes. As long as there are pirates and violent deaths and a villain with a glass eye.' Leo smiled and then shivered again, as though a draught had passed over him. He bent his head over the box and began examining the other books.

'Papa,' I said, 'did you ever open that book Aldebaran left you?'

He shook his head.

'Maybe you should,' I said. 'Maybe it would help. If Aldebaran was trying to tell you something, it would be in that book, wouldn't it?'

'Why do you say that?'

'It just seems to me that's how he thinks.'

I had expected him to argue. But he only nodded and went upstairs. I heard him go heavily across the living room. He paused for a moment, then came back down. 'Maybe there is some clue in it,' he said. 'Maybe you are right. At least it might set my mind at rest.'

'Open it, then.'

His hands shook. I leaned over his shoulder as he took off the paper. Onto the counter fell a battered hardback, with the gold type on the cover nearly worn away. He turned up the dial of the lamp, and I made out the title: *The Darkness Has a Thousand Voices*, and under it 'Harlan Smith'.

'Harlan who?' I said.

'I don't know. I have never heard of him.'

'Did Uncle write in it?'

Leo fanned out the pages carefully and shook his head. 'Nothing.'

It was not what I had expected, and I saw now why Leo had not opened it. The book was a disappointment. It did not alter the fact that Aldebaran was gone, and now we had nothing left to rest our hope on. Leo examined it half-heartedly. A yellow watermark ran halfway up the spine, and the words were obscured by stains. He turned over the title page. 'It's only two years old,' he said. 'And published here in the city. Look at the figures here – this one is a first edition. First and last, I suppose.'

'I have never heard of Harlan Smith,' I said.

Leo shook his head. 'You can tell they hardly printed any copies of this. Look at the way it is bound. I wouldn't be surprised if it was printed privately. Seven Sisters Press. John Worthy, Printers and Bookbinders. Have you heard of either of those?'

'No.'

I went on watching him. He was absorbed in the first page now, leaning close to the lamplight. I finished sweeping the floor and washed up the plates that lay about the back room. When I came back into the shop, Leo was still studying the book. 'Anselm,' he said, touching my arm. 'Listen to this.'

'What?' I said.

He read quietly, so I had to stand very still to catch all the words. ' "Midnight," ' he began, ' "and still no one came. And outside the window of his cell, in the restless darkness, voices rose up and spoke to Jean-Michel. The voices of everyone he had ever lost and everyone he loved. These voices haunted him. It is a fact not well known among the rulers of this world, that the darkness speaks to the lonely." '

The silence hummed. 'What?' I said.

'It sounds like something, doesn't it?'

'Like what?'

'I don't know.'

Leo was still studying the first page of the book. In the square, the church clock chimed twelve. 'Go to bed, Anselm,' he said, and put a hand on my shoulder. 'It's late. I will come up in a minute.'

I went upstairs, but I sat awake for more than an hour

and did not hear him come up after me. Eventually I blew out the lamp and slept.

When I went down to the bathroom, somewhere near dawn, Leo was still there at the counter. His face was grey with too little sleep, and he was on the last pages of the book. 'Anselm,' he said hoarsely.

'Yes,' I said. 'I'm here.'

'I think it means something,' he said. 'I can't tell what, but it does.'

'What kind of thing?'

'I don't know.' He coughed and rested his head against his hand. 'It's the first time,' he said. 'It's the first time in years that I've read a book and it's said anything to me. I mean, here.' He put his fist against his heart. 'Do you understand that?'

'Yes,' I said.

'I don't think Aldebaran is gone,' said Leo. 'I think that's what he's trying to say. Either that or . . .'

'Or what?'

He closed the book and opened it again, then ran his hand backwards through his hair so that it stood up untidily. 'You'll think I'm crazy,' he said. 'If I tell you, you won't know what to say.'

'Tell me anyway.'

'It sounds like Harold North,' he said. 'It's like he could have written it.'

There was a long silence, in which all the antique clocks on the walls of the shop ticked out of time with each other. Then he pushed the book across the counter towards me.

'Should I read it?' I said.

'Just a few pages.'

I turned to the beginning. Leo leaned across the counter,

and I could see his hands trembling. All the time that I was reading, they went on shaking. Eventually he reached across and touched my arm, and I looked up. 'Well?' he said.

'Yes,' I said. 'It's like him.'

'A lonely man,' Leo said. 'A journey. Politics. There is even a ruined church, like in *The Sins of Judas*.'

'Or *The Shattered Wheel*. You know, when they get lost out on the moor and they come to the hermitage. That's what it reminds me of.'

'It's something about the way he tells it.'

In the dim light, our eyes met. Leo had spent half my childhood searching the city for Harold North's books, looking for copies that had not been destroyed under the old regime, and I knew them almost as well as he did.

'It's strange,' he said. 'That's why I became a secondhand trader, because of those books. I mean, for that reason more than anything. I fell into it by accident. I know that he's gone, and I've still spent my whole life thinking . . .' He shrugged. 'I've spent my whole life pretending that he's still guiding me. Is that stupid?'

'No.'

'This sounds like him,' said Leo, and shook his head. 'I swear it does.'

'Do you think that's why Aldebaran gave it to you?' I said.

'I don't know.'

Leo lit a cigarette carefully and closed his eyes. I watched him. 'Maybe it's just because they are similar,' he said. 'Maybe he thought it would say something to me, because it's like what Harold North used to write. Or maybe . . .' He shook his head again. 'Maybe he meant something else.'

'Harold North can't be still . . .' I said, and did not finish.

'I know,' he said. 'I know.' The wind lulled, and the silence came down more heavily than before. I could hear every coal in the stove shifting among the dying flames. If it hadn't been so quiet, we might not have heard the gunshots.

They came from somewhere in the city and made Leo start and raise his head. 'What was that?' he said, his eyes on the window. The lamp had gone out. I felt for Leo's matches and tried to relight it, but he put his hand on my arm. 'Listen,' he whispered. 'It sounded like . . . my God, Anselm—'

The sound had come again, two sharp cracks, and closer. 'What?' I said. 'Leo, you're scaring me.'

'It's gunshots. I know it is.'

I had heard gunshots before. But never this close and never four or five within a minute. We both stood listening, separated by the darkness. A sliver of moonlight cut down through the window and turned Leo's head to silver. 'It was probably just a trader with a shotgun,' I said. 'Someone killing rats—'

'It didn't sound like that.'

At the same moment, there was another burst of gunfire. 'Anselm, listen!' Leo said.

We stood there without speaking, listening to the silence. It drew out so long that my heart slowed. Leo did not move. Eventually I dared to light the lamp. I went to the back room and turned over the cold ashes of the stove. They did not need turning, but I wanted to make a noise, because I knew Leo wanted silence. I cannot explain it. He was far away, and I wanted to bring him back.

'Anselm, shh,' he said. 'Listen again.'

I listened. A drum was beating somewhere. It came closer and faded again on the faltering breeze. 'What is it?' I said.

'I don't know.'

I was afraid suddenly, and I didn't know why. It was not the noises in the darkness outside – it was the way Leo was standing transfixed, as though they held him prisoner. The music was coming closer. Across the street, someone opened an attic window. I started towards the front window.

'No,' said Leo. 'Let's go upstairs.'

I followed him. The living room was in darkness; the last traces of the fire were dying in the grate. Through the narrow window over the stairs, I thought I could see lights moving. Jasmine's door was ajar, and she was still asleep, lying sideways across her bed with her thumb in her mouth. The light of the streetlamp lay across her face. Leo went in and closed the curtains. The drumming was quite clear now, in spite of the rain and the wind outside. Men were chanting something over it.

'What are they saying?' whispered Leo.

'It's too far away to hear.'

He watched the lights moving. The men were passing our street by a wide margin and marching towards the castle. We watched them until they were lost in the rain and the darkness. Dawn was approaching now. The eastern sky was a dull grey, and the wet tiles of the houses gleamed. 'You should get some sleep,' I said. 'It's nearly morning.'

'What do you think it means?' said Leo.

'I don't know.'

He was standing frozen again, in front of the window. I touched his arm, and he started. 'Try and get some sleep,' I said.

'What if they come back?'

'They won't. Not now that it's daylight.'

'Anselm, what do you think they were doing?'

I shook my head. I did not know either.

I did not sleep again that night. There were too many thoughts in my mind, chasing quickly on each other. And from the creaking of the living-room floorboards, I could tell Leo was still there, pacing up and down in the dark. Apart from the gunshots and those chanting men, I could not help thinking of Harold North. I knew he was dead; we all knew it. But I had never properly considered the pain it caused Leo not to be sure.

Before Mass, when the city was still cold with the early morning shadows, there was a knock at the side door. It was Mr Pascal, with the newspaper folded under his arm. 'Well, well,' he said, coming in and shaking the dust off his boots. 'And did you hear the gunshots last night?'

Leo was lighting the stove, but he straightened up now, hitting his head hard on the stove lid.

'What gunshots, Mama?' murmured Jasmine.

'It was nothing,' said Leo.

'Jasmine, go upstairs and get your boots,' said my mother.

Jasmine ignored that. Mr Pascal glanced about the shop as if settling for a long stay. Then he unfolded the newspaper and spread it out on the counter. It was a tradition with him to bring it into the shop nearly every morning and lecture us on the contents, and we had never been able to think of a way to dissuade him. But today was different; today there was something in it. The front page was half taken up with a line drawing depicting men with torches and rifles marching in ranks past the castle rock.

'Look,' said Mr Pascal, pointing to several different places in the text. 'Militant members of the Imperial Order . . . rebel government officials . . . illegal rally.'

'What do they want?' said Leo.

'They want to take over the country,' said Mr Pascal. 'Listen here: "Shots were fired and a disused shop burned. The police moved in after a local trader alerted them to the situation. Sixteen arrests were made."'

The newspaper had all the spelling mistakes of a rushed morning edition; they must have reprinted it in the last hour.

Jasmine was clambering onto a chair, trying to see over my mother's shoulder. 'Mama, Mama!' she whined, tugging my mother's sleeve. 'What does it say?'

'Nothing important,' said my mother. 'Come on, put on your shawl. It is nearly time to leave for Mass.'

'It all makes sense in my view,' said Mr Pascal, lighting a cigarette and turning to address Leo. 'The new Alcyrian government are criminals; they effected what was no more than a military coup, and yet no one has been able to bring them to justice. So now the New Imperial Order wants to do the same thing in every country on the continent. And it gives those old supporters of Lucien something to hope for. They say this will be the hardest winter for a long time, and not only that, they say—'

But whatever else they said was interrupted by another knock at the door. It was Michael and his parents.

'Did you hear the gunshots?' Mrs Barone asked my mother as soon as they were over the threshold.

'No, we were asleep. But Leo and Anselm did.'

'Why won't anyone tell me what's happening?' Jasmine was demanding, tugging my sleeve now.

'Hush,' said my mother. 'Go and put on your boots.'

Mrs Barone was questioning Mr Pascal anxiously. As the only possessor of the morning edition of the newspaper, he knew more than even they did. Mr Barone said nothing, just shook his head and ran his hands over his hair. He looked very old and helpless standing there in the doorway. Michael touched my shoulder. 'Are you going to Mass today?' he said.

'Yes, I think so.'

'Some people aren't.'

'Who?'

'The pharmacist is refusing to leave her house.'

'Is the city dangerous?' Leo demanded, looking up from the newspaper.

'No,' said my mother. 'It will be fine. We'll go to Mass.'

Leo caught hold of her arm. 'Maybe we should not . . .'

'We are going to Mass,' she said.

As if in answer, the church bell began to chime. 'Jasmine, get your shawl,' my mother said. 'Leo, Anselm, put on your boots.'

Leo looked as if he would argue, but he did not. He just went and got his boots in silence.

'I dare say there is nothing to fear,' said Mr Pascal. He sighed, refolded the newspaper, and got up to leave. He was not religious and neither was Michael, but the rest of us set out. Leo kept a firm hold of Jasmine's hand all the way down Trader's Row. He did not need to; the city was deserted. There was no sign that anyone had been marching in the streets the night before. And yet I had never seen it so quiet either.

My grandmother was waiting for us at the church door. The sun had risen just high enough to cross the roofs of the houses, and a few birds were hopping about in the dust. The fountain was the only sound in the empty square. Jasmine broke free of Leo's hand and ran over to the edge of the pool. The horse statue was broken; it had never recovered from the revolution, and now the water sprayed only inter-mittently from its mouth, making arcs in the still air. A few people were hurrying through the church doorway. 'Come along,' said my grandmother, and we followed her. The church was half empty.

'Papa, you keep yawning,' Jasmine whispered as we stood side by side in the pew. She elbowed Leo, and he started and raised his hymn book higher. My mother smiled at that. The light fell through the stained-glass window in rays and carved deep lines in the corners of the priest's face. Father Dunstan was not much older than my mother and Leo, but he looked like an elderly and distinguished man as he proclaimed the Gospel. I could not concentrate. My eyes were aching with too little sleep. I watched the dust spiral in the rays of light. My grandmother listened tensely to every word, as though she would be examined afterwards, and every time I looked away, she nudged my shoulder hard and tutted. By the time the service finished, my shoulder was aching from it.

After the service, my mother went to speak to Father Dunstan, and Jasmine dragged me out into the square. 'Watch me!' she said, scrambling onto the edge of the fountain and running in circles with her arms outstretched. I watched, but I was thinking of other things. The city had come out of its silence at last. People passed occasionally, in their best clothes or in rags as their luck decreed. There were even a few wealthy couples in open carriages. 'Is Grandmama coming for Sunday dinner today?'

Jasmine demanded, coming to a halt in front of me.

'Yes,' said Leo. 'Apparently she won't be dissuaded.'

He had come up beside us without my noticing. His face was colourless from lack of sleep; it made his grey eyes darker and more piercing.

'Papa!' said Jasmine, and leaped into his arms. He caught her and set her down.

'Come on,' he said. 'We should start for the graveyard.'

We went every week after Mass. Half our family was buried there – Grandmother Margaret, and Grandpa Julian, and Leo's brother Stirling. Aldebaran's grave was a mass of flowers that Sunday. We left shilling bouquets on each of their graves and stood for a long time at the end of Stirling's while Leo studied the worn inscription.

'Did you know?' Jasmine said, tugging my sleeve. 'Did you know, Anselm?'

'Did I know what?'

'Stirling is twenty-four.'

'Yes,' I said.

Stirling had died when I was still a tiny baby, and now he had been gone twice as long as he had ever lived. Leo stood on the end of the grave for a long time without speaking. 'Come along, Leonard,' said my grandmother eventually. 'It will be three o'clock before we start dinner at this rate.'

She marched ahead of us, the scarf about her head tied stubbornly tight and her heeled shoes clicking. The sunlight threw the chaos of the shop into relief, and my grandmother tutted when she saw it. 'Dear me, it gets messier every week,' she said, folding her shawl and going to the stove. 'Give me the potatoes, Maria. Let me do it.'

'I can manage,' said my mother.

'You shouldn't, in your condition.' My grandmother lit the stove and sent Jasmine out to the yard for water, then started the potatoes boiling. My mother fried a piece of pork, cutting it into slices to make it go quicker, which caused my grandmother to shake her head again. Leo picked up an oil lamp from the cupboard and polished it absently with an old rag.

'So there is going to be another war,' said my grandmother. 'That's how it looks, with these vagrants marching about in the streets and the king refusing to leave his castle. I must say, I never thought I'd see the day.'

'Is there going to be a war?' said Jasmine.

'No,' said Leo, ruffling her hair.

'Anselm, do something,' said my grandmother sharply. 'Don't just stand there.'

'He is – he's setting the table,' said my mother.

It was true, but I did not say anything. My grandmother straightened the plates and shook her head. 'When do you go back to school?' she asked me.

'September. If I go.'

'What do you mean, if you go?'

'If I go back to school and don't stay and help Papa in the shop instead.'

'Help Leonard in the shop?' she said. 'But surely you want an education?'

'I have an education,' I said. 'I've been at school for ten years, Grandmama.'

'What future is there in secondhand trading?'

I did not know how to answer that, so I kept quiet. My mother began serving up the food. 'Our family was meant for better things,' said my grandmother. 'If poor Julian was still with us, he would turn over in his grave.'

'That doesn't make sense,' said Jasmine. 'You said if he was still with us, he would turn over in his grave; that doesn't make sense.'

A silence followed. Then my mother laughed out loud. 'Come on,' she said, clapping her hands. 'Your food is going cold, Mother.'

My grandmother ate slowly, stabbing each potato with her fork as though she had a personal grievance against it. Jasmine ate her dinner under the table. She had done that since Aldebaran died, and none of us questioned it, but today my grandmother kept leaning back in her chair to frown at her.

'Light the lamp, Anselm,' said my mother quietly. It was growing darker; already the brief sunlight had faded away. Clouds banked over the city, shutting out the light from Trader's Row. 'This weather,' said my grandmother. 'You can never rely on it.'

Silence fell again. It was broken when Jasmine dropped a potato and crawled across the floor after it. On her way back under the table, my grandmother cornered her and caught her by the wrist.

'Let me go!' said Jasmine at once.

'Stop that noise. You are to sit at the table until you have finished your food. Do you hear me?'

'Mother, don't nag her—'

'It is bad manners. Jasmine, do you hear?'

Jasmine tried to struggle free, but my grandmother kept hold. There was a silence while Jasmine glared. Then the lamp in my hands began to tremble. 'Hey, Jas,' said Leo warningly. 'Jasmine, stop. Anselm, put that lamp down!'

The lamp exploded as I dropped it. Leo swore and threw out his arm to shield my mother's face. My grandmother let out a shriek. 'I didn't mean to! I didn't mean to!' Jasmine said.

There was a silence while the glass dislodged itself from every corner of the room and fell shivering to the floor. Jasmine started to cry and ran to Leo.

'It's all right,' he said shakily. 'No harm is done.'

I raised my hand to my face. There was glass in my hair, and a faint line of blood was running across the back of my hand. I rubbed it off absently. Hot oil was spilling out of the lamp, ruining what was left of the varnish on the table. My mother cleaned it off with a pile of rags and threw the glass-encrusted potatoes into the stove.

'Well!' said my grandmother. 'I think after that performance, Jasmine, you should spend the rest of the day in your room.'

'It's not her fault,' said my mother.

'Maria, the child did it on purpose. She wilfully broke that lamp!'

'She didn't do anything wilfully, Mother.'

'I did!' said Jasmine through her tears. 'It was my fault, wasn't it?'

'I don't know why you tolerate it!' said my grandmother, getting to her feet. 'The child's behaviour is already out of control. If poor Julian was here—'

'Poor Julian doesn't come into it!' said my mother. 'Jasmine, go outside and wash your face.'

'Papa, come with me,' Jasmine murmured.

I got up and followed them too. When Jasmine came back out of the bathroom, my mother and my grandmother were arguing loudly enough to rattle the loose side window. Leo lit a cigarette and exhaled slowly with his eyes closed. Jasmine sniffed intermittently, and we waited.

'No one trusts them. She will come to a bad end unless she stops this nonsense!' my grandmother was shouting. 'If you would just *discipline* her, Maria—'

'How do you discipline powers out of a child, in the name of heaven?'

'She runs about doing exactly what she likes. Letting her eat under the table—'

'She's upset. We are all upset. It's been less than a month since Uncle—'

'It's long enough. And as for Anselm, I can tell that boy is going to go wrong. I've been telling you so for years.'

'There is nothing wrong with Anselm. Don't you dare talk like that about him!'

'They need firm treatment. You are their *mother*!'

'I have brought up my children in the way I see fit!' my mother said, her high-class accent catching up with her. 'Just like you did.'

'What is that supposed to imply?'

'Nothing. I'm not implying anything—'

'If you are not careful, Maria, they are going to turn out exactly like you!'

There was a silence. Then my mother shouted something else, but Leo spoke quickly over her. 'Come on,' he said. 'Let's leave them to get on with it.'

Jasmine gave a token smile and put her hand in his. We crossed the street and sat down on the bench in front of the pharmacist's shop, where an old tree cast its spindly shade across the pavement. Starlings were settling in the branches, though it was still early. Outside the empty shop on the corner, the pharmacist's two small sons were playing soldiers in their Sunday clothes. Leo lit a cigarette and watched them clutch their chests and expire in the mud of an imaginary trench. Since the newspapers had been full of rumours of war, they had developed an obsession with fighting. 'Can I go and play with Billy and Joe?' said Jasmine.

'Go on,' said Leo, ruffling her hair. 'But not soldiers.'

'Not soldiers. I know.'

We watched her cross the hard mud of the street, walking very elegantly, the way my mother did, as Billy and Joe broke off their game and came to meet her. There was a pause; then they began throwing stones against the wall, ducking every time and shouting, 'Freedom! Death to the old regime!'

Leo shook his head and lit another cigarette. 'Not soldiers,' he said. 'Revolutionaries. I don't know where they pick these games up.'

The gusting wind carried a few words to us: 'So bloody-minded!' came my mother's voice, and 'You are a fine one—' came my grandmother's. As we sat there, Michael appeared at the corner of the street. He ducked to avoid Billy and Joe's stone throwing, patted Jasmine on the head as he passed, and crossed the road towards us. He was wearing an old hat of his father's that he thought gave him an air of distinction, but the material was worn so shiny in places that you could almost see through it. He had stuck a red feather in the band. 'Anselm,' he said. 'Come to the Royal Gardens. My father has been lecturing all afternoon, and I want to go out for a walk.'

'You're just on your way back from a walk,' I said.

'I know.'

'Go on,' said Leo, putting his hand on my shoulder. 'I will be all right here.'

'Are you sure?'

'Yes. Of course.'

I got up and went with Michael. When I glanced back, Leo was studying something across his knees. It was that book again, *The Darkness Has a Thousand Voices*. As I watched, he took a scrap of paper and a stub of pencil from his pocket and began writing.

'What is your father doing?' said Michael.

'I don't know.'

'What's the book?'

'The one Aldebaran left him. He has been reading it since last night.'

We went through the demolished part of town and past the government hospital. People were queueing outside, some of them lying on stretchers and others sitting wrapped up in coats on the steps. We passed the Heroes' Monument on Castle Street, and I glanced up at the memorial to Harold North. His date of death was fixed in the year he had left the country – twenty-two years ago now. 'And also his wife, the singer and dancer Amelie' was inscribed under his monument.

As we stood there, thunder began low over the houses, and lightning flashed. The rain came out of nowhere and pounded on the roofs. 'Come on,' said Michael, catching hold of my arm, and we ran for the nearest doorway. We stood and watched the rain fall.

'Do you think there is any way Harold North could still be alive?' I said.

'Where did that come from?' he said.

I told him about the book. Michael considered it for a long time. 'Maybe,' he said at last. But he did not sound convinced.

'I know,' I said. 'It sounds impossible. But I wish there was some chance.'

'If he was still alive, why hasn't he come back?' said Michael.

I sat down on the step, and he sat beside me. The rain was falling hard now, soaking the red dust of the city so that it ran like blood. 'Maybe if he was too scared,' I said.

'Of what?'

'Of facing his old life. Of seeing Leo again after all this time.'

'Maybe,' said Michael.

'Or maybe if he couldn't come back,' I continued. 'If he was in prison, or ill, or . . .' I shrugged. 'I don't know.'

'But if he could have come back, he would have, wouldn't he?' said Michael.

'People do stupid things,' I said. 'Without meaning to hurt themselves, or even wanting to.'

'That's true.' He turned his hat round in his hands and replaced it on his head. 'Very wise, Anselm.'

It was something I had learned from Leo. In truth, nearly all my wisdom was secondhand. We fell into silence again. The storm raged briefly, then wore itself out. 'Come on,' said Michael as the rain dwindled. 'Let's go to the Royal Gardens and then home.'

'What about your father?' I said as we resumed our walk. 'What was he angry about?'

Michael jammed his hat down harder on his head. 'He wants to leave the country.'

'Is he serious? You told me before—'

'I don't know,' said Michael. 'I don't know if he's serious, but he keeps ranting on about it, day and night. I swear to God, it's all he ever talks about!'

I was startled by the real exasperation in his voice. 'Do you think he would make you—' I began.

'We are in a bad state,' he said. 'We have very bad debts. My father is trying to be the first honest pawnbroker in the family, and it's going to finish the business. He gives people back their things when they can't pay. A few weeks ago, we had the debt collectors in—'

'Are you serious?'

'Yes. Of course I am.'

I didn't know what startled me more – that the debt collectors had been at the Barones' shop or that Michael had not told me. We walked on in silence, along the alley beside the Five Stars Inn. The wind cut sharply, as though it was already winter. I pulled my jacket tighter around my shoulders. It was an old leather jacket of Leo's, with his cigarette burns in the sleeves.

'I don't want to leave,' said Michael. 'But I don't want to stay if things get as bad as they are supposed to.'

'Where would you go?' I said.

'South.'

'Where south?'

'I don't know, Anselm.' The exasperation was creeping back into his voice. I kept quiet and waited for him to continue of his own accord. 'The fact is,' he said, 'I don't want to live in a country ruled by the Imperial Order. And they wouldn't want me. So maybe it would be best just to get the hell out of here.'

'But, Michael—'

He shook his head then. 'Let's not talk about it,' he said. 'It might not even happen.'

He had a way of dismissing a matter just when you reached the heart of it, and it exasperated me, but I knew from experience that I could do nothing about it. We ran the last few streets to the Royal Gardens. They were almost deserted tonight. A few boys our age were throwing stones into the empty fountain. A couple of children were dodging in and out of the old maze. Hardly anything remained of it now except a few overgrown hedges. The government had never been able to afford to restore the gardens. We took the least weed-choked path to the far fence, behind which an old house stood. It was where we always came to get away from Trader's Row.

The house had been boarded ever since I could remember, and red signs warned trespassers away. Michael and I knew how to get under the barbed wire, and when we were younger, we made a den in the broken carriage that stood in front of the doors and spent every waking hour of one summer there. But we did not go inside tonight. I watched the starlings settling in the pine trees on the other side of the fence, and through the branches, I saw the lights of the castle, appearing then vanishing again as the wind moved the trees.

'Look,' said Michael suddenly, making me start.

'What?' I said.

'I thought I saw a light. Look . . . there.'

'What, in the castle?'

'No. In the house. The first floor.'

We both stared at the house, but no light came again. 'Where?' I said. 'Tell me which window.'

'It was somewhere near the middle.'

The darkness around us was suddenly charged with energy. When we were children, we had firmly believed the house was haunted; that was part of the attraction of the shut-away world on the other side of the fence. And now those old fears stirred in my mind and made me stop breathing as I stared at it. But no light shone from the windows, though we watched in silence for several minutes.

'Maybe I imagined it,' said Michael eventually. 'Come on, let's go home.'

By the time I got in, the argument had burned itself out, and my grandmother was leaving. My mother was sweeping up the broken glass from the floor.

'Let me do that,' said Leo. As he took the dustpan and brush from her, I saw his fingers rest against hers for a moment.

'I see *you've* decided to grace us with your presence,' my grandmother remarked as she crossly swept past me at the door. 'I will see you all next week.'

We listened to her heeled shoes vanishing along the street. 'Jasmine wanted to speak to you,' my mother said as I took off my jacket.

'What about?'

'I don't know. She told me to send you upstairs. I think she wants some help with her newspaper cuttings.' My mother smiled tiredly and touched my arm as I went past her up the stairs. I knew it was a kind of apology for my grandmother.

Jasmine was sitting up in bed, cutting up a newspaper with my mother's dressmaking scissors. 'Anselm, help me cut along the edges,' she said. 'I can never do it right.'

'Is that what you wanted to talk to me about?' I said.

'No,' she said. 'But help me first, Anselm.'

I sat down on the edge of her bed. There were two articles – one was about the king and the second about Aldebaran, another testament from a great man who had once known him. Jasmine had already cut out a picture of the king looking tired and handsome, and she was arranging it in the last remaining space on her wall. She collected every article about them both; if someone raided our house, they would think it the hideout of some out-lawed band of royalists. I cut around the articles carefully and handed them to her. 'There,' I said. 'Will those do?'

'Thank you, Anselm.' She laid them carefully on the chair beside her bed.

Aldebaran's wooden box was there beside them. She glanced at it and sighed. I had not looked at it properly until now. The lid was carved into a neat pattern of stars, and the inside was balding velvet. I opened it and then closed it again, then set it back down beside her bed. 'It's a nice box,' I said. But I did not really understand why he had given it to her.

'Anselm, are you sad?' she said.

'No.'

'Are you sure?'

I hesitated. But I could not tell her about Michael leaving. I felt as if I could make it less likely by forcing myself not to even think about it. 'Nothing,' I said. 'It's really nothing at all, Jas.'

Jasmine picked up the box and began tracing the pattern of stars with one finger. 'Anselm?' she said, pausing halfway along the line and gazing up at me.

'Yes.'

'Why doesn't Grandmama like you?'

She was looking up at me intently, her thumb in her mouth, and I could tell this was what she had wanted to ask me all along. 'She does . . .' I began. But it was no use. Jasmine had been able to see my thoughts since before she could talk. 'I don't know,' I said. 'Sometimes she doesn't act as if she likes any of us very much.'

'But she's different with you,' said Jasmine.

'Maybe.'

'She is. Can't you remember when she started being like that?'

I hesitated. 'She's always acted like she disapproved of me, as long as I can remember. Not all the time, but sometimes. My seventh birthday – that's the first time I can think of.' I made to leave. 'To be honest, Jasmine, I gave up trying to understand her long ago. I wouldn't pay it too much attention.'

'You've never told me the story of your seventh birthday,' she said.

I smiled at that. 'There isn't a story.'

'You could make one.'

'No, I couldn't.'

'Please. Make me a story about your seventh birthday.'

It was something to think about instead of the storm that was rising again outside and Michael's talk of leaving. 'All right,' I said. 'But only a short story. It's half past nine already.'

'All right,' said Jasmine, replacing her thumb in her mouth. 'A short story.'

It started with Leo's writing. On winter nights when I was a small boy, he used to sit by the fire writing pages and pages, and I tried to copy him even before I could spell out my own name. The year before my seventh birthday, my mother was working late as a governess, and the evenings were long. Leo and I used to sit and write while we waited for her to come back. And it was on these evenings that Leo talked to me about his past life. One night he told me about Stirling. I was struggling to copy a line of a poem out of my school textbook, and Leo stubbed out his cigarette and said, 'You remind me of him, you know.'

'Who?' I said. He had been thinking aloud.

'Stirling,' he said. 'My little brother.'

I closed my book. In the metal coal bucket, I could see my reflection, a large-eyed boy with reddish brown hair and a mouth just like my mother's. 'It's not that you look like him,' said Leo, seeing me studying it. 'I don't mean that. But there are certain things about you that are the same.'

'Tell me about him,' I said.

He lit another cigarette and inhaled slowly. 'I remember this one time,' he said. 'We were planning a picnic, and your mother decided we shouldn't bring you. You were a tiny baby. So Stirling promised to remember and take you on a picnic too, one day. That's what he was like, you know? Things like that mattered to Stirling. I think that's what I remember most about him, that he cared about things like that. They don't matter to everyone else.'

'What was the picnic like?' I said.

Leo shook his head. 'We never went. Stirling fell ill and . . .' He shrugged and drew on his cigarette.

'Maybe we should go on a picnic now,' I said.

Leo watched the flames waver in the grate. 'Look,' he whispered, pointing with his cigarette. 'A horse rearing. Quick, or you'll miss it.'

'I see,' I said. It was a game we'd always played. We sat in silence while the wind troubled the flames, but no more shapes appeared.

'We should go,' he said then. 'Maybe you're right.' I waited for him to continue. 'In April, for your birthday,' he said. 'What do you say?'

'I'd like to.'

He ruffled my hair, then got up and rolled yet another cigarette, standing in the light of the fire. We did not speak about it again, but that was how it was decided. And for the next two months, I remembered.

The twenty-second of April dawned grey and cheerless. I got up and dressed and went to the kitchen, where my mother and Leo were wrapping up a basket of food. 'Are we still going?' I said.

'Of course,' said Leo with a quick smile.

'What's a few raindrops, after all?' said my mother.

She hugged me tightly, and Leo swung me up onto the top of the cupboard and set me down there so that I was on a level with them. 'Open your presents,' said my mother, taking down two parcels from the shelf. 'Go on. I can't wait until your grandparents get here.'

I opened the parcels. She had bought me a fur hat that I had dearly wished for. Leo gave me a box of coloured pencils that were so good they made the rest of our possessions look grey and dismal. While I was still thanking them, Aldebaran arrived at the door, stamping his feet against the cold. 'Uncle!' I said, and jumped down to run and meet him.

Aldebaran made a great impression on me as a child. His face was so thin when he smiled that you could imagine every bone under it, but he had Leo's young grey eyes, and he was the cleverest and most impressive man we knew. 'Anselm, you look older already,' he said, which made me laugh. He had brought me a book of stories wrapped in brown paper and a rose in a jar.

'Where did you get a rose at this time of year?' said my mother.

Aldebaran only smiled. 'Are you looking forward to the picnic?' he said, ruffling my hair.

'Yes, Uncle. Can you come?'

He nodded. 'They will not miss me at the meetings. I told them my great-great-nephew's seventh birthday was more important.'

'Tell us how you are, Uncle,' said my mother. 'We have not seen you for days.'

'Sorry. I have been so busy. Losing Rigel has made things harder.'

'When will he be back?' said my mother. 'I read about it in the papers.'

'It is a long-term mission,' said Aldebaran.

I did not understand this conversation, though I listened. I learned, years afterwards, that Rigel had once been the head of the secret service and that Aldebaran had sent him away on some important mission from which he never returned. At the time, I thought he must be some kind of animal – how else could he get lost? 'Will you find the poor thing again?' I asked, which made my mother laugh.

My grandmother and grandfather arrived not long after. We set out in a hired carriage. The frost was disappearing from the roofs of the city, and my mother called it the first real day of spring, though the sun hardly glanced out between the clouds all that morning. We spread out rugs in a valley of wild flowers. At that time, the factories and metalworks had barely advanced into the eastern hill country, and you could lay out a picnic anywhere you chose. As soon as we arrived, my mother and Leo unveiled an iced fruit cake.

'Very good, Maria,' said my grandmother in almost an approving tone. 'That looks just the proper thing.'

'Oh, Leo was the one who made it,' said my mother. 'I just drew the pictures in the icing.'

'Making your husband do the cooking!' said my grandmother. 'Whatever next, Maria?'

'Don't worry,' said my mother, cutting the cake carefully into pieces with our old kitchen knife. 'Leo is not my husband.'

She laughed and made my grandmother shake her head. But my mother's face turned serious as we sat there. A darkness passed over her and made her shiver. I could not take my eyes away from her, after I noticed that. 'Anselm,' said my grandfather then, ruffling my hair. 'Come and take a walk with me.'

My grandfather could not walk far, on account of his leg, which was damaged in the war, but he led me around the valley and pointed out the flowers and butterflies to me with his walking stick. He was a man who knew everything, and yet he passed on his knowledge quite carelessly. 'Look,' he said as a tiny blue butterfly spiralled past us. 'Princess Marianne Blue. There are hardly any in the city, but you see them sometimes out here. They live just one day, you know.'

'Just one day?' I said, startled by that. It made seven years seem an age of some importance.

'And look at that flower,' said my grandfather. 'Bleeding heart, they call it. It looks so like the bloodflower that people still confuse them, and hearts have been broken that way.'

'Why?' I said.

'Because people who find it are convinced that it is the cure for silent fever, and they bring it home for their relatives. And of course, this flower, this bleeding heart, can't do anything at all.'

Leo got up and wandered away, towards the crest of the nearest hill. I watched him go and lost the thread of my grandfather's voice. 'Stop lecturing the poor boy, Julian,' said my grandmother then. 'He doesn't want to hear your stories.'

'Oh, he does not mind it,' said my grandfather.

'No, Anselm is a clever boy,' said Aldebaran. 'He will be a great man when he grows older.'

'Perhaps he will be a priest,' said my grandmother.

'A great author,' said my grandfather.

'Writing is in the family,' said my mother. 'On Leo's side, I mean.'

'I don't see why that should affect Anselm,' said my grandmother.

There was a sudden silence. No one answered, but everyone's eyes were on her suddenly.

'Well, I don't,' she continued, glancing around at us all but meeting none of our eyes. 'You are confusing the child, Maria. I think he should be told the truth.'

'Anselm,' said my mother, putting a hand on my shoulder. 'Go and get Leo. It's time for lunch.'

I got up and started away across the grass. Behind me, I heard my mother's voice rising and my grandmother's quick reply. I tried to listen, but I could feel my mother's eyes on my back, willing me to walk faster. Leo turned when I reached him. He had been gazing at the horizon, where I could just make out a grey shadow beyond the hills. 'It's time for lunch, Papa,' I said.

'Stay up here with me for a while,' he said. 'I want to show you something.'

'What?'

'Look – over there on the horizon.'

'What is it?' I said.

'Ositha,' said Leo. 'I went there once, when I was training as a soldier. During the war. It is just a ghost town now.'

'What does that mean, a ghost town?'

'It means no one lives there. The army destroyed all the buildings, and no one went back.'

We stood for a while looking at that abandoned town on the edge of the sky. Then he took my hand, and we wandered back down to the valley. The argument was over. Aldebaran and my grandfather were talking about the unseasonable weather. My grandmother took bread and cheese and slices of meat pie out of the basket, and Leo handed round the cake, and for a while everything was all right. The sun even emerged.

'Just to think,' remarked my grandmother after the food was finished.

'Just to think what?' said my mother.

'Well,' said my grandmother. 'Seven years since.'

The silence settled again, more menacing than before. 'That is enough,' said my mother. 'Don't talk any more about it.'

'I'm only remarking, Maria. There is no need to take that tone.'

'There is every need to take that tone!'

My grandmother raised her eyebrows and brushed an invisible fly from her skirt. 'I'm just saying that it's seven years since that whole sorry business. That's all. There, I've said it, and you're free to condemn me as you always do.'

My mother moved so quickly that none of us saw until it was over. She slapped my grandmother hard across the face. Suddenly everyone was on their feet. The apples rolled off their plate and bounced away down the hill. They were good apples, and I wanted to pick them up, but I was fixed to the ground and could not move.

'After what I've done for you,' said my grandmother, her voice shaking. 'After everything I've done for you, Maria, and you treat me—'

'I won't listen to this,' said my mother. She picked up our rug and our basket, took my hand, and started for home, though it was five miles. Leo ran after us; none of the others dared. There was such a fierce anger coming from my mother that I thought I could see the air trembling around her. None of us said anything all the way back to the city.

When we got home, my mother locked herself in their bedroom, and we could hear her crying bitterly behind the closed door. Leo's hands shook as he smoked a never-ending chain of cigarettes. 'Come on,' he said eventually. 'I'll take you to a restaurant and buy you a cake. As it's your birthday. Anselm?'

'No,' I said.

'Please.'

'No, I don't want to.'

'Anselm, please. Come on.'

He badly wanted my birthday not to be ruined, but I kept up the resistance. Eventually he gave up and sat down at the table and rested his head against his hand.

'Papa?' I said. 'What did Grandmama mean about a sorry business?'

'Nothing,' he began; then he shook his head. 'Anselm, listen. Just before you were born, some bad things happened, and your grandmother can't help remembering them.'

'What bad things?'

Leo traced a line in the flour lying on the table. 'They

lost their money and had to move to Citadel Street. Your mama has told you about that, hasn't she?'

'Yes, she's told me.'

'Your grandmother sometimes talks as though you had something to do with it,' said Leo. 'But you didn't, and no one thinks you did – just remember that.'

We sat for a long time listening to my mother cry. Then Leo got up and went to the bedroom door. I could hear their voices, my mother's tear-choked and Leo's gentle, saying, 'Come on, Maria. Come on. Shh now.' After a long time, she stopped crying. I remained where I was, in the silent living room. I was suddenly certain of the truth. If Leo told me the misfortunes of the family weren't anything to do with me, it meant – somehow – that they were.

Jasmine listened to that story in silence, then lay down quietly. 'Well,' I said, 'that's the best story I can make of it. It all happened so long ago, years before you were born.'

'Yes,' she said.

'So?' I said. 'What do you think?'

'I don't know.'

The clock in the square chimed ten. 'You should probably go to sleep,' I said. She was already yawning. She reached up to kiss me goodnight and let me arrange the blankets around her. I turned out the lamp and left. But I could tell from the glint of her eyes as I closed the door behind me that she was still awake and thinking. Maybe it was remembering all those people who were gone now – Aldebaran and my grandfather, and somewhere far back the ghost of my real father – or maybe it was because I had never really worked out the truth about what happened the year I was born, but I could not sleep either that night.

★ ★ ★

The Imperial Order marched every night during those last days of July, and every morning the newspapers carried more reports of rioting in the north of the city. Leo did not sleep. He sat up at nights in the back room of the shop, smoking an endless line of cigarettes and studying that red book. And in those days, the world began to change.

We did not realize it at first. No one spoke about it, only the newspapers. First there were those reports of militants rioting in the north. Then General Marlan of Alcyria threatened the states to his east with war, and Titanica threatened retaliation. Marcovy, a country I knew only from geography lessons, threatened Titanica in return to protect its coal-mining interests. Maybe we did not pay enough attention. But those places were hundreds of miles from us, and Aldebaran's death still went unresolved. The king's face appeared on the front of the newspaper every day, looking old and tired. 'My duty to you is to promise you what Aldebaran always promised,' he stated. 'Our country will not go to war.'

The last days in July were national holidays, and in former years we had shut up the shop and gone to the Royal Gardens every evening to dance as the stars came out. Neither Leo nor my mother seemed much inclined to go this year, and we kept the shop open. Then, one morning, Mr Pascal came to our door before seven o'clock. Leo was still lighting the stove, and I was out in the yard fetching water.

'I just spoke to Mr Barone,' he said breathlessly, shoving a newspaper at Leo. 'Alcyria has declared war on all the states along its eastern border. It's official. It's no longer just a threat, North.'

Leo took the newspaper; I leaned over his shoulder. On the front page was a line drawing of General Marlan with his fist raised. Below it a map was striped in black arrows that covered half the continent. Leo ran his hand backwards over his hair. 'What does this mean?' he said.

'I hardly know,' said Mr Pascal.

Jasmine came skipping down the stairs at that moment. Leo threw Mr Pascal a quick glance. 'We are getting on well with those old books,' he said in a voice that hardly faltered. 'Come and see.'

Mr Pascal folded the newspaper. They went to the counter and turned over the contents of the box he had given us. I followed them. Jasmine wandered into the room and looked up at Mr Pascal. She could tell when something was wrong in half a second; our only hope was to conceal what the trouble was, and from Leo's fierce glance, I knew Mr Pascal wouldn't dare say anything more about the news-paper report.

'What's this?' he asked absently instead, picking up another book from the counter. It was *The Darkness Has a Thousand Voices*, still lying there from last night.

'That's something else,' said Leo.

Mr Pascal picked it up and flipped over the pages, from front to back and then the other way. 'Harlan Smith,' he said.

'Do you know anything about him?' said Leo.

Mr Pascal shook his head and studied the first page of the book. 'This is old-fashioned writing,' he said. 'I don't know if there is much call for it nowadays.'

'I'm not selling it,' said Leo.

'Seven Sisters Press,' said Mr Pascal. 'It doesn't sound like a real publisher to me. Not that I know much about book dealing, but if it was a real publisher, I would have seen it about the city. What about John Worthy, the printers?'

'They closed down two years ago,' said Leo.

I glanced at him. He must have looked that up some-how. Mr Pascal set the book down again distractedly and said, 'I don't know what we are going to do. I'm worried, North, and I don't mind telling you so.'

'Maybe it will all turn out all right,' I said, but I did not sound convinced.

'Anselm?' said Jasmine. 'What will turn out all right?'

'Nothing,' I said.

That was too much for Jasmine. She stamped her feet and pulled the box of books off the counter. 'Why doesn't anyone tell me anything?' she demanded, fighting Leo's attempts to restrain her. 'And why haven't we gone to the gardens to dance like everyone else? It's not fair!'

'You'll have to go tonight, North,' said Mr Pascal, shoving the newspaper into his pocket.

'Why?' said Leo.

'The twenty-ninth of July,' said Mr Pascal. 'The king's speech. You'd be a fool to miss it at a time like this.'

With that he left. 'Shh, shh,' Leo told Jasmine, taking hold of her arms. 'If you want to go to the gardens, we'll go, all right?'

All that day, people were hanging out their flags again and decorating their windowsills with white flowers. It was the tradition; the twenty-ninth of July was the day on which the Liberation had started, the day Lucien had been assassinated. The contents of the newspaper seemed to have brought out new patriotic feelings in the city. At six o'clock, the Barones called round to ask if we would go with them to watch the procession.

'Come on,' said Jasmine firmly, and put up the CLOSED sign.

'I don't know, Jas,' said my mother.

'Papa said we could go,' said Jasmine.

'Did he?' said my mother.

'He promised, Mama.'

'Then let me go and get ready.'

She disappeared upstairs. We stood out in the street to wait. From the gardens, music was drifting over the rooftops in the still evening air. People hurried past in twos and threes.

'Anselm, go upstairs and check to see if Maria is all right,' said Leo when several minutes had passed.

I ran up the stairs. The evening sunlight was falling in rays through the high window. 'Mother?' I said. 'Are you coming?'

'I won't be long.'

Her voice sounded strange, as though it was coming through a thick wall. 'Are you all right?' I called.

'I'm fine.'

I went back down again, and we waited. The clock struck seven. We could already hear the muffled applause as the king and his procession moved through the gardens. 'Come *on*,' Jasmine said. 'We'll miss the whole thing.'

'You go ahead,' I said. 'I'll wait for Mother.'

'Are you sure?' said Leo.

'Yes. I'll meet you by the fountain, where we always stand.'

I watched them start along the street, Mr and Mrs Barone arm in arm, Jasmine with Michael, and Leo glancing back every few yards. I gave him what I hoped was a reassuring smile. The house seemed very quiet after I went back upstairs. The whole city must be at the Royal Gardens tonight. I sat down on the top of the stairs and watched the sunlight turn golden on the rooftops. From time to time, a wave of applause rose in the still air.

As I sat there, I began to hear another sound, so soft that at first I thought I had imagined it. I stopped breathing and listened. My mother was crying.

I went to the door of the bedroom. I wanted to speak, but the sound of her crying constricted my throat, and I could not make a sound. 'Mother?' I said at last. 'What's wrong?'

'Nothing.'

But she went on crying. I pushed open the door. She was dabbing at her eyes with her old coloured shawl and searching about for her shoes, and all the while, the tears ran down her face. 'What is it?' I said.

She sat down on the edge of the bed and reached out for my hand. I thought she would tell me it was the war or Aldebaran. But instead she shook her head and said, 'This was the day your real father died.'

The silence closed around us, and neither of us could speak. I tried to several times, but I could not. Then the clock chimed the quarter hour, and my mother looked up. 'Is it past seven already?' she said. 'Anselm, we have missed half the speech. It's my fault. Why didn't you tell me?'

She was brushing the tears from her face and struggling to lace up her boots, and then she took me by the hand and hurried me after her down the stairs. A thousand questions were burning in my mind. But then we were out in the street and running along the deserted alleys. The voices still rose from the Royal Gardens. A few white flowers lay trampled in the dust. All the way there, I wanted to ask her.

But as we reached the gates of the gardens, the crowds came surging back towards us.

'What is it?' said my mother, tightening her grip on my hand.

'I don't know.'

'Can you see them?'

'No.' I glanced about. 'Wait – over there.'

I made out Jasmine on Leo's shoulders, somewhere near the fountain. We struggled towards them through the crowds. Halfway there, they met us. Jasmine was crying. Mr Barone and Michael were arguing loudly.

'What's going on?' I said.

'The king has declared war on Alcyria,' said an old man close by. 'Get back home, because there's going to be trouble.'

The gunshots started just after we reached Trader's Row. They were all over the city, quick rifle volleys and angry shouts. People were still hurrying past the shop windows or calling for their relatives. Leo put up the grilles on the shop windows. Next door, I could hear Michael and Mr Barone still arguing.

'I just don't believe it's true,' my mother kept saying. 'Another war. I just can't make myself believe it.'

'If Aldebaran was here . . .' said Leo.

The shouting and the gunfire went on until the early hours. Eventually we went upstairs and tried to sleep, out of disbelief more than anything. There was nothing else to do. On the way to Mass the next morning, we passed people leaving the city. They were driving north in old horse carts with their belongings piled around them, avoiding our glances as if they thought we would condemn them for their loss of nerve. The church was more crowded than it had been for weeks. Father Dunstan preached about the steadfastness of the Lord in times of trouble.

When we came out of the church, Michael was waiting by the fountain.

'Michael!' called Jasmine, and ran towards him, but he did not swing her up into his arms as he usually would have done.

'You had better come,' he said.

'What is it?' said Mrs. Barone.

Michael led the way back towards Trader's Row, and we followed at a jog. I could see nothing wrong at first. Then I made out the letters on the wall of the shop and the black space where the front window used to be. Leo ran ahead and went in at the side door, and I heard him go quickly up the stairs. 'I was in the back room,' said Michael. 'I heard the noise and came out, but they had guns.'

'Who was it?'

'I don't know. The Imperial Order, I think, but I don't know.'

We caught up with him and stopped in front of the building. 'They didn't take anything,' said Michael. 'They ran away down the alley as soon as I came out.'

'This is it,' said Mr Barone, shaking his head. 'I can't stay here any longer.'

It could have been worse. But my skin turned cold all the same, looking at the destruction. While we had been at Mass, someone had smashed all our windows and the Barones', and NONE OF YOU ARE SAFE was daubed in six-foot letters on the wall.

I wanted to talk to Michael that night, but the light never appeared at his window, and when I called his name, he did not answer. There was only air between us now that the windows were smashed, and I could hear him walking about his room. 'Michael, I need to talk to you!' I said in exasperation, but he did not stop his pacing. Eventually I gave up and put a board across my window and went to bed. The whole city seemed in a stupor the next day. No one went out.

'Have you spoken to Mr Barone?' Mr Pascal asked us when he came into the shop late that afternoon. Leo shook his head. 'All he has been talking of today is getting out of the city,' said Mr Pascal. 'North, I think he is really going to do it.'

'I should go and talk to Michael,' I said.

'Yes, do,' said Mr Pascal. 'And perhaps you can put some sense into their heads. I told him this whole thing will blow over—'

'Will it?' said Leo, startling us both. He had been silent all day, but he got up now and began locking the windows. 'Let's close up,' he said. 'No one will come in anyway. Jasmine!'

'Yes, Papa,' she said sullenly. She was lying under the table drawing. Leo had forbidden her to go out and play with Billy and Joe in the street.

'Nothing,' said Leo. 'Are you all right?'

'Yes, Papa.' Jasmine rolled over and began kicking the underside of the table.

'Stop that,' he said. 'Anselm, help me tidy up.'

As soon as we had finished sweeping the floor and rearranging the boxes in the shop, I went next door to the Barones'. The door was locked, but Mrs Barone let me in. 'Is Michael here?' I said.

'Yes. You had better go up and see him.'

The place was strangely silent today. I knew the

Barones' shop as well as our own; it was a bare and dusty place, with a crucifix on the back wall and a grille across the counter and a shabby sign that said NO GUNS BOUGHT OR SOLD. Our two shops were the only ones in the street that still clung to a no-firearms policy. Today the shop looked barer than usual. 'Have you opened today?' I asked Mrs Barone.

She shook her head. 'Michael is in his room,' she murmured, then hurried out of sight into the back of the shop.

Michael did not answer when I tapped on his door, so I went in. He was lying on his bed with his arm across his face. 'Anselm,' he said when I came in.

'Are you sick?' I said.

He shook his head and rolled over but did not say anything.

'Can I sit down?' I said.

He nodded.

I moved his hat aside and sat down on the rickety chair beside the bed. The glazier had already been in and replaced the windows in both our shops, though Dr Keller had complained about the bill. The broken shards of the old window were still lying on the floorboards. 'You should clear this up,' I said, for want of anything better.

'All right! Don't fuss, Anselm!'

'What are you angry about?'

'It's not you.'

I waited. Eventually he sat up and looked at me. In the dim light of the falling evening, with his black hair that went in all directions and his dark grey eyes, he looked like the picture of some melancholy sufferer. 'My father wants to leave the city,' he said. 'He isn't joking – he says next week or the week after. And I don't know what to do.'

'Can't you talk to him?'

'I've tried.'

'But if you tell him—'

'Anselm, I've tried.'

He got up and went to the window. 'Talk to me,' he said. 'Tell me about something else, Anselm. I can't stand all this.'

I watched the dark falling across his face. 'The day before yesterday,' I said, telling him out of habit what was first in my mind, 'when you went ahead to the Royal Gardens, my mother told me something. Out of nowhere, she just told me. The twenty-ninth was the day my real father died.'

Michael glanced up. 'She said it just like that?'

'It was terrible, to be honest with you.' I stood up and went to the window, then came back. 'She was crying, and I didn't know how to ask her. I can't now. The moment passed, with all the trouble that happened afterwards.'

Michael turned and studied my face. 'So what do you think about it?'

'I don't know what I think.'

'Did she say anything else?'

I shook my head.

'But you didn't ask her?'

'I couldn't. It would have made her too upset.'

'But you could find out, couldn't you? I mean, you could try and find out who he was some other way?'

'How?'

Michael thought about that, studying the glass on the floorboards. 'Go to the graveyard and see who died on the twenty-ninth of July.'

'Maybe,' I said.

'Or look in the government register of deaths, or . . .'
He shrugged.

We fell into silence. The fact that he was leaving overtook the room again. Darkness was coming down outside.
Nightfall had invaded the alleyways and was creeping
further in. Starlings began to settle in the trees, circling
downward in clouds that shifted endlessly. Michael got up
and lit the lamp.

'Michael, if you leave—' I said.

He shook his head and went on shaking it, like an old
man. 'I thought about staying and letting them go without
me. I was almost sure I was going to. But if there really is an
invasion . . .'

'Do you think there will be?'

'From the way my father is talking. The Imperial Order
are maniacs, I swear. I couldn't live in that world. There are
things about me that government will never accept.'

'Maybe if you just kept your head down—' I began.

'Is that what you are going to do, Anselm? Keep your
head down all your life?'

Mr Barone called from downstairs.

'I had better go,' I said. Michael nodded. But as I left, he
reached out his hand to me, as though in apology. I took it.
He had strong fingers, like an artist's. I had always wondered
if it came from the ten generations of Barones before him
who had made their living as jewellers, or if it was just
chance.

'We will always be friends,' he said. 'Won't we?'

'Yes,' I said. 'Of course we will.'

'Because otherwise—'

But Mr Barone's voice cut off whatever else he had

been going to say. I turned and went down the stairs and into the street, closing the front door behind me. The stars were shining over the castle, crossed by the last birds flying home. I glanced up at Michael's window, but he had put out the light.

The next day, there were soldiers in the city, marching east. And Mr Barone was true to his word. Within a week, the Barones' shop was sold.

Dawn,

the thirtieth
of December

*A*fter I got to that point, I ran out of words. The dawn was rising white beyond the windows of the inn, extinguishing the lamps and creeping over the bleak snow outside. Mr Hardy sighed and stretched out his legs. We were old friends now, after sitting awake and talking all through the blackest hours and drinking his cheap spirits. He had told me a good deal about himself. He had once been a rich man and a scholar and had lost everything after Lucien took power. Since then, he had been wandering from place to place. He told me this with no trace of self-pity. It was as though he was sure that no one was to blame for it. And he listened very intently to my story. Every few minutes, he would question some detail or nod and cough and pour out another glass of spirits. 'What I don't understand,' he said at last, 'is how you ended up here.'

'Here?' I said, glancing around at the dingy front room of the inn.

'I mean travelling like this – on your own, with no belongings, like you're running away from something.' He said it without any accusation.

'I have some belongings,' I said. It had become an important point to me. I turned out the contents of my pockets. But they looked a dismal array like that.

'What are those papers you are carrying with you?' said Mr Hardy.

'Just a story.'

He poured out half an inch of spirits and sipped them thoughtfully. 'Talking of stories, did your father ever find out about Harlan Smith?' he asked.

'I was coming to that.'

'Will you go on?'

I shook my head. I could not. He seemed to understand, because he said, 'Perhaps we should talk of something else. Tell me about this other story instead.'

'That's part of it too,' I said.

'I see.'

'Read it if you like,' I said. 'I don't really understand it myself.'

'What's it about?' said Mr Hardy, turning over the pages.

'Another country. Rigel. Nothing that relates to my life at all.'

'Rigel who was head of the secret service? Rigel who disappeared?'

'Yes.'

He studied the first page of the story. 'I can't make it out,' he said. 'My eyesight failed young, I'm afraid, and I can't read in this dark.'

'Then I'll read it to you,' I said. Talking was better than sitting there in silence, listening to the wind howling and shuddering at the walls. He nodded, and I picked up the stack of papers and began.

'Once, many years ago,' the lord Rigel began, 'there was a boy who wanted more than anything to study magic.'

'Where are we going, Papa?' said Juliette. She was huddled opposite him on the carriage seat, wrapped in his overcoat with only her face showing.

'Shh,' said Rigel. 'Just listen to the story.'

Juliette rested her face against the misted pane of the window. Outside, dawn held off a while longer, and the countryside was outlined in dismal grey. A light snow drifted across the moorland. 'When will we come back?' said Juliette. 'Will it be soon?'

'I don't know.'

A streak of dust lay across her face from the carriage window, and he reached across and brushed it away. His heart ached sometimes to look at her. She was still so small; her hand on his was no weight at all.

'Go on with the story,' she said.

'This boy was born in Angel in the south,' said Rigel. 'His mother was a poor woman. She used to go out cleaning for wealthy people and washing the steps of their houses. She had worked for the great Markov family and other rich families. In the icy weather, she came back with her hands bleeding. It was hard, Juliette, very hard.'

'Yes,' said Juliette. 'It must have been. And what about his father?'

'Well, the boy's father was a mystery,' said Rigel. 'A soldier who had come and gone without leaving even a name. The boy – Richard, I will call him – at first he did not think much about his father. But as Richard grew up, it became clear he had powers. He could perform strange feats that no one understood. He could guess what his mother was thinking without asking her, and he dreamed once about the future and saw himself in a cold northern city where people fought in the streets, and once he saw himself as a rich man in a tall white house. These dreams began to unnerve his mother. She believed that her son had been born into a family with powers, without either of them knowing it. Richard used to ask her again and again to tell him about his father.'

'Did she know much about him?' said Juliette.

Rigel turned to glance out the window, at the snow falling on the bleak moorland and the lights of the harbour ahead. 'Not really,' he said. 'It was a cause of shame to her. She talked very little about him. But I always wondered, when I was growing up.'

'Richard always wondered,' Juliette corrected him.

'Are you cold, Juliette?' he said, reaching forward to grip her hands. 'You are. Perhaps we should stop at an inn for half an hour.'

'No. I'm not cold. Papa, where are we going?'

'Let me go on with the story.'

'I don't want a story,' said Juliette.

Rigel had been going to continue anyway, but her next question took the words away from him. 'Is Mother going to be there?'

He had been planning to carry on the story over the miles of bleak moorland, spinning it out according to the length of the journey. He had been going to tell her about his mother's death when he was still a young boy, and his troubles under Lucien's government, and how he finally studied magic. But he could not tell it now. 'No,' he said. 'No, she's not going to be there. You know that.'

'Papa?' said Juliette. 'Do you still work for Mr Aldebaran?'

'Yes, angel. He is going to come and see us off.'

'Then why is he sending us away?'

'He isn't, Juliette. I was the one who suggested it.'

'I don't want to go away.'

Rigel wanted to say something, but a heavy silence was constricting his throat, and he could not speak. They were approaching the harbour now. Juliette traced a line in the window; it became a heart, then vanished. Through the clear lines in the glass, Rigel could see the ships stretching out against their moorings and men unloading crates by torch-light. The flames leaped wildly in the wind.

'Where are we going?' Juliette asked.

'Another city,' said Rigel.

'Papa, why are you crying?'

'I'm not crying,' said Rigel, but he was.

Juliette leaned forward carefully and touched his face. She traced the scar that ran from his mouth upwards across his cheekbone, then vanished against the line of his hair. Rigel could feel her fingers trembling with cold. The crying threatened to cut him in two; it rose so violently in his chest that he could not hold it back.

The whole tragedy of his life came over him like the crashing sea beyond the harbour wall. He saw himself, the brilliant and self-taught student of magic, the only pupil Aldebaran had ever taken, and the woman he fell in love with – Juliet Delmar, the only heroine of the resistance, a woman so bright to him that she made the stars look dim. This was the end of the story, Juliette's favourite story, and it had turned bitter now. He had always been ambitious. Was that the fault that had brought them down? If he had not been the head of the secret service – if he had not been responsible for the imprisonment of half the leaders of the New Imperial Order – Juliette's mother would still be alive. They had come to his door with guns, shouting for him, and the fearless Juliet Delmar sent the servants to the back of the house, hid Juliette in the cellar with the housekeeper, and went to answer it.

'Juliette,' said Rigel. 'It's all my fault.'

Juliette sat hunched in the seat opposite him and said nothing. The carriage had come to a halt now. The guards were standing there waiting for him to get out. Rigel laid the fur rugs on the seat, pushed open the door, and lifted Juliette down, taking care not to hit her head against the door frame. In his other hand, he bundled up the few things he was taking with him – his books and papers that he needed to communicate with Aldebaran. But he did it carelessly. It did not matter any more.

Juliette pressed her face against Rigel's overcoat, trying to block out the icy wind. Her nose dug into his shoulder. Aldebaran had been standing in the shadows of an outbuilding, but he came towards them now. 'There you are,' he said, and reached forward to grip Rigel's hand. 'You are certain about this—'

'Yes,' said Rigel.

'And you will send me a message when you arrive?'

'Of course.'

'All the details are here. Plus enough money and a few things you can sell if you have trouble with the false account. There is nothing I can foresee, but—'

'Very well,' said Rigel, and took the black case that Aldebaran held out. 'I have my books. I can send word to you straight away.'

'Good,' said Aldebaran, studying Rigel's face. 'That's good.'

'What is it?' said Rigel.

'It is so soon, Rigel,' said Aldebaran. 'That was all I was thinking.'

'I need to go,' said Rigel. 'I need to be away from here.'

There seemed nothing else to say. The plan had been so carefully rehearsed that Rigel was already thinking of what came next, and he did not know how to bid Aldebaran farewell. So he gripped the old man's hand again and turned. He carried Juliette down the steps into a small boat and began to cast away the moorings. 'Teacher?' he said, pausing for a moment. 'Why did you promote me over everyone else? Why did you always show me so much favour?'

He knew that he would not return to his country – he had decided it, in the bleak kind of calm that came over him in the days after his wife died – and now that he was leaving, he wanted to ask.

'You were my pupil,' said Aldebaran. 'That's why.'

'You never taught anyone else. You said you would only ever teach a relative, and you took me as an apprentice.'

'There are mysteries in my family,' said Aldebaran. 'In both of ours. I had a brother, Harold Field, who spent several years in England. He was a soldier and a very reckless man. After he came back from England, the year before you were born, he was on active service at the southern border, just outside Angel. And you told me much the same story about this father you never knew.'

Rigel had thought it was something like this and had long since dismissed it as arrogance on his part. 'Teacher?' he said again. The boat was pulling away from the quay, and the rope rattled through the ring and fell loose. They were out on the water now.

As the night divided them, Aldebaran said, so quietly that Juliette could not hear, 'Listen, whatever comes into your head, Rigel, don't let me down.'

Rigel raised his arm vaguely in a kind of wave that became a salute, then pushed off from the quayside and drove the boat round into the waves. The tide carried them, and there was no point in raising a sail in this storm, so they drifted instead.

'Papa, I'm scared,' said Juliette.

'It's not far. Just a few yards across the river mouth.'

'Where are we going? Holy Island?'

'Holy Island is far to the north of here, Juliette. No, we are going somewhere else.'

The waves surged and lifted them. 'Papa!' said Juliette.

'What? Don't be scared.'

'What did Aldebaran say?'

'I don't know. I don't expect it was anything important. Just goodbye.'

Rigel told himself the story again as he held the boat steady. It was something to fix his mind on, to keep it from rolling and plunging like the restless sea. What if now, after everything, they were both pitched overboard? But he could not think of that. The recklessness that had taken possession of his soul became a kind of bravery. The end of the story – the truth about Aldebaran – seemed to close the whole chapter of his life until now, and what lay ahead was uncertain. He glanced at Juliette. She was staring out into the driving snow, his overcoat pulled close around her shoulders. She made no sound; it seemed a point of honour with her. Perhaps Juliette had suffered too much already in her life, because no matter what he did, he could never make her spoiled. He almost wished she would cry and scream and demand to be taken back.

'Are we going home ever?' said Juliette.

'No,' said Rigel.

'What – never?'

'Never.'

Juliette started to cry then. 'Hush now,' said Rigel, regretting his honesty. 'It's for your own good, Juliette. You'll be safe where we're going.'

Juliette did not answer. Rigel ducked as the boat swung precariously. 'There is the island,' he said.

'I can't see it.'

'Just ahead, not far,' said Rigel, who could not see it either.

A tale came to him from a long way off about a magician and his daughter who were cast out on the heartless sea. An English story. He had always been drawn to that place. 'This is a very important mission,' said Rigel. 'Magic is dying out, and Aldebaran is sending me to this other city to find all the people with powers who are living there, people who belonged to our country once, long ago. Someone has to teach them and pass on the skill so that it doesn't die altogether.'

But he wasn't going to do it, he realized. It had been an excuse to leave the country – that was all. He was going to take the money and run.

The boat jolted suddenly and ran aground on a gritty mudbank half covered in snow. 'Come on,' said Rigel, lifting Juliette out and taking back his overcoat.

'Where are we?' she said.

'Check by the stars,' said Rigel. He took a battered compass out of his pocket and handed it to her. Juliette rubbed the mist from the lens and bent close to it in the darkness. The needle was twisted and jammed, as though something had struck it violently. Juliette started to cry. 'Come on, it's all right,' said Rigel. 'I'll carry you.'

They started up the bank. The darkness was thick around them, and every few yards, Rigel would stumble on a broken stick or a hidden line of wire and force back a curse. Stones clicked under his boots. The snow clouds were clearing now, and when they looked back, there was only black mud and marshes and far away the definite line where the sea met the horizon.

'What's happened to the land?' whispered Juliette.

'It's there,' said Rigel. 'You just can't see it.'

They were walking beside a river now. Rigel kept his hand on the back of Juliette's head, as if she were still a baby.

'Talk to me, Papa,' said Juliette. 'I don't like the silence.'

'Well,' said Rigel, 'I'll tell you about our new life. We are going to find a place here where we can live. You can go to school.'

'Where will we live?' said Juliette.

'I'll buy us a house. Do you know how much money we have here?'

Juliette shook her head.

'Fifteen million English pounds,' said Rigel. 'It's in the bank in my name and I can take it out tomorrow. Do you know how much that is?'

'A lot.'

'Yes. A lot. In this age it is. Our whole street back in Kalitzstad.'

'Back where?'

'Sorry – in Malonia City,' said Rigel. But he was less certain of the name suddenly, as though they had left ten years ago and he'd forgotten the place. 'Malonia City,' he repeated. 'Our street in Malonia City.'

'What was it like?' said Juliette.

'You know our street. It's on the east side of the city, and the houses face out across the city wall. You can see the eastern hills and the mountains beyond, and you can watch the sun rising over them if you wake early enough.'

'Yes,' said Juliette uncertainly. 'I remember that.'

'Well, you were very small. Anyway, we'll have a big house here and servants.'

'What's the city's name?' said Juliette.

'The City of Long Down,' said Rigel. 'At least that's what we always used to call it, when we were in the resistance. But, no, that's not quite right.'

'I don't like it,' said Juliette. 'Going to a city when we don't even know what its name is.'

They passed under a bridge that trembled and shuddered above them. Rigel knelt down in the darkness and clutched Juliette's hand so tightly that she held her breath. 'Papa, what was that?' she whispered when the noise had faded.

'Nothing,' he said. 'Just a carriage passing.'

He stood up, shaking, and watched the car's tail-lights recede into the dark. 'We will get used to this place,' he said. 'You will like it here. It's a good place to live.'

Juliette did not answer. As they walked on, he could see the stars, and he tried to point them out to her.

'Why are they so faint?' Juliette murmured.

'Because it's nearly morning,' said Rigel, which was not the truth. The stars were fainter here, but there was no reason for it that he could understand. Something about poisoned gases that came between the earth and the constellations. It struck him that he had never asked Aldebaran where the poisoned gases came from. Perhaps they were just one of the old man's superstitions, like his belief that magic was stronger here. Perhaps he should not think about it, now that he and Juliette were alone in this country.

Rigel did not take out the compass, or the maps that were sewn into the lining of his overcoat. He could not shake off the feeling that he had made this journey before, and a strange calm came over him. He had always believed that it was his powers that gave him this sense of returning. It was as though the whole of his life was there in the back of his mind, and all he had to do was follow a path already set out for him. That was how he had felt when Aldebaran agreed to let him set out on this mission. As though he had been prepared for it years ago. To find a place far away from insecurity and fighting. A place where Juliette could sleep in a cool white house with alarms on its walls, away from the criminals whose grudges made Rigel wake up shouting in the blackest hours of the night and who had taken her mother from him, a place where Juliette could grow up and be safe. Because there was nothing like having a child of your own to make you lose your courage.

Rigel stopped on the muddy bank of the river and set Juliette down. Across the water, a single light was burning. Rigel took out the bundle of papers – all his books on magic and the papers he had used to communicate with Aldebaran. Then he threw them into the river. They sank out of sight, and the dark water covered them.

Around one o'clock, they stopped at a cold white building at the edge of a main road. Rigel hesitated outside the door. Through the glass, he could see a woman in a uniform. She stood at a metal box, counting out coins and sorting them into transparent bags. She gave him a quick smile as they entered, and glanced at his shabby overcoat. It was probably not quite right for this country, he thought. He took it off and folded it over his arm.

Rigel had practised this scene with Aldebaran, and it stabbed at his heart now. 'A portion of chips, please,' he said, and counted out the few coins she asked for. He waited with his eyes on the tiles under his feet. They had some strange marbled pattern, but they were softer than marble. He wondered if he would one day be so used to this country that he could see tiles like this and not marvel at them.

'Would your little girl like one?' said the woman, holding out a tray of sweets.

Rigel started. 'No,' he said without thinking about it. 'Thank you, but no.'

'Yes, I would, Papa,' said Juliette, and reached out for one. Her accent was stronger than his and made the woman smile.

'Are you here on holiday, then?' she said.

'Yes,' said Rigel.

'Where from?'

'Australasia,' said Rigel.

'Australia?'

He had mistaken the name. Still, they would be gone in a minute, and the worst thing was to appear uneasy. He nodded and smiled. 'Must be warmer there this time of year,' said the woman as she handed the package of food across the counter.

'Yes, a good deal warmer,' said Rigel, and picked up Juliette and turned to leave.

Outside, he was shaking, and he had to sit down on the edge of the pavement as soon as they were out of sight of the building. He sat there and ate pieces of fried potato out of greasy paper and did not let go of Juliette. She had drifted back to sleep in his arms. When she woke, he gave her the last few chips, then put the paper in his overcoat pocket and picked her up. They set out again across the dark countryside. Lights were winking all around them now, the edges of the nearest towns and ahead, the vast city.

Rigel could not stop his heart from beating heavily. But Aldebaran has done this before me, he thought. I am only following in his footsteps. I am following in the footsteps of countless others, like a pilgrim. That's all. These people who once belonged to our country, these people with powers I was supposed to find. They might have been weary of their old lives too. They might have been heartbroken and desperate to escape.

At last they came up over a low rise, and the city spread out before them. Rigel stopped and set Juliette down and straightened her overcoat. Behind him he could hear the occasional car passing, but he was already used to that sound. Ahead the city stretched so far that he could not see the end of it. A strange orange mist hung over the buildings in the last of the darkness, and lights winked here and there. 'Juliette,' he whispered. 'Look ahead.'

'What is it?' said Juliette.

Rigel's heart ached. It came from being glad and terrified in equal measure, and for a moment he could not speak. But then the name came back to him. 'The city of London.'

THE THIRTIETH OF
DECEMBER

By that part of the story, the weak sun was rising, and the guests in the inn were beginning to stir. I folded up the papers. Mr Hardy watched me thoughtfully for a moment, then got up and walked to the window and back again. 'That story troubles me,' he said. 'It makes Rigel a traitor.'

'I know,' I said. 'That was what made me think it was just a story.'

'On the contrary,' said Mr Hardy. 'That is what makes me think it is true.'

I watched him consider it, then turn and walk back to me and sit down heavily at the table. 'Will you carry on telling me?' he said. 'Another evening.'

'Yes,' I said. 'All right.'

Soon after that, the innkeeper came down and gave us bread and water. We had hardly any money; it was an act of charity on his part. Then the coach driver sent for someone to mend the wheel, and before twelve o'clock, we set out again into the snow and the bleak moorland, leaving that village behind.

We did not travel far that day. The snow was banked high on the sides of the road, and no one came out to clear it. After darkness fell, the coach driver began looking for another place to stop — another bleak inn in an unknown village somewhere. I slept with my head on my rolled-up jacket on the table in the front room. When I woke, I was confused. It was just past midnight, and the stars were shining outside over a landscape I did not know. It took me several seconds to remember where I was.

Mr Hardy was sitting with his arms folded, gazing out into the dark. 'Anselm,' he said. 'Are you all right?'

'Yes,' I said.

I got up and went to the window. Drifts of snow like mist were crossing the dark moor. The whole thing made my heart turn cold.

'Come and sit here,' said Mr Hardy. He had been saying his rosary, but he put it away now and drew out a chair for me.

I sat opposite him. 'Thank you,' I said. I did not know why my heart was still so heavy and why I still had not written one word of the account I had planned.

Mr Hardy was evidently thinking of the same thing, because he said, 'How is your story progressing?'

'It's not,' I said. 'Not really. I don't know how to tell it.'

'How you told me,' he said. 'Just write it down.'

'Maybe,' I said.

'Go on telling me, if you like,' he said. 'I would rather listen to that than sit here in the dark.'

I still had a wish, however childish, to explain myself. I wanted someone to tell me it would be all right. 'Can I go on?' I said. 'Don't you mind it?'

He shook his head. 'Where did you get to?' he said. 'Ah, yes. Your friend was about to leave the city.'

It all came back to me, as though it had never been gone, and I started to tell him.

AUGUST

On Michael's last night in the city, we went out after dinner and walked through the streets. The night was starlit. There had been no riots in the past days, and the city had begun to come alive again. Wealthy people were gathering around the theatres and bars. We wandered through the markets. I did not know what to say to him; now that the Barones' shop was packed up and Michael was really going, there seemed to be no words between us any more.

We passed a gold and silver stall where the traders crowded so thickly that they shoved each other into the road. Michael slowed to look. A well-dressed man with greased black hair was shouting loudest and banging down crown notes on the stall. He had a suitcase in his hand and a necktie slung casually around his collar, as though it would have fatigued him too much to tie it properly. His accent was something like Alcyrian. I knew half the traders in the city by sight, but not this man. 'Look at him,' I said. Michael nodded with a kind of awe.

'You are robbing me,' the man was saying, holding a gold medallion to the light. 'This is not real gold—'

'Yes, sir, I assure you,' a voice interjected.

The man bit the medallion. Half his own teeth were gold. 'Ten crowns,' he said. 'It's gold plating, for God's sake.

And throw in those four rings for me as recompense for being so dishonest.'

An argument broke out. But he must have succeeded in his bargain, because the next moment he was shoving the jewellery into his jacket pocket and turning to leave. He picked up the suitcase and strode off down a side street.

'Who was that man?' said Michael. 'Have you seen him before?'

'No, I never have.'

We watched him until he was out of sight. 'I wonder what he meant by "gold plating",' I said.

'It's something they have invented in Alcyria,' said Michael. 'They pass a lightning current through water, and the gold sticks to the surface of the metal and covers it. Then you can pretend it's real gold, and people who don't know will buy it. Mr Pascal told me.'

'Does that work?'

'Oh, you know Mr Pascal's stories.'

'And where do they get the lightning from? Do they draw it down out of the sky?'

Michael laughed. 'Probably.'

But his laugh faded quickly as we turned away from the markets and wandered on listlessly. 'I don't want to go home until late,' Michael said. 'I will only argue with my father again.' We stopped at the Five Stars Inn, halfway to the Royal Gardens, and Michael ordered spirits. His drinking troubled me sometimes. He did it so blindly, as though he was already desperate. When we left to go on, we could see the guards changing posts on the castle road and troops moving slowly down. 'Going to the borders,' said Michael.

My heart hurt, and I tried to say something, but I couldn't. We walked along an alley where the homeless sat huddled around an old brazier. The wind was rising.

'Spare any change?' someone called, but I had nothing to give him.

'Let's go to the old house,' said Michael.

We crossed the Royal Gardens, still divided by our silence. As we approached the fence, he caught my arm. 'There!' he said. 'I told you there was a light. The other day, when we were here before.' We stepped closer to the fence. The light was flickering behind a ragged curtain on the first floor. 'Come on,' said Michael. 'I want to see who it is. I can't leave without knowing.' He crawled along the fence to the gap in the barbed wire and began edging his way under it. I could hear shouts beginning close to the castle, but I did not want to go back yet. I followed him. We crossed the grounds at a run and stopped under the lighted window. 'I can get up into one of these trees,' he said.

'You'll break your neck,' I said.

'I won't,' he said.

He stopped ahead of me, staring up into a pine tree that stood close against the front wall. Its branches scratched the glass when the wind moved it. The lighted window was one of the only ones that had not had the panes shot out of it in the Liberation or been smashed by children's stones. Michael began to climb, leaning precariously as he swung round the trunk from branch to branch. I waited, then grew sick of the dark and the silence and climbed up after him. It was not hard to do. I kept my eyes fixed on Michael above me and did not think about falling. He reached down and pulled me up onto a branch that was stronger than the rest. We sat there in the tree, with the wind howling around us, and looked at the lighted window. 'Come on,' Michael said then. 'I'm going across to the windowsill. And, Anselm, if I die, say a prayer for my soul.'

'Don't,' I said, but he ignored me and edged out along the branch. 'Michael, come back,' I said. He turned and grinned at me. His eyes were steady, as though he didn't know what danger was. The branch creaked and sighed. 'Come back now,' I said, and reached out my hand to him. 'Michael, I'm not joking!'

The branch gave way as he caught my hand, and we both went down together.

It was not far to fall in the end, but it still knocked the breath out of my lungs. We lay for several long seconds without letting each other go. Then Michael said, 'Anselm, are you all right?'

'Yes,' I said, and coughed.

'Are you sure?'

'Yes. Are you?'

'I think so.' He sat up. 'I tell you, if these plants hadn't been here . . .' There was a tangle of briars and thornbushes growing up against the wall, and they had broken our landing. I was still gasping for breath, so I lay where I was. The wind was rising all the time, and there was drizzle in it now. 'Let's go to the old carriage,' he said. 'Before it gets any worse. I'm sorry; I thought that branch would hold out.'

We were both limping when we stood up, and it made me laugh, though it was not really funny. We struggled to the old carriage, and Michael struck a match to light us up the steps. In the wavering flame, his face was paler and older. He blew out the match, and we could see faintly by the moonlight alone. Damp had eaten away the coach furnishings, but the leather seats were still intact in places. The wheels on one side were broken, making the coach lean drunkenly, its two lamps out of line. The front window was cracked, and a light dusting of mould covered the cushion behind my head. We always kept candles here, under the coach seat. Michael reached for one of the lamps, took off the mildewed glass globe, put a new candle in, and lit it. The flame steadied and brightened. The sky outside turned to a deep indigo against the glass, a thousand miles wide. 'Do you remember that summer when we came here every day?' said Michael.

'And the time when we came looking for ghouls.'

'My God, I've never been so scared in my life.' He shook his head. 'Except maybe now.'

I waited for him to continue, but he didn't. 'What are you scared of?' I said.

'I don't know.' He rested his cheek against the window and sighed. 'Anselm, everything is wrong with the world. Our shop is finished. My family has been here for generations. What do we have now? My father says when the Alcyrians arrive, it will go hard for us, because he was in the resistance. He says it's better to leave now with our dignity. But dignity doesn't keep you safe. I wish I had something to believe in. And I keep thinking . . .'

'What?'

'Anselm, what if the Imperial Order does win? I don't want to be fighting against the world all my life. But I don't want to keep my head down.'

'They can't win,' I said. 'The king won't let them. And Titanica is the strongest country on the continent, and they've already sent troops in.'

'But it's not just a country, the Imperial Order. It's everywhere.'

As if in answer, there was a burst of gunfire. It had been

too much to hope that the rioting was over for good. 'We should get back,' I said. But neither of us moved.

'Anselm, look at this,' said Michael.

He took a crumpled sheet of newspaper out of his pocket and put it into my hand. It was too dark to see it properly. 'What is it?' I said.

'People are disappearing,' he said. 'Not just in Alcyria, but also here. A man who was with the resistance under Lucien's government. A woman teacher who spoke out about the Imperial Order in her town. They can get you for anything. If you go to Mass when they have called a curfew, or come from the wrong country, or have powers, or if you fall in love with the wrong person. That's two years in jail.'

The candle spluttered with a strange human sound and went out. I struck a match. Michael was sitting far away from me, his coat pulled up to his face, and shadows moved in his eyes. 'Anselm, sooner or later, people who don't agree with them will have to fight,' he said. 'And I'm scared to think of where it's going to end.'

'It might not come to that,' I said. 'In between his pessimistic moods, Mr Pascal is saying it might all blow over.'

'But how can it? They have everything. They are building all kinds of new roads, and railroads too, with carriages powered by steam, and they have the best navy, the strongest army, all the money. Anselm, I swear I have to do something. I swear.'

'What?'

'I don't know.'

His voice was shaking with anger or fear; which it was, I could not tell. 'Michael, listen,' I said.

'What?'

'We'll be all right,' I said. 'I know we will.'

'Are you just saying that?'

'Maybe.'

He laughed without mirth. I knew his face so well that looking at it was some reassurance, even in the dim light of the carriage, where I could hardly make it out. 'I'll miss you,' I said, 'when you go off south and leave this god-forsaken city.'

A breeze troubled the match, and he raised his hand to shield it, but it fell from my fingers and our hands came together instead. His was cold. We sat there palm to palm as though we were divided by glass. The match on the floor was still burning, but the light barely reached our faces. 'Anselm, this is why I'm angry,' he said. 'Because the whole world is against people like me.'

'Then it's against me too,' I said. The wind howled around the abandoned carriage, but as he leaned forward, it seemed to falter.

'Write to me,' he said. 'If you find out anything about Harold North or your real father. Write to me anyway. It won't be the same, when I don't see you all the time.'

'I don't have your address,' I said.

'I'll send it to you,' he said.

'Do you promise?'

'If I can.'

'How will we ever see each other again, unless you do?'

'We will,' he said. 'People find each other. And whatever happens, don't forget me.'

'I won't.'

I could not help thinking of two years in jail for falling in love with the wrong person. 'It's not justice,' I said, and he nodded, still shaking with anger, and kissed me.

★ ★ ★

I don't know how long it took me to realize how I felt about Michael. It was not gradual; it was more like the twist of a knife. I woke one day and saw him differently, and after that my life grew harder, not easier. Real love is a fierce thing. It never lets you go, no matter how miserable it makes you, no matter how unforgivingly it sets you against the world. Two years in jail. You might as well imprison people for the turn of their accent or the colour of their eyes. That was what I thought. Because as surely as I knew, I was in love with the wrong person, and there was nothing I could do about it.

The next morning, the Barones closed up their shop, put the grilles on the windows, and left. And when we woke, the Imperial Order had declared war on us all. Posters had appeared on every wall of the city, with an eagle and a scythe and the Imperial Order's crest. 'We declare war,' they proclaimed, 'against the king and his government, the followers of religion, the resistance traitors, the Unacceptables, the homosexuals, the practitioners of magic arts.'

The day Michael left, Jasmine and I went together to meet my mother after work. A grey wind ran through the city, sending the Imperial Order's posters spiraling along every street. No one seemed to want to remove them. Even the shopkeepers left them stuck to their front windows. Towards evening, the police came out and began to take them down.

We walked fast, towards the east of the city. Jasmine jogged beside me, in her last year's winter boots; they were stretched out of shape with wearing them too long. 'What are you thinking?' she asked me.

'Nothing, really.'

'Are you missing Michael?'

'He has been gone only a few hours.'

I had not answered her question, and she knew it. There is no deceiving a magic child. 'I miss him,' she said. 'Will he come back?'

'Maybe when all this trouble is over.'

'Does that mean never?'

'I don't know. I hope not.'

She tossed her hair impatiently and walked ahead of me, her faded shawl wrapped very tightly around her shoulders. She had to walk along every broken wall we passed; it was a kind of superstition with her. By the time we got to Regent's Place on the east side of the city, the day had begun to lose its light. This was where all the rich of Malonia City lived. Dr Keller's house was at the end of the row, and the merchant banker whose children my mother taught owned the tallest house in the middle. The window frames were painted in gaudy red and green, as though the family was too rich to take even their expensive house entirely seriously. There was a small brass sign under the upstairs window: THE LORD RIGEL, REVOLUTIONARY HERO AND FORMER SECRET SERVICE LEADER, LIVED IN THIS PLACE. I wondered if the family had known that when they bought the house, and whether it added to or diminished the value.

'Anselm,' Jasmine called. 'Watch.'

I turned and my heart nearly choked me. She was walking along the top of the city wall, with the street on her right and the drop to the river on her left. I did not know how she had got up there; I had turned away for only a minute. 'Jasmine, come down from there!' I said.

'No.'

'Jasmine, in the name of—'

'Don't distract me, Anselm.'

She walked slowly, putting one foot in front of the other. The wind off the hills was fierce enough to unsettle her balance; every time she took a step, she swayed. I did not dare to move once she had told me not to. She kept walking until she reached the end. Then she launched herself into the air, and I ran forward and caught her.

'Jasmine, what the hell did you think you were doing?' I demanded.

'Nothing. Put me down.'

'Do you want to give me grey hairs like Leo's? Honestly!'

'I wasn't going to fall.'

'The wind could have knocked you off.'

'It couldn't. I knew. Put me down.'

I put her down but kept hold of her wrists. I could not argue; I knew from hard-won experience that it was pointless. But I kept hold of her hands tight enough that she could not break free. I almost hoped it would hurt her. 'Let me go,' she was whining, but I wouldn't. I kept my hands closed around hers until we saw my mother coming down the steps of the house. 'Mama!' called Jasmine then, and broke away from me. My mother smiled and knelt down on the steps to put her arms around Jasmine. At the window of the house, I saw the curtain move. Those two rich children were very curious about us but were too shy to ever let us see them looking out.

Jasmine and my mother began talking at once. I walked behind them. My heart was still beating fast. Every few weeks, Jasmine did something like this, and ever since Aldebaran had died, she had been worse. My mother was walking slower than usual; she kept shifting her handbag from her right hand to her left.

'Let me carry that,' I said.

'You're a prince, Anselm,' she said. It was heavy with all the children's schoolbooks.

'How are the two little duchesses?' I asked.

'Oh, the same as ever. Juliana wanted to know today if there were really people who had babies without being married, so I told her certainly not.'

Jasmine choked with laughter and had to be hit on the back several times before she regained her composure. She saw it as a point of principle to look down on those two children, with their white dresses and their high-class manners.

'Tell us about places you've been?' asked Jasmine when she finished coughing.

'Oh, I'm tired tonight,' my mother said.

'Please!' said Jasmine. It was a favourite game of hers. As we walked through the city, my mother would point out each house she had danced at when she was a rich girl and every street she had visited with her well-to-do friends.

'All right,' she said. 'You see that chapel on the corner? It's a private chapel that used to belong to the Marlazzis, and Agnes Jean was married there. They had seventeen brides-maids, so many that the front of the procession finished before the end had even begun. I started laughing when I saw that, and my papa had to take me out. And the confetti was real gold leaf—'

'Real gold leaf?' said Jasmine, wrinkling her nose.

'Real gold leaf, not one word of a lie. The beggars came out and collected it afterwards. Come on.'

Jasmine linked her arm in my mother's. She had to reach

a long way up to do it, but it made them very alike. The weak sunlight in their brown hair was a thousand colours. My mother drew strangers' eyes as the north draws a compass, and Jasmine at almost seven years old was already beautiful. It only made me lonelier today. Nothing was right now that Michael had gone. It seemed like the worst kind of sign.

As we passed by the Royal Gardens, Jasmine ran to the railings to stare through at the boarded house. The place looked more dismal in the daylight. The dark surrounded it and gave it stature, but now it was just a derelict building, with the light shining through the gaps in the roof and all the windows smashed. It seemed already a hundred years since Michael and I had sat in the abandoned carriage with the wind howling around us.

'Mama, did you ever go to that house in the old days?' said Jasmine.

'No,' said my mother.

'Whose house was it?'

'I can't remember.'

'It must have been someone's.'

'Oh, Jas, it was a long time ago. But, yes, it must have been someone's.'

We walked the rest of the way in silence. By the time we got back to Trader's Row, the street was in shadow, and starlings were wheeling in the sky. 'It will be autumn before long,' said my mother, glancing up.

'Mama?' said Jasmine. 'Can I please not go to school any more?'

'Why do you say that?' said my mother, looking down at her anxiously.

'I just don't like it there. I don't want to go back.'

'You have to go to school, Jas,' said my mother. 'You want to learn and get clever, don't you?'

Jasmine sighed. 'When do I have to go?'

'Next week.'

'I want to go and train with a great one, like Uncle did. Can I?'

'Maybe one day.'

'That means no, doesn't it?' She tugged my mother's hand. 'Doesn't it?'

My mother rubbed her forehead. Her face was very serious tonight; the laugh that usually lingered at the corners of her mouth was quite gone.

'Come on, Jas,' I said. 'Mama is tired.' I took Jasmine's hand, and we followed her inside.

Leo was writing when we came in, resting on the accounts book. He looked up as the door opened, then closed the book and put it into the drawer under the counter. We sat in the back room and drank tea while the storm rose again in the city. 'Anselm,' Leo said when we had finished. 'Will you help me sand down these old cupboards? I want to start varnishing them before the cold weather sets in.'

It was something to do, and I set myself to it fiercely. I took the oil lamp out to the yard and worked in its circle of light. I thought Michael must be thirty miles away by now, if they had met no problems on the road. The wind troubled the lamp and made its light stretch and waver. I worked for hours, until it was quite dark. I glanced up only when my mother called me for dinner. And as I looked up, I started. Someone had been standing by the yard gate looking in at me.

As soon as I met his eyes, he turned and vanished. I

could not be sure how long he had been there. Fear caught hold of me suddenly. I picked up the lamp and went inside.

'What is it?' said my mother as I closed the door behind me.

'Nothing.'

'You look as if you've seen a spirit.'

'Not a spirit,' I said. 'It's nothing.'

'Dinner is ready.'

I nodded and set down the lamp. But my heart was still beating fast. I kept glancing at the front window, expecting to see someone looking in at us. And even after everyone else had gone to bed, I could not sleep. I went down to the shop and polished a box of old lamps at the counter instead. The wind growled disconsolately around the house and made me think of the shop next door standing empty and Michael further away now – forty miles or fifty, and getting further with each minute that passed.

At half past one, I heard people shouting outside. They had been shouting for several minutes, but I had not heard them at first, because the wind and my thoughts had drowned their voices. I glanced up at the front window. The lamplight made reflections against the glass, and beyond it figures were moving with lighted torches. Through the grilles, I could see people dressed in blue, half of them boys my age and others older, running up and down the street. They were shouting, 'The king is dead!' and rattling the grilles on the shops.

'Anselm!' said Leo, making me start. He was standing on the stairs with his clothes pulled on hastily. 'What is it?' he said.

'I don't know. It's a group of men in blue clothes.'

'Blue clothes? Put out the lamp.'

I turned to blow it out. The scene outside the window emerged from the darkness. Eight or ten men were running up and down in the street, proclaiming that the king was dead. 'Where are the police?' said Leo. 'Where the hell are they?'

Lights were coming on in the shops now. The starlings leaped from the tree opposite the Barones' shop, rising in a cloud past the castle.

'Join our cause!' shouted one of the men. 'Come out of your houses and join our cause!'

'Piss off and let me sleep!' called someone from the pharmacist's highest window. The men threw themselves against the grille of her shop, their torches leaping wildly. I thought I recognized one of them for a second. He looked like Isaiah, from the class above mine at school. Then the light fell again, and I could not make him out.

'Where are the police?' Leo kept saying. Someone thumped the grille on our window, and we both started and drew back. My mother was on the stairs then, with her arm around Jasmine's shoulders.

'Come back upstairs,' she whispered.

'Maria, listen!' Leo whispered. 'Listen to them!'

'Come back to bed. They will not do anything.'

'You three go back,' he said. 'I'll stay here.'

But none of us moved. It was half an hour before the police came and read the riot notice outside our door. 'The king is not dead,' they shouted; then, 'By order of the government of Malonia and His Majesty King Cassius, disperse and return to your homes. You are charged with disturbing the peace, an offence punishable under Malonian civil law. Disperse and return to your homes. This is your first official warning.'

The men went on shouting and running. The crowd had multiplied; there must have been twenty or thirty of them now. Then, without warning, there was a volley of gunshots. Jasmine shrieked and clapped her hands to her ears. The police were firing rifles off their shoulders.

'It's all right,' said my mother. 'Shh, it's all right.' The gunshots came again, and the crowd broke up.

'None of you are safe!' shouted the nearest man as the crowd fled down an alley. 'None of you royalists are safe in this city any more! Remember that!'

The silence hummed. Somewhere down the street, two traders were calling to each other from their upstairs windows: 'Bloody nerve' and 'Get back to sleep; the police will sort it out.' A man opened a window and threw out a cigarette, lazily, as if to show he was not afraid.

'Come back upstairs,' said my mother. 'All of you. Come on.'

We went to bed, but I could tell no one else was sleeping. Eventually I got up again. Leo was there in the living room, smoking and staring out the narrow window at the roofs beyond. The whole city had a strangely subdued air now, like the atmosphere after a party. 'Are you all right?' I said.

He nodded and stubbed the cigarette out on the windowsill. 'Things are changing,' he said. 'Aren't they?'

'I don't know.'

He did not go on. I sat down on the sofa and stared into the dwindling fire. After a while, Leo stirred and crossed the room and sat down in Grandmother Margaret's old rocking chair. There was no space in the tiny living room, and it stood jammed against the wall, where it could not move. He leaned forward and lit another cigarette. 'There is something

I want to know,' he said. 'Why do they always choose our shop?'

My skin felt cold, as if the fire gave no heat at all. 'Do you think they really do?' I said.

'The windows,' he said. 'And shouting about royalists. It can't just be chance.'

And the man standing in the shadows, I thought. He was watching us for some reason.

'They know our name is North,' said Leo. 'They must know that this is a royalist family. They must. Either that or . . .'

'Or what?'

He sucked in smoke as if it was the only thing sustaining him. 'I don't know. Nothing. I was thinking about something else.'

The silence came between us again. I wanted to say something, but I didn't. His hands were shaking.

'Listen, Anselm,' he said. 'I'm thinking about going somewhere else for a while.'

'Where can we go?'

'Not you three. Just me.'

There was a silence. I let it draw out on purpose, to force him to speak.

'You three could move to another apartment,' he said. 'I'll sell the contents of the shop at the auction rooms, and it will be enough to live on for a long time. A long enough time. And . . .'

'But where would you go? Papa, what are you even talking about?'

He studied the cigarette in his hand, as though he didn't know how it had got there. The wind in the chimney sounded like a crying child. 'Mr Pascal says they will be bringing in compulsory labour soon. And when they do, I'll have no choice.'

'But you can claim exemption. On account of your cough, or the baby.'

'Maybe I could, but—'

'Don't you want to?' I said.

He did not answer. He sighed instead and took down *The Darkness Has a Thousand Voices* from the mantelpiece and turned over the pages. 'I wish I knew what kind of country this baby will be born into,' he said. 'I wish I knew that everything would be all right. Anselm, my heart just feels like stone, as heavy as stone.'

'It will be all right,' I said. 'The king has withstood all kinds of troubles.'

'Has he? It feels like – I don't know – like something is starting that no one understands. Or like the end of something. Like the end of the world.'

'How do you know what the end of the world feels like?' I said.

'I can't see any future any more.'

'You shouldn't talk like this, Papa. You only do it because you get so melancholy.'

'Maybe you're right.' He stood up and stubbed out his last cigarette. 'I'll try and get some sleep,' he said. 'You should too.'

But I did not sleep until the light started to rise behind the houses, and every half-hour, I heard him turn over quietly. I knew he only let himself turn every thirty minutes, so as not to wake my mother, who slept lightly. It seemed to me the loneliest sound, to hear him turning over like that in the darkness, and I could not sleep because of it. That, and thinking of Michael.

★ ★ ★

When we woke the next morning, the city was different. The people who passed our shop were strangely agitated as they hurried to work, laughing too loudly or talking in furtive groups. Mr Pascal came in before we had even opened up the shop. My mother was still upstairs dressing for work.

'You had better come and see this, North,' he remarked in his most ominous tone.

We followed him out. There was a chill of autumn in the air this early. Leo was shivering faintly as we walked. Mr Pascal led us down an alleyway and pointed up at the wall. Letters were daubed there in streaking blue paint: THE NEW IMPERIAL ORDER WILL TAKE BACK WHAT LUCIEN LOST. JOIN US OR DIE.'

'It's all over the city apparently,' said Mr Pascal, shielding his eyes to gaze up at the words. 'They must have been everywhere. It must have taken hundreds of people to do it. I wonder what the king will have to say about this.'

Leo was still shivering, with his arms folded tightly across his chest.

'Maybe it doesn't mean anything,' I said.

'I wouldn't be so sure,' said Mr Pascal. 'It looks like civil war.'

The pharmacist and her husband came out and studied the letters. The greengrocers across the road still had their grilles up. They had taken a cautious attitude since food prices went up the year before, and now with the slightest hint of trouble, they did not open.

'And I'll show you something worse,' said Mr Pascal.

Leo was already following Mr Pascal along the alleyway.

I went after them. We came to a halt at the side of a half-demolished house.

'Look,' said Mr Pascal with a certain pride in his discovery. One whole side of the building was covered with a face – a man with a scar across his right cheek and his hand raised in a gesture of defiance. It must have taken them half the night to do this. I thought at first it was Rigel, and that was the famous scar they said he gained in the revolution. But the way Mr Pascal was sighing and shaking his head, I could tell this was no revolutionary hero.

'Ahira,' said Leo very quietly.

'That's right,' said Mr Pascal.

'Ahira?' I said, startled. 'Why would someone paint Ahira on the wall?'

'It's a criminal offence,' said Mr Pascal. 'You are not allowed to paint a war criminal on the walls of this city. Whoever did that will be afraid to show their face again.'

'Who's Ahira?' said a small voice, and I turned. Jasmine was standing beside me, her thumb in her mouth.

'Jasmine, go straight back to the shop,' said Leo. 'Anselm, take her.'

'No,' said Jasmine. 'I want to know who that man is.'

'I'll tell you on the way back,' I said. She followed me for a few steps, then dragged her feet in the dust. 'Come on, Jasmine.'

'Tell me now,' she said.

'He's no one. Just a man who worked for Lucien. Come on.'

'Who's Lucien?'

'You know Lucien.'

'No, I don't.'

I had never thought about Jasmine not knowing these things. 'Who's Lucien?' Jasmine repeated.

'He used to rule this country, until I was three months old,' I said. 'He was – what was the name?'

'Commander of the Realm,' said Leo, who had fallen in beside us. 'Jasmine, will you please hurry?'

'Billy and Joe are playing out under the tree,' said Jasmine, pointing towards the pharmacist's sons. 'Can I go?'

'No,' said Leo. 'You'll have to stay in the shop today.'

'Why?' Jasmine wailed. 'I don't like it in the shop. There's nothing to do!'

'You can go out to the yard later if things quieten down.'

'No!' Jasmine lay down on the doorstep and began crying. People glanced at her as they passed.

'Jasmine,' I said. 'Hey, Jasmine. I'll take you for a walk later—'

'No,' said Leo, picking Jasmine up and carrying her, screaming, through the door. 'You are both staying inside.'

We opened up the shop, and my mother insisted on going to work, but all day Leo was glancing at the door, and every customer made him start. We saw the police passing several times, sweating in their red uniforms. The summer seemed determined to finish with a flourish. Even the shade shimmered black and restless. The other traders kept calling into our shop, as though we were under siege and had to raise each other's spirits. Leo closed at four o'clock. We had taken nothing all day.

I could tell Leo was not sleeping, because I could not sleep either. Lying awake in the moonlight, I could see the faint light of the oil lamp on the shop counter creeping up the stairs and across the living-room floorboards and coming to rest against the bottom of my door. A few nights later, we were woken by shouts again. A building somewhere was on fire, and people were running up and down the street with guns. Smoke billowed thickly across the clouds. We all stood in the living room, not speaking, while the police ran about and people clamoured in the street. Then, after a while, it fell silent again. Even the dogs did not dare to bark.

My mother made tea, and we sat around the back room in silence. Jasmine was on Leo's knee with her face buried in his shirt. Across the table, his eyes kept meeting mine. 'I wish to God that Aldebaran was here,' he said eventually.

'Don't blaspheme,' said Jasmine, her voice muffled.

Leo hugged her more tightly. 'I wasn't, Jas.'

My mother started talking about the baby. It was kicking tonight, she said, as though the riots had woken it too.

'Does he sleep?' said Jasmine.

'Yes,' said my mother. 'It sleeps and wakes up like anyone else.'

'*He*, not *it*,' said Jasmine. 'It's going to be a boy.'

'If it is a boy,' said my mother abruptly, 'I want to call him Stirling.'

No one spoke, but the silence this time had a different quality. 'Stirling is a good name,' said Jasmine. 'Would you have called me Stirling if I was a boy?'

'Your middle name is Stella – that's the closest we could get.'

'My middle name is Stella?' Jasmine demanded. 'Why didn't you tell me ever before?'

'It's on your certificate of birth,' said my mother. 'I must have mentioned it, haven't I, Jas?'

'Let me see that certificate,' said Jasmine.

Leo got up and searched through the drawer where we had once kept important documents, but they had long since been swamped by other contents. 'It must be here somewhere,' he said.

'I wrote it down in my journal,' I said. 'Remember those journals I used to keep?'

'Go and find it,' said my mother.

'I don't know where they are. Maybe in that box under the sofa.'

'Go on, Anselm,' said Jasmine.

I took another lamp and went upstairs. The box was furred with dust, but I could see the journals there on the top. I had kept them as a child when I saw Leo writing and wanted to copy him. I found the one from the year of Jasmine's birth and carried it back down.

'Is that your writing?' said Jasmine when I opened it.

'Yes. Look – here it is.' I had recorded it carefully, in Leo's ink pen, borrowed for the occasion. ' "I am glad to report that Jasmine Stella Andros North was born safely in our apartment in Citadel Street, delivered by Sister Mary Fuller, AMC." '

'What's AMC?' demanded Jasmine.

'Me being pompous,' I said. 'It's on the plaque outside her door.'

'It just means Advanced Midwifery Certificate,' said my mother. 'Sister Mary Fuller. I liked her. Perhaps I'll have her again for this baby.'

'Go on,' said Jasmine.

I read on: ' "I, Anselm Andros North, ran to Paradise Way to fetch the midwife. My sister is called Jasmine because of the jasmine flowers growing in the gutter outside the window. And Stella in honour of my uncle Stirling. She is nine years and one month and thirty days younger than me. Jasmine looks red and small, but I can tell already she will be a beautiful lady. She cried in the church when the priest baptized her. She cries a good deal." '

Jasmine laughed at that. ' "She cries a good deal"! Did I?'

'I forgot about Anselm running for the doctor,' said my mother. 'And, yes. Yes, you did cry a good deal, at least at the start.'

The firelight and that account held us against the dark outside.

'Why did you name me after a flower that grew in the gutter?' Jasmine asked, looking up at my mother with something like disappointment.

'Because it was the one beautiful thing in that place,' my mother said.

After we went back upstairs, I sat at my desk under the window and turned over the pages of those old journals. Some of them went so far back that I could not even remember the circumstances in which I had written them; they were like a stranger's words. Others I could recall, even down to the look of my small hand gripping the pen and the light outside the windows. I turned to the year that we moved into the shop and found an entry I remembered well: 'I have a new friend next door whose name is Mikeal. We are going to signal to each other from the windows and when we grow up we are going to travel around the world together and be the best of friends always, even when we get married and go to different places.' And Michael had crossed out his name a few weeks later when he insisted on reading my journal and had written the proper spelling very firmly underneath it.

That only made my heart ache, so I closed the journal and went back to the earlier ones. I found an entry from the year before that made me pause and turn up the lamp. 'Jasmine looks like Leo and my mother already,' I had written, 'and I keep thinking about my real father. Sometimes when I look in the mirror I can see something about his face in mine. I think he had red hair and a strong kind of look. I wish I had seen his grave. I wish I knew what his first name was and whether he would have been proud of me.'

I turned a page back and found 'my real father' again. He was there, too, in the journal from the year before, every few entries, and he took up six pages of speculation in the one before that. And suddenly it came back to me clearly, the way I had felt about not knowing – before Leo became my father and I decided not to think about it any more.

I closed the journal and watched the clouds drifting over the stars. They looked like the continents of another world. I wondered where Michael was by now. I wondered how long he would remember me.

Everything felt wrong with my heart since Aldebaran had died, as though his absence had set the whole world out of joint. That night, I decided two things as I watched the clouds and shivered and could not sleep. I would find out who my real father was, before things grew too uncertain. And then, before life divided us, I would find Michael again.

THE NIGHT OF
THE FIRST OF JANUARY

'You were in love with your friend Michael,' said Mr Hardy. He did not ask it; he just said it.

'I suppose so,' I said.

'And are you going to find him?' he said.

'I don't know.' He waited. 'I don't know if I'll ever find him again now,' I said. 'With everything that's happened since.'

'I think you should find him,' Mr Hardy said. 'One day. No matter what has happened since.'

I got up and refilled his glass of spirits, more for the sake of avoiding his glance than for any other reason. 'I thought you would be shocked,' I said.

He shook his head. 'I probably look old to you,' he said. 'But that means nothing. People have fallen in love since time began. Sometimes with the wrong person, as that newspaper put it, but always irrevocably and in spite of the fuss it has caused.'

I could not help smiling at that. He was strange, Mr Hardy, and I did not know what to make of him, but already he had become a kind of relative to me in the loneliness of the journey. He sipped his spirits thoughtfully, then said, 'I was in love once.'

'Just once?' I said.

He considered it. 'Yes,' he said. 'Just once.'

I had expected him to have a whole line of women in his history; he was a traveller and a man who knew about the world. 'I'll tell you the story, if you want to hear it,' he said.

'I do,' I said. 'Tell me.'

'Well,' he began. 'I used to write copy for a company that sold encyclopaedias. I wanted to be a great writer, but the newspapers wouldn't have me.' He gave a dry laugh and sipped his spirits again. 'Anyway, they assigned me the worst letters, and I worked on those. X and Z. I was seventeen years old and just out of school. I had a four-mile walk home across the city, and in the winter it froze your blood. I used to walk home past a convent where poor girls took rooms. They went out to work as clerks or housemaids in the town, and in the evenings they helped the nuns at their chores.'

I did not know where this story was leading, but I knew better than to interrupt.

Mr Hardy studied the spirits in his glass and went on. 'Anyway, one night I was late coming home, and as I was walking by this convent, I heard someone singing. If you had heard it . . .' He shook his head. 'It was the most beautiful thing in the world. I suppose I was very young, but I know it was beautiful. Like an angel's voice. I stood there listening for half an hour and didn't even notice that my fingers were numb with cold. And the next night I came home late again, just in the hope of hearing her singing.'

'Did you hear her again?'

'Yes. Before I knew it, I was staying for an extra hour every night, just so I could be outside the window when she came home. I used to stand in the cold outside the convent walls, even when the snow was falling like tomorrow would never come. And I was in love, I swear.'

'Without ever seeing her?' I asked.

Mr Hardy laughed, and his eyes glittered in the lamplight. 'Yes, I suppose so. It was weeks before I really saw her face. It took me that time to work up the courage. I waited one day until she came out of the convent door on her way to work. I didn't go up to her; I just watched her pass. She had lovely grey eyes and a way of walking.'

'How did you know it was her?'

He shook his head. 'I just knew. She was just how I imagined her, from that angel's voice. She walked like an angel, like her feet didn't touch the ground. I know it's an old and hackneyed way of speaking, but I swear it was how I felt. And she had a way of dressing, too, like she refused to be poor. I remember that about her. In the years afterwards, even when we were struggling—' He broke off then and laughed. 'But I have given the story away now.'

I was sure that he had meant to. 'So you got the courage to speak to her eventually?' I said.

'Eventually. I sent word by one of the nuns, and she met me at the convent gate. I had thought she would refuse altogether, but she came down to meet me. She was very proud and indignant. She wanted to know what I had been doing standing under her window every night. I told her the story.'

'What did she do?'

'Thought I was a very foolish boy and marched away in a high temper.' He laughed. 'And eventually became my wife.'

I waited for the moral of the story. The tales he told me of his past life always had some meaning, like the chord that resolves an old song. 'So I know what love is,' he said at last. 'And let me tell you, I'm glad I had the courage to go up to that door. I'm glad, even though I lost all hope when she turned and marched away. It was weeks before she relented and let me see her. To try and find out the truth, or change the world, or make your own life better is like jumping from a cliff – you risk losing everything. But the cautious lose everything anyway, because they try to hold onto it. Either you cast it to the four winds and trust to faith that it will come back again, or it falls through your fingers by degrees.'

'Are you telling me to go and find Michael again?' I said.

He shook his head. 'I would never do that. I am just telling you what I think.'

The snow threw itself against the window and made the little boy sleeping in the corner murmur softly and turn his head.

'Go on with your story,' said Mr Hardy. 'It is of much more consequence than my sentimental ramblings.' He gave a quick smile.

'No,' I said. 'It was interesting.'

'Well . . .' He acknowledged that with another smile and poured me more spirits. 'Go on,' he said.

'I don't know how to go on,' I said. 'That's where I've got to so far. I'm writing it down, but I don't know what to write next.'

'Then you can always read to me, if you aren't too tired.'

I nodded and got out those papers. When he was not listening to my story, he wanted to know all about them, and it was easier to read to him than listen to the silence of the country around us.

'This part is somewhere else,' I said. 'It's part of the same story – I think it happened at the same time – but it's not in the same place.'

'Did you write it?' he said as I unfolded the papers. 'I have been wondering.'

I shook my head. 'I don't even understand it.'

'Who did, then?'

'Someone else.'

'Someone you know?'

'Yes.'

'Someone,' said Mr Hardy, 'who knows about other places.' Then he was silent for so long that I thought he had forgotten the inn and the story and the night outside.

'Yes, go on, read it,' he said eventually, and came back.

★ ★ ★

The car was packed, and Anna and her son stood side by side in the rain. 'Is that everything?' she said without expecting an answer. The old Rolls-Royce was caked in dried mud and dented where a low branch had hit the roof. Anna rearranged the pile of boxes across the back seats. To have reached twenty-two years old and still be able to fit all that she owned into a dozen battered cardboard boxes seemed to her dismal, as if this was all her life on earth amounted to. She turned and gave a smile she knew was false. Ashley did not return it. He stood there silently, wearing a worn red coat with the sleeves all chewed and a mutinous expression. Anna knew that look well. 'What is it?' she said.

'I don't want to leave.'

'I know. But listen, Ash— '

Monica appeared at the side door. 'Can't you manage that box?' she called, and raised a hand to shield her eyes from the rain.

'I'm fine,' said Anna, jamming the last box back into place. The side burst, and records slid out across the gravel at her feet.

'Here,' said Monica, bustling forward to help her.

'It's all right; I can manage.'

'No, let me do it.'

Anna stood back and let Monica pick up the records. 'They aren't scratched,' Monica said. She polished them on her jacket sleeve and stacked them back in the box.

'They were my father's,' said Anna. 'I don't even have anything to play them on.'

'They might come in useful. Are you ready to go? And are you sure you will be all right driving all that way?'

'We'll be fine.'

'I hope the old car will last.' Monica patted the car's roof. It clanged with a minor note. 'I'm sure Mr Field would have wanted you to have it.'

The rain was driving the mud down the sides of the car now. Anna slammed the door and dusted off her hands. Monica touched her arm as she turned to open the driver's door. 'Listen,' said Monica. 'I never meant for things to turn out—'

'I said, it's fine.'

They stood a while longer in the driving rain, but there seemed nothing else to say, so Anna opened the driver's door. 'Let me go in and put on a coat, and I'll see you off at the gate,' said Monica.

She turned and started back towards the house, her heeled shoes sinking into the wet gravel. As soon as she vanished, Ashley tugged Anna's arm. 'Mam?' he said. 'Tell me about my father.'

'What?' said Anna. 'I can't hear you for this rain.'

But she could tell Ashley knew that she had heard. She was always startled by the guilt that his six-year-old's honesty could make her feel. He stood there now, with his arms folded and the same mutinous expression fixed in his eyes. 'Ash, I've told you,' she said. 'I have told you the story a hundred times.'

'But it's not true,' said Ashley.

Anna reached for his shoulder, then decided against it. Her hand rested in the air between them. 'It's the only truth I know,' she said. 'Come on, Ash. Don't be too hard on me; I do my best.'

The rain was driving in gusts now across the surface of the lake. It clouded every mountain and dragged the sodden leaves from the trees. 'Was it really him, that time up on the hill when I was little?' said Ashley.

'It was only a year and a half ago.'

'But he wasn't real. He was like a ghost.'

'He was really there,' said Anna.

'I don't believe you. Tell me the truth about him.'

'I've always tried to tell you the truth, Ashley. Always.' The rain was falling harder now. 'Come on,' said Anna. 'Get in the car.'

'Not until you tell me. I'm not leaving until you tell me.'

'Ash, listen . . .' The rain shook the trees now and pounded her skin. 'Come on.'

'No. I'm not.'

'Monica wants us to leave so she can lock the place up. The new owners want the keys; they want to come in this afternoon. We have to go. We can talk about it on the way down.'

'You won't. You'll say you want to concentrate on driving, and we won't talk about it.'

'When we get to London, then. Just get in the car.'

'We won't talk about it,' said Ashley.

'We will. I promise I'll tell you on the way down, all right?'

'No,' said Ashley. 'I don't want to go. I dream about him here. And I don't know if I will in London. I didn't dream about him when we were living there before. And if he comes back to find us, then how will he know where we are? And—'

'Ashley, get in the car. Your dry clothes are packed, and I can't get them out again.'

'I won't leave. I'm going to stand here until you tell me.'

Anna unclasped the chain around her neck. The single

blue jewel caught the grey light and glittered the same colour as her eyes. 'Here,' she said. 'This is the necklace your father gave to me. And if you wear it, I promise you, you will still dream about him.'

It was a measure she had been saving for the most desperate of circumstances. 'Why?' said Ashley. 'How do you know?'

'Because I dream about him. It reminds me, you know? You can look at it and know this necklace belonged to him before you were born.'

'No,' said Ashley sullenly.

'Why not?'

He shrugged. 'It's your necklace.'

'It was for you,' said Anna. 'That was who he really meant it for. Not me. You can remember him by it, all right? Even when we've gone away from here. And I'll tell you about your father on the way down; I promise I will.'

Ashley stared up at her for a moment, and she did not know which way the argument would fall. Then he took the necklace, and she picked him up and bundled him into the car before he could change his mind.

The rain made the engine cough and rattle. Anna always drove gripping the steering wheel so tightly that her knuckles turned pale; it was a habit she could not help. Ashley sat in silence, a box of plates and cutlery balanced on his knees under the battered road atlas. Monica waved until they were on the road. Then she turned and went back into the empty hotel.

'She doesn't care about us,' said Ashley.

'She has lots of things to do before this afternoon, that's all. She can't stand out in the rain waving goodbye.'

'If she cared about us, she would have given us some of the money,' said Ashley.

'People are complicated,' said Anna, and gripped the steering wheel tighter. 'She gave us the car, after all.'

As if in answer, the car gave a low cough. Ashley opened the road atlas and directed his mutinous stare at the pages.

'The A591 through Lowcastle,' said Anna. 'Find that and tell me the way. The fastest route south and east.'

It was a game they always played, and it distracted Ashley now. Anna turned onto the road out of the valley. As they passed the stone circle on the hill, she saw Ashley look up. The clouds were drifting over it strangely, but Anna did not give it more than a glance as they rounded the hill – the car coughing angrily all the while – and came down into the next valley. 'There is something wrong with the engine,' said Anna. 'Listen, Ash. It sounds like an old man dying.'

'It's because we haven't used it for so long,' said Ashley. 'It will be all right in a minute.'

'If you say so.'

Ashley glared at the page of the atlas, and Anna thought she saw it crumple. The roads contracted and slid together. She breathed in and stared at him. 'Don't look away from the road,' said Ashley. A van was swinging round the corner ahead. And when she looked again, he had turned to the next page. The windscreen wipers shuddered, and the silence fell between them again. 'I'm sorry,' said Anna, staring at the road ahead. 'I'm sorry we have to leave.' Ashley did not reply. 'Uncle Bradley will let us stay for a while,' Anna persisted in a falsely bright tone she suddenly remembered her own mother using. 'And I'm hoping you can go to his school. You won't be in the class he teaches, but Bradley will look out for you. It won't be so bad, Ash.'

'What I don't understand,' said Ashley, 'is why you don't just marry Uncle Bradley. Because my father isn't coming back, is he?'

'No,' said Anna.

'So why don't you marry Uncle Bradley?'

'Because I'm not in love with him.'

'That's not the only thing.'

'No,' said Anna. 'No, it's not. But it is important.'

'He's in love with you,' said Ashley.

'No,' said Anna. 'He isn't, and, anyway, there's nothing I can do about it if he is. You know who you love, and I'm not in love with Bradley.'

'Did you love my father? Did you know about that?'

'That was different. We were so young.'

'But did you love him?'

Anna had thought she would answer that question, but she changed her mind. She reached for the gear lever, the car running more smoothly now, down the other side of the pass and between rain-darkened fields, every one of which Anna knew. 'I wish we weren't leaving too,' she said. 'Did you know that, Ash? I wish we could stay.'

'Yes.'

Anna tried to loosen her grip on the steering wheel, but she could not do it. The silence drew out between them like the winding road. Through the clouded glass, the familiar hills passed and receded again. 'The M6 south,' said Ashley. 'That's the next road, isn't it?'

'Yes, it is,' said Anna, hoping desperately that the question meant he had forgiven her.

* * *

Darkness came down while they were stuck on a motorway in the Midlands. 'Ashley, try to get some sleep,' said Anna, though it was early. He closed his eyes obediently and after a while lay still. The road atlas slid from his hands. Anna caught it and turned over the pages, tracing their route in reverse. She came to the crumpled page and studied it. The creases looked old. It must have been an illusion, but she could not quite dismiss it. She had dismissed too much of what Ashley had done in the past few months. It had looked as though he frowned at the page and it crumpled under his glance.

She reached across and touched his face. He would not have let her if he was awake; he already thought himself too old to be treated like a child. Ashley's cheek was warm, as if he had a fever. Anna rested her hand on his forehead to cool it, then bent over and kissed his hair. Car horns were blaring ahead, but the traffic was locked in motionless lines. Anna shut off the engine. 'I'll tell you the story of your father,' she said. 'Like I promised.'

The car was very silent without the engine running, and Anna heard her own voice, like a stranger's. She rested the side of her face on the steering wheel and spoke to Ashley like that, as if the cars on every side did not exist. The rain obscured the windows now, and mist crept over the glass. 'Listen,' she said, 'I don't know what parts of it are true any more. It was so long ago. But this is the story. I was in Lowcastle with your aunt Monica, working at the old hotel, and your father lived down the road in the house called Lakebank. He was a handsome boy, Ash. You should have seen him. He had your black hair and your dark eyes. He used to walk past and talk to me. He came from somewhere else. Not exactly another country. He used to tell me about that place. A long way back, my grandfather's family came from that place too.'

Ashley turned his head restlessly. 'Shh,' said Anna. 'Anyway, he had to go back, and after that I never saw him again. He left me just that necklace – that's all. I don't know if I believe the story about another place now. It was so long ago, like I said, and . . .' She shrugged and trailed off. The story seemed feeble even to her ears, and she wondered if there were other things that should be part of it. 'And then when we saw him on the hill that night, was it real? I don't even know. Ash, if there was some way I could find him, if there was some way we could be together, I would still take it. I don't know if that's stupid. Bradley has been a father to you more than he ever has. But, yes, I loved him. Love is not a good thing. Don't be deceived in that. Not always a good thing, because it makes you forget about everything else.'

The cars were rolling forward now, their red tail-lights drawing away from the old Rolls-Royce as they moved on into the rain-washed dark. Someone blared a horn behind them.

Ashley sat up and said, 'Mam, what is it—'

'It's all right.' Anna turned the ignition key. Ashley closed his eyes again and murmured something. 'It was a magic necklace,' she said as they edged under a concrete bridge and over the crest of a hill. 'That was the other thing I should tell you. At least, that was the game we played. A magic necklace that could let you see other worlds.'

The road spread out ahead of them, marked out in lights, swinging down over this low hill and another, as far as Anna could see. 'Listen, we'll stop next time we pass somewhere, and I'll buy you something to eat,' she said to drive out the bleak silence. 'And then we can plan what we'll do in London. It's going to be a new chance for us. I mean, the chance for a new life. Ashley, are you awake?'

Ashley did not answer. Anna smiled at nothing and touched his face again. 'Go on sleeping,' she said. 'It's all right.'

It was midnight by the time they reached London. Anna was driving in a stupor, as though the road alone was drawing her on, across one more junction and round another deserted roundabout and into the suburbs of the city, where the famous skyline was too far away to see. The street was where she had thought. Forest Park Mansions. She parked the car close up to the pavement, between a white van and a splintered tree, and shut off the engine. Ashley was asleep beside her, and she did not want to wake him and leave the silence of the car. She thought, This car is all I have of my old life – this car and the necklace in Ashley's hand, and that's all. They had moved three times in as many years. Anna wondered if she would always be travelling like this. As if it was her destiny to pack up her belongings again, persuade a mutinous Ashley to follow her, and drive off – the car coughing angrily – in search of another life.

Anna looked up at the row of houses and searched for Bradley's window. Most of them were darkened now. She made out an old woman, crossing the lighted room with a kettle in her hand and wincing at every step. Bedraggled plants stood on another windowsill, and behind them music was thumping.

'Come on,' she said then, shaking Ashley by the

shoulder. 'Let's go inside and find your uncle Bradley. He will be waiting for us.'

'Where are we?' said Ashley.

'Here,' said Anna. 'Wake up, Ash. We're in London. At Uncle Bradley's house. Remember?'

As they got out of the car, a man with an umbrella came out of the dark to meet them. 'Anna?' he said. 'Is that you?'

'Bradley,' she said. Her legs were aching from hours on the road, but he covered the distance between them and put his arms around her and picked up Ashley, who smiled reluctantly. Bradley held Ashley close to him, like a returning soldier reunited with his child. 'Have you been waiting for long?' said Anna.

'Not long. I thought you would arrive about now, so I came down to wait for you. I thought you might need help with the cases. Here, let me . . .'

He set down Ashley and dragged out a box, making an act of struggling with it as though it was the greatest weight. Ashley laughed at that.

'Leave them,' said Anna. 'We can take them up in the morning. You two go ahead. I'll lock up the car.'

Bradley gave her a quick glance, then led the way, Ashley carrying the umbrella. She could hear them beyond the lighted door of the building, clattering up the stairs. She put a hand on the dent in the roof of the car, then locked it and turned and followed them. The Rolls-Royce looked like something from the past as she glanced back. It was gleaming under the streetlamps, a car left behind when some romantic age came to an end. She closed the door of the building behind her and started up the stairs. Bicycles were lying tangled in the hallway; old newspapers were stacked up in front of the ground-floor flat. Behind one door, she heard a couple talking. She tried to see these things as the future details of her life, but she was too tired, and they just made her heart ache.

Bradley was waiting at the door. 'Come in,' he said. 'Anna, you look asleep on your feet. Was it a bad journey?'

'Not so bad; just long.'

'I still can't believe you drove all the way here in that old Rolls-Royce. I doubted you, didn't I? Didn't I say it would collapse somewhere near Birmingham?'

She smiled. 'Yes, it's true. But the car held out. After the first few miles, it stopped complaining, didn't it, Ash?'

'The engine was just cold, because you hadn't used it,' said Ashley. He was at the table already, making a careful sandwich out of an old jar of jam and the end of a loaf of bread. 'Do you want one, Mam?' he said.

She shook her head. The stupor of the road still hung over her, and she stayed where she was by the door. Bradley began searching through the cupboards, muttering about tea and sugar. Anna glanced about. The kitchen window was curtainless and looked out over a grimy glass roof where pigeons slept. Beyond, she could hear the traffic surging. 'It's a bachelor's house,' said Bradley with an apologetic grin.

'No,' said Anna.

'Come and sit down. I'll find you something else to eat.'

Anna watched him search the cupboards and turn over the unpromising contents of the fridge. The cold fluorescent light made his eyes look puffy. 'Are you working hard these days?' she said. 'You look tired, Bradley.'

'I don't mind it.' He threw a few things into a saucepan and lit the gas under it. 'I always wanted to be a teacher,' he said to Ashley. 'Since I was your age. Your mother will tell you.'

'It's true,' said Anna. 'Since we started at school and Bradley learned to write his own name and thought he was a genius.'

They laughed, but after that, none of them could think of anything to say. Ashley finished his sandwich and sat watching them. 'It's kind of you to let us stay, Bradley,' said Anna.

'Stay as long as you want to.'

'Now that we're here, we can find somewhere of our own—'

'Really, stay as long as you want. I like having you here; it's good company.' Ashley yawned. 'You're falling asleep,' said Bradley. 'I've made up the spare room for you, Ash.' He pointed through the living room to the farthest door. Anna picked up Ashley and carried him to the spare room.

Anna and Bradley sat up late that night, and when they were both exhausted, the conversation ran more easily. 'What will you do here?' said Bradley eventually. 'Anna, I've been meaning to ask. Will you work in a hotel again?'

'I suppose. It won't be like it was with Monica, though. I'll have to ask my mother to look after Ash in the evenings. I was thinking about finding some way to dance again, but you know how it is. He's only small.'

Bradley got up to wash the plates. 'Talking to you, I sometimes think I know nothing about life,' he said.

'You make me sound like an old woman.'

Bradley laughed.

'I'll go and check on Ashley,' said Anna. 'He gets these nightmares, and when he wakes up, he wants someone to come and talk to him.'

'What does Ashley have nightmares about?'

Anna hesitated, then gave him the truthful answer. 'Not knowing where he is,' she said. 'And falling through the world and disappearing.'

'Existential for a six-year-old,' remarked Bradley.

'Maybe,' said Anna. 'I'll go and check on him.'

Ashley was lying awake when she opened the door of the spare bedroom. She sat down on his bed and listened to the steady drone of the traffic beyond the glass. 'Can't you sleep?' she said then.

'Mam?' he said. 'Do you ever feel like you don't belong here?'

'Don't belong where?'

'Here. In London.'

'We have only just arrived. It always feels like that coming to a new place.'

'I don't mean that. I mean, like you don't belong in this whole place and you want to get up and leave.'

'What do you mean?'

'I don't know.'

Anna went to close the curtains. One of them was broken and creaked mournfully when she tried to pull it across. 'Well, what, Ashley?' she said, turning to face him. 'It's two o'clock in the morning; tell me what you mean.'

'Don't get cross.'

'I'm not cross. I'm sorry. I'm not cross, but I want to know what you mean about not belonging here.'

'Why are you scared, then? If you're not cross, you're scared.'

'I'm not scared,' she said. But she was not certain that was true. 'It just makes me worried when you talk like this.'

Ashley picked up the necklace from the table beside him

and studied the single jewel. 'Did he really used to wear this?' he said.

'Yes,' said Anna. 'I told you about the bird necklace I used to have when I was a little girl. That jewel was the eagle's right eye.'

'How did he have it and you have the rest of it before you even met each other?'

'It was just chance,' said Anna. 'When you are young and foolish, you think signs like that have to be obeyed. A boy has a necklace and you have the other half of it, and you think it means you are meant to be together.'

'So you weren't?' said Ashley.

'What?'

'Meant to be together?'

'Oh, I don't know. It's late – you should be asleep.'

Ashley clenched his fist around the jewel and closed his eyes. She sat there beside him and waited for him to sleep. She seemed to have sat waiting for Ashley to fall asleep a hundred thousand times in the past years. In the orange half-light of the streetlamps, the room looked strange and lonely. That light illuminated the old boxes piled on top of the wardrobe and glistened on the leaves of the spidery plants and lit up the broken television set in the corner. Anna studied these things without seeing them properly, until Ashley slept. She told herself it was superstition to take the jewel out of his grasp and put it back on the table. But she did it anyway.

EVENING
THE SECOND OF JANUARY

It was another night and another bleak inn, somewhere close to Angel City, when I went on with my own story. The route we were taking had grown more and more circuitous as more of the country was barred to us. The woman and her little boy spoke in whispers and stared bleakly out at the night, then went to sleep side by side. Mr Hardy drank his spirits in silence. I began to write, and the words came more easily now, and when they didn't, I sat and watched Mr Hardy.

'I had a family once,' he said abruptly. 'I had a wife and two little boys.'

I put down the pencil. 'What happened?' I said.

He sighed and said very quietly. 'We were separated. Years ago. My wife and I had to leave the city, and we left our two boys with a relative. I was a wanted man. There was a price on my head under the old regime. I came very close to being assassinated several times; people were watching the house. We could never have gone back while Lucien was in power.'

'And then what happened?' I said.

'And then . . . I don't know. Things changed. I think I was half mad for a while after my wife died. I changed my name, and I changed my identity, and I pretended I didn't exist. I mean, I pretended to myself. I made up another life, because my old life had stopped existing. There was no old life to go back to any more. Because one of my sons was gone and the other was grown up, and

I didn't know how . . . I could not think how I would face him
again.'

He rested his head on his hand. His face was very sad and old
in the lamplight of the inn. He had a look about him of someone
who had once been happy, a long time ago, and it made me
melancholy to think of the years since then that had shadowed over
his once-handsome face. 'But what about you?' he said. 'I still don't
know how the story finishes.' He poured out spirits again. 'Carry
on telling me,' he said. 'Please. It would make my heart less heavy
to hear you tell me.'

And I felt so sad on his behalf that I went on with the story.

SEPTEMBER

'Anselm Andros, you are not concentrating,' said Sister Theresa. I glanced up and came back to the real world. The rest of the class was staring at me; outside the windows, a fine drizzle was falling.

'Sorry,' I said, sitting up straighter.

'Try to keep your mind on the lesson in progress,' Sister Theresa told me with a frown.

'Sorry,' I said again.

I bent my head over the textbook. I could not remember what the lesson in progress was. They were all the same, lists of facts that half the class copied down studiously and the other half ignored altogether. There were thirty of us left this year and still not enough desks to go round. I was sharing with Gabriel Delacruz. He had divided the desk very precisely with a line of chalk. Michael's place, beside John Keller, the doctor's son, was no longer his.

The restless sounds of the classroom troubled the air as Sister Theresa went on writing. 'Second year of King Cassius's reign: Alcyria imposes reparations on Malonia,' she scrawled on the blackboard. It was history, I decided. Though it could just as well be political studies. I wrote that sentence down, then drifted away from the classroom again. Sister Theresa was describing the breakdown of the national economy, writing figures on the board with a flourish.

The school clock chimed four, and Sister Theresa set down her chalk and raised the moth-eaten orange flag at the front of the classroom. We pushed back our chairs and stood up for the national anthem. We now had to sing it every day when school finished. As soon as it ended, I threw my jacket around my shoulders and began piling up my books. People were already racing out of the other classrooms, the girls from one side of the school and the boys from the other.

'Anselm, one moment,' said Sister Theresa. 'I want to talk to you.'

I waited. 'Do you know where Michael Barone is?' she said. 'I understood he was coming back to school.'

'His family left the city,' I said. 'Last week. They sold their shop, and I don't know when they are coming back.' I could not say 'if', but we both knew that was what I meant.

Sister Theresa made a note in her register, frowning, then straightened up and looked at me over her battered spectacles. 'Tell me, Anselm,' she said. 'Why did you choose to stay on this year?'

I murmured something vague about wanting to be well educated.

'On some points you are a very good pupil,' she said. 'But you have been in another world since the start of term.'

'Sorry, Sister.'

'I don't want you to lose your way,' she said. 'These are difficult times.'

She meant the boys in the class who had joined the Imperial Order; I knew it. There were three or four, and though none of us had betrayed them, everyone knew who they were. 'My family are royalists,' I said. 'They have been royalists since my father's father, and I'd rather die—'

'Would you?' she said. 'Yes, that's what I was afraid of. Concentrate on your studies and you will do well, Anselm.'

I opened my mouth to question her, but I did not know what to say. She began cleaning the chalk off the board.

'You may go now,' she said.

I picked up my books and left, along the corridor and across the desert wasteland of the front yard. The mud here was packed hard enough to jar your feet; here and there, the younger boys had excavated holes with bits of stick, then given up. I was the last to arrive at Jasmine's school, though I ran half the way there. All the way, I was wondering what Sister Theresa had meant.

Jasmine was waiting outside the gates, sitting alone under an elderly tree that grew up through the pavement. She was frowning at something on the ground in front of her, and as I approached, my skin turned cold. She was making the stones creep across the ground. They edged over the dusty paving of the street, as though they were racing each other, and fell through the grating of the basement opposite. I heard the soft plinking sound as they struck the bars. A crow with a broken wing leaped from the tree, and Jasmine looked up. 'Anselm, you're late,' she said.

'Is that a new trick?' I asked.

'Uncle taught me, before. Anselm, you're late like you always used to be.'

'I'm sorry. I won't be this year. It was just today; I couldn't help it.'

She rolled her eyes with an old weariness and picked up her books.

'Sorry, Jasmine,' I said. 'My teacher was lecturing me; I could not get away.'

'What what she lecturing you about?'

'Not paying attention. And not losing my way.'

'Losing your way? What does that mean?'

'I wish I knew. Come on.'

We set out for home. Our route was the straightest possible; it crossed a patch of waste ground where broken glass clinked under our feet, then came out across the new square. Carriages swept past us on their way north and south, and I kept hold of Jasmine's hand as we crossed it. At the centre was a statue of the king, and a few traders had broken away from the market and set up at its feet, spreading their goods out on old rugs and rickety tables. Their shouts rose around us, and people argued and picked up the goods restlessly and swore at the traders when they did not like the prices. I stopped at my grandmother's stall to buy vegetables and bread for dinner.

'Why doesn't Jasmine come up and say hello?' she enquired as she counted out shillings for change.

'Oh, you know – she's only small, and the crowds.'

'That's as may be,' said my grandmother. She glanced over at Jasmine and frowned. 'And where is that friend of yours today?'

'Who, Michael?' I said. She knew him well, but she always called him 'that friend of yours'. 'He has left,' I said. 'He left last week.'

'Oh?' she said. 'Yes, I noticed the shop standing empty. His father was a pawnbroker, wasn't he?'

I did not answer. The crowds divided us, and I struggled back to where Jasmine was waiting and took her hand. A light rain was beginning. 'Come on,' I said. 'Let's go home.'

Jasmine was gazing up at the statue of the king, and she did not hear me. The white stone was streaked with mildew now, and people had attacked the inscription underneath until it was barely legible. THE CORONATION OF HIS HIGHNESS KING CASSIUS III, it read. JUSTICE, INTEGRITY, PEACE. And someone had added words below it.

'Anselm, what does that end part say?' Jasmine asked, pointing. 'Lying . . . bas . . . lying bastard? Is that what it says?'

'Come on,' I said. 'Jasmine, hell itself will break loose if Grandmama hears you shouting "lying bastard".'

She laughed and followed me. We ducked under the old barbed wire onto St. Stephen's Lane. This street was half demolished; the slum housing was supposed to have been rebuilt years ago.

'I don't like school,' remarked Jasmine, balancing along a ruined wall.

'It's only been one day, Jas. Why don't you like it?'

'Because of my teacher. Stupid Mr Victoire. I can already tell I don't like him; he's just like horrible Mrs Simmonds last year.'

'How can you know already?'

'He made me sit in the cupboard. There are spiders in there. I felt them crawling in my hair; I swear I did. He said I needed to learn discipline. I know discipline. I just don't listen to him when he tells me to do something stupid.'

'He made you sit in the cupboard?' I demanded.

'Yes. That's not one word of a lie.'

'Wait – come back and tell me properly,' I said, trying to catch hold of her arm, but she jumped onto an abandoned newspaper stand, then swung round a lamppost, and I could not catch her. 'I'm the queen of all I survey!' she proclaimed from halfway up the lamppost.

'You look more like a monkey to me,' I said, and made

her laugh and slide down to the ground. 'But seriously, Jasmine,' I said, catching her arm. 'He made you sit in the cupboard? That doesn't seem right.'

'It's not so bad,' said Jasmine. 'I like it better in the cupboard, because I don't have to see his ugly face. Will you carry me home? Listen, let's pretend I'm a princess and you're my servant.'

I picked up Jasmine and ran with her. 'Faster, servant!' she shouted at intervals as we made our ungainly voyage over the rubble at the end of the street and through the next alley to the end of Trader's Row. As we raced along the street, Jasmine reached up to catch hold of the flags that were still hanging from the washing lines. They were left there from the end of July, mingled with the washing on the lines. It was the tradition to leave them until the end of September, when the king had formed the first government.

'Look,' Jasmine called as we passed the Barones' shop. 'Stop, servant! Stop! Someone has moved in.' We stopped to stare in through the window. 'What are they doing?' said Jasmine.

Three men in shabby clothes were stripping the old paper from the walls and sawing up planks. Behind the dust on the window, they moved like ghosts in our vision. The old letters on the window, MICHAEL BARONE, JEWELLERS AND PAWNBROKERS FOR FIVE GENERATIONS, were already half scratched away. A few of the other traders were standing at their shop doorways, watching the three men work. 'Anselm?' said Jasmine, and dropped down to the ground again and put her hand in mine. 'Do you miss Michael?'

'Why do you ask?'

'You never talk about him.'

'Did I used to?'

'Sometimes. And when people go away, you have to talk about them, don't you? Because that way you keep remembering them, and they aren't really gone.'

'Michael hasn't died, Jas,' I said.

I watched the nearest workman taking a sledgehammer to the old counter and throwing each dismembered plank into a corner of the room. 'Can we write him a letter?' said Jasmine.

'I don't know his address. He said he would send it, but he hasn't. Maybe they are still looking for somewhere else to live.'

'But what if he doesn't send it?'

'Come on,' I said. 'Let's go.'

Mr Pascal was standing in the shop doorway, berating Leo over something. He raised his arm to let us under it and went on talking. 'It is a solid gold venture,' he was saying. 'If you don't make a fortune, I solemnly promise you, you can have everything I make out there in repayment for the inconvenience. You will be rich, North; may God strike me down if I tell a lie.'

Jasmine glanced up at me with a grin. She thought Mr Pascal's outrageous bargaining the funniest thing on earth.

'I'll put the water on to boil for tea,' I said. Leo nodded. He was listening intently to Mr Pascal, and as we passed him, he kissed Jasmine and ruffled my hair without really noticing us.

'It would only be until Christmas,' Mr Pascal continued. 'Listen, North, this country is as good as occupied already. The economy is a tower of cards. But Holy Island is ruled by no one, and that is where money is to be made. Everyone is going west.'

'I don't believe these stories about gold paving the streets of Holy Island,' said Leo, putting the pieces of an old lamp together with a steady hand. He had his spectacles on. They still looked strange on him, but Leo's eyesight was deteriorating young, and Father Dunstan had recommended them.

'They aren't stories, North. Come on, give me an answer.'

'I can't, not just like that.'

'Well, let me know by the end of the week. One way or the other. I had better go, but don't forget.'

Leo nodded and raised his hand as Mr Pascal stepped out of the door. 'It's all changed next door,' he remarked from the step. 'I still can't get over Barone leaving like that. The shop has been in his family since the first King Cassius. I hope his view of the future turns out to be wrong, or we are all in trouble.'

With that dismal thought, Mr Pascal left us. I put the water on the stove to boil, all the time watching Leo. He carried the lamp carefully to a shelf and set it there on a faded piece of velvet. Then he jammed a cigarette into his mouth and lit it.

'What was Mr Pascal lecturing you about?' I asked him.

'He wants me to go with him to Holy Island for the winter. He's shutting up his shop to go and trade there; that's what he says.'

'But you're not going to?' I said. Leo did not answer. He just took the cigarette out of his mouth and exhaled carefully.

It was only then that I heard the silence. The street had been noisy, but now only the birds were singing, and their voices seemed artificially loud and bright. 'What is it?' I said. 'Listen to the silence.'

'I can hear it too,' said Jasmine, and ran to the door.

'Don't go out there,' said Leo suddenly. 'Jasmine, come back here.'

He stepped forward and shot both bolts home. At the same moment, three men in blue uniforms appeared farther up the street, sauntering along with rifles on their shoulders. 'Jasmine, Anselm, go into the back room,' said Leo. 'At once.'

'No, I want to see,' said Jasmine.

'I'm not joking, Jasmine! Go!'

I had not heard Leo shout for as long as I could remember. We both obeyed him. We stood in the doorway of the back room, watching the street, Jasmine leaning forward desperately to try and see. The men were coming this way. They stopped opposite the pharmacist's, and one of them took out matches. I thought that he was going to light a cigarette. But instead he struck a match and held it up in the still air. Another man took out what looked like a can of paraffin. I bent down, trying to see what they were doing, but they had moved out of my vision.

'Papa,' Jasmine murmured once or twice, and Leo said, 'Shh.' The men marched away down a side alley.

Then there was a roaring hiss, like a stove catching. The men had set light to the nearest flag, and from the way the flames engulfed it, it looked like they had drenched it in paraffin first. The fire was racing along the washing line, burning the pharmacist's shirts and a stained old blanket. It caught the next flag and leaped towards the sky with a triumphant roar. Trails of paraffin in the dust blazed like spirits. The next washing line caught and burned, and the people out in the street were shrieking and coughing and running for shop doorways. The flags were all catching now; the man must have thrown the paraffin upwards in-discriminately, drenching everything. The washing lines blazed like cords of fire and crumbled. People ran out with buckets then and threw water from their upstairs windows. The lines fell in a tangle of scorched rope, and the shrivelled remains of the flags went with them. It had all taken less than a minute, and for a long time nothing broke the stunned silence in the street.

People began emerging from their houses at last, though Leo was still holding us back. 'Could have set the whole house on fire,' someone was muttering, and someone else said, 'Bloody fools.' A baby above the old stationer's was screaming in outrage. Billy and Joe began parading around with a half-extinguished flag, but the pharmacist slapped them both so hard they staggered. Into the chaos, serene and beautiful, walked my mother. 'What is all this?' she said. Then, 'Leo! Anselm! Jasmine!'

I will not forget her face before she saw us. It was the start of something, that expression, like the reflection of terrors still to come. The look of someone who suddenly saw their family taken from them, torn apart or scattered in what would soon be an open war. Then Leo said, 'It's all right; I'm here,' and she was with us again. Someone, maybe Mr Pascal, tried to turn it into a joke. The siege atmosphere returned. And we pretended that everything would still be all right. But the men had been in blue uniforms; we had all seen it. Those were uniforms I knew well, from pictures in history books. They were the clothes Lucien's soldiers used to wear.

That night, after the others had gone to bed, a kind of restlessness came over me, and I went down to the shop to search for evidence of my real father. There must be something, I was certain, some record of his name. I began in the back room, with the drawers of the old desk. But I found no sign there. Only a pile of unpaid bills, and a thousand letters, and a bundle of Jasmine's drawings. I put them back and carried the lamp with me to the front room.

We had only lived here five years, but in that time, the shop had grown cluttered with half-forgotten objects. In a corner, I unearthed a box of books that Leo had never been able to sell but that he could not stand to part with either, half of them copies of Harold North or old things from before my grandmother was born. I opened a worn-out third edition of *The Sins of Judas* and read the last page. 'Some things that I have lost I will never find again. Like the river that flows and becomes a different river, I have stepped out of the world and it has gone on without me. And I wish wholeheartedly that I could return and live differently. And I wish I could tell my younger self that it would have been all right.'

When I closed the book, a cloud of dust rose like a phantom and vanished in the draught. Underneath a pile of secondhand clothes, I found a case of letters that Mr Barone had passed on to us. People left them in his shop sometimes, forgotten in the drawers of desks and locked in writing cases. As I turned over the first bundle, moths rose and threw themselves against the glass of the lamp. The quiet whir of their wings went on as I continued to search. In the drawers of the counter were brooches that had lost their jewels, and books without covers, and a china swan with a broken neck, wrapped in newspaper. I found all my school reports, and a lock of Jasmine's baby hair in a yellowed envelope, and a tarnished ring. The ring made me pause for a moment. But how could it be anything to do with my real father? He would never have given my mother a sign like this when they were not even married.

Something made the drawer stick, and I had to reach in and pull a sheaf of papers out before I could close it. I hesitated before I put them back. They were not old, and the writing was Leo's. I held them to the lamp.

' "Once, many years ago," the lord Rigel began, "there was a boy who wanted more than anything to study magic." '

That was how the page started, and it made no sense to me. But as I read it, I heard Leo's tread on the stairs. I moved without thinking. I put the papers back and turned down the lamp.

'Anselm?' he said.

'Yes,' I said. 'I'm over here.'

He came down the stairs slowly, his head bent to avoid knocking it on the low door frame, then straightened up and looked at me. 'Can't you sleep?' he said.

I shook my head.

'Neither can I.' He sat down at the counter and watched the moths thudding softly against the lamp. He did it without really seeing them. I pulled up a rickety dining chair priced half a crown and sat opposite him. I thought I knew what kept him awake, more than anything. Mr Pascal's talk of Holy Island.

Leo leaned on both elbows on the counter and lit a cigarette. 'Anselm,' he said at last. 'If I ever had to leave . . . I mean, if I went away . . .'

'Is this about Mr Pascal?' I said.

The smoke gained a life of its own, making ghostly patterns that hung between us. 'No,' said Leo.

He breathed in smoke, and his voice shuddered when he did it. I could hear it catching on something in his chest. It was a strange sound, like listening to an old man, but he was only thirty-one. He leaned on the counter and coughed.

'Your cough is starting already,' I said. 'It's only September.'

'I know.'

'I don't understand,' I said. 'Why are you talking about leaving?'

'Anselm, the other night,' he said, 'there was a man standing outside the shop watching us.'

I did not answer. The silence was charged suddenly, as though lightning had run through it.

'Do you know anything about this?' said Leo. 'Have you seen him before?'

I did not know how to answer. I could not tell him that I had seen the man; it would only make him more anxious. 'I don't know,' I said. 'I've seen people outside, but they might just have been walking past.'

'When?'

'Weeks ago. It was probably nothing.'

'Not this time,' said Leo. 'This time, there was a man standing outside watching us.'

'What did he want?' I said. 'Do you know who he is?'

'He could be anyone,' said Leo. 'He could be a debt collector. I owe money. Doctor Keller has sent a final demand; the bills are piling up. Someone is going to stop being lenient sooner or later.'

I did not answer. I had seen the bills just now, searching through the desk in the back room, and the situation was bad.

'Or he could be someone from the government,' Leo

went on. 'All able-bodied men older than eighteen are supposed to have signed up for National Service; it's all over the city on those government posters.'

'I know that's the law,' I said. 'But they aren't going to enforce it for months, Mr Pascal says.'

'Yes, Mr Pascal says.'

'Everyone says.'

He stubbed out his cigarette and lit another.

'So is that who you think he is?' I said. 'A debt collector or someone from the government?'

Leo shook his head. 'Anselm, there are things you don't know,' he said. 'I think people are looking for me. I can't help believing that he's someone from the Imperial Order who means no good.'

'Why would they be looking for you?'

He did not answer. He went to the front window instead and stood looking out. The wind was driving pale clouds across the narrow strip of sky. 'Is it just because our family are royalists?' I said. 'You weren't even in the resistance, Papa.'

'But I was involved with the resistance,' said Leo.

I watched the back of his head. He did not turn. 'I never knew,' I said eventually.

'No one knew. It was just a mistake. I was in the wrong place at the wrong time. I'm not saying it wasn't my fault. It was. But no one knew about it, because I haven't told anyone.'

'But then if no one knew, how could this man—'

'I can't be sure,' he said. 'That's the thing. The Imperial Order seem to know everything, and I can't be sure any more. I can't be certain that there wasn't someone who saw or heard about it and who could have spoken to them since.'

'Papa, do you really think they are going to take over here too?' I said.

He did not answer. His silence was worse than anything he could have said. I ran my fingers along the worn leather of the counter to try and convince myself that it was still really there and that everything was the way it always had been. 'Why didn't you tell me?' I said again. I was half proud of him, in spite of his talk about mistakes, and half shocked. The resistance men were all hardened fighters in their time, and I could not imagine Leo ever being one of them.

'I don't know,' he said. 'I was never part of it; it was just a mistake better left forgotten.'

'How was it a mistake?'

'It doesn't matter.'

Leo ran his hand backwards over his hair and came back to the counter. When he did, I noticed the letters on the window. Something was different about them. I picked up the lamp and crossed the room, then raised the light to the glass. Half the sign was gone. Where L. NORTH & SON used to be, the letters were scraped away. A network of scratches shifted in the lamplight, arranging themselves into circular patterns. It looked as though someone had taken a file to it. 'Who scratched off the sign?' I said. 'Did you see someone do it?'

'I did it,' said Leo.

I stood there stupidly, the lamp still raised in my hand.

'I did it,' Leo said again. 'Anselm, sometimes it is better to be anonymous, you know? The Norths are Aldebaran's family – I don't think there is one person in the city who doesn't know it. Do you remember when we used to have well-wishers coming to our door, in the old days? People who thought Harold North was some kind of martyr. You probably don't remember; you were too young.'

'I remember,' I said. 'A woman brought a wreath once.'

'Yes.'

'But, Papa, why take our name off the window now—'

'Because I'm frightened,' he said. 'I'm frightened of what they will do when Harold North is no longer a martyr.'

'Is everything going to be all right?' I said.

'I don't know,' he said. 'I don't think so. Anselm, I have such dreams.'

I had always admired Leo for his honesty, but sometimes I would rather have heard him lie. I would rather he had said, Yes, forget about the men outside the door; it will be all right. I rested my forehead against the window and stared out. Somewhere in the east, a fire was blazing. The Imperial Order burning old buildings was no longer a new occurrence. A derelict building on Citadel Street, two doors from our old house, had gone up in smoke.

'It is not just because of my father,' Leo said. 'Anselm, it was a very bad thing that I did. If it ever comes out – if anyone ever learns about it – I will be in trouble. And so will you – all of you.'

'What did you do?' I asked, turning to him. The way he spoke about it made my heart turn cold. 'Maybe if you just told me—'

'I can't tell you.'

'But it was something connected to the resistance?'

'Don't ask me. I know telling you would be dangerous. Anselm, don't tempt me to do it.'

'All right. All right, I won't, Papa.'

My own voice sounded frightened, like a child's. 'I wish Aldebaran was here,' Leo said. 'I never knew how much I relied on him before.' He sat down at the counter again and lit a third cigarette. 'Sometimes when I can't sleep, I start wondering where he is now. Is that madness? I don't know. I can't think of him as just gone away for ever.'

'He's still watching over us,' I said. 'I believe that much.'

'When you lose someone,' Leo said slowly, 'they watch over you. I know they do. But the fact is, they can't always help you any more. They can't be there to catch you. That's what troubles me about it. To think that if I died, I would see you and Jasmine and Maria suffering and not be able to do anything about it. Is there anything worse than that?'

I did not know what to say. I did not like to think of it. 'Papa?' I said, changing the subject as far as I dared to. 'Did you ever find out about that book? The one that Uncle left you?'

He shook his head. 'Nothing of consequence. I asked Markey about it.'

'You asked Daniel Markey?'

'Yes. I met him by chance, and Mr Pascal thought he would be the only person who would know.'

'I suppose he would be the only person.'

Daniel Markey was the best antiques valuer in the city, and a long time ago, when Leo was training as a soldier and every next man was in the military, Daniel Markey had been his sergeant. They acknowledged each other but hardly more than that.

'So what did he say?' I asked.

'Nothing. He didn't know the publisher. No, I'll just have to leave it. I don't think it's a sign – not really. I think it's just something Uncle thought would occupy me for a few hours. It was a bit like Harold North. As if he had written another book. I think that's all Uncle meant by it.'

Asking Leo about the book seemed only to have added to his melancholy, so I gave up and made tea instead. Leo drank shakily; in the silence, I could hear it sliding down his throat each time he swallowed. I picked up the newspaper and turned over the pages. The rich people in the portraits stared back, people whose concerns were politics and wars. INVASION IMMINENT, the headline threatened.

'If a war could really be coming, we should try to stay together,' I said. 'Shouldn't we?'

I knew it was childish to be so afraid. I had asked it because what he had just said made me think about him dying. Leo put his hand on the back of my head, like I was a little boy. 'You talk more sense than anyone sometimes, Anselm,' he said. 'It's true. We should always stay together.'

He took the newspaper from me and leafed through the first few pages. His hand came to rest at a picture of the king, under a report on the minute details of the split in the government.

'He would give us a few hundred crowns,' I remarked, half joking. 'To pay those debts.'

'No,' said Leo. 'No, he has sold all his furniture to give the money to the poor. It says so here. All the state furniture is gone. He must be desperate.'

'What does he do now?' I demanded. 'Eat his banquets sitting on the floor?'

The idea was not particularly funny, but we both laughed, and once we started, it seemed better to keep laughing, in the cold shop with the wind howling outside, than to stop and let the darkness advance on us. I fetched our overcoats from the back room and turned down the lamp, and we waited for it to get light.

★ ★ ★

The next day, a fine frost clung to the dust of the city, and slogans had appeared overnight on every wall. The side of Mr Pascal's shop bore Ahira's and Talitha's faces. The pharmacist's front window was obscured with black slogans. Jasmine walked very close beside me all the way to school. The police were wandering about in every street, with their guns across their shoulders.

'Don't leave me,' said Jasmine when we got to the gates. 'I don't like it at school.'

'Jasmine, don't start this,' I said. My eyes ached from yet another sleepless night. 'Of course you like school. Go on.'

'No. Anselm, I don't. Don't make me go.'

I pushed her towards the gate. She whined and clung to my hand. 'Jasmine, just go inside,' I told her, but she would not, and it turned into an argument. I was so late for school that I had to sit at the back of the classroom, far enough from the heat of the stove that the window was still frosted. I could barely hear Sister Theresa, and my mind drifted.

On the shelf at the back of the classroom were stacks of dusty old history books. They were left over from before Lucien's regime, and no one used them any longer, but nothing was thrown away in Queen Anneline Government School. I reached for one now and turned to the back, where the genealogies of the noble families were. When I was a little boy, I used to wonder if one of these names was my father's. It seemed stupid now. I studied each name in the St. John family and half of the Markovs, then turned over to the de Fiore family and traced the line down again. It was cut off before the last descendant, a Jean-Cristophe. I supposed it meant they had disowned him.

Since resolving to find out the truth about my real

father, I had done nothing about it. I thought of Michael telling me to go to the graveyard or the records office. If he had still been here, I would have done that. But it was not simple. It felt like a betrayal of Leo, to try and find the man he had long since replaced. And it was as though I was breaking some unspoken promise to my mother too.

'Change places!' called Sister Theresa, bringing me back. We changed at the end of every lesson now; the people at the back of the class got too cold otherwise. I shoved the book onto the shelf again and moved further forward.

The sun fell below the houses as we walked home from school, and the city grew as cold as death. The wind skinned your knuckles as though there was grit in it. Jasmine and I walked without speaking, our scarves pulled up to our eyes. 'I can't believe anywhere could be so cold,' Jasmine said through rattling teeth as we crossed the new square.

'Explorers in the north survive in places much colder than this,' I said.

She trekked out ahead of me, pretending she was wading through snow. 'What do they discover?' she said.

I did not know. We read about them in the newspapers, but they were mostly Alcyrian. 'Oil and gas, I think. So they can invent machines. They say it's going to be a new era, across the whole continent, when these machines are perfected.'

I had heard this from Mr Pascal. Jasmine wrinkled her nose under her scarf. 'Imagine going somewhere colder than this just for oil and gas. They must be looking for something more important.' She stopped then and took hold of my arm. 'What's that sign?'

I looked where she was pointing. It was an arrow,

painted in black on the side of a house. 'I don't know,' I said. 'Come on, it's too cold to stop.'

'There's another,' said Jasmine as we passed the next end building. 'Shall we follow them?'

'I think it's getting ready for snow.'

'Look. Another one, Anselm! Stop and look.' She tugged my sleeve. A fresh blast of wind drew the tears from my eyes. 'Can we follow them?' she said. 'Please.'

'Let's just get home,' I said. The police were still about, and it was growing colder all the time. I tried to pull her on. In response, Jasmine turned and ran away down a side street. 'Jasmine, come back!' I shouted. She did not slow. I hesitated, then followed her. The wind drove into my eyes running in this direction and forced the tears faster out of them. At the end of the street, there was another arrow – a whole line of them, leading away along an alley.

'It's a secret trail,' said Jasmine. 'Like in *The Beggar King*.'

'Let's go back,' I said. 'It's cold as hell.'

'Not now, Anselm. We can't turn back now.'

'Come on, don't be stupid.'

But Jasmine was determined. She ran ahead of me from arrow to arrow. I realized as we approached that the trail was leading us to Citadel Street. 'Jas, come on,' I said, ducking under the barbed wire. 'Enough of playing games now. Let's just go back.'

'Isn't this where we used to live?' she asked, keeping a few yards between us so that I could not catch her.

'Yes,' I said. 'And I know there's nothing down here, so let's just go.'

'No. Not yet.'

The street was deserted, half the houses demolished and the other half boarded. The wind howled around them and became strange voices that followed us as we walked. Every building in this street had an arrow now as well as a red cross on the door. Crows were gusting to and fro in the wind. We came to a halt abruptly, like soldiers in a comedy. I collided with Jasmine and dropped my books. 'Look,' she whispered. The arrows met on the front wall of our old building. Above them were the words THIS IS THE PLACE. Ahira's face glared down at us in blue.

'It's something to do with the Imperial Order,' I said. 'Come on, Jas; let's just go.'

Jasmine needed no further encouragement. We turned and ran. Perhaps it was childish that I was glancing back too. I stumbled as we climbed under the barbed wire, and the books in my arms slid across the frozen ground again. 'Go on; I'll catch up,' I said, but Jasmine waited, hopping up and down with cold and fear. I picked up the books, and we ran again, along the alleyway and back into the light and bustle of the new square. Once we were surrounded by people, we glanced at each other and almost managed to laugh. But it had been actual fear that drove us, and we both knew it.

We did not speak as we resumed our walk home. Jasmine was studying the frosted ground thoughtfully. 'Shall we tell Mama and Papa?' she said at last. 'Or not?'

I hesitated. 'No,' I said. 'No, let's not tell them. But listen . . .'

'What, Anselm?'

I wanted to say, But Leo thinks the Imperial Order are following him. But a man stood outside the door and watched us. But they smashed the windows in our shop, and now they have written their slogans on the house where we used to live, and it can't just be coincidence. They must have some plan. 'But nothing,' I said, and took her hand. 'Don't say anything, all right? Let's go home.'

'You had better cheer your father up,' said Mr Pascal when
we got back. 'He has been so downhearted all day that I
despair of him. North, I don't know how you will make
money in the auction rooms tonight if you are so
melancholy.'

'You are going to the auction rooms tonight?' I asked.
Leo rarely went to the auction rooms any more; they were
the haunt of market traders.

'Desperate times,' said Mr Pascal.

It was bitterly cold that night after Leo and Mr Pascal
set out. I tried to tidy some of the things in the shop, but I
knew I was losing the battle and my bones ached. My
mother and Jasmine were upstairs by the fire, acting out
some noisy drama in my mother's best dresses and heeled
shoes. I put up the grilles on the shop windows and bolted
the door, then got out that writing of Leo's instead. But I
was not certain I should read it at all.

Michael would have told me to do it. But Michael was
far away; I didn't know where. And I was certain Leo had
put the writing in that drawer to be out of sight.

The shop was sinister on these autumn nights. I did not
like the shadows or the way the oil lamp guttered in
invisible draughts. With the wind howling down Trader's
Row, I thought I could hear voices out there. It made me
think of Harlan Smith's book and the people who spoke to
him out of the darkness, in words he could not quite
recognize. That was what happened in the story, right at the
start. I had read bits of it, but I did not quite understand it.

Before I could decide whether or not to read what Leo
had written, someone banged on the door and made me

drop the pages. 'Let me in; it's perishing out here. Anselm! Is that you?'

It was my grandmother, rapping on the door and frowning in through the grimy pane of glass. I ran to let her in. 'What are you doing sitting down in the shop on a night like this?' she demanded as soon as she had crossed the threshold. 'And what is that frightful noise from upstairs?'

'Just Mother and Jasmine.'

'I came to see how Maria is.'

She was already starting up the stairs. I shoved the papers into the drawer, picked up the lamp, and followed her. As we came into the living room, the laughter stopped abruptly. My mother was in an old red dress that she was falling out of, her rouge and lipstick clearly Jasmine's work. Jasmine was wearing a skirt that came up to her armpits and Leo's soldier's boots.

'What on earth are you doing?' demanded my grandmother. 'Maria, you are expecting a baby. You are supposed to be resting. And this child should not be wearing makeup like a common hussy.'

'Common husky yourself,' said Jasmine, which made my mother snort with laughter. 'We're doing a play, Grandmama. Come and watch.'

My grandmother did not come and watch. Instead, she lectured us from the doorway on the vices of the theatre, the serious danger the baby was in, and the indignity of the whole performance. My grandfather Julian would be turning over in his grave to think of such behaviour. What was more, we were Androses and once part of a great family, and if the family name was going down like a sinking ship, it was because of spectacles like this. (Jasmine sniggered at the word *spectacles*, which started my grandmother off again.)

'And another thing,' my grandmother finished. 'Do you let Leonard smoke in here?'

'He sometimes does,' said my mother.

My grandmother raised her eyes to heaven and opened the window to let in the freezing night air. 'Have some mercy!' said my mother, still trying not to smile. The laughter was leaving her in stages, like a shaking fit.

My grandmother glared round at us all. I went downstairs to boil water for tea. When I came back up, my mother and Jasmine were dressed in their ordinary clothes again, and a cold silence hung over the room, clinging to everything far worse than Leo's cigarette smoke.

'Mama?' said Jasmine as I set down the tray of tea on a pile of boxes. 'What does "This is the place" mean?'

I glanced at her. 'Has she been reading the newspapers?' said my grandmother.

'No,' said Jasmine. 'It says "This is the place" on the front of the house where we used to live, and I want to know why.'

'I don't know,' said my mother, frowning. 'Is it a line from the Bible?'

'The Imperial Order went round writing it,' said my grandmother. 'There was something in today's newspaper.'

'I'll go and find it,' I said.

'No—' began my mother.

'Go on, Anselm,' said my grandmother. 'Find it if you want.'

I stood fixed in the doorway. My grandmother frowned. 'Go on,' she repeated. 'Maria, there is no harm. Anselm, I told you, go and find it.'

This time my mother did not argue. I went downstairs. Usually the newspaper was lying on the counter of the shop or on the table in the back room, but it was not there tonight. I searched everywhere, then opened the stove to add more coal and found it there. It was torn into shreds and nearly burned, shoved into the back of the flames. I did not know who had done that. I turned and went back up the stairs. 'We don't have today's,' I said as I came back into the living room. 'Maybe Papa never went to get it.'

'Oh,' said my grandmother. 'Well, the story was not very nice, but I suppose' – she glanced at Jasmine – 'she doesn't understand. Anyway, the Imperial Order have been writing "This is the place" on the walls where the famous war criminals were shot. I suppose they see them as great heroes now.'

Jasmine put her thumb in her mouth and whispered, 'Who was shot at our old house?'

'Ahira,' said my grandmother with half a glance at my mother. 'He was shot just out there in the street. Anselm was a tiny baby at the time; you weren't even born.'

We exchanged uneasy glances, but no one spoke. 'I never knew that,' I said when the silence had drawn out a long while.

'Well, I don't suppose you did,' said my grandmother.

'Down Citadel Street?' I said. 'No one ever told me that. You mean to say during the revolution?'

'Yes,' said my grandmother.

'His blood must still be there,' said Jasmine. 'It must be all over the street. I'm not walking there ever again. Who shot him?'

'Were we there at the time?' I said.

'Did you see it?' said Jasmine. 'Mama, did you see him get shot?'

My mother stood up abruptly and began clearing away

the half-finished tea. The cups rattled as she carried them down the stairs; her hands were shaking badly.

'What is it?' I said.

'Nothing,' she said. 'Nothing. The baby is just kicking. I would rather get up and walk about.'

'I was drinking that tea, Maria!' my grandmother called. My mother did not bring it back. 'Well,' said my grandmother, shaking her head. 'I'm sure you children have a right to know the truth as much as the next person.'

There was a crash, and we all started. My mother had dropped the tray. The three of us ran to the top of the stairs and collided; my grandmother won the struggle. 'Oh, Maria!' she wailed as she ran ahead of us down the stairs. Strewn across the floor of the back room were the shattered remains of the cups. 'Maria, those were mine!' my grandmother cried. 'We brought those from Cliff House – your father bought them for my wedding present! Oh, Maria! How could you be so careless?'

My mother did not answer. She just turned and went out into the yard and closed the door. I helped my grandmother pick up the cups, more to stop her lamenting than anything else. 'I should never have given Maria half the set,' she said. 'Never, never—'

'They are not all broken,' I said, setting aside two that were only chipped at the edges.

'Let me help,' said Jasmine.

'No,' I said. 'You'll cut your hands. Stay on the stairs, Jas.'

She ignored me and picked up two halves of a cup. 'Look,' she said, frowning and piecing them back together on the sideboard. 'It's not broken, Grandmama.'

'Don't be silly!' said my grandmother with a sob.

'Look,' said Jasmine, and stepped away from the cup.

When she took her hands away, the two halves remained together. It was only when I got closer and still could not make out the cracks that I realized what she had done. I picked it up. It did not fall into two pieces as I had expected it to but held fast. 'How did you do that?' I said.

'Willpower,' she said.

'But, Jasmine . . .' I held the cup to the light of the oil lamp and tried to snap it again. It would not break. 'Jasmine, that is not possible,' I said.

'Why not?'

'Because even the great ones can't mend what is broken,' I said. 'Uncle told me so when I was a little boy. It's like a law of the world.'

'There aren't any laws,' said Jasmine. 'That's stupid.'

'There must be certain rules,' I said. 'Otherwise what is magic?'

'Just people doing what they want to,' said Jasmine vaguely, and went on piecing together the cups.

My grandmother shivered and stood close to the stove. Jasmine worked carefully, lining up each broken piece and frowning at it until the cracks disappeared. When she had finished, there was a silence. Even the wind lulled outside, as though in respect.

'I don't know how you did that,' said my grandmother. 'But you are an angel, Jasmine.'

'See,' said Jasmine. 'There isn't anything wrong with powers, Grandmama.'

My grandmother did not answer. But she gave Jasmine an apple and ruffled her hair. Earlier the apple must have been withheld on the grounds of bad behaviour, but Jasmine had won it now. We stood around the back room waiting for my mother to come back.

When several minutes had passed, I went out to the wind-racked yard and tapped on the bathroom door. 'Mother?' I said. 'Are you all right?'

'Anselm,' she said. 'Come in.'

I went. She was sitting on the edge of the scratched shower with her head resting on her hand. In the light of the single candle, her eyes were deeply shadowed. 'Are you all right?' I asked her again.

'Yes, of course. I'm sorry about all that.'

'There's no harm done. Jasmine fixed the cups. What's wrong?'

'It was just that story of your grandmother's. I get so frightened for the baby, and I don't want to hear about . . .'

'No,' I said. 'Grandmother can be insensitive sometimes.'

Her mouth twisted at that. ' "Insensitive sometimes"? More like a coal train going down a mountain. She could make insensitivity into a profession.'

There was a silence in which my mother's worry was a solid presence, then we both smiled. The traces of Jasmine's make-up still lingered in the corners of her mouth and made her cheeks glitter. 'Come on,' she said, and wiped her eyes. 'Let's go in.' It was only when she did it that I realized she had been crying.

The wind was rising as we climbed the stairs. The clock in the square chimed the half-hour.

'Where is Leo?' asked my grandmother. 'I expected him to be here tonight.'

'He's at the auction rooms,' said my mother. 'He will be back before long.'

'All the same, it is irresponsible of him to leave you alone with the children in your condition.'

'Anselm is sixteen. And I am perfectly able to be

left alone in my condition. Mother, don't fuss about it.'

'Well, so you say,' my grandmother remarked. 'So you say, you are perfectly able, but I'm not so sure. And where is Leo really tonight? That's what I'd like to know. Out drinking probably.'

'Leo never drinks,' said my mother.

'Besides, Jasmine should be in bed,' said my grandmother. 'It's half past eight.'

Jasmine frequently stayed up past eleven, but none of us thought this the time to mention it. After my mother had told her a story, and I had told her two, and my grandmother had been prevented from opening the window to give her some fresh air, Jasmine fell asleep.

'What are all these newspapers doing stuck about the child's room?' my grandmother whispered, glancing about.

'Just Jasmine's cuttings,' said my mother.

'They are hardly edifying subjects for a young girl.'

I had never thought much about it. But my grandmother's disapproval made me see everything as she did. 'At least she learns something from them,' I said, but I sounded defensive, and my grandmother had the victory. She set her mouth firmly and closed Jasmine's bedroom door with a snap.

'You need to get this house in some kind of order,' she remarked.

'It is in some kind of order,' said my mother.

'Boxes and old furniture everywhere! Maria, you can hardly cross the floor.'

'We like it like this.'

'I've a mind to start sorting it out.'

'Please don't. Just sit down and rest.'

My mother sat on the sofa and started marking books.

My grandmother wandered about the room, picking up various objects and setting them down again. Then she began shifting the boxes around restlessly. 'Anselm, help me lift this,' she would remark at intervals, or 'Turn over those cushions; they are full of dust. No, not like that!'

I was trying again to read that book, *The Darkness Has a Thousand Voices*, but with my grandmother's fussing, I could not concentrate. My mother fell asleep on the sofa eventually, the half-marked schoolbooks sliding off her knee. I picked them up and piled them on the cushion beside her, then spread a blanket over her.

'And another thing,' said my grandmother. 'That story you told Jasmine was hardly suitable, Anselm. I wonder at you sometimes.'

'It's her favourite,' I said. 'Uncle used to tell it to her; it was the story she asked me for.'

My grandmother gave a sniff. I tried to ignore her but could not quite manage it. 'What's unsuitable in it?' I demanded.

'All the characters were criminals, it seemed to me.'

It was a story about smugglers, and a cabinet with a secret compartment with a map hidden in it, and a band of robbers who sailed on the sea. Aldebaran had told us once that it was a story from England and that there had always been sea robbers there. In the old days, everyone used to hide their most valuable possessions in secret compartments in their cupboards and chests, because they had no bank vaults. I tried to explain that to my grandmother, but she only sniffed again, and I could tell she was not really listening.

The clocks chimed ten, and I wished Leo would come home.

★ ★ ★

I must have fallen asleep beside my mother, because when I opened my eyes, I was slumped on the sofa with *The Darkness Has a Thousand Voices* digging into my chest. My grandmother was in the doorway; she must have come up from the back room. She was not tidying now. She was just standing there watching me. She leaned against the door frame and sighed. The light was dim, and she must have thought I was still asleep. I lay and watched her. She made no move to advance further into the room but just sighed again. It was a sound like the heartless wind in the streets outside and did nothing to raise my spirits. I hesitated, then whispered, 'What is it?'

'Anselm!' She put a hand on her heart. 'I thought you were sleeping; you startled me.'

'I just wondered what you were sighing about.'

'It was nothing.'

'What were you thinking?'

'You have changed; that's all I was thinking.'

'What do you mean?'

'I only noticed it now, when I came in and saw you. You look less like Maria than you did when you were a little boy. That was all.'

I sat up. I could not have slept for more than half an hour, but it felt like coming back a long way. 'Maybe it's my hair,' I said, still half asleep. 'It's turned redder since then, but my eyes are still like Mother's. Is Papa back yet?'

Her mouth straightened. 'No.'

I rubbed my aching neck. 'What time is it? Eleven? Twelve?'

'Almost half past eleven. I don't know what Leonard is thinking, staying out so late.'

'The auction rooms close at eleven,' I said. She did not

answer. I got up and went to the window. A few tiny rain-drops clung to the glass; the street outside was dead with sleep. 'Where is he?' I demanded.

'Yes, where is Papa?' said Jasmine from her bedroom doorway, and we both started at her voice.

'You should be asleep,' said my grandmother. 'What are you doing up again?'

'I can't sleep when Papa isn't back.'

'Maybe I should go and look for him,' I said.

'Certainly not. You can't go out at midnight, with the Imperial Order about and who knows what other vagabonds. Sit back down, Anselm.'

In the quiet, we could hear every clock ticking in the shop below. We sat and waited. Jasmine was half asleep, though she claimed not to be. I rocked her on my knee for a while, and she closed her eyes. My grandmother sat in the hard chair by the fire. 'Anselm?' she said then. 'Do you think Maria looks thinner?'

I glanced up. My grandmother was studying my mother's face in the dim light, her forehead creased in concern. I followed her glance. It was hard to tell in the darkness, but asleep my mother looked pale and not like herself. 'I don't know,' I said. 'Do you think so?'

'She is not as well as she should be; I know that much. I worry about her. When I was expecting Maria I'm sure I never worked.'

'Things are different now,' I said. 'I mean, with our family. You never worked then at all.'

'Yes, I know that very well.'

'Sorry. I didn't mean anything.'

My grandmother set her mouth so sternly that her lips disappeared, and she poked the fire. Time passed.

★ ★ ★

I must have slept again, because the next thing I knew, Jasmine was shaking my shoulder and hissing, 'Anselm. Wake up. Anselm!'

I sat up and heard it. Someone had closed the back door of the shop. My mother was still asleep on the sofa. My grandmother was in the chair beside the fire, sitting very stern and upright with her eyes closed. 'Is she asleep?' I whispered. Jasmine nodded. 'Shh, then; don't wake her. Let's go downstairs.'

For some reason we went slowly, and Jasmine took my hand. The clock in the square was chiming twelve. 'Is it Papa?' she whispered.

'It must be.'

'Why isn't he saying anything?'

'It's late – he doesn't want to wake anyone.'

There was a thud somewhere below, and I started.

'Anselm,' she said as we turned the dark corner of the stairs. 'What if it's not Papa? What if it's those men in blue and they've got him?'

'Shh.'

There was another thud and a low scraping noise. It was not coming from the yard; it was coming from somewhere in the dark back room. 'What is it?' said Jasmine, her voice rising.

'Stay here,' I told her. I raised my hand to keep her back and crossed the back room. A dark figure was at the door, shooting the old bolts across. Those bolts had been rusted since we moved into the shop, and we never used them. I made out the figure's gold hair and the lit cigarette in his mouth. I knew it was Leo, but he looked like a stranger. 'Papa?' I said.

He frowned for a moment, then seemed to recognize me.

'Where have you been?' I said. 'And why are you bolting the door like that?'

'He followed me back. I know he did. I could feel him there behind me in the street. I had to walk miles to get away from him.'

'Who?' I said.

He did not answer. His eyes were wild and restless and made my heart thud fast. I was shivering from waking so suddenly. 'What on earth are you thinking?' I said.

'Shh,' he said so fiercely we both started. 'Shh. Stay there.'

The wind juddered around the side of the house, and over its noise I thought I heard something. In the cold dimness, I could barely see what Leo was doing. He went silently to the dresser in the corner and took something out.

'Papa—' Jasmine ventured.

'Shh,' said Leo again. Then everything happened all at once. Someone appeared outside the door and stumbled over a box in the yard, and Leo raised the thing in his hand and said, 'Don't move. Don't come closer.'

In the moonlight, the thing in his hand glinted. He was holding our kitchen knife.

'North?' said the voice outside the door. 'North, is that you?'

'What do you want?' said Leo.

The person outside stumbled over another box, and Leo breathed harder and steadied his grip on the knife. 'If you come closer, I swear—'

'North, I just came to check that you were home safe. I lost you at the corner of the road.'

'It's Mr Pascal, for heaven's sake!' I said.

Leo stared at the door for several long seconds, then dropped the knife and covered his face with his hands. Mr Pascal was trying to unbolt the door now, muttering, 'North, what have you done to this door? Are you all right?'

'He's all right,' I said.

Mr Pascal gave up his struggle. 'I'll leave you, then,' he said. 'I just wanted to check. It's bitter cold out here, and I should get back.'

'Yes,' I said. 'Thank you.'

'Goodnight, Anselm.'

I tried to call goodnight, but my voice failed me. Leo was still leaning against the table with his head in his hands. I picked up the knife and put it back in the drawer. When I did it, I noticed how badly my own hands were shaking. 'What were you thinking?' I said.

Leo was still breathing fast. He turned and tried to light the lamp, but his hand on the match was unsteady. Jasmine lit it for him. He took a few steps towards us, swayed, and caught hold of the table.

'Papa, are you ill?' I said.

He swayed again and collapsed into the nearest chair. I was close enough now to smell the spirits in the air about him. They were hanging round his head like an air of guilt. 'Are you drunk?' I said.

'No.'

'You are,' I said.

'No, I swear I'm not. I only had a couple of . . .' His voice slurred and became incomprehensible.

'You are drunk. How could you be so bloody stupid? Don't you know how worried we've all been?'

'Shh, shh,' he said, raising his hands and trying to fix his eyes on me. 'Is Maria asleep?'

'Yes, finally. She was worried enough about you.'

'Don't wake her. Anselm, I'm sorry.'

His voice faltered, and I thought he was going to cry. I had taken Michael home countless times when he got like this, and the crying state was always the worst. 'I'm taking you up to bed,' I said. 'If Mother finds out about this, you know what she will say.'

'I'm sorry. It was all a mistake.'

'I know. Come on.'

I put my arm around his shoulders and pulled him up the stairs. 'It was all a mistake,' he kept telling me at intervals, already sobbing.

'I know,' I said. 'Shut your mouth now or you'll wake Mother.'

'I'm sorry, Anselm. I'm a terrible father to you.'

I steered him across the living room and into the bedroom, took off his boots and threw the covers over him, all the time divided between concern and anger. 'It's cold as hell,' he said, shivering now. 'Will you turn over the fire? Please, Anselm?'

'Turn over your own bloody fire,' I told him, and blew out the lamp and left him. My mother was still asleep on the sofa, one hand resting on her stomach where the baby must be kicking. I took the blanket from my room and covered her with it before turning down the light. Jasmine went back to bed, and I told her stories until she fell asleep.

Leo was coughing worse than ever. That coughing echoed hollowly through the house, and the sound of it made me more angry. I sat at my desk and looked down at the dark and frosted street and hated Leo for his coughing and his drunkenness. It was easier to be angry than to worry about him. I wished Michael was here. I tried to summon him out of the darkness, to imagine he was at his window and we were talking like we used to do. 'It's out of character,' I would say. 'That's what worries me. When people act out of character, they are usually desperate. There is usually something badly wrong.'

'Not always,' Michael would say. 'Sometimes they are just sick of being treated the same day after day. Every few months, my father goes out walking all day without telling us, just to prove he still can.'

'Not with Leo,' I would say. 'Leo isn't like that.'

And then Michael would say . . .

But it was no good. I was making his replies out of fragments of our old conversations, and here the words ran out. I wondered if this was how Harold North felt, or the great Diamonn, when his words ran dry. I turned up the lamp and read *The Darkness Has a Thousand Voices* instead, until I felt myself falling to sleep, with my head on the desk and Leo still coughing and the light just starting beyond the window. And in the street, a man was watching the house. I was too far gone into sleep to wake myself and go down and check. But he haunted all my dreams, and I was certain that I had seen him there.

MIDNIGHT,
THE THIRD OF JANUARY

'How did you go so long without finding out about your real father?' said Mr Hardy. 'You must be . . . how old?'

'Sixteen,' I said.

'I would have wanted to know,' he said.

'I did,' I said. 'I did, but I never asked.'

I could not explain it. Leo had won my absolute loyalty when I was still too young to realize it, and my mother's dismal moods at every mention of those days were terrible, because they were so rare and unnatural. I loved Leo and my mother so fiercely that I knew their weaknesses — or perhaps I loved them because I knew their weaknesses. I always knew I had to make things right for them, because they were not so far from despair as they appeared to be.

'I was worried about hurting them,' I said eventually. 'They had been hurt too much already by the time I was born, and I didn't want to hurt them any more.'

'Very admirable in a young boy,' said Mr Hardy, and smiled.

'Not really,' I said.

'You don't think very highly of yourself,' Mr Hardy remarked.

'No,' I said. 'You wouldn't either, if you knew.'

He did not ask me to tell him. He knew by now that it was useless to ask me to go on with the story when I couldn't. I had told him all last night, and this night, too, and then had run out of words again. 'After that,' I said, 'after Leo got drunk that night, I did think about my real father. More and more.'

'So that story,' he said. 'Leo was the one who wrote it.'

'Yes.'

'And did you read it, in the end?'

'Not then.'

'But you have it with you now. It's the same story.'

'Yes.'

Mr Hardy waited for me to get out the papers. 'Do you think your father would mind me hearing it?' he said as I opened them.

I had already thought about this. I had done enough harm already to be cautious. 'No,' I said. 'I'm certain he wouldn't mind. Not someone like you.'

'What do you mean, someone like me?' said Mr Hardy with a faint smile.

'I don't know,' I said. 'Someone who understands.'

It was true. He understood more than I did, though I was the one telling him. Even though I was the one who had read the story long before.

Years later, when Ashley looked back at his first school in London, the only thing he could remember was drawing maps. He sat at the back of the class and filled every exercise book with them. There were other schools and other drawings, but maps were what he began with. The teachers tried to stop him, then gave up.

He started by copying pages from Bradley's book that had every London street. At first Ashley wondered if London was where he belonged after all. It was a city that seemed to have no end, and within it were a hundred other places, with ancient and mysterious titles: Seven Kings, Swiss Cottage, Gipsy Hill, the Isle of Dogs. But sometimes as they rode home on the underground, Ashley close to Anna's side with strangers' elbows and handbags digging into his head, strange thoughts came to him. Why was there a network of tunnels under this city with trains running through it? And why did everyone go down into the dark without complaining? And when they went down, who had said that no one could look at each other? Who had invented that rule? At first he thought it was a game the others were playing, like trying not to step on the cracks in the pavement. When he asked Anna these questions, she smiled and said a lot of people wondered about it. But he had not meant it like that. He had been thinking about another place that came to him in dreams, where there were no underground trains and no crowded escalators, and these things would look like inventions out of the future.

After the plans of London, Ashley moved on to the school atlases and found that the places with the mysterious names were not just in England. You could travel across the sea or fly in an aeroplane and reach them. North was Archangel, west were Sacramento and Bitter Creek; in Australia, the place that everyone seemed to think his father came from, he found Cape Catastrophe and Ninety Mile Beach and Alice Springs. He used to ask Anna, 'Do we come from one of these places?' It became a joke between them. For several years of his childhood, he was convinced that the area of the city called Belgravia was a separate country.

At his next school, there were no more maps to copy. So Ashley drew other things. The old maps lay in the bottom of the wardrobe in Bradley's spare room. And sometimes he took them out again and wondered if one of these places was where he was meant to be. He fixed his eyes on the signs when they went out into the countryside in the old

Rolls-Royce, looking for places that might be the one he was searching for. But then Anna sold the car, and there were no more journeys, and Ashley forgot about other places and went on growing up.

For several years, Juliette was haunted by a dream in which she and her father walked along a riverbank in the darkness of winter. There had been a boat, and a view of the black estuary, and something before that, so vague that she could not recall it. When she asked her father, he said, Yes, that was the Thames estuary. But beyond that he would say nothing at all.

Juliette believed for several years that they led a charmed life. It was a sentence that she found in a book on her father's shelves, and it seemed to define their luck. Whatever Richard Delmar wished for, it came to him. A white house in a leafy square, and a fathomless supply of money, and an ancient but fixable Rolls-Royce in which their driver and guard, James Salmon, took them out for drives in the rolling hills beyond the city's far edges. Juliette did not know what her father did for a living. He sat shut up in his study sometimes, and sometimes he drove away and was gone for days. His business cards said RICHARD DELMAR, SOLICITORS. When she asked him if he had once been called something else, he said no, that had always been his name.

Perhaps the strangest of the things that came to Richard were the people who asked him for work. These people arrived at the door with bundles of their belongings and foreign accents, and Richard always sent them away. Juliette never heard what they said, but Richard always told her afterwards that they had been asking for work – that was what they came for. There was something about them all that

Juliette could not fathom. She was eleven years old by the time she worked out the question she wanted to ask. 'Papa,' she said eventually. 'Why do such eccentric people always come to talk to you?'

They were sitting in the drawing room. It was an afternoon in autumn. 'What, angel?' said Richard, folding his newspaper. It took a single question to command his whole attention.

'The people who come and talk to you,' she said. 'The ones who come to the door.'

'They are just asking for work or money.'

'Why?'

'One of the hazards of living in Belgravia.'

'Where do they come from?'

'All over the country.'

'So how do they know to come here?'

'Oh, I expect they just go along the street knocking on every door.'

'They don't. I've seen them. They come to our door and then they go away again.'

Richard took off his glasses. 'Well, I don't know,' he said. 'Do you want me to employ them, Juliette?'

'No,' she said. 'I just wondered, that's all.'

'They are lost people,' he said. 'Just people who don't know where they belong.'

There was a silence in which Richard rubbed his eyes and Juliette sat on the edge of the sofa and looked at him. In her new school uniform – a green skirt and a green jacket and a strange green bowler hat that was always getting misplaced somewhere – she felt like a character out of an English comedy. 'I don't understand our life sometimes,' she said.

'Why not?'

'I don't know. I just don't understand it. I don't belong here.'

'But you're getting on so well at Elmlea School for Girls. Aren't you? And all your friends—'

'I don't have friends!' said Juliette, throwing down the green bowler hat. 'I don't have friends. No one understands me! And why do I have to wear these stupid clothes? These aren't my clothes!'

Richard replaced his glasses carefully.

'We don't come from here,' said Juliette. 'Years ago, there was a boat and a river, and I didn't know I was English, and I want to go back.'

Richard sat up and gripped the arms of his chair. He did it suddenly and then released them, but Juliette saw. 'I don't know why I can't remember,' she said. 'I can't even remember my mother; that's the worst thing of all. Why can't we go back and visit that place? Why don't we ever talk about it?'

'All right,' said Richard quietly. 'All right, I can tell you about it.'

Juliette waited, the force taken out of her anger suddenly. 'We used to live in a country that was very dangerous,' said Richard. 'And I made enemies. I was the head of the secret service. Your mother was part of the secret service too. But I put several members of a gang in jail, a gang called the Imperial Order.'

'The Imperial Order?' said Juliette.

'Yes.' Richard studied the mock-medieval figures on the rug. It was a pattern in which three hunters chased endlessly after a leaping stag, and tall maidens bestowed their smiles from the windows of a castle. 'They came to the door one night,' Richard said, so steadily that his voice had no feeling in it at all. 'I wasn't at home. Your mother answered. You were just a little girl. They came to the door with guns, and your mother . . .'

Juliette stopped breathing and covered her mouth with her hands. She sat like that without moving, and Richard did not go on. 'So we left,' he said at last. 'The man I worked for agreed to send me to another country. When we got here, I broke with him. I threw away my papers, took all the money out of the account he left for me, and changed my name. Then we came here. It is an easy city to hide in. So there you are. That's why we left our country. That's why we are not going back. Because I wanted to keep you safe, Juliette. I'll die rather than let anything happen to you. I swear I'll die.'

His voice broke down altogether, and he got up and went to the window and stood there with his back to her. Juliette stared at her green hat on the floor. It looked stupid, lying there, and she could think of nothing to say. 'What country is it?' she said.

'It's better that I don't tell you.'

'Is there anyone else from that country here in London?'

Richard did not answer. Juliette wanted to question him further, but the story had frightened her more than she could say. And after that day, her life did not seem charmed any longer. Her father had committed a crime to keep her safe, and Juliette could not help glancing over her shoulder as she walked about the city guarded by James Salmon, as though that old fear from across the sea would somehow catch up with them.

FOUR O'CLOCK
THE FOURTH OF JANUARY

'This is the bleakest time of the night,' said Mr Hardy. 'Did you know that? When it's so long since the day before you can't remember the sunlight, and the morning still seems a hundred miles away.'

It was true enough, but we were all on edge that night, and it was not just the darkness. Earlier, driving up towards the coast, we had come to some kind of roadblock. What its purpose was no one could say. Soldiers without uniforms had stopped us and muttered between themselves for several minutes, brandishing their rifles. Then they had searched our belongings and let us continue.

It was still dark now, and it would be dark for several hours, but the driver was already preparing the coach in the grey yard outside the door. A few stars were shining over the town, and smoke drifted low over the snow-covered ground, driven on the east wind. The little boy was pale with too little sleep. He and his mother were sitting close to the fire with their suitcases piled around them. Then, after a while, they went out to the hall to wait for the coach to set off.

'We won't leave yet,' said Mr Hardy. 'It is too dangerous to travel in the dark.'

'Yes,' I said.

'What I don't understand,' said Mr Hardy, 'is why your father never studied magic.'

'He lost all interest in it,' I said. 'And maybe he had a point. What can magic do to make things all right?'

Mr Hardy nodded. Then he got up, went to the window, and walked back again. His hands were twisting together all the time, and he kept nodding vaguely.

I was startled to see tears in his eyes. 'What is it?' I said. 'Is there something wrong?'

He shook his head and looked as if he would speak. He looked like that for a long time. Then he said, 'Anselm, will you go on telling me? My heart is so heavy suddenly.'

'All right,' I said. 'If you want to hear it.'

He nodded and sat down at the table. But his hands were still twisting underneath it. They went on like that, as if he had no power over them, all the time that I was telling him.

OCTOBER

I woke one morning to hear my mother and Leo arguing. 'I wouldn't suggest it unless it was for everyone's good,' he was telling her, nearly crying with anger.

'What is this?' demanded my mother. 'You are going to leave me to bring up your children because life gets tough, Leo?'

'It's the law,' he said. 'I'm supposed to sign up. It's the law, Maria!'

'Leo, you know perfectly well you could avoid it if you had any wish to stay!'

'No,' he said. 'No, it's not that. It would break my heart to leave them. It would break my heart to leave you all – you know it would – but I swear you don't know the half of what's happening, Maria. I don't even understand it myself.'

'Do you want to never see us again? Is that what you're saying, because—'

'I didn't say never! Maria, I didn't say that!'

'Anselm,' murmured Jasmine, at my door. She slid round into the room and reached for my hand. Her thumb was damp where she had been sucking it, but I let her take my hand anyway.

'Shh,' I said, and stepped closer to the doorway. Through the narrow crack, I could see them, face to face on opposite sides of the room. My mother was leaning over the back of the sofa, one hand clasped to her mouth.

'You got up too suddenly,' Leo said, halfway between exasperation and concern. 'I was making you a slice of toast. You are supposed to eat before you get up; otherwise the sickness hits you worse.'

'I got up, Leo, because you told me you wanted to leave us—'

'No,' said Leo. 'No, you don't understand. Maria, you're pale. Will you just sit down?' He tried to push her down onto the sofa.

'I won't sit down!' she said, throwing off his arms. 'Damn you, Leo North, I'm not some invalid. Let me go!'

She looked like a girl my age when she was angry, white-faced and shaking and convinced of her own righteousness. Leo ran his hands through his hair as though he wanted to rip it out.

'You would be better off if I went,' he said desperately. 'You don't understand. You don't see what I am saying. Please—'

'Of course I understand!'

'Maria, please!'

His voice was growing hysterical now; he did not sound like the father I knew. 'You can live with your mother; there is space for you three. Without the rent to pay, I can borrow the money we need, and I'll be back before the baby is born, so why won't you just let me—'

'Because we need you here, you complete bastard,' said my mother, and slapped him hard across the face.

Leo gave up abruptly. He went out onto the stairs and lit a cigarette. A cold silence fell over the house. My grandmother tutted incredulously as she gathered up her things to leave. And when I went down to the bathroom that afternoon, I found Leo in the yard, breaking up firewood with a blunt axe and his bare hands. I watched the shabby gilt doors of a cupboard fly into pieces in the frosted air. 'We could have sold that,' I said.

'It's worth more like this,' said Leo.

I stood there watching him destroy the cupboard with a ferocity I had not known he had. He was so far away in his silence that I could think of nothing to say. Jasmine wandered down the stairs with her thumb in her mouth. 'Anselm, Mama is busy working,' she murmured. 'Can we go for a walk?'

'All right,' I said. 'Get your coat and scarf.'

'It's going to snow,' said Leo, pausing for a moment and glancing at the yellow clouds gathering over the castle. He was out of breath, and sweat was standing out at the edges of his hair.

'Not yet,' I said, and closed the door on him. We put on our overcoats, and Jasmine took my mother's red shawl, and we set out. As we left the back room, my mother kept her head bent stubbornly over the schoolbook she was marking. But her eyes gave her away. Every time Leo struck the cupboard, her eyelashes flickered, as though she was afraid.

Out on the doorstep, the wind cut sharply. Half the shops in the street had closed early today. Saturday used to be a good evening for trade, but since the Imperial Order had taken to roaming the streets, Trader's Row had grown silent and dismal. The wind only gained in cruelty as it narrowed itself to drive through the street.

'I would have liked to go and see Michael,' said Jasmine sadly.

I put my hands in my pockets. 'Yes.'

'Anselm, look!' she said then.

'What?'

She tugged my sleeve and pointed to the Barones' window. For the first time in weeks, there were no workmen sawing up planks or sanding down the shop walls. And as we turned to look at it, the lights began to come on, until the whole street in front of the shop was illuminated. The new letters on the window stood out blackly: J. W. FORTUNE, ESQ.

People were glancing out of their windows now, but no one came out. We were alone in the windswept street. 'Look,' Jasmine said again, pressing her face against the glass. There were no longer any grilles on either of the windows. One of them was taken up with a large painting; in the other was a heap of gold and silver chains worth thousands of crowns, lying there like an invitation to thieves.

'Can we go in?' said Jasmine.

'Why not?' I said. 'It's open.' Without thinking much about it, we stepped inside.

It was like standing in the middle of a nobleman's house. The furniture was all old and valuable, piled high in corners and stacked up to the ceiling. The paintings above were dark oil portraits of beautiful women and noblemen standing in front of their fine houses. There was no one at the counter. I noticed a shelf of books and wandered over, but I recognized none of the titles. *The Glorious Liberation* and *Heroes of the Iron Reign* were there in several editions. While I was running my finger along the spines, someone appeared at the door of the back room.

'Good afternoon,' said Jasmine politely.

I turned. It was a man with oiled-back hair and a gold-toothed smile, and I knew his face. He was the man Michael and I had seen that last evening, at the jewellery stall in the market, the man with the suitcase and the Alcyrian accent who tested a gold medallion with his teeth.

'Good afternoon,' he said. 'My first customers.'

'We're traders too,' Jasmine told him. 'Not customers.'

'Oh?' said the man.

'We live next door. Are you J. W. Fortune?'

He shook his head. 'That's just what I call my shop.'

'What's your name, then?' said Jasmine with an air of suspicion.

He laughed and lit a cigarette. 'Jared,' he said. 'To you.'

He smoked some perfumed tobacco, unlike the cheap cigarettes that turned Leo's fingers yellow and racked him with coughing.

'Everyone has been wondering about you,' said Jasmine, going up to the counter.

'How so?'

'Because we never saw you. At school, Billy and Joe said they climbed up the back wall and saw you making kidnapped children into meat pies to sell in your shop.'

He laughed, a slow laugh that had a studied air. 'Who are Billy and Joe?' he said.

'Their mama is the pharmacist just over there.'

'Ah,' said Jared. 'Well, I think they were mistaken. I have been out of the city on business. I have been back from Alcyria only a few weeks, and I've been so busy that I had no time to open the shop until now. And in any case, these bloody workmen have taken so long to set it up—'

'Are you from Alcyria?' said Jasmine.

'Not originally.'

'Where are you from, then?'

'Nowhere in particular. Here, I suppose.'

He did not look Alcyrian, and he had a wanderer's

accent; it moved from place to place and never settled down. 'I spent a few years living out there,' he said. He drew on his cigarette, then dropped it and crushed it under his heel. Leo would have smoked it down to the end. It was the mark of a rich man not to do that. 'Look around if you want to,' he told Jasmine.

She wandered between the rows of tables. In the new gas lighting of the shop, she looked sadder than I had ever seen her. I wondered if Leo and my mother were arguing again next door. I wondered if there was any trace left of the Barones' old shop.

'Look at this,' said Jasmine, bending to stare at a castle made from glass crystal that shone with a thousand lights.

'Four hundred crowns,' said Jared.

'Are you joking?' I said.

'No.'

'Sorry, I didn't mean—'

He laughed, and the tension vanished. 'You seem very interested in those pictures,' he remarked to me.

I was not looking at the pictures. I had been looking at the walls between them, trying to find a single trace of the old red paint that used to be there. 'Yes,' I said. 'Are they famous?'

'They used to be,' he said. 'They pass through my hands, and I keep them for collectors. They are not to everyone's taste nowadays, of course.'

'They are copies, though?'

He gave a quick laugh. 'Originals. That one is a Joseph Cortez. You have heard of him?'

'Cortez? Yes.'

It was a lie, and I think he knew it. I had never heard of

Cortez. I looked away, and my eyes fell on a rack of guns glinting over his head. They were the only objects in the shop that were not old or valuable. 'You sell firearms?' I said.

'Evidently,' said Jared. 'You say it as though you have principles.'

'We have a no-firearms policy.'

'An eccentric way of working in these times.'

I did not answer. It was true; it was eccentric.

'Mr and Mrs Barone never sold guns,' said Jasmine sternly. 'So I don't think you should either.'

'All I've heard this week is Mr and Mrs Barone did this; Mr and Mrs Barone didn't do that.' He did not say it with exasperation; he just said it. 'Don't you think progress is a good thing, little one?'

'No,' said Jasmine. 'Not if progress is just selling stupid guns.'

Jared leaned on the counter and began polishing some kind of old dagger on a leather cloth. I went on studying the guns and wondered if I should apologize for Jasmine. I decided not to. Over the counter was a green flag that I did not recognize. The symbol in the centre was a black constellation with a red circle behind it. 'What is that flag?' I asked him.

'Oh, that? It's the government's symbol.'

'The Malonian government?' I said.

'A certain division of it. Not the royalists.'

'Don't you like the king?' demanded Jasmine from the corner.

Jared glanced over. 'Who says I don't like the king?' he asked, very reasonably. 'Our aims are different; our outlook is broadly the same. That's philosophy for you.' He pointed the dagger at us, half mocking, like a teacher driving a point home. 'King Cassius is not a strong leader,' he said. 'The Party wants a strong leader.'

'The Party?' I said.

'The Malonian Ruling Party, this division I'm talking about.'

'But they are not ruling,' I said.

'They very soon will be.'

'Is that really true?'

'I don't think you should have that flag up there,' said Jasmine. 'I don't think that's very civilized when the king lives just up there, and people want to kill him.'

'People want to kill him?' said Jared. 'Who does?'

'Everyone. It's why he has guards all the time – that's what Uncle said.'

'Your uncle sounds like a wise man,' said Jared.

'He was. But he's not here any more.'

'Are you an antiques trader, sir?' I asked before Jasmine could say anything else.

'Antiques,' he said. 'Fine art, jewellery. I suppose we deal in the same things. To a point.'

I did not answer. Our shop was a poor imitation of this one, no matter how many years longer we had traded in this street. L. North & Son was full of secondhand goods, and gaudy prints and line drawings, and gold and silver people had already pawned a hundred times.

'Go on, look around,' said Jared to me. 'You are an antiques trader. Give me your expert opinion on my stock.'

I began examining a cupboard without touching it. It was well restored, like nothing I had seen. 'Do people buy these things?' I asked.

'Yes, of course. That's why I sell them.'

'I only thought . . .' I shrugged. 'They are very good quality.'

'Certain people will always buy them,' he said. 'I don't concern myself with the others. I don't think much of these junk shops you see clinging on everywhere, when the economy is in such a state that they will only wither and die. These pedlars should break free and leave while they still have a few coins to their name. Still, life is tough and perhaps I should not judge.'

It came to me that he did not think much of L. North & Son and was trying to tell us so. But perhaps that was uncharitable. I was still trying to make out his expression when Jasmine gave a muffled cry. The glass castle, glittering, had slipped off the edge of the table. I heard myself shout, 'Jasmine!' and saw her horror-stricken face, like a tragic mask. Then she reached out her hand, and the castle leaped back into it, and the disaster was averted.

Jared drew in his breath. 'Did she just—'

'No,' I said.

'I could have sworn,' he said. 'I could have sworn on my own life that it came back to her.'

'It was good luck,' I said, crossing the room and replacing the castle on the table in front of Jasmine. I could see my hands shaking.

'Yes,' he said. 'Good luck, or else your sister is a magic child.'

'She doesn't have powers,' I said.

'She would be rare, in this city. They say magic is dying out.' He ran a hand over his oiled hair thoughtfully. 'Ah well,' he said then, as if to dismiss it. I pushed the castle further onto the table. 'That piece is very fine,' he remarked. 'I would have been sorry to lose it. Well caught.'

'I'm sorry,' Jasmine said.

He raised one hand, as though to push away all apologies. 'It's no matter. Do you know why it's valuable? This is an interesting story. Would you like to know?'

'Yes,' said Jasmine, all her former hostility crushed under the weight of the disaster that had almost befallen us. 'Why is it valuable, sir?' she said.

'It once belonged to Ahira.'

'Ahira?' I said. 'The war criminal Ahira?'

'He was many other things. But, yes.'

I bent down to study the castle. I did not want to touch it. Every window was etched into the glass with painful care; the towers glittered like diamonds. I had never thought of the war criminals caring much about beauty. Jasmine tugged at my sleeve, but I was transfixed by the lights in that crystal. I thought of that man, whose face I had studied in a hundred history books, staring into the crystal too, seeing the same lights I saw. Then the wind blew more fiercely beyond the windows, and I came back to the present. The sky was losing all its brightness now. 'We should go home,' I said.

'Wait one moment,' said Jared as we crossed the threshold.

'What is it?' I said.

'Perhaps you will think this a strange question. But have I met you before?'

'Me?' I said.

'Yes. Not your sister, just you.'

'I saw you once at the markets,' I said. 'I was with my friend, and you were at a jewellery stall.'

'When was this?'

'A few weeks ago.'

He shook his head. 'I don't mean then. I never saw you at the markets; not that I can remember. It was a long time ago, but I know your face. I knew it as soon as you walked into the shop. It's only that I cannot place you.'

I must have looked blank, because he raised his hands to dismiss the question. 'Think no more about it,' he said. 'I am probably mistaken.'

I looked at him properly. He had what people call an honest face, made strange by his gold teeth. The lamplight revealed every detail of his appearance, even the lines in his oiled black hair where he had smoothed it back with his fingers. He was like no one I had ever met, and I was certain that if I had ever seen this man before, I would remember it. 'No,' I said again. 'No, I have never met you, except that one time, and then I just saw you from a distance.'

'Very well,' he said thoughtfully. 'Good evening, then.'

Once we were out in the street, Ahira's face glared at us from every wall. 'Ahira,' said Jasmine. 'Everyone talks about Ahira. What did he do?'

'Bad things,' I said.

'What bad things?'

'It was a long time ago,' I said. 'Let's get inside.'

'All right, but I want to know what bad things.'

I did not answer, and she followed me reluctantly, back round the side of the shop where Leo's axe lay abandoned beside the wreck of the cupboard. 'And why did he say he knew you?' she asked as we reached the side door.

'I don't know,' I said. 'He must have made a mistake.'

'No, he didn't. I saw his face, and he didn't. He knew you, Anselm, for sure.'

'I'm certain it was someone else he was thinking of.'

But there was something about the man that made me uneasy. Perhaps it was just that old trader's law, never trust the rich. Because this man, in spite of everything, was rich. The contents of his shop could have paid the debts of the rest of the street. 'Come on,' I told Jasmine, glancing back at his lights. 'Let's go inside.'

We passed Jared again on Monday morning, gingerly polishing the window of his shop as though he had never cleaned a window in his life. But that day things changed, and I had no time to think any more about him. When I got to school, the rest of the boys were crowded around a notice at the front of the classroom. 'Settle down!' Sister Theresa was calling vainly, rapping with her knuckles on the blackboard.

'What's this about?' I said.

'It's about National Service,' Gabriel Delacruz muttered to me. 'They want us to sign up.'

'This is a *provisional* list,' Sister Theresa said, parting the crowd and striding forward to rip the notice off the wall. 'The king has tightened the laws on National Service and has asked that all able-bodied sixteen- and seventeen-year-olds sign up too. There is no compulsion.'

'Good,' said John Keller, the doctor's son. 'Because I'm damned if I'll fight for the king.' A few people muttered their agreement.

'I am under orders to put this notice up,' said Sister Theresa. 'Don't come to me with your complaints. The government has ordered that this notice be put up in every school and that I read it out. Which, if you will be quiet, I might be able to do. Sit down!'

The class drifted reluctantly to their desks. Sister Theresa cleared her throat and read, in a voice without emotion, ' "A statement issued by His Majesty King Cassius in alliance with the government of Malonia, now the Malonian Ruling Party." ' People shifted mutinously. ' "During the early hours of last night, the Alcyrian army made hostile advances across the border of Malonia. As a result, the government has taken full control of the ruling of the country. The government orders all able-bodied men of eighteen and above who have not yet signed up for National Service, either labour or military, to do so within the next two days. Those who fail risk arrest and prosecution—" '

'Prosecution, indeed?' said Gabriel, who thought himself something of a politician. 'Where was the king's government when the poor were dying in the streets last winter, and where was the king's government—'

'Silence!' said Sister Theresa. ' 'The government also asks that all able-bodied sixteen- and seventeen-year-olds register their willingness to volunteer, in order that the government can draw up a list for the quicker deployment of labour should a state of emergency arise.' '

The class glanced round at each other, and I could see the same expression on their faces that must be on mine. None of us wanted to sign up. 'This whole thing is ridiculous,' said John Keller. 'Why should people like us have to sign up just because we're still in the country, when half the class has already got the hell out of here?'

'Half the class?' said Sister Theresa, fixing him with a cold glance. 'What do you mean, half the class?'

'People like Michael Barone. He must have known this was coming and decided to get out, because he was too scared to fight.'

'That's not why he left!' I said, startling even myself.

'Why did he go, then?' said John Keller, turning to me. 'Did you have some kind of lovers' quarrel?'

I began to stand up, but Sister Theresa said, 'Sit back down at once, both of you!' I could feel my face turning the darkest red. John Keller knew nothing about Michael or me, and yet he could still drive me to anger.

'But I don't see,' he continued from his seat, 'why people like us have to sign up and bloody cowards and debtors and criminals are still hiding in their houses dodging the draft.' He flashed another glance at me, and I was certain suddenly that he meant Leo.

'What the hell are you talking about?' I demanded.

'You don't *have to sign up*,' said Sister Theresa. 'This list is provisional and voluntary. Now please be quiet, both of you. Let's get this over with and carry on with our severely disrupted lesson. Does anyone want to sign?'

We were still glancing about uneasily. No one wanted to. And yet under the pressure of those glances and the silence, everyone except John Keller did.

On the way home from school, we passed a line of men queueing at an old butcher's shop with a paper sign on its front window. Jasmine ran to look at it. It was a volunteering post, and the men, shifting from foot to foot with their hats in their hands or smoking grimly, were signing up for National Service. We passed another line and another. In the third was Mr Pascal, studying a newspaper and lecturing the man beside him between paragraphs. 'Ah!' he said. 'Anselm and little Jasmine. How are you two?'

'Well, thank you,' I said. 'Are you signing up, sir?'

He spread out his hands, losing several sheets of his newspaper to the wind. 'There is no point avoiding it,' he said. 'And perhaps it is not so bad. A man like me will never be called on to fight. No, they'll ask me to repair some uniforms every fortnight and then leave me alone, I shouldn't wonder.'

He nodded to us, and we carried on along Trader's Row to the door of the shop.

'Anselm,' said Jasmine. 'Is this a real war?'

'I suppose so,' I said.

'It doesn't seem like one.'

'No.'

It was not how I had imagined war either, when my mother and Leo talked about it. Although people were dying for our nation all along the eastern border, it felt like a bad dream that the country would wake up from. And yet by order of the king, or his rebellious government, Leo should be in that queue where Mr Pascal stood. He should have signed up by now.

Leo was out in the yard when we got back. Jasmine ran to him, but he did not pick her up. He had piled up half the contents of the shop against the back wall and was sorting through them.

'What's all this?' I said.

'Nothing,' said Leo.

I stepped forward and turned over the most recent layer. Two history books, a dingy oil painting, and a coronation medal in its box. 'What is this?' I said again.

'Papa, why is everything out here?' Jasmine murmured.

'No reason,' said Leo.

'Papa?' she said, tugging his sleeve.

'I'm working – leave me. Jasmine, for heaven's sake, can't you behave?'

Jasmine caught my glance, and for a moment I saw tears

start in her eyes. Leo never spoke sharply to her. Then she drew herself up to her full four feet, marched inside, and banged the door. We listened to her stamp up the stairs and across the living room. 'If Aldebaran was here, he would tell her to behave,' said Leo, and went on working.

'Papa, what's wrong?' I said.

'Nothing is wrong. Honestly, it's nothing, Anselm. Go on inside.'

I watched him from the doorway. His hair was troubled by every wind that blew; his eyes were glittering from the cold. He looked like someone I did not know. He was wearing a holey old scarf that Jasmine had knitted him; that was the only clue that he was still Leo. As he worked, he kept throwing the scarf back over his shoulder with a quick impatient sigh. 'Papa, tell me what you're doing,' I said. He did not answer.

I went inside. The shop was different – I could see it at once. It looked strange and bleak with half its contents gone. I boiled water for tea and stood at the misted back window watching Leo work. After a while, I began to see what connected every object that had vanished. They all had some royalist link, from the medallions with the king's face to the patriotic history books. And I knew what Leo was going to do even before he did it. He took out his matches, threw paraffin over the pile, and set it all alight.

Jasmine and I were at the back door at the same moment. 'Stay there,' I told her. I stumbled out into the thick smoke and caught hold of Leo's coat. 'What are you doing?' I said. 'What the hell are you doing?'

'Let go of me.'

'Those are worth hundreds of crowns! In God's name, Leo!'

He shook me off and poured more paraffin onto the pile. The flames rose high enough to turn his eyes to a fierce red. I pulled him into the back room and slammed the door on the smoke. Jasmine was huddled in the corner, coughing. I emptied out the coal bucket and began filling it with water from the tap in the corner. I threw it over the flames and went back, again and again, although I knew there was no point in it. The fire dwindled and became a smouldering pile of wreckage.

Everything was ruined already; there was no salvaging it. I turned over a shattered lamp with one foot and bent to pick up a lucky coin in its charred display case. 'Papa, what have you done?' I said. The coin burned my fingers, and I let it fall again. 'Do you think people will stop troubling us if you pretend not to be a royalist?' I said. 'Is that it?'

'I've had them in here, Anselm,' he said. 'They come in every day, when you're at school, and say, "Why are you selling these things? Don't you know you shouldn't be selling these things?" They come in with their blue uniforms and their guns, and they do it to every trader who looks like a royalist. The police don't stop them because they can't, Anselm. So tell me what else I should do.'

'Who are they?' I said.

'I don't know. The Imperial Order.'

I kicked at the ashes that had once been a history book. 'So this is a solution?' I said. 'This melodrama.'

'I'll do whatever I have to,' he said. 'And don't you condemn me for it, Anselm!'

'You're supposed to have signed up,' I said. 'John Keller was talking about it at school. Everyone is talking about it. So why draw attention to yourself, Leo?'

Jasmine started to cry and reached for his hand. The cold

wind drove ash against us. It clung to our boots and misted all our clothes. 'Let's just go inside,' said Leo.

I turned and went to the yard gate instead.

'Anselm?' he said. 'Where are you going?'

'A walk.'

'When will you be back?'

'Later.'

'But, Anselm—'

I turned and left.

As I crossed the city, the air turned very still, and I heard what sounded like gunshots. I stopped on the corner of the square, beside the church, and listened. They were faint but real, somewhere in the east beyond the hills. They must be explosives, diminished by the distance into a faint cracking sound. I shoved my hands down in the pockets of Leo's old jacket and decided to go to the graveyard. I had put it off too long.

The graveyard was different, I saw, when I approached it. Torches were burning at the gate, and shadowy figures stood at the end of the bridge, looking in. I was too close to turn back when I realized they were the Imperial Order. They saw me hesitate but made no move. In the lamplight, I could see them clearly. They wore modern rifles across their backs, not like the battered ones the police carried, but their uniforms were stained and worn through with age. I wondered if they had salvaged them from a trench some-where. One man had a captain's badge and the other a sergeant's. The sergeant, a man about Leo's age with wiry brown hair, gave me a grin and an exaggerated bow. I had no choice but to pass them. My heart thumped dis-honourably fast, but I did it.

The graveyard was deserted. I walked quickly until I was lost among the ancient tombs, then stopped. Here on the edge of the city, I could hear the silence of the eastern country. I stood there watching the dark beyond the far gate. Alcyria was over those mountains, the army's machine guns trained on all the passes, their armoured vehicles rolling slowly across our soil. That was what their army was like; it had been in the newspapers. 'An unstoppable force', the reporter had called it. A strange kind of panic twisted my heart. It came to me that no one really knew the rules. The castle lights, blazing over the city, seemed no protection at all.

I started among the old tombs, more to keep out of sight of the Imperial Order than anything else. These graves belonged to the noble families, and their names were carved over the entrances. They were names from the history books – MARLAZZI, ST. JOHN, MARKOV. Most of them had no living descendants. A cold thought came to me out of nowhere, that maybe this country was already the past. Maybe the new places, the nations with armoured vehicles and automatic rifles, were the real world now. Michael once talked to me about England, about how he could not believe in it, because how could the people living there be as real as us, and how could their lives matter as much to them? But perhaps we were the ones who did not matter. I had never thought about that before, and it made me melancholy.

As I was wandering along the line of tombs, the last one made me pause. The stone angels on the walls were damaged, as though someone had attacked them with a heavy object. And the name – 'de Fiore' – was nearly destroyed. I wondered what this ancient family had done wrong. Was it the Imperial Order who hated them? But when I looked closer, I could see that the damage was old and weathered. This had happened years ago, probably when I was a young boy or even before. Or perhaps it was just chance. I knew people stole the marble off these tombs and sold it in the markets; maybe that was how this grave had been damaged.

One of the Imperial Order men outside the gate laughed and coughed, and when I glanced back, I saw his breath scudding upwards in the frosted air. I left the old tombs and wandered along the lines of newer graves. The sky in the east was a fathomless blue; the graveyard walls stood out darkly against it. The wind sighed in the branches of the trees. Aldebaran's tomb still bore the skeletons of the flowers people had left there weeks ago. I passed it and started towards the far corner, beyond Stirling's grave, looking for graves with the twenty-ninth of July as the date of death.

Suddenly I came upon them, a whole row of headstones. Forty people or more had died on that day. I read the names: John Worthy, Ishmael Salter, Andrew James Goldhart. They were resistance members and Lucien's soldiers; they had all died on that day, because that was the day the old regime had fallen. And I had never thought about it. I had been stupid to think I would find my father's grave by looking here. I thought of all the other graveyards in this city and in the countryside about it and suddenly knew it was hopeless.

I had tried to make up a story about my real father, years ago when I was still a young boy. I had written the title 'The Lost Son' in my journal, naming it after a story of Diamonn's, and had written seven very grand pages in Leo's ink pen. In the story, my real father was a reckless young man who drifted through my mother's life by chance. He was a soldier, and he truly loved my mother, but they fought, and the war separated them before they could make amends. He had heard of my birth from a military camp and tried to come back and see me, but he was killed before he reached the city. 'And the soldier left a fortune for his son, but it was never discovered,' the story finished. 'So, alas, the boy grew up poor and fatherless.'

But that seemed such a betrayal of Leo and so far from the truth that I could not leave it as it was. I was neither poor nor fatherless. I ripped it out of the journal and burned it and tried to stop thinking about my real father after that day. But now I was thinking about him. I could not help it.

As I left the graves behind, I noticed something strange. Every few yards, there was a space the size of a grave, with a rough square of turf that did not exactly match the rest, but with no headstone. It was as if one in every five graves had vanished from this part of the graveyard, when everywhere else they were packed closely. I stopped beside the last one. Had someone dug it up, or was it just a space that had never held a grave? The breeze raced low over the ground, making the grass shiver.

'Anselm?' said someone, and I turned.

Father Dunstan was standing a few yards away, his cloak drawn up to his neck and the faint light of the city gleaming in stripes on the side of his thick grey hair.

'What are you doing here?' I said.

'Keeping watch,' he said. 'People were damaging the graves, so a few of us have agreed to come here and keep vigil every night.'

'Is it not dangerous?' I said.

'Perhaps it is.' He came closer and studied my face. 'Is there something troubling you?'

I shook my head. 'Nothing.'

'And how are your family?'

'Well,' I said. 'They are all well.'

'I have been meaning to call and see your father. I have hardly spoken to him since his uncle passed away. How is he?'

'He's all right,' I said.

'Good,' said Father Dunstan. 'That's good.'

The wind troubled the grass and set an empty can somewhere rolling with a mournful note. 'I should go,' I said. 'It's getting late.'

He nodded. 'Goodnight, Anselm.'

Father Dunstan left me and went on his way, pacing among the graves with his hands behind his back. I wondered how many of these names on the stones had once been part of his congregation, and how many of them he had tended in their last illnesses. Then the wind caught at my hair, as though trying to hurry me away, and I turned and walked in and out of the graves towards the gate. I had to pass between the Imperial Order men to get out, and I did not turn back after that.

I didn't want to go home after I reached Trader's Row, so I went into Jared's shop instead. The last customers were leaving as the clock struck five, and the glittering lines of furniture stood serene and empty in the front room. The Barones' shop had never seemed large, but Jared had imposed a kind of grandeur on it. He was at the counter, packing something carefully into a leather suitcase. 'Ah,' he said, smiling when he saw me. 'My young neighbour. Come in and close the door. Here, this will interest you.'

I crossed to the counter. He returned his attention to the suitcase and unfolded a couple of leather cloths. I breathed in quickly, and he laughed at that. The case was full of jewels. They looked like they were worth what our shop turned over in a year. He rifled through them carelessly. 'Diamonds, more diamonds, sapphires, and rubies.' He glanced up. 'You look dismal. I thought these might lighten your spirits. Value them for me, if you are a trader.'

'Which of them?' I said.

He handed me the biggest of the sapphires. I did not know what he meant by it, but I was captivated in spite of myself. I studied the jewel in the harsh light of the gas lamp on the wall. I had never seen a sapphire this size, but I multiplied by eight from the ones the Barones had sold once in their shop and added another hundred crowns for its clarity of colour. The way it was cut was some technique I had seen Michael's father doing once. If you got it right, the value was doubled. 'Eight hundred crowns,' I said, looking up.

'Very good,' said Jared, taking back the jewel. 'Very good, indeed. Do you deal in gold and silver?'

'No,' I said. 'Not things like this. Mr Barone did.'

'So I'm told,' said Jared. He put the suitcase into a safe in the wall but left it unlocked. 'It is amazing, what Alcyria is mining now. I have seen the machines they are using. They drive the pumps with steam, drain out the water, and go down deeper than anyone could before. Have you heard about this?'

Mr Pascal had given us his own version of the story. 'Is it true, then?' I said. 'They have new technologies there?'

He nodded. 'The military technologies are what I would watch. Armoured vehicles, and ships powered by steam, and the newest automatic rifles. No one can match them, I shouldn't think, on this continent.'

'They will take over for sure,' I said. He was only confirming what I already knew.

'There is no point in being sentimental about it,' said Jared. 'When a country falls apart, traders should be there to divide the spoils. It is our inherent nature – it would be dishonest to fight it.' He laughed. 'Don't look at me like that. I don't want them to invade any more than you do. But I am not going to complain if the political uncertainty makes me a fortune.'

My heart felt so restless that there was no accounting for it. I supposed it was thinking of my real father and Aldebaran and Michael. In my head, all the people who were gone from me drifted like spirits, gaining in strength the more I tried to ignore them.

'Tell me, Anselm,' he said. 'What's on your mind?'

'What?' I said, startled.

'What's on your mind? You seem troubled.'

'I'm just thinking.'

'What about?'

'My friend who used to live here,' I said. 'And other things.'

'What things?'

I studied the nearest picture and waited for him to ask me a different question, but none came. 'I'm trying to find out about someone who died years ago,' I said. 'But I don't know how.'

'I'm told Daniel Markey is the man to ask. He is a veritable mine of information, according to that Pascal gentleman from the clothes shop over there. Apparently, he lost everything when the old regime fell. He is not a man whose company I like, but he knows a lot about those days.'

'Yes,' I said. 'I could ask him.'

'What do you want to know?' said Jared.

'Just his name,' I said. 'I know the date he died, but I want his name.'

'Go to the government records office and file an enquiry. That's what I'd do. Not that those records are very reliable. Especially the ones from around the Liberation.'

'Thank you, sir,' I said, though it was no help really. I went to the wall and studied the pictures that were leaning there.

'How is your young sister?' he asked.

'She is well.'

'You know, I could have sworn she was a magic child. But you don't come from a family of great ones?'

I shook my head. He went on watching me. 'I have heard that those born with powers sometimes see visions and write or draw what they see with no knowledge of it, and it's accurate to the smallest degree. Fascinating. Think what use they would make as spies; no wonder the great ones used to be in such demand. Does your sister ever do that?'

'No,' I said.

'Do you know,' he said, 'I heard a rumour that Aldebaran had written a last prophecy. Someone said that to me. "He wouldn't have died without leaving one" – that's what this man said. Imagine that. Imagine how rich you'd be if you discovered it.'

'Yes,' I said.

'When I heard your name was North, I thought you might be related,' he said.

'You heard our name was North?' I said.

'Isn't it?'

'I don't know how you found out, that's all.'

'Mr Pascal,' said Jared. 'Who else?'

I smiled because he expected it. He was still studying me thoughtfully, and I could tell he wanted me to look up. I turned to the nearest picture and examined it instead. It was a portrait of a red-haired man with a patch over his eye, standing on a hilltop looking outward. His head was outlined in gold like a saint's. Ahira again. I did not know what a picture like this was doing for sale in an ordinary shop. 'Is this an original too?' I said by way of changing the subject.

He did not answer. And when I turned, he was staring at me so strangely that I forgot the picture altogether. 'What is it?' I said.

'My God,' he said. 'It's not what I thought at all. You're Maria Andros's son, aren't you? You're Anselm.'

I did not know what to say. I opened my mouth to speak, then stopped. 'You are Anselm,' he said. 'I am convinced of it.'

'Yes,' I said.

He reached out and gripped my hand. 'My God,' he said again. 'How old are you now?'

'Sixteen.'

'Sixteen years? Is that how long it has been?'

'Sorry,' I said, taking my hand back out of his. 'But how do you know my mother?'

'Oh, Maria? We were childhood acquaintances. Close friends at one point. But to tell the truth, you do not look much like her, and it was only when . . . it was only . . . my God.' He lapsed into silence, still staring at me. 'I've seen her,' he said. 'I've seen her walk past the window of my shop a dozen times, and I never once realized. I thought the Androses had left the city.'

He went on staring at me, running his hand absently over his hair. 'But I must visit her,' he said. 'The coincidence is so strange. I never thought I would see you again. And the man you live with – North, the secondhand trader – is that your stepfather? I heard rumours that Maria had taken up with someone after you were born.'

I hesitated.

'How is Maria?' Jared went on without noticing. 'What does she do now? I cannot see her as a trader's wife, to tell you the truth.'

'She is a governess,' I said.

He nodded and his teeth flashed. 'Very like her. Has she ever mentioned me?'

'I don't know. Maybe she has.'

'Jared Wright.'

I remembered then. She had mentioned him once, years ago when we were walking through the city and she was pointing out places she had been. 'The Wrights lived there,' she had said, and pointed to an old mansion. 'The father was in the government, and I was engaged to the youngest son for a day.'

'Were you the youngest son of the Wright family?' I said.

'Yes,' he said.

I nodded. 'She has spoken about you.'

Jared regarded me like a lost relative. I did not know what to say, so I stood there between the counter and the door, putting my hands in and out of the pockets of Leo's old leather jacket. 'Anselm Andros,' he said again. 'I can hardly credit it. I must come and see Maria at once. I had no idea that she was still in the city.'

The wind moaned through the door, and we both started. Two men had come in and were lingering in the draught. 'Pierre, Westwood,' said Jared Wright, nodding to them. 'I will be with you at once.'

'I had better go,' I said.

'Wait,' said Jared, turning back to me. 'Isn't there anything I can do for you? As the child of an old friend, it is only right.'

The men were stepping forward now, throwing me suspicious glances. I turned to leave. 'It is kind of you,' I said. 'But I don't need any help.'

'I'll come and see you,' he said. 'Later tonight, or tomorrow, when I finish with this.'

I nodded. Then I was out in the street, the wind attacking my face and whipping my scarf out fiercely. There was no snow in it, but I could feel it about to fall in the merciless cold of the air. The two men hurried into the back room of the shop, taking Jared with them. I turned and went inside.

I could not concentrate that night at dinner. I was thinking again of the graveyard, and everything the others said passed me by. Eventually I went upstairs, under the pretence of a headache, and sat at the table in the corner of my room, turning over the books on it aimlessly.

At seven o'clock, my mother came to the door. 'Anselm, what's wrong?' she said.

'Nothing,' I said.

'There is; I can tell. You are just like Leo – easy to read. Can I come in?'

I nodded. She sat down on the edge of the bed and kicked off her shoes. It was not just my real father that troubled me; it was the way Jared had recognized me. From what my mother had said, that youngest son of the Wright family had not been a good man. And she had never been happy to see a single old acquaintance. They came into the shop sometimes, always driving up in carriages – well-spoken women with their babies, and gentlemen who had once been her admirers. 'Mother,' I said. 'Have you met the man who has moved into the Barones' shop?'

'J. W. Fortune? No. I've seen him once or twice, from a distance, but I've never spoken to him. Why do you ask?'

'Jasmine and I met him the other day. And I went in today, and he told me – it came out – that he used to know you. Years ago.'

'I never knew a man whose name was Fortune.'

'That's not his name,' I said. 'He's called Jared Wright.'

The pitch of the silence changed. I turned. She was watching me without breathing, one hand raised to push back her hair. 'What?' she said.

'Jared Wright.'

'Anselm, what do you know about him?'

'Nothing,' I said. 'I was in there and he recognized me. He said he was a childhood acquaintance of yours.'

'Yes.'

'Is he the one you were engaged to for a day? The one whose father was in the government?'

'Yes. That's him. Anselm, are you sure he said Wright?'

'It's him. I told you, he recognized me. He said, "You're Anselm Andros. You're Maria's son."'

'But you don't look like me.'

There was a silence. The window rattled in the night breeze, and the lamp gave a strange cough. 'He said he was never coming back,' she said.

'He has been in Alcyria,' I said. 'He has been in the city for only a few weeks. I suppose it got too dangerous there.'

'Yes,' she said. 'Yes, I suppose that's . . .' She trailed off and rubbed her forehead, as though she was trying to work something out. 'Anselm, he said he was never coming back. He was a collaborator, and they wanted him imprisoned.'

'What did he do?'

'Nothing terrible, not exactly. But he was a collaborator. He joined Lucien's government as a boy of fifteen and filed papers for them until they lost the war. But listen to me – what has he told you?'

'About what?'

'About those days.'

'Nothing. Just that you once knew each other. And he said he would call round.'

'When?'

'Tonight or tomorrow.'

She stood up so suddenly that the lamp shuddered. 'I had better go round there,' she said.

'Shall I come with you?'

'No. Stay here.'

'Mother, what's wrong?'

She put on her shoes and threw her shawl about her shoulders. At the doorway, she managed to smile briefly at me. 'Nothing is wrong,' she said. 'But Leo seems melancholy, and I hardly think a visit from that man will cheer him up. No, it would be better if I went and put him off.'

I heard her quick footsteps as she went down the stairs and out of the side door. Leo was down in the shop shifting boxes around. Jasmine had disappeared to her room with today's newspaper and my mother's scissors. I listened to the silence. I heard my mother knock once at Jared Wright's door, then again. But he did not answer. She knocked four or five times before she gave up. Then I heard her come back through the side gate and up the stairs. 'Anselm?' she said. 'Can I come in?'

'Yes.'

She stood just inside the door, still in her shawl and Sunday boots. 'Anselm, listen,' she said. 'About Jared Wright. I don't want you to go there again. I don't want you to speak to him. I'm going to tell Jasmine as well.'

'Why not?'

'He is not a good man.'

'He seemed all right. I mean, he must have changed since then, if he was only a boy when you knew him.'

'Anselm, promise me you won't go in there again,' she said.

'But I don't see—'

'Please,' she said.

'He is our neighbour,' I said. 'I can't avoid him.'

She did not answer. 'And, anyway,' I said, 'I don't under-stand this. You've told us that you were engaged to him, and we know he was a collaborator. What else is he going to say to me that you don't want me to hear?'

My mother's eyes flashed very dark, and I was startled. 'Just don't go in there again,' she said quietly. I did not answer. She reached forward, as if to touch my shoulder, then seemed to decide against it. She left me like that, closing the door behind her, and went slowly downstairs. I leaned on the table, staring at the scratched-up surface of the wood. The others were going to bed now, although it was still early; a general depression had fallen over the house. One by one, the lights went out. I watched the street darken and wondered whether it was just that brief engagement that my mother was upset about. Out of nowhere, the thought came to me that Jared must have known her on the twenty-second of April in the last year of Lucien's regime. Jared must have known all the circumstances surrounding my birth. And that was the one thing she had never wanted me to know.

The next day, I passed a man with wiry brown hair as I went down the road for a newspaper and passed him again as I went in at the shop door. It took me several minutes of thought before I recognized him. He was the Imperial Order sergeant from the graveyard gate. I glanced out of the shop window. There was no sign of him out there, but it made me uneasy. He had been standing opposite our shop smoking a cigarette, and every now and then looking up at the windows.

I did not tell the others. My mother was quieter than I had seen her in a long while. Leo had not spoken since yesterday and the incident in the yard. Jasmine alone seemed cheerful.

'I've got an important announcement,' she told us at dinner. 'I'm going to be in a play.'

'A play?' said Leo.

Jasmine put a school library book down on the table with a loud thump. It was Diamonn's *Complete Works*, tied together with string to stop the pages from falling out.

My mother picked it up. 'What play is it, Jasmine?'

'It's *The Beggar King*. It's going to be in the Royal Gardens, and the king and everyone is going to come and watch, and I'm going to be in it.'

'*That* play?' said Leo.

We had watched it every year; it was a famous tradition. Every year, a different school was chosen to act it, but it had never been Sacred Heart. And ever since she could talk, Jasmine had wanted to be in it, with the same tearful desperation that had made me long for powers.

'I can't believe they have chosen your school this year!' said Leo.

'Usually it's one of the schools from the east,' said my mother. 'It must be destiny, Jas!'

Jasmine's announcement thawed the cold atmosphere that had lain over the house for the past days. In between my mother's excitement and Leo's questions, none of them noticed the shadow that crossed the front window. Someone was out there, walking up and down.

'Anselm,' said Jasmine. 'Aren't you pleased?'

I drew my eyes away from the window, and smiled and ruffled her hair. 'Of course.'

'Why do you keep looking out of the window?'

'I don't.'

'What's your part, Jas?' said my mother. 'Is it a big part?'

'Quite big,' said Jasmine.

'Who?'

'The storyteller.'

'The storyteller is the best part in it,' I said, which made her smile more widely.

'I think I might be an actress,' she said. 'I mean, when I grow up. I think it's what I'd like to do. This can be the start of it.'

'Your grandmother used to be a dancer and a singer,' said Leo.

'*Grandmama?* She used to dance on a stage?'

Jasmine was so incredulous that we could not help laughing.

'Not her,' said Leo. 'No, I mean your other grandmother.'

'Amelie North,' said Jasmine solemnly. 'I'd like to be like her.'

'Read us your part,' said my mother. 'The table can be your stage, Jas – here.'

She and Leo began piling the plates into the sink to clear a space. My mother threw Leo's overcoat about Jasmine's shoulders, and he lifted her onto the table.

'Go on, Jas,' he said, and handed her the book.

Jasmine drew herself up impressively and opened it, ignoring the few battered pages that fell out. '"Good friend, draw close and hearken to my tale,"' she began.

And someone hammered on the door.

Jasmine dropped the book, and my mother started out of her chair, then laughed at her own surprise. 'That gave me such a shock,' she said.

'Who can it be at this time?' said Leo.

'It's not late. I'll go—'

'Don't answer,' I said.

She was already halfway to the door. 'Why not?'

'Just don't. I can't tell you why – just don't.'

The knocking came again. Leo was on his feet now. 'Anselm, what's going on?' he said.

'There was a man outside the house today,' I said, speaking very fast to keep my mother from going to the door. 'He's someone from the Imperial Order, and he was outside our house. I saw him before at the graveyard.'

Leo took two steps towards the door, then back towards Jasmine. I turned down the lamp. In the dark street, I made him out clearly enough to be certain. It was the man with wiry hair, the man who had been in the street outside our shop twice today already. 'Don't answer the door,' I said.

The man rapped on the door so hard that the windows rattled. Leo blew out the lamp.

'Let's go upstairs,' said my mother.

'Come on,' said Leo. 'Quickly, Jasmine.'

He lifted her down from the table, and we went, falling over boxes in our hurry. Upstairs, the fire was dying and the room was dark. 'Stay still,' said Leo. 'He may not know we're in here at all.'

The wind was growling around the house now. We all stood still trying to listen. After the man had knocked four times, there was a long silence. Then we heard two people walking past, well-spoken women with heeled shoes, laughing over some story. If that man had been in the street, I was sure their conversation would have faltered. Jasmine ran to the window; none of us tried to stop her. It was too dark for her to be seen. 'He's not there any more,' she said. 'He's gone away.'

'Shh,' said Leo. 'Jas, keep your voice down.'

We glanced at each other. Then my mother stepped forward and closed the curtains. 'I won't be frightened,' she said. 'Jasmine, go on with your play.'

'Maria . . .' Leo began, taking half a step towards her.

'No. I won't let them frighten us.' Jasmine stood shivering at the window. 'Anselm, go and get the book,' said my mother. 'Jasmine can go on with the play up here.'

'But listen . . .' Leo began, then gave up. Jasmine went on with the play like a soldier in a battle, ignoring the silence that threatened to engulf us. But we could not get back the brief safety of that moment before the man knocked at the door. The shop no longer felt like a place of security, and the light threw shadows, no matter how far my mother turned up the lamps.

Leo did not sleep that night, and I did not either. I sat beside him, and we watched the fire and said nothing. I felt far removed from him. It was as though he had travelled a long way in his thoughts, and I could not reach him. And I suddenly began to see everything going wrong. I could not explain it, only that I felt strange forces working to divide us. 'Papa?' I said. 'Would there be any reason for the Imperial Order to hurt you? I mean, do you think that's what they want?'

'Yes,' he said. 'I think that's what they want.'

I tried to touch his arm, but I couldn't do it. 'Is it about what happened before? About the resistance?'

'Anselm, I can't stand this any longer,' he said. He stood up. The fire blazed behind him and turned him to an outline of black against its flames. 'Sixteen years ago, the year you were born, I did a very bad thing,' he said. 'I can't tell you what it was, because it would put you in danger. But I feel . . .' He shook his head. 'I feel as if it's catching up with me. Like a dark shadow over my shoulder, you know?'

'Is it really as bad as you say? Papa, I can't imagine you doing anything wrong. Lots of people were involved with the resistance. Lots of people regret what they did. But surely—'

He shook his head. He went on shaking it, then looked up at me. A picture came to me from nowhere: Leo standing in the dark of the back room, holding our kitchen knife. Suddenly I could imagine him doing something wrong. If circumstances drove him to it.

'Tell me, is it going to be all right?' he said.

I could not tell him so. He lit a cigarette and stood at the window, looking out at the lights of the city. They came out and vanished again as the Imperial Order ran through the streets. He lit another cigarette, then seemed startled to see two in his hand.

'Papa?' I said. He did not turn. 'Sometimes I think I don't even know you any more,' I said. 'You are scaring all of us. Burning those things, and drinking, and arguing with Mother – it's not like anything you ever do.'

He did not answer. He just smoked the first cigarette down to the bitter end. Away over the houses, beyond the edge of the city, I could see the dark line of the eastern hills and a greyish light over the mountains. And something else. All along the horizon, dim orange lights were burning. 'What are those?' I said. 'Those lights over there.'

He pushed the window up and leaned out. The lights were so far away I could hardly make them out.

'Maybe I imagined it,' I said. 'The stars are very bright.'

'That one,' said Leo, pointing with his next cigarette. 'In the sign of the bull, low down on the horizon there. It's Aldebaran.'

'The orange one?' I said.

'Yes.'

'Where do you think he is?' I said. Leo did not answer. We stood there until our teeth were rattling with cold. Then we closed the window and went back to the fire. Leo did not speak to me. He seemed locked in some private torment, and I could not reach him.

I could not help thinking of him differently after that. I could not help wondering what it was, this strange crime that haunted him. After that night, I was not so certain of his innocence any more. This history of his, this involvement with the resistance, was not just a boyish allegiance that he now regretted. It ran much deeper than that.

The next morning, we found the reason for the strange lights on the horizon. The Alcyrian army had advanced. And on the walls were a thousand posters. They had the Imperial

Order's crest, and they called for the arrest of the unknown revolutionaries who had killed Ahira and Talitha and Darius Southey and for the arrest of all royalists and every member of the old resistance. 'And others known only to us,' the list proclaimed ominously. While we were in school, the police came and tore the notices down. But at the end of the day, when we stood to sing the national anthem, half the class remained at their desks. As if by some agreement, they sat there with their arms folded and would not sing. They just sat there stubbornly, their eyes fixed too closely on the ground in front of them.

Sister Theresa read out a statement issued by the king. He would enter into diplomatic negotiations with the new president of Alcyria; occupation would be avoided at all costs. But none of us really believed him. The Imperial Order was here already, gathering force. And I knew Leo was one of those on the list known only to them. Sometimes, when things start to go wrong, you gain a kind of vision. Not enough to change anything – just enough to suspect, when life deals its next blow, from which direction it will come.

That evening, Jared Wright called at the shop. My mother was just home from work, sitting in the back room with her feet up on the sofa, and Leo was out in the yard chopping up firewood. Jared came in quietly and closed the door behind him. 'Hello?' he said. I looked up and saw him, standing at the counter with his hat under his arm.

My mother stared at him, and he looked at her. 'Maria?' he said then, very quietly. 'Lord, you are just the same when I look at you now. Just exactly the same.'

'Jared,' she said. 'Jared Wright.'

'So you are still – ' he began, and she said, 'Anselm tells me—' They both gave a quick laugh and she came forward, and they gripped each other's hands.

'It's cold as hell out there,' said Jared, lighting one of his expensive cigarettes. 'I'm just back from a meeting on the other side of town. Aren't you going to offer me a cup of tea?'

My mother went to the stove and began boiling water. Then she stood beside the table, rubbing her hands together as though she was cold, and tried to fix a smile on her face.

'I cannot believe I am seeing you,' said Jared. 'How long has it been?'

'Sixteen years.'

'Yes, that's it. Sixteen years.'

'I thought you were never coming back.'

He smiled. 'Never is a long time. Still, with the political situation the way it is, no one knows how long they are staying. I am back for now.' He drew up a chair and sat down.

'How are you, Jared?' she said. 'Well?'

'Very well. And you? Expecting a baby?'

'Yes.'

'And is the little girl your daughter?'

'Jasmine. Yes.'

'Jasmine? How exotic.' Jared made to ruffle Jasmine's hair as she ran past with the teacups, but she dodged out of his reach. 'She is very like you,' he said.

'Yes,' said my mother, stroking Jasmine's hair. 'Yes, she is.'

The water boiled, and in silence my mother poured it out and set a cup on the table. Jared ran his finger round the rim of the cup. My mother stood beside the wall, one hand resting absently on her stomach, and watched him.

'Tell me,' said Jared. 'You didn't have the Imperial Order

here last night, did you? Because I'm told they were everywhere.'

'Yes, we did,' I said. 'What about them?'

'They want to investigate the deaths of the war criminals; apparently there has not been a proper inquiry. It all seems very tedious to me.' He yawned and stretched out his legs. 'You know, it was quite by chance that I recognized Anselm,' he said. 'We met twice, and I could not place him the first time. It was only when he was standing there in the shop, in a certain light . . .' He raised his hand as though he was a painter describing a sketch, then let it fall and laughed. 'You know,' he remarked. 'The last time I saw you properly, Maria, was in Cliff House. Where the drawing room was the size of this whole shop, I dare say. How are your parents now?'

'My father died a few years ago,' she said. 'My mother is well. She still goes out to work at the markets.'

He raised one eyebrow. 'She was a very fine lady once,' he said.

We listened to him drink his tea. Outside the window, the light was already gone. Clouds were drifting slowly across the sky, throwing their shadows onto the city. 'And where have you been since I saw you?' said my mother.

'All over the continent,' said Jared. 'I was in Alcyria for six years. And other places. Titanica. The Western Gulf Islands. Holy Island, too, briefly. There is a good deal of money to be made.' He glanced about the shabby back room. 'But you are married now, Maria? And the mother of a family.'

'Not married,' she said.

'Ah?' he said with a quick smile. 'Very like you.'

'Jared, I'm not sure what you are doing here.'

The pitch of the silence changed when she said that.

Jared raised his hands and grinned more widely, but with less goodwill. 'I came here out of courtesy,' he said at last. 'Merely that.'

'It has been sixteen years. Maybe you should just—'

'Go?' he said. 'Fine. Perhaps that is best, after all.' He drained his teacup and nodded round at us all. 'I am glad to see you well anyway. We are neighbours; I'm sure we will see each other again.'

My mother caught Jasmine's hand as Jared got up to leave. We watched him throw his jacket around his shoulders and push back his chair. As he passed me at the door, he put a hand on my shoulder. 'This boy will go far,' he remarked. 'He is a first-class trader.'

'Is he?' said my mother.

'Yes.' Jared gripped my shoulder tighter. 'Yes. He's a good boy. I recognized him at once, you know.'

Then he turned and was gone. I could still feel the weight of his hand as I watched him close the shop door and saunter past the front window. My mother turned away and began washing out the teacups, with her head bent low over the sink. 'Anselm, Jasmine,' she said. 'Don't tell Leo about that.'

'Why not, Mama?' said Jasmine.

'Oh, you know how he gets. He will only worry.'

Jasmine nodded and disappeared under the table with Diamonn's *Complete Works*. I began setting the table for dinner. My mother moved about the back room, putting things away. But in all the time she was doing it, she never once met my eyes.

On Sunday, new posters covered every wall of the city, with the government's crest stamped in the corner. The king would be making a speech that afternoon, and all were invited to attend. A stage appeared in the square, guarded by police in red uniforms. Soldiers cordoned off the streets; the factory bands played their brassy patriotic tunes into the freezing air. We all went, except my grandmother, to stand among the crowds and listen.

The first snowflakes were falling now. They lodged in my mother's and Jasmine's hair and clung to Leo's black coat. We were too far away to hear the king's voice, but we could see him from where we stood. He walked up onto the platform heavily and spoke from between bodyguards. Watching him, I could not believe this was a man my mother and Leo's age. He looked already old. 'People of Malonia,' went the mutters that ran back through the crowd. 'We are currently under threat, and for this reason I have called you here to speak to you.'

Though the king went on, we missed the next part of the speech. 'The Alcyrian government has asked,' someone repeated then, a few yards away, 'that we repay all reparations in full by the end of this month. This is not possible, and I have to announce that it is likely . . .' Here the king paused and turned over a paper in his hand. The crowd was silent now. I could hear a baby crying half a mile away. 'It is likely,' he went on, 'that the new government of Alcyria will invade our country.'

The king's words were engulfed after that in the shouts of the crowd. 'Shh! Shh!' Jasmine was saying furiously and stamping her feet. Leo and my mother did not move. They stood there side by side, watching the king on his makeshift stage, as though their hearts had stopped beating. My mother had one hand against her cheek like a fine lady at some concert. Leo's cigarette hung ridiculously from the corner of his mouth. I wished they would move. I thought that if they moved, this news might somehow stop being true. 'I know,' someone said near to us, 'that you will face this threat with courage and determination. I am proud to stand here among you, my fellow citizens, knowing what we have achieved together, what is still to achieve. This cannot be taken from us. I pray you will stand beside me in the struggle.'

But whatever the king said next was lost in the shouting that ensued. People were pushing through the crowd, forcing us apart, men in blue uniforms with rifles on their shoulders. Someone fired a volley of shots into the air.

'Jasmine!' my mother shrieked. 'Jasmine!'

'All right, I've got her.' Leo dragged Jasmine out of the crowd, wrenching her arm, and picked her up and began struggling towards the edge of the square, his other hand around my wrist. The crowds around us were surging and receding like the restless sea. A war veteran on two crutches, his medals jingling ridiculously, limped across our path at a run and fell to the ground. 'Come on,' said Leo. His fingers on my wrist were so tight that the pain was all I could think about. I stayed close behind them as Leo fought his way to the edge of the square and towards Trader's Row.

Everyone was shouting, not only the Imperial Order. Traders we half knew from the markets had joined the stampeding crowd. And everywhere people were pulling out guns, in complete defiance of the king and all his laws. We struggled all the way to our door, then stumbled inside and slammed it behind us. Leo shot all the bolts home.

It was very quiet in the shop. My grandmother was pouring out tea in the back room. 'Back so soon?' she said. 'I thought you would not stand this cold.'

Jasmine was crying, clinging to Leo's jacket. 'Are you all

right?' Leo said. 'All of you? Are you hurt? Did I hurt your arm, Jasmine?'

She shook her head and went on crying.

'What is all this fuss?' said my grandmother.

'There was trouble at the speech,' my mother said. 'The Imperial Order, rioting. And, Mother — there's going to be an invasion. That's how it looks.'

Nothing troubled my grandmother when you wanted her to be troubled. She made us sit down, and poured us out tea, and ignored the rioting outside. 'You young people,' she said, shaking her head at my mother's and Leo's stunned faces. 'You think these things have never happened before.'

'No,' said my mother quietly. 'No, I know that they have, and that's why I'm frightened.'

'We will weather this again, like we have in the past. That is life, Maria.'

'We lost everything,' said my mother, still in the same quiet voice. 'We did not weather it so well, Mother, if you recall.'

My grandmother could not answer that. In her two-room apartment in Old College Lane was all the furniture she had managed to salvage from Cliff House. It stood there, out of place and self-conscious like the contents of Jared Wright's shop, and the rest of their old life was history.

We all stood at the upstairs window and watched the crowds run unchecked through the streets. They did not stop until long after dark, and even then they would not be quieted.

'Listen,' said Jasmine when we were all sitting around the fire. 'I'm going to draw a magic circle around us, and then no one can do us any harm.'

My grandmother frowned. 'No, Jasmine,' she said. 'It's wicked to play these games on a Sunday.'

'Not games,' said Jasmine. 'It's real. Look.' She circled us slowly. 'This line is magic, and no one can cross it. Uncle showed me.'

'Does it work?' said Leo.

'If you believe in it,' said Jasmine.

She completed the circle and sat down on the sofa beside my mother, one hand on her shoulder. My mother gave a quick start.

'What is it?' said Leo.

'Nothing,' said my mother. 'Just the baby waking up.'

'When he's born,' said Jasmine, 'I'll teach him too.'

'Good heavens,' said my grandmother. 'If the child has powers, it will be more than a God-fearing person can stand.'

My mother sat up and stared into the fire. 'What are you thinking?' said Leo. But she would not answer.

And I know it was my imagination; I know no real great one can draw a magic circle. But after that moment, the crowds seemed more distant and their voices less hostile. And after that moment, the night began to grow calm.

The next night, just after darkness had fallen, Leo put on his coat and scarf and announced that he was going to the markets. 'Can I come with you?' I said.

'No,' said Leo. 'Stay here.'

'I don't mind. You might need help carrying the things back.'

'I'll be all right,' said Leo.

I was about to go down to the shop; he had just come up. Something about his voice made me uneasy, and I lingered at the top of the stairs.

'It's so cold,' said my mother, getting up to kiss him. 'Don't be long, Leo.'

'I won't.'

She had been marking books on the sofa, and she still had Juliana's arithmetic in her hand. Leo took it silently, placed it on the sofa, and closed his fingers on hers. Then he kissed her and said, 'I'll be back soon,' and kissed her again, and once more. There was something about the way he did it that was not right. It was too fierce, and I could tell she noticed it too, because she watched us go down the stairs, a faint frown troubling her eyes and the arithmetic book left forgotten on the sofa.

'Papa, will you be home in time for dinner?' said Jasmine as he left.

'I don't know,' said Leo.

'I'm learning my play well now; I almost know it.'

'Good,' he said, and kissed her forehead. 'That's good.'

He turned and looked at me as though he was about to say something. Several times he almost did. Then he shook his head, and the next minute he was outside. The darkness took him quickly from our sight.

Jasmine glanced up at me, suddenly close to tears. 'Something is wrong with Papa,' she said. 'Isn't it?'

Fear gripped me. The way he had left was so strange that I could not dismiss it. 'Shall I ask Mama about it?' said Jasmine, halfway up the stairs already.

'No,' I said. 'No, don't, Jas. Don't worry her.'

'Then what are we going to do? Anselm, I'm scared.'

'I'll go after him,' I said. 'I'll just follow him and make sure that he's all right.'

I threw on my jacket, and Jasmine ran to fetch my boots, as if it was urgent that I leave at once. I tied the laces hastily and half ran out of the door.

'Anselm,' she said as I left. 'Be very careful.'

'I'll be fine,' I said.

The cold showed no sign of relenting as I stepped out into the street. The very darkness seemed charged with ice. Leo had already disappeared round the corner. Mr Pascal appeared at the door of his shop, wanting to tell me the story of some solid silver lamp he had bought for almost nothing from a market trader with a wooden leg, but I made my excuses and left him. I ran for several yards, then caught sight of Leo and slowed. He was walking without urgency, both hands in his overcoat pockets and his head bowed against the wind. The cigarette in his mouth kept dying in the rising breeze.

It was strange to see him like that, when he did not know that I was walking after him and thought himself completely alone. He looked very young, in spite of his greying hair, and without any defence. Every few yards he would pause to light his cigarette again. I wanted to call his name, but I knew he would send me back at once. So I followed him in silence, under the streetlamps and back out again into the dark, along alleyways and across boarded yards and along the sides of inns where music played and people stamped their feet. I pulled the collar of my coat up high so that only my eyes could feel the cold. The streets were worse than freezing at nights. Leo was not walking towards the markets, I realized. He was heading towards Citadel Street.

I fell behind. He had a way of half glancing over his shoulder that made me constantly think he would discover me. Citadel Street was deserted anyway; I could not lose sight of him here. It was a dismal place tonight. The homeless and the dispossessed had set up camps in the empty houses. In one of them, a brazier was burning and twenty people or more stood huddled around it. A blackened painting still hung over the mantelpiece on the exposed back wall. Leo stopped in front of our old building and glanced up at the boarded windows. Then he tried the door. He went around to the side and struggled with that one too. He struggled for a long time, then gave up and rested his head against the red cross on the wood.

When he set out again, his steps were more definite, and I had to jog to keep up with him. The waste ground that surrounded Citadel Street was unlit and treacherous. We came out at last in an alleyway beside an inn. Leo shrank away from the lights of the windows and paused for a moment to light a cigarette.

In that moment, I heard someone else move. I did not dare to turn. But I suddenly knew that I was not the only one following Leo. Carefully, I edged into the doorway of the inn and pretended to be struggling with the buttons of my coat, as though to fasten it more tightly against the cold. In the corner of my vision, I could see a man in blue. He had not seen me. He was beside the nearest wall, with a gun raised in his hand.

I moved before I knew what was happening. I caught hold of Leo and pulled him through the doorway of the inn at the same moment the man in blue fired.

People shrieked and turned over their chairs as we fell into the inn. And then something happened that I swear saved both our lives. A group of men in red uniforms, sitting smoking in the back corner of the inn, got to their feet. 'What's going on?' said the tallest, taking out a pistol.

'It's the Imperial Order,' I said. 'The man out there had a gun—'

The police picked up their rifles and stormed out into the street. Leo just lay where he was, staring at the false chandeliers that hung from the beams. 'Papa?' I said. 'Are you hurt?'

He turned over and saw me properly. He said nothing, just breathed fast and coughed and searched about him for a cigarette. Then he said, 'Anselm, in God's name, I told you not to come with me.'

'He's vanished,' said the tall officer, appearing at the door again. 'Do you have any idea who that man was?'

'Someone from the Imperial Order,' I said. 'He had the uniform.'

'Did you recognize him?'

'I didn't see his face.'

'Please raise your hands,' said another officer, training his rifle on us and squinting through his gold spectacles as though to intimidate us more completely. The inn had emptied by the other door; it was remarkable how quickly everyone had fled the scene. Even the barman had shut himself up in the back room. 'Please raise your hands,' the officer said again. 'Let me see your papers.'

We had papers, but we never carried them. 'We don't have them with us,' I said. 'They are back at the shop.'

'Names, then,' said the officer with the spectacles.

Leo raised his hand to stop me from speaking and got slowly to his feet. 'He had nothing to do with it,' he said. 'And I'm Leonard North.'

'Leonard North of the North family?' said the officer. 'Aldebaran's relative?'

'Yes,' said Leo.

'Then we need to talk to you. You are supposed to have signed up for National Service. If you don't come quietly now, you risk prosecution.'

'But there are hundreds of other people—' I began.

'Shh,' said Leo. 'It's fine; I'll come. But one thing – you have to promise me.'

'What is it?' said the officer wearily. He was glancing at his unfinished glass of spirits on the table.

'It has to be far away,' said Leo. 'Do you understand? And they can't know. The Imperial Order can't know. They are following me and threatening my family, and I'm afraid they are going to try something. Do you understand what I'm saying?'

'We'll see about that,' said the officer. They were putting on their jackets now and hastily finishing their abandoned drinks. 'We will escort you to your house,' said the officer. 'You can collect a few things and leave by the next ship west, to the munitions factory on Holy Island. We will ensure the matter of the Imperial Order is looked into.'

'Munitions factory?' I said.

But Leo just raised his hand again and nodded.

'Quickly please,' said the tall officer, in what he must have hoped was a kind voice. 'We are not supposed to be on duty, and the police have more than enough to do as it is.'

I could not speak to Leo; the officers divided us all the way back to Trader's Row. At the door, they hesitated.

'My wife is expecting a baby,' said Leo with a strange kind of calm. 'I don't want her to be worried by anything.'

'We will wait outside the door,' said the officer. 'You can go inside and collect your things. We will then escort you to the harbour.'

Leo went in ahead of me and closed the door behind us and leaned against it. I could hear Jasmine shrieking with laughter at some game in the living room above. The kind chaos of the back room seemed like the remains of someone else's life. 'I told you not to come,' Leo said at last.

'He was going to shoot you!' I said. 'If I hadn't been there—'

'Anselm, maybe it would have been better.'

'Don't be bloody ridiculous!' I didn't know why I was angry with him, but I was. 'Papa, he wanted to kill you! He wanted to—'

'Listen,' he said, still in the same calm voice, as though he had heard nothing I'd said. 'After I leave, pack your things and go to your grandmother's. Tell Doctor Keller that he can rent out the shop. You will all have to stay there until—'

'No. You can't just order us to pack up our whole life.'

'Listen to me!' said Leo, losing his composure. 'Anselm, in the name of God, just listen to me!' Jasmine's laughter faltered upstairs. 'Sixteen years ago,' Leo whispered, 'I shot a man. He was an important man in Lucien's government, and people know what I did. The Imperial Order know; they have a price on my head and it's thousands and thousands of crowns. When I told you I was involved with the resistance, I wasn't honest. I couldn't tell you the full truth. But I'm telling you now.'

I stared at him. I could say nothing.

'I have to go,' he said. 'I have to, because if they take control of this country – if they find me – we will all be in danger. We will all be wanted criminals. You and Maria and Jasmine, even the baby. Anselm, there is nothing we can do. Don't make this harder. I'm not Maria's husband; I'm not your father. If I leave now, it will be better for all of you, and you can pretend you were never connected to me, and maybe it will be all right.'

'But, Papa . . .' I said, and could not go on.

'Anselm,' he whispered. 'Please, just help me. I don't think I can do this otherwise.'

He turned and started up the stairs. I followed him. There was nothing else to do. Jasmine came running to the door when we arrived, still shrieking with laughter. She was wearing my mother's heeled shoes and best dress, with rouge daubed liberally across her cheeks. 'Look at me,' she said. 'I'm a rich lady.'

'Very smart,' said Leo.

My mother was on the sofa with her eyes closed, but she opened them now and smiled and reached out her hand to Leo.

'Are you all right?' he said, taking it gently.

'Just tired. The little duchesses were a handful today. I swear I am more a police officer than a governess to them half the time. Leo, your hand is like ice. Where have you been?' She sat up and pushed back her hair. 'Jasmine and I think Stirling Harold for the baby. Or Stirling Julian. What do you say?'

Leo said nothing, just gripped her hand in both of his own. Her face darkened. 'What is wrong?' she said. 'You both look as though you've met a ghost.'

'It's nothing,' I said. My voice didn't sound right and only made them stare at me more anxiously. Leo went down to the shop and brought up an old suitcase we had never been able to sell.

My mother was on her feet in a second. 'What is this?' she said. 'Leo? Answer me.'

Leo said nothing, just began throwing things into the case. Jasmine was the first to understand. She stared up at me, her face serious now behind her bizarre make-up. Then she ran into the bedroom and began pulling the things out of the case. 'No!' she said. 'You're not leaving, Papa! You're not leaving!'

'Stop it,' said Leo quietly. 'Jasmine, just let me do this.'

'No! I won't let you! You're not coming back, are you? You're going away for ever.'

'Just let me pack my case.'

'No, I won't!' She took out his clothes and threw them across the room. His shirts fell in the fireplace, sending soot flying.

'What is wrong with you, Jasmine?' Leo shouted. There was a silence. He knelt on the floor, one boot in his hand and the other somewhere out of his reach under the bed. Then he started to cry.

'No,' said my mother. 'Leo, you swore to me that you wouldn't leave.'

'I can't help it,' he said. 'It's the police – they have called me up for National Service. I tried to say no—'

'You can tell them that your wife is expecting a baby. You can, because I checked on the way back from work last week, when you were talking like this before, and I don't see why—'

'You're not my wife,' said Leo. 'That's why.'

'No, Leo, damn you!' She slammed the case closed and stared at him over it, her eyes fierce and wild.

'Maria, please. I don't have any choice. Don't make this harder.'

We all sounded like we were acting some tragic play. We were unequal to this, and no one could find the right words. Leo pulled the case away from my mother and went on crying. He wiped his eyes with the back of his hand and shoved his old army boots and his Sunday shirt into the case, then the scarf Jasmine had knitted him.

'No!' said Jasmine. 'You can't have that scarf if you're leaving. You're not my papa any more!'

She caught hold of the end and tried to pull it away from him. He tried to hold onto it, stupidly, and it ripped in two, the wool unravelling. 'I hate you!' shouted Jasmine, kicking him. 'I hate you, and I don't care if you're crying. You're a bastard. I wish you'd go straight to hell!'

'Jasmine,' I said, trying to hold her back. 'Jasmine, it's not his fault. Stop it.'

My mother was crying now, but she refused to let Leo see that. She stood against the door frame and swiped angrily at her tears. I knelt there with my arms around Jasmine and let her struggle. But maybe she was the only one who realized it properly. He was going to do this, pack all his things into that suitcase with the broken clasp and walk away into the dark, and none of us could stop it.

As if from a hundred miles away, I heard a voice on the stairs. 'The door was open, so I came up,' my grandmother called. 'Maria? What is going on up here?'

She appeared at the top of the stairs and took one glance at our tear-streaked faces and the suitcase between us. 'Heavens,' she said. 'Is he leaving, then?'

Leo began trying to fasten the suitcase shut with an old belt. My grandmother went to my mother in the doorway, throwing dark glances at him. 'Didn't I always say?' she burst out eventually. 'Maria, didn't I always tell you Leonard was no good?'

I was still struggling with Jasmine, and I lost hold of my temper. 'It's not his fault, you bloody-minded old cow!' I told her.

There was a silence while she puffed herself up with indignation. 'You're just like your father,' she said then, very steadily. 'You're just exactly like your father. I hope you know that, Anselm.' Then all hell broke loose.

Leo turned without looking at any of us and ran down to the back room to fetch the rest of his things. Jasmine began wailing in earnest, and my mother knelt down and put her arms around her. I edged out of the doorway and down the stairs. Leo was working fast, piling everything into his case in the dark.

'It's not justice,' I said. 'It's not justice that they are chasing you.'

'It is justice,' said Leo.

'Who was he?' I said. 'This man who you . . .'

The word *shot* rested in the silence between us. Leo did not answer. The silence fell heavily as he fastened the belt around the case and tried to pull it tight. He struggled to light a cigarette, but his hands were shaking too badly. He crumpled the whole box suddenly and threw it at the wall.

'Papa, tell me it will be all right,' I said.

'It will be all right,' he said, still crying. 'Everything will be all right. You have to have faith, Anselm.'

'Is that all?' I said. 'This country is falling apart. You've just told me you're a wanted criminal. When will we see you again if war breaks out?'

'Anselm, please . . .' He began climbing the stairs again slowly, dragging the case behind him.

'What is this?' I said. 'Goodbye for ever, or what?'

'I don't know.' Snow thudded against the window. It was coming down like the end of the world, as if it wanted to extinguish everything. He turned and looked at me. 'Anselm,' he said. 'I have loved you more than I could ever love a son of my own. And I will, after I go. Even if I die. Love is stronger than anything; it never lets you go. I don't deserve you – not any of you. This is my own fault. I always had it coming to me.'

My mother was too angry or too unhappy to kiss him, so he turned away without saying goodbye. Jasmine wailed and tried to drag him back as he left. My mother just stood crying in the doorway. He went down the stairs like that, Jasmine clinging to the handle of his suitcase all the way, her nose running and her hair dishevelled, screaming at him not to go. At the bottom of the steps, the suitcase broke. Everything fell out onto the floor and scattered.

I stepped forward. All his Harold North books were there. 'You can't take those,' I said.

He tried to gather them up, shoving *The Golden Reign* into his pocket and turning to pick up the others. Jasmine began gathering them, too, clutching them to her chest.

'No,' she wailed. 'No, I won't let you have them. I won't let you go.'

He tried to pull them out of her arms, then gave up. 'Keep them for me,' he said. 'Both of you.'

Someone was hammering on the door suddenly. Leo raised a hand to his head. 'Go upstairs,' he mouthed to me. I caught his eyes and tried to tell him in a look that I was still his son no matter what happened now, no matter what divided us. Then I had to turn and push Jasmine inside and close the door behind us both. The cheerful firelight of the living room seemed absurd, like a stage set for someone else's life. A fierce snowstorm was howling round the house now; we did not hear the side door close. Jasmine ran to my mother and buried her face in her dress and cried.

Leo had forgotten one of his old boots in the hurry; it lay stupidly between the bedroom and the door. I could not stay there and let him leave on his own. 'I'm going after him,' I said, picking up the boot. 'He might need this. I'll be back.'

When I opened the door, the snow howled through it in a torrent. It was pouring out of the sky so fast it was a solid force in the air, an early storm that would barely settle but that obscured the whole city. The flakes clung to my eyelashes and drove into my mouth. I turned and started towards the harbour. 'Father!' I shouted. 'Leo!'

I was running downhill; that was the only way I could tell I was going in the right direction. The houses on either side were just black shadows; the gas lamps were plastered with ice and gave no light at all. Someone was shouting behind me. Whether it was one of the Imperial Order or the police or just a trader in the nearest market, I could not tell, but I ran on. The wind was so merciless that it snatched my breath; I could not shout for him. I ran instead. Eventually I made out the dim lights of the harbour through the storm. Figures in red uniforms were ushering a few men towards the end of a long line. 'Papa!' I shouted.

One of the men broke away and started towards me. We met in the driving snow between the harbour and the buildings. 'Anselm, why did you follow me?' he said.

'I don't know.'

He put his hand on my shoulder. His fingers were very strong in that moment; his hand on my shoulder was the only real thing in the snowstorm that surrounded us. 'Listen,' he said. 'Whatever happens – whatever wrongs I've done – I did love you, Anselm. And your mother and Jasmine. Will you tell them?'

'Yes,' I said.

'You were the one who saved me,' he said. 'It was you most of all, in the end. Did you know that?'

I shook my head. The wind drove the tears from my eyes, and they burned my face with cold. 'What about the baby?' I said. 'What about Mother?'

'Anselm,' he said. 'It breaks your heart, but I believe you find a way of surviving. I really believe it.'

'Move along now; move along!' the officers were shouting.

'Take care of them,' he said. 'I promise you, I will try to find a way, but I just don't know any more.'

A well-dressed woman in the nearest house glanced out at us, her lamplight illuminating suddenly the square of grey slush on which we stood. She frowned, then pulled her shawl tighter around her, as if to shield herself from such a pathetic sight. Leo was standing there with his nose running. I was crying and did not care.

'Anselm, I'm sorry,' he said. Then he broke away from me and joined the line. They were all men like him, with shabby overcoats and old suitcases and tired smokers' eyes. I watched them descend towards the harbour. Then, after a while, I could not tell which one was Leo any more. It was only then that I realized his old army boot was still in my hand. I had run all the way to the harbour with it and had forgotten to give it to him.

I was in darkness now; the snow in the air was the only light. The gas lamps stood obscured by the blizzard. The snow slid down their panes and made the lights flicker feebly. Then, as I reached the end of Trader's Row, it began to recede altogether. It hesitated, as though drawn back up into the air, and the gaslight spread its glow across the silent street. I walked slowly through the last flakes to the door of the shop.

The back room was full of melting snow; it lay in a drift from the door to the bottom of the stairs, with the moonlight shining coldly on it. I must have forgotten to close the door behind me. I tried to kick it aside, then gave up. I heard it dripping below me as I walked up the stairs. Jasmine was still clutching the Harold North books when I got back. Her face was pale and blotched with crying. My mother was staring at the fire, sitting awkwardly in the armchair because of her swelling stomach. I closed the door quietly behind me.

'Well!' said my grandmother. 'Now that Leo has given up his responsibilities, someone must take charge. I will go and fetch my things tomorrow morning. In your condition, Maria, you cannot be in the house on your own.'

'Mother, I'm fine.'

'Nonsense.'

We were all too dejected to argue. We let her lecture us, detailing her plans as though this was some army campaign. There were two police officers in the alley opposite; I could make out the blazing red of their uniforms in the dark. Even so, none of us slept that night. We sat up around the fire, watching the wind trouble the flames. 'Will Father be at Holy Island yet?' said Jasmine at about eleven o'clock. I'd had to tell them where he was going.

'He might be halfway to the west coast by now,' said my mother. 'If the snow has not stopped them. He will have to go all the way along the river, and then cross the country-side by coach, and then take another ship to Holy Island.'

We fell into silence again. Traces of Leo's presence were everywhere, things he had left carelessly as he fled and things that he could not have taken. The ring with his initials, which my mother turned around on her finger, and his old leather jacket that I still wore. And the look of him in Jasmine's eyes.

'He'll be back for my play, won't he?' she said.

My mother stroked her hair. 'You know your papa – he never misses anything if he doesn't have a good reason.'

'That means no,' said Jasmine. 'Doesn't it?' Neither of us

answered. 'If he doesn't come back, I won't ever speak to him,' said Jasmine. 'Why did he have to go away?'

'It was not his fault,' I said.

A dismal silence fell again. 'Where's Holy Island?' said Jasmine.

'Get the atlas and I'll show you,' said my mother.

Jasmine ran to fetch it. It was my old atlas; Leo had bought it for me from a trader he knew in my second year at Sacred Heart Infant School. The borders were already out of date. 'There,' said Jasmine, pointing to Holy Island on the map. 'A hundred miles.'

'I thought you could see it from the highest tower of the castle,' I said. 'That was what Papa always told me.'

My mother shook her head. 'People like him can. No one else.'

I supposed she meant people with powers.

'There,' Jasmine said, drawing a line in red pencil straight from Malonia City to Holy Island.

'Don't do that,' said my mother. 'It won't come off.'

She drew another line defiantly. 'I hate Malonia,' she said. She scribbled over the page, pressing so hard that the pencil went through the paper.

'We should have gone with him,' said my mother, and shivered.

At midnight, I wandered down to the yard and stood in the snow. It was already melting. I thought perhaps Leo would come trailing back up the street and tell us he had changed his mind. And standing there in the dark, I thought of Michael. When his father had been taken to the government hospital two years ago with a failing heart, he had stood under my window and thrown gravel at the pane until I woke. I had sat beside him while he waited, and he would have done the same for me, but now he was gone and I didn't know where. And Aldebaran could have helped us, but he was unjustly killed, and no one seemed to remember. I wondered if this was how it always was when someone went away from you. It only made you miss the other people the more fiercely.

The snow began to fall again, robbing the city of all colour. I turned and went back inside. I wandered about the shop performing Leo's usual tasks – sweeping the floor and turning down the stove and bolting the doors and windows. I counted up the day's takings and took them to the safe. I never usually opened it, but it could not be helped today. I turned the dials to the combination Leo had set and hit the side to shake the broken lock free. It let out a mournful clang when I did it. I put the money into the case on the top shelf.

As I pushed the door closed again, I noticed something. On the bottom shelf, under a dusty box of jewellery and the parcel from Aldebaran marked *To the baby*, there was a pile of papers in Leo's writing. I pulled them out and held them close to the lamp. Half of them were the story I had already seen, stapled to the other pages so that they formed a makeshift book. And there was more, several pages, and the word FINISH at the end. The sheets were bound together neatly with string.

'Anselm,' sniffed Jasmine from the doorway, making me start and turn. 'What's that you're holding?'

'Nothing,' I said.

'Let me see.'

I handed the pages to her. 'It's something Papa wrote,' I said.

'What is it, then?'

'A story. I don't know.'

'Read it to me?' she said. 'Please. Then it will be like Papa is here.'

'Oh, Jas.' I shrugged. 'I don't think it's that kind of story.'

She sniffed and handed it back. Perhaps that was worse than anything. On any ordinary day, Jasmine would have snatched the papers out of my hand and begged me to read them to her until I gave in. But tonight she just trailed back upstairs with her blanket wrapped around her and went to her bedroom and put out the light. I closed the safe again.

I left the papers on my desk while I lay awake in the dark; they gleamed palely under the moon. Every time I drew near to sleep that night, it escaped me. But I must have slept eventually, because when I did, I dreamed. I could see Leo struggling through the blizzard at a grey stone port and the sea foaming white with the snow that troubled it. And then it was another man, a man with reddish hair like my own, who turned and walked away into the night. I started and sat up. After that dream, I could not sleep again. I was more and more haunted by him, my real father. Perhaps it would be worse now that Leo was gone.

There was nothing I could do, and the night stretched away from me in all directions. I lit the lamp and began to read those papers. It was a strange story, and I did not understand it. It began with the lord Rigel and his daughter and Aldebaran and England. But at least it kept the dark at bay.

MORNING,
THE FOURTH OF JANUARY

Mr Hardy shook his head after I finished telling him that story. It was ten o'clock, and the coach was about to leave. He went on shaking his head. A muscle twitched under his eye with a flickering movement, making him look very old and frail suddenly. 'Are you all right?' I asked him.

'Yes,' he said. 'Yes, I am all right.' He coughed. 'Go on. Tell me what happened next.'

But we were leaving now. The others were already climbing up into the coach. He could not get to his feet, so I helped him, and we crossed the yard like that. 'Go on with the story,' he said again. 'As soon as we reach the next inn, you must tell me.'

'I will,' I said. 'But, sir, I don't understand. Why are you so interested?'

He just shook his head.

I gave him those papers to read instead. I could tell from the way his eyes moved restlessly that something troubled him, and I knew them almost by heart anyway. I knew how the story went on. I stared out at the dark moorland, towards the black line that must be the sea beyond the snow-covered cliffs.

'Here,' said the woman then, touching my shoulder. She was handing round biscuits and cold tea.

We had hardly spoken a word to her since we set out. Mr Hardy smiled and took a biscuit, and I took one, and she gave us a nervous smile and hid herself behind her little boy again, making much of stroking his hair and checking if his hands were cold. But the boy was looking up at us both now with interest.

'What's your name?' he asked me.

'Anselm,' I said.

'I'm Matthew,' he said.

'Esther,' whispered his mother.

The little boy looked up at Mr Hardy. 'Harlan,' said the old man after a minute.

'Harlan?' I said. He gave me a quick glance. He must have got it from our talk of Harlan Smith and that book, but I did not know why he had given a false name.

The woman and her son were watching us curiously. Mr Hardy met my eyes, then turned away and drank his tea carefully. The tin cup rattled in his hand, which was shaking badly. He seemed to be growing weaker on this journey. I watched the line of the sea draw close to us, then run alongside the coach road, its waves breaking close and very black against the edge of the snow. After a while, Mr Hardy went on reading. I knew the words he read, and I repeated them in my mind. It was something to drive out the cold.

Juliette woke because she was troubled by strange dreams. Outside, the orange London darkness showed no sign of lifting. She rested her head against the window frame, and her heart felt cold in her chest, as though she was still in the dark beside a strange river and did not know what was ahead.

Richard was out. She did not know where the offices of his solicitors' firm were, but she supposed that was where he was now. The clock on the mantelpiece stood at twelve. Juliette threw a dressing gown around her shoulders and crossed the carpeted landing to her father's door. The study was darkened, but she thought she would go in and wait for him. It was what she often used to do when she was small.

Richard had always had a study, though he never worked in it. Juliette stood in front of the desk and spun the old-fashioned globe, and stared at it and made it go on spinning longer than was possible. She pretended she was a great woman, and the globe was enchanted to go on spinning for ever. She could not remember how she had learned these tricks. She had tried to ask Richard about them once, but he had shaken his head and refused to see the paper that was crumpling in her hand. Afterwards, she did not dare to tell him again. That was just after he'd told her about their old country and her mother dying. Ever since then, she had been able to do impossible things.

Juliette put one finger on the globe to stop it spinning. Beside it was a stack of old volumes of Shakespeare. Her father thought there was no English writer higher and read and reread those old plays. Juliette turned over the pages, looking for the quote about the charmed life, then gave up and put the volumes back on the pile. Standing on the desk in front of them was what looked like an antique typewriter, with a blank page in it so old that dust dulled the edges of the paper. It must be something her father had picked up in an antiques shop. Juliette bent close to the machine and made out each ornate letter, standing out in shiny metal. She brushed the dust from the keys, then frowned and tried to make them move by themselves. She had no reason for doing it, except to make something speak to her out of the lonely silence. She knelt in front of it and fixed her eyes on each key. She tried to make her mind become the old metal and the ink and the page between its rollers. Outside, a car door slammed and broke her concentration. She went on staring at it. She felt herself go outwards, through the empty air and into the dead metal of the machine, and give it life. The letter R sprang up and printed itself on the paper.

Juliette started. The other letters were clattering now. 'R-I-G-E-L', typed the machine, and fell silent again.

Juliette fought the wish to run out of the room and slam the door behind her. Instead, she bent down and examined the printed page. Then she went to the table beside the sofa and poured out a glass of water from a plastic bottle. She watched her hand shake as she drank. Her head ached, and she wished she had never tried to make the typewriter move. It was a long walk back to the desk. The room was too big and too white and cold. It must be something about the rich, thought Juliette, that made them colour their houses every shade of white. Perhaps it was to prove that dirt and dust were no object. She could never see herself as wealthy, though she knew it for a fact. She always felt like an impostor in this house.

Juliette went back to the desk, took down the English dictionary, and turned over the pages, looking for the word Rigel. Something about it was already imprinted in her memory. But the word was not there. And yet there was something about the dictionary that made sense to Juliette. Every word, even and and but, was defined for her within its pages, as though it was made for someone who could never see the world as familiar. And this was how she understood her life. As something she could never get used to.

It was while she was still studying the dictionary that the machine came to life again. It rattled so loudly that she dropped the book. 'Rigel,' it was typing. 'Rigel. Rigel. Rigel.' The rattling was enough to wake the servants. Juliette tried to hold the keys down, but they were dancing now, forming new words on the yellow paper. 'Rigel, are you there?' wrote the machine. 'Help me.'

Juliette watched the machine type, and she knew she was not the one who was making those letters move. 'Help me,' the machine wrote again. 'They want to kill me. Rigel, you promised not to let me down.'

Juliette backed away and slammed the door behind her. As she did it, she heard her father in the hallway.

'Juliette?' he said quietly, bending his head to peer up the stairs. 'Are you awake?' He threw off his coat, unwound his scarf, and came bounding up the steps two at a time. 'What's the matter?' he said. 'You look like you have seen a spirit. What's that noise?'

'Nothing.'

He opened the study door and stopped. The machine was spilling a ream of paper, still writing frantically. 'Juliette, have you been playing about with that?' he said.

'No,' she said. 'I didn't mean to do anything.'

He crossed to the desk and knelt down, trying to unjam the paper. And then he stopped. He was studying the words that still unreeled themselves line by line. 'Go back to bed,' he said then, very quietly. 'Go back to bed at once. I want you to stay in your room.'

Juliette went out, but only as far as the corridor. She stood in the alcove at the top of the stairs and listened. The typing went on, unevenly, then stopped. Then she heard a violent smashing sound, somewhere down in the garden. She ran to the bathroom and pushed up the window. The typewriter was lying in the low yard outside the cellar, smashed into several pieces with its keys around it on the ground. Richard had thrown it from his study window.

Juliette went to her room and sat on the edge of the bed,

shivering. James Salmon went and stood outside the door, and she could tell from the shape of his coat that he had a gun. She did not usually like her father to let his bodyguard patrol outside the house with a gun; she was sure it was not legal here in England. But tonight she was almost glad of it, because the whole world seemed suddenly hostile. She sat awake until dawn rose over London and extinguished the orange light of the streetlamps. At six o'clock, Richard tapped on her door.

'Come in,' she said. He came in slowly and sat down on the bed beside her and rubbed his eyes. His glasses slid precariously down his nose. Richard looked older and tireder this morning. 'Listen, Juliette,' he said. 'I think we might have to go away.'

'What do you mean, go away?' she said.

'Move to another house. Maybe another country.'

'Back to our old country?'

'No.'

'Then I don't understand—'

'I can't explain. I can't explain, but I have decided. We are going.'

'What are we running away from?' said Juliette.

Richard started and looked up at her. She did not know why she had asked it; it was the first thing that came into her mind. 'What are we running away from?' she said again. 'What did those words mean? Why did you break the typewriter?'

Richard shook his head. He went on shaking it.

'I'll find out,' said Juliette. 'If you don't tell me, I'll still find out.'

'Juliette, I'm trying to protect you.'

'I'll still find out.'

'I don't want to tell you.'

'You told me about my mother, that other time.'

'I know.'

Juliette watched his face. He got up and went to the window. The London dawn had almost reached its height. The fenced garden in the middle of the square was illuminated, like a window into some promised land. 'Those words,' said Richard, 'were from my old employer. The man who sent me on this mission, the man I broke with ten years ago. He has now been assassinated. And now that they know I'm alive, I'm afraid they are coming for me.'

Juliette listened for a long time in silence, but no more words came. Then she went with her father silently through the house, helping to pack up their most valuable possessions and burn every paper that bore their names. They went two miles across the city to a drab hotel beside the railway. James Salmon came with them, carrying his gun. Juliette did not dare to ask any questions. But after that, she could not sleep without the nightmares returning to her.

EVENING,
THE FOURTH OF JANUARY

'That was the night Aldebaran died,' said Mr Hardy as soon as we were alone that evening. 'The night when Rigel and his daughter left their house; it was the same night.'

'Yes,' I said. 'I think so.'

He handed the papers back to me. The sea crashed outside. This inn stood right on the cliff edge, facing out across the black water. Snow spiralled down and was lost among the waves. 'How did Leo know these things?' said Mr Hardy. 'That's what I want to know.'

'I never asked him,' I said.

He looked up at me. 'What happened after he left?'

'Shall I finish telling you?'

'Yes.'

In truth, I had almost given up on my story. It was still less than half written, and the pages lay abandoned in the inside pocket of my coat. I did not know how to tell what came after. But Mr Hardy still wanted to hear, and I felt a strange kind of duty to him now, as though I had to go on telling it until the bitter end.

'Go on,' he said. 'Just as before. I want to know what happened.'

NOVEMBER

I never understood, until that night when Leo left, how the truth gets swallowed. But after that night, when the early snow melted and the winter mists invaded the city and the cold grew less bitter and yet ran deeper into my bones, I never once thought about the man with the gun. He had been about to shoot Leo, and we had both known it, but I tried not to even consider it. And I never let myself think about Leo killing someone, though he had told me quite clearly that he had done it. But what could I do? And who was there to tell? I was the only person who knew, and so those things stopped being true, because I wanted them to. They had happened once, like a story, but not to me.

After Leo left, my grandmother moved in, with her carpetbags and strict rules of conduct, and took up residence in Jasmine's room. And my mother, as if to prove her justified, fell ill. She went to work the first day, looking sick and pale. On the second day, the merchant banker and his wife sent her home. We sat up by the fire, the two of us, after Jasmine and my grandmother had gone to bed. My mother kept stirring to put on more coals, and I tried to get up before her each time and stop her from tiring herself out. She looked very young in the firelight, like a girl expecting a baby, not a woman of thirty-one. I wondered if that was how she had looked in the months before I was born. I had never much thought about it before, but my real father and those years I could not remember were haunting my thoughts now more and more.

Someone coughed down in the street and made us both glance up. I went to the window. The gas lamps gave no light at all, but when I frowned, I could see a man pacing up and down in front of the house opposite.

'What is it?' said my mother.

'Nothing,' I said. He was a police officer; I could make out his red uniform. I rested my forehead against the glass. The man paced and turned smartly, a thin man with a cigarette jammed in his mouth. 'Nothing,' I said again, and drew the curtains across. The fact that they had taken Leo's wish seriously made me almost more anxious than if they had ignored it. I wondered what it was they were defending us from.

'Mother,' I said, 'are we staying here for good?'

'What do you mean?'

'Are we going to stay in the shop? We haven't even opened since Leo left; we are not making money. And next month's rent—'

She ran her hands through her hair and kept them there, and I wished I had not asked.

'Leo wanted us to go and stay with Grandmama,' I said.

'No,' she said. 'No, we are not doing that. There is no space in that house. We will kill each other before a month is out. We will manage here. All right?'

'Yes,' I said, like a scolded child. 'All right.'

'Anyway,' she said, 'we might be forced to leave, and we can think about it then.'

'Forced to?' I said, thinking of the Imperial Order.

'Leo left us in a bad way,' she said. 'Did you have any

idea? I've been looking through the accounts book. We are so far in debt that I don't think we can recover.'

I did not know what to say, so I listened in silence. I'd had some idea.

'So when Doctor Keller loses his patience, we'll have no choice,' she said. 'Unless we think of something to do, and I can't, Anselm. I really can't. I've tried.'

'So we'll end up at Grandmama's anyway,' I said. 'Is that what you mean?'

'I want the baby to be born here,' she said. 'I want to stay here. This is our home. Leaving seems like a bad omen.'

Her words made the back of my neck turn cold, and though I moved closer to the fire, it gave no heat.

'I know it's just superstition,' she said. 'But this is the place where everything was good.'

'We won't have to leave,' I said, suddenly determined. 'I'll think of something. Mother, maybe if you let me give up school—'

'No,' she said. 'No, you are not giving up school. That is absolutely final.'

We sat in silence, listening to the fire murmuring. 'Wake me at seven tomorrow,' she said eventually, and got to her feet. 'I think I will be well enough to go back to work by then.'

She went to bed soon after, and after a while she fell asleep, but I could not. Father Dunstan had said her illness was no more than a winter chill, but it seemed like a bad sign. The baby was due in six weeks' time, and all of us were worried. In six weeks' time, it might be born into occupied territory. It might be born into a country at war. And how could we stay in the shop for long if things were really as bad as she said? Dr Keller was not a lenient man.

I paced through the empty house. Jasmine was in my mother's room now; she slept with her head against my mother's shoulder and her thumb in her mouth. I went down to the back room and polished up some old jewellery and laid it out in the window. By the time I had finished, it was past four o'clock. I sat down at the counter and rested my head on my arms. I thought I would just rest for a while. I thought perhaps if I rested, I might think what to do.

I woke up shouting, as I had only when I was a small boy. 'Papa!' I was calling. I half expected Leo to come running into the room.

'Shh, be quiet!' said someone, putting a small hand over my mouth. It was Jasmine, in her nightgown and my mother's boots.

I came back. I had fallen asleep with my head on the shop counter. The lamp was still burning. 'What time is it?' I said.

'Six o'clock,' said Jasmine. 'What were you shouting about?'

'Nothing. It was a dream.' I sat up. 'Why are you awake?' I said. 'It's early; you should still be in bed, Jas.'

'I couldn't sleep, so I came down here.'

She went to the window of the back room. 'Anselm, the snow has settled at last,' she told me solemnly. 'Come out in the yard and make a snow statue with me.'

'It's below freezing out there.'

'Please. Papa would have.'

I could not argue with that. We went upstairs and dressed in the dark. The light outside was cheerless, but Jasmine would not be dissuaded. I took a lamp out with us to guard against the dismal grey morning, and we began. Jasmine worked intently, her forehead fixed into a permanent frown. When she glanced up, the lines remained there. 'Anselm, how shall we make his head?' she asked.

'Here, roll the snow up.' I pulled the sleeves of Leo's jacket down over my hands and began rolling a ball. Jasmine watched, her thumb in her mouth.

'Bigger than that,' she commanded. But we were acting out the scene, and it was no good. I stuck the head of the statue onto the body and stepped back.

'What do you think?'

'It's all right.' Jasmine carved the eyes and mouth carefully with one finger, then lost interest. 'Anselm,' she said. 'You know that box Uncle gave me?'

'Yes,' I said.

'I think it's not from here. I think it's from somewhere else.'

'Where could it be from? One of his journeys, do you mean?'

'I don't know,' she said thoughtfully. 'But not here.'

My grandmother was downstairs now, banging the poker on the bottom of the stove. The clocks chimed seven. 'I had better go and wake Mama,' I said. Jasmine followed me up the stairs, but she did not say anything more about the box; she just disappeared into her room to get ready for school.

I stood still at the door of my mother's room for a long while before I woke her. She was sleeping on her side, her arms wrapped around the space where Leo would have been. My mother was so beautiful that even if you had known her all your life, you sometimes stopped and noticed it. She turned her head and murmured something into the pillow. I did not want to wake her. I suddenly felt that I would rather die than go over there and wake her and see her face when she came back from wherever she was. But it was already past seven, and I had promised. While I stood there, she stirred and looked up at me.

Her eyes moved through several degrees of confusion as she sat up. 'Anselm,' she said then.

'How do you feel?'

'Better. Better than yesterday.'

'Shall I bring you a cup of tea?' I said, and went down to fetch it. When I came upstairs, she was lying back on the pillows again.

'I didn't know where I was when I woke up,' she said with her eyes closed. 'I was dreaming of other times.'

'I could tell,' I said.

'Thank you for waking me.'

I watched her drink the tea in silence. 'You had better get ready for school,' she said then.

She left for work at the same time as we set out. Jasmine dragged on her hand all the way to school, crying that she did not want to go. I was late, and the only desk free was at the back of the class, already occupied by John Keller. I sat down beside him in silence. Sister Theresa was lecturing the class on the history of the monarchy.

'You haven't paid your rent,' John Keller wrote on a scrap of paper and glanced at me.

My heart gave a quick jump. I hesitated, then wrote, 'We have.'

'You haven't,' whispered John Keller, crumpling the paper. 'Your father pissed off without paying. Times are hard; tell your mother so.'

'I won't tell her anything,' I said.

Perhaps I said it too rashly, because John Keller narrowed his eyes and said, 'Your family are all the same.'

'What do you mean by that?'

'The poor scum we have to deal with to make an honest living—'

I pushed back my chair. John was already doing the same.

'Sit down,' said Sister Theresa.

'You don't know a damn thing about my family!' I said, ignoring her.

'Your father is Leonard North,' said John, raising his voice. 'And the Imperial Order are after him, and when the Alcyrians come, they will be after him too. Your family think they are better than everyone just because of some story about once being famous. But people like you are going to have to learn. So you should watch out, Anselm Andros, and not take money that you can't pay back.'

'And you should shut the hell up,' I said. 'You're a spoiled rich boy who knows nothing about the world.'

'Anselm!' shouted Sister Theresa. 'Sit down at once!'

John Keller was laughing at my outrage, and it made me angrier. 'I've seen your father,' I went on, abandoning all caution. 'And everyone says he cheats his tenants. He's the meanest old bastard that ever lived.'

'At least he's my real father,' said John Keller very quietly.

I started forward, but someone held me back. Someone else called, 'Fight!' and ducked below his desk again. John Keller swung a clumsy punch at me, but I had hold of his shirt and his face grew startled. For all his bravado, he was not used to fighting. I was struggling, but someone had tight hold of my arms. I wrestled free of his grip and knocked

John Keller over. Then he hit me, hard, and blood was in my mouth.

'Silence!' shouted Sister Theresa.

The fight was over before I realized what had happened. 'Anselm, John,' said Sister Theresa. 'Into my office, now.'

We were still struggling as she marched ahead of us towards her office door, but I was only struggling now because I had to; all the will to fight had gone out of me. Sister Theresa divided us and made us stand facing the wall. 'I have never seen such bad behaviour,' she said. 'You, John, need to think seriously about whether you have a future at this school. Anselm, I am quite frankly shocked and appalled by the violence you have just displayed. You will both stand there for the rest of the day. If I hear either of you talk, you will be expelled.'

It was very quiet in Sister Theresa's office. Outside the window, snow was falling. Blood ran steadily into my mouth; John Keller had broken one of my teeth. The fight stood unfinished between us. But we could only wait there, while the rest of the class went on in an unnatural silence next door. Sister Theresa came to the door of the office at lunchtime. 'Anselm, go and get some paper to put on that tooth,' she told me with no trace of sympathy. 'And clean that blood off my office floor.'

'Can I go out to lunch?' said John Keller. 'My father will be expecting me.'

'No,' said Sister Theresa. 'And you should both know that I will be writing to your families in very serious terms about this incident. I will also be including it in any future references I write.'

The snow thudded lightly against the glass, and the wind howled. Sister Theresa went away again. A group of younger boys were running about the yard in coats and scarves, kicking an empty bottle against the fence. 'Bastard,' muttered John Keller. 'Bastard. How will I get a place at medical college now?'

'John Keller, I hope you were not talking!' shouted Sister Theresa, appearing abruptly at the door. 'Anselm, I told you to get some paper and clean the blood off the floor.'

I did it, then stood there and stared at the woodworm in the floorboards under my feet. I could not help thinking of Leo. He had been gone only a few days, and already I was in bad trouble. I could not have faced his disappointment at this. I knew how he would have reacted. He would have refused to believe I was guilty. Even when my mother was disappointed in me, he would have gone on defending everything I did.

My whole head was aching, and my tooth throbbed with a steady rhythm. We stood there miserably, my mouth still bleeding and John Keller sniffing as though he was about to cry over his medical career. The afternoon drew on and dusk began to fall. Eventually Sister Theresa began the national anthem, and the others filed out. 'You may both go,' she said. 'I will escort you to the gate.'

We walked in silence, on either side of Sister Theresa, along the empty corridors and out into the snow. A gang of John Keller's friends was waiting for him. As Sister Theresa walked back to the school, he tried to lunge towards me, but they held him back. I turned and started towards Sacred Heart.

When she saw me, Jasmine stopped in the middle of, 'You're late, Anselm,' and started to cry.

'Hey,' I said. 'It's all right.'

'What happened to your tooth?' she said.

'John Keller broke it.'

'Anselm, it looks bad. And there's blood all over your face.'

'I'm all right. Hey, Jas, don't start crying. Please. Don't worry about me.'

'I am worried, though,' she said. 'Anselm, I am.'

My tooth was still throbbing, and a heavy tiredness came over me suddenly. 'Come on,' I said. 'Let's just get home.'

Our feet on the close-packed snow were the only sounds as we walked. We crossed the new square, past the half-empty market and the statue of the king. He had a coat of snow now and snow lying on his head and encrusted on his eyelids. The lights of the city were brightening. Among them were lines of Advent lanterns, arranged early along a few of the windowsills.

'Oh, Anselm!' Jasmine burst out eventually. 'What are you going to say to Mama?'

'Nothing,' I said. 'Jasmine, you can't tell her I was fighting.'

'She'll notice.'

'I'll wash it off before she gets home.'

'Shall I help you? Or shall I go and meet her and make sure she stays away until your face looks better?'

She was looking up at me with such concern that it startled me. A few snowflakes drifted down out of the grey air and lodged on her overcoat. I brushed them away. 'Thanks, Jas,' I said. 'But I'll be all right.'

The shop was in darkness, and the fires had gone out. I began to relight the stove in the back room, but Jasmine said, 'I'll do it,' and sent me out to wash my face instead. There was blood streaked across my cheek and caked in the edge of my hair; I looked like a desperate criminal. The water was so cold it felt like there was ice in it. But I washed my face anyway – there was no time to light the gas burner and wait for the hot tap to grow lukewarm. When I straightened up, I shivered. My face looked altered. It was just one missing tooth, but it changed everything about me, the way each ruined building altered the whole face of the city. I looked like an untrustworthy stranger. After I went back inside, a fit of repentance came over me, and I helped Jasmine with her newspaper cuttings, and corrected her homework for her, and listened to her reading her part from *The Beggar King*. But I kept thinking about John Keller's father now; I could not help it. 'Jas,' I said. 'It was a bad idea to start a fight with our landlord's son. It will mean nothing good.'

Jasmine, with more wisdom than I had expected, made no answer. The clocks in the city were striking five. 'I didn't realize it was so late,' I said. 'I thought they might send Mother home early, since she was ill.'

'Yes,' said Jasmine. 'I want Mama to come back.'

'Go on with your reading,' I said, and tried to convince myself that John Keller's father would see the situation in a favourable light.

By six o'clock, we were growing anxious. The city was dark, and the explosives on the border were clearer tonight than they had ever been. Mist rose and drifted over the snow. When I looked out into the night, I could see figures in it, just out of sight, where no people stood at all. We sat at the upstairs window and watched the empty street. Mr Pascal was walking about, putting up posters with the king's face and some propaganda message and singing a song about how he married the most beautiful girl in Angel City.

This was as far as his war work extended, and the relief had made him more talkative than ever over the past few days. But he did not come near our shop today. I almost wanted him to, to drive out the silence.

As we sat there waiting for something to happen, a carriage drew up with all its lights blazing.

'Who's that?' said Jasmine, jumping up and pressing her face to the window.

'It looks like a gentleman and two fine ladies,' I said.

'It is.'

'So what are they doing outside our shop?'

'Let's go down,' said Jasmine.

'We can see better from here.'

The people were getting down from the carriage, one of the ladies supporting the other, who looked weak and pale. 'Put the lamp out,' said Jasmine. I did it. And it wasn't a gentleman and two fine ladies at all. It was a gentleman, a lady, and my mother. The woman supporting her was the merchant banker's wife. The man was Dr Keller.

Surprise kept us fixed in our places until they knocked at the door. Then Jasmine ran down to open it, and I followed. The shop was open, and they were already inside.

'Hello,' said the lady. 'Mrs Andros's children?'

'Yes,' I said.

'Your mother is not well; I brought her home in our carriage.'

Jasmine ran to my mother and put her arms around her, saying, 'Mama, what's wrong?'

'I'm all right,' she said. 'Really, it was very kind, but there is no need—'

'I took the liberty of asking Doctor Keller in,' said the banker's wife. 'He is a neighbour and our own doctor, and

I knew he was acquainted with your family. I wanted someone to see to her after she fainted.'

'You fainted?' I said, turning to her.

'Really,' said my mother. 'It is nothing serious.'

'I'll help you upstairs.'

She leaned on my shoulder, protesting all the way that she was fine. 'You had better go down and talk to them, Anselm,' she whispered when I had helped her onto the sofa and Jasmine had run for a blanket to cover her. I hurried back down the stairs. They were lingering in the middle of the room, not touching anything, as though they had never been in a shop before and were afraid the goods might be infected.

'Thank you for bringing her back,' I said, avoiding Dr Keller's eyes. I was not sure why he had accompanied my mother home, but I took it as a bad sign.

'It is no trouble,' said the banker's wife. 'I was anxious about her, I must say.'

'She will be right again in a day or two,' said Dr Keller. 'Rest and good food, and a tonic if you can get it.'

They were already starting towards the door. 'Thank you,' I said, and my stomach wrenched with guilt suddenly for the kindness with which Dr Keller was treating us. 'Do I – do we owe you—'

He raised his hand. 'No charge.' Then he was helping the banker's wife into the carriage. He reached out as if to grip my hand in farewell. But when I made to take it, he handed me an envelope, so quickly that no one else could have seen. He put on his hat and got into the carriage, and they swept away down the street.

I stood for several seconds in silence. Then I went back into the shop, bolted the door, and opened the envelope.

Inside was a page, handwritten, with FINAL DEMAND stamped across the top. I raised it to the lamplight. It was a short note to the effect that our rent had been raised without notice, and as a result, we must 'either find the requisite monies or vacate the premises'. The new rent was five times what it had been. The requisite monies totalled three thousand crowns.

I threw the letter into the stove. It was not only that he was turning us out of the shop. It was the way he was doing it. The way he covered his tracks so that he would look like an honest man. And what cut to my heart most bitterly was that the whole thing was my fault.

When I went upstairs, my mother was lying very still, her hand resting on her stomach. The fire had gone out; a drift of snow down the chimney had drowned it altogether. 'Are you all right?' I said.

'Yes, I'm fine.'

'You don't look it. Mother, what's wrong?'

Jasmine was trying to light the fire. I took the matches from her. 'No,' she said. 'Let me do it.' The draughts were so strong in the room that I had no choice. Jasmine took the match and frowned at it, and the flame straightened and caught the wet coals.

'You know what Uncle said . . . about using your powers for things like that . . .' my mother murmured.

'You look so ill,' I said. She did not answer but just lay there, looking grey and sick. I rested my hand on her forehead. It was feverish, in spite of the cold.

'Anselm, you're shaking,' she said. 'Why are you shaking?'

'I'm not.'

'You are. Look at me.'

It was the first time I had met her eyes, and she started. 'What happened to your face?'

'Nothing,' I said. 'I broke my tooth at school.'

'Are you hurt?'

'No. It's just one tooth.'

'Is that all? Are you certain?'

'Mama, I'm more worried about you,' I said. 'Shall I go for Father Dunstan?'

'I don't want to trouble him.'

Footsteps came up the stairs at that moment, and we all glanced round. 'It's only me,' said my grandmother, approaching the door. 'Why are you burning so much coal? It's like a Christmas bonfire in here. I wonder you can afford it.'

My mother fell back on the pillows and let out a groan that my grandmother surely must have heard. It did not deter her. She came in and scolded and fussed until Jasmine went stamping to her room in tears. But in the end, my grandmother's arrival was what decided things. She would not listen to my mother's protests. She found the midwife's old address, crumpled under a pile of letters in the desk in the back room, and told me to go and fetch her.

The midwife lived in an apartment like ours, at the top of a house on Paradise Way. She came with me at once, throwing her shawl about her shoulders. 'Who is treating your mother?' she asked as we walked. 'Is it Doctor West? Or Doctor Sarah Law, I suppose, if you live on Trader's Row.'

'No one,' I said. 'I mean, the priest comes to see us if we are ill, but no one else.'

She frowned and asked me nothing else the rest of the

way home. She was a small woman and younger than my mother, and she had grown shabbier since Jasmine was born, but there was something of my grandmother about her; perhaps that was why my grandmother approved. She ushered Jasmine and me back into the stairwell as the midwife came in, then closed the door on us.

'Come on,' I said. I took Jasmine's hand, and we trailed down to the back room.

'Why can't we stay?' said Jasmine, kicking the stove. 'It's my brother.'

'Jasmine, come away from there,' I said. I began boiling water for tea. 'Tell me about your day at school.'

'I don't want to talk about my stupid day at school. I already told you about it.'

'Did you practise your play? You didn't tell me that.'

'Be quiet, Anselm. Let me listen.'

I fell silent. We could hear their voices above us, but not the words. 'I wish Papa was here,' whispered Jasmine.

'Yes.'

'I'm worried about him.'

'I know, Jas.'

I tried to hear their voices again, but it was no good. 'But he will be all right,' I said. 'He always is. Papa is luckier than he looks.'

I had thought that would make her smile, but it didn't. 'The thing I'm worried about with Papa,' she said, kneeling in front of the stove so that its light shone in her grey eyes, 'is that he doesn't . . .' She looked up at me earnestly. 'He doesn't want to live.'

'Doesn't want to live?' I said.

'Yes. He's not like you and me and Mama. He doesn't want anything for himself. So he needs to be with his family, because otherwise what does he have any more? He doesn't care about being all right like everyone else does.'

'So what do you think we should do, Jas?' I said, with the sinking truth in my heart that she was right. 'If you tell me what to do, I'll listen, but I don't see what—'

'We can go to Holy Island,' she said. 'We can go and find him. That's what we can do.'

She was gazing up at me, waiting for a response. I could tell she had been saving up this question. I shook my head. 'Mama is ill now. It's a long journey.'

'How long?'

'Two days or more.'

'When the baby is born, we could go.'

'But when the baby is born . . .'

'I know. Anything might happen.' Jasmine poked the coals in the stove disconsolately. 'Anselm, when will Michael write to you and tell you his address so we can send him a letter? Everyone goes away. Aldebaran and then Michael and then Papa. When will Michael write?'

'I don't know!' I said.

'Don't shout at me.'

'I wasn't shouting,' I said, too loudly. But I felt beleaguered by her questions, and my tooth still ached, and in pieces in the stove was a demand for three thousand crowns we had no way of paying. We fell into silence again. But I did not want to listen to their voices above us, not knowing what they said. 'Here,' I told Jasmine, picking up her copy of *The Beggar King* from the sideboard. 'Let's practise your play.'

'I don't want to,' she said.

'Go on. I want to hear how it's going.'

'No.'

'Please. It will make the time pass faster.'

She began reluctantly. I took all the other parts. While we were still reading, my grandmother appeared. 'You can come back in now,' she said. The midwife passed us on the stairs and went out by the side door. My mother was lying on the sofa under blankets, tears rolling down her cheeks. 'What is it?' I said, and alarm began to constrict my throat.

'The baby is not well,' she said. 'It is much too small.'

'Maria.' My grandmother gave a quick sigh. 'I have told you already – I'm sure it is nothing to worry about. The midwife said this was a normal winter fever.'

'But that it could be dangerous. That's what she said. It could be dangerous because the baby is small! And I have to give up work, and how will we pay the rent then, and I'm so afraid—' My mother's voice rose and choked her.

Jasmine reached out and tried to brush the tears from her face. I could think of nothing to say. I felt like it was filling the whole room, my helplessness, and suffocating me and everyone in it.

'But it will be all right?' I said at last. 'Won't it, Mother?'

'I don't know.'

'You will be all right?' I said.

She did not answer. Jasmine started to cry too.

'Of course it will,' said my grandmother. 'Maria, this is an overreaction.'

We sat dismally in front of the fire, my mother lying very still on the sofa, with the tears leaking occasionally from her eyes. Jasmine kept trying to bring her cups of water or read to her or bring her toast balanced shakily on a plate, until my grandmother scolded her and made her cry again. And all the time the shop stood closed, and our debts weighed heavier. Eventually I could not stand it. 'I am going out,' I said.

'Where?' said my grandmother.

'The markets. I want to sell a few things Leo left. I will not be long.'

I took the best jewellery out of our shop window and made the circuit of the stallholders in the new square. There was one merchant in the corner who everyone avoided, a woman who sold relics of Lucien's regime – old army badges and paintings of war criminals and books with titles that proclaimed war and revolution. Out of desperation, I tried her; she was the richest of the stallholders now. She gave me half a crown for a chipped bracelet. 'Good fortune to you,' she called after me as I left. To be shown charity by a collaborator was too much. I dropped the half-crown into a beggar's cup as soon as I reached the next street.

Carts rolled past me, piled high with people's possessions. They were still leaving the city. In some of the streets, there were now lines of TO LET signs, and the houses stood locked and barred. The snow began to fall onto the grey drifts that still lay in the streets. No snow remained clean in this city; the smoke and the dust clung to it within an hour of falling. I thought about where to go. Standing in the snow, a kind of purpose came over me. It was too cold to stay still and deliberate. I started for Dr Keller's house.

I stood for several minutes in the street outside, looking up at the black front door. Then I walked up the grand old steps and rang the bell. A maid in uniform opened it, a girl about my age. 'I want to see the doctor,' I told her. She disappeared, throwing her hair over her shoulder, and left me in the snow.

Police on horseback went by, the horses' hooves falling

heavily in the slush of the road. I waited, fixing my eyes on the boot scraper at the top of the steps. It matched the plaque beside the door with the doctor's name on it. That boot scraper was shaped like the gate of a country house, done in some brassy metal that gleamed against the snow, and there was even a little brass bird on the corner of the gate.

The maid appeared at the door again at last, and frowned at me for looking too closely at the scraper. 'The doctor won't see you,' she said. 'He is with his family, and his hours of work are over.'

'I don't want him to come out,' I said. 'I am here to talk to him.'

'About what?' said the housemaid, refining her high-class accent.

'He is our landlord. There's some mistake in the accounts. That's all.'

'I'm afraid I can't fetch him.'

'No,' I said. She was already halfway to closing the door. 'Listen, you have to. It won't take long, but I want to talk to him. You have to fetch him.'

'What is all this?' said the doctor, appearing behind the maid in the hallway. He regarded me in silence for a moment, then stepped out the door and pulled it closed behind him. He had a glass of spirits in one hand. 'Yes,' he said. 'It's perishing cold. What is it?'

'I came because . . . sir . . .' I hesitated. 'Thank you for treating my mother earlier.'

'It was a favour to my neighbour, that's all. Look, why are you here?'

'That letter you gave me,' I said. 'This final demand.'

'Yes. I know what it says.'

'I think there was a mistake,' I struggled on. 'I mean, not a mistake, but I think . . .' He watched me in silence. 'Sir, you must know we can't pay it. I came here to ask you to treat us fairly. The rent is five times what it was. You must know we can't pay.'

'Mr North, your finances are your own concern. I charge what I charge.'

'But you must know—'

'Look,' he said, lowering his voice and stepping closer to me. 'You are the boy who assaulted my son, aren't you? Answer me.'

'I didn't assault him,' I said. 'He was the one who started it; he said things about my family he had no right to say.'

'Listen to me very carefully,' he said. 'I want you off my property in the next five seconds.'

'I'm not on your property!' I said.

'You are on my steps. I have seen the bruises on my son's face, and I will be taking it up with the police.'

'Look at my tooth, then,' I said. 'Look what he did to me – it's much worse. And he said things about my father.'

'Oh, you people are all the same,' he said with a kind of exasperated smile.

'What people?' I said. 'What people are all the same?'

'Goodnight.' He slammed the door and drew the curtain across behind it.

'What people are all the same?' I said again. The door remained shut. No one in the house had heard. I sat down on the steps. I had not meant to say what I just had, at least not the way it came out. I had intended to reason with him, to apologize for giving John a black eye and make him see that it was not justice to raise our rent because of it. Pointless schemes drifted in and out of my mind. I thought about walking to the palace gates and telling the guards I was a relative of Aldebaran's and asking the king to help us. But the king's debts were worse than ours. Dr Keller's probably were, too, I thought. Half the wealthy in this city lived off money that was not theirs. And that made me think of Michael, because it was like something he would have said. I wondered if I really could go and find him when all this was over.

The thought passed and the snow fell harder. I got up and started down the steps.

As I went down, I heard voices laughing behind the yellow glow of the curtain. I stopped. 'Anselm Andros?' John Keller was saying and laughing as if his ribs would break. If I had not heard that, I might not have done what I did. It was a stupid thing to do; I knew it even at the time. I walked home and waited until everyone had gone to bed. Then I put on my overcoat and an old hat of Leo's and covered half my face with a black scarf my mother used to wear to church. I went back to Dr Keller's with a file and a crowbar. I dug the boot scraper out of the old concrete it stood in and prised the brass plaque with his name off the wall. It was not hard to do. Then I took them to the all-night pawnbroker's and sold them for scrap metal. Behind the curtain, they never stopped their laughing.

I had to pass by the auction rooms to go home, and I could hear shouting and stamping from an upstairs room. I stopped and listened. I thought I would go in for a while and listen to the trading, and maybe my heart would be less restless. I was already regretting what I had just done. The clocks were striking ten, but what sounded like a packed auction was taking place inside.

I went in. The building had a dingy stairwell with barred windows, and when no one lit the lamps, it was impossible to find your way up without stumbling. But I made out a square of light around the third door at last. I opened it and went inside. The room was crowded. People sat in front of the walls on benches and old crates and stood packed in the centre. There were rifles everywhere and blue flags hanging from the ceiling. At the front, under a guttering gaslight, a man was shouting from the stage. I saw all this before I realized that it wasn't an auction. Then it was too late; they had shut the door behind me. 'That's right!' shouted the man on the stage. 'Come in, come in.'

Suddenly all the eyes in the room were on me. He regarded me for a moment, then resumed his shouting. 'The Imperial Order are coming,' he said. 'And when they do, those with loyalty will be rewarded. There is a reason why our nation is poor. It is not because of Lucien's government. It's because of the king and his followers. The Alcyrian government knows this!'

I had frozen when the crowd was watching me, but now their eyes were fixed on the stage again. There were some hoarse shouts that might have been approval or disagreement. Under the harsh light, I could see the sweat rolling down the sides of the man's face, like some picture of a martyr. 'That's right,' he said, licking his lips and glancing around at us all. 'That's right – the Alcyrian government continue to demand reparations from the king, not because they want to steal our wealth but because they want to redistribute it.'

I did not understand this theory, but it seemed to grip the crowd like an infectious disease. After each sentence, the cheers grew stronger. They made the lamps shiver in the ceiling and rattled the blacked-out windows. 'Redistribution,' shouted the man. 'It has already begun, and I encourage you to further it. But when the Alcyrians come, they will help us. They want to take back what belongs to the true nation. They want to take it from the Unacceptables, the priests, the foreigners, the homosexuals, and when they come, they will give it to those who deserve it.'

There was an outbreak of cheering so loud it made me shiver. People glanced at me because I was not clapping. But that cheering had brought me back to my senses. I turned and pushed through the crowd, not slowing when people elbowed me, until I reached the door. 'Leaving, are you?' shouted the man from the stage. 'Stay and hear the next speech at least.'

I went out and closed the door behind me. Leaving took all the courage left in me, but I had no choice. I knew that if I had stayed, I could never have spoken to Michael again.

Fear overtook me after that brief act of defiance, and I ran down the steps and out into the dark. As I turned down an alleyway, someone caught me by the shoulder. 'Anselm,' he hissed. 'What were you doing at an Imperial Order rally?'

For a crazy moment – I don't know why – I thought it was Leo. But I turned and saw Jared Wright there instead. 'Jared?' I said blankly. The cigarette smoke was different; I should have known.

'I wasn't at an Imperial Order rally,' I said.

'You just came out of one.'

'No, I didn't. It was a mistake.'

He raised one eyebrow.

'I didn't mean to go to it,' I said. 'I thought it was an

auction, so I went up. I came straight back down again when I saw.'

He looked at me for a moment, taking in the hat and the black scarf and the raised collar of my overcoat.

'Honestly,' I said. 'I know it doesn't look like it, but I went by mistake.'

He hesitated, then threw his head back and laughed so hard his gold teeth flashed. 'My God, Anselm,' he said when he had finished. 'You really did think it was an auction.'

I waited while he continued laughing and stamped the snow off his shoes. 'Come on,' he said. 'I'll take you home.'

'I don't need taking home, sir.'

'Come on, I'm going that way anyway.'

We walked without speaking for several streets. The stars had come out overhead. I made out the one Leo had shown me – the orange star in the sign of the bull that was supposed to be Aldebaran. Or perhaps I had mistaken it. It was shining very brightly tonight, like a fire far off on a hill. Jared might have noticed it too, because he glanced up, then said, 'I don't suppose Maria has told you to avoid me?'

'No,' I said.

He grinned as though he did not believe it. But his face grew serious again. 'So what did you think?' he said.

'Of what?'

'The rally.'

I shook my head. 'It doesn't make sense.'

'They are not sane,' he said. 'The whole lot of them are not sane. It worries me, and I don't mind telling you. I've pledged half a million crowns to the government. Not that I support the king, but his advisers are better than these maniacs.'

I stopped and looked at him. It was not his political

views that startled me, but the casual way in which he had disposed of half a million crowns. 'Are you such a rich man, sir?' I said.

He raised one eyebrow. It was a look I was coming to know well. We walked on past an inn that was closing up and through a square where the snow drifted over the ground. 'How is your mother?' said Jared.

'Not well,' I said. 'Not at the moment.'

'I'm sorry to hear it,' he said. 'She is not in danger?'

'I don't know.'

'I haven't seen your stepfather about either.'

'No,' I said.

'He must be one of the famous Norths,' Jared said. 'I know it, whatever you say. I envy him, you know. People would pay for anything Aldebaran left, and I'll bet good money there was a last prophecy. I would pay thousands for that, really I would – so would half the political men in this city. Was there one, do you know?'

I shook my head. 'Ah!' said Jared, delighted with his cunning. 'So your stepfather is one of the Norths, then? You admit that much.'

'His surname is North,' I said. 'That's all. And, sir . . .'

'Yes.'

'Why do you call him my stepfather?'

'Well, he is, isn't he? What else do you want me to call him?'

I started to speak, and so did Jared, but neither of us finished. We were on the corner of Trader's Row. I wanted to ask him how he knew that and what he knew of my real father. But I could not do it. I had promised my mother not to even see him again. I knew it was superstitious, but with her lying so sick inside the house, I could not bring myself to disobey her. 'I should go inside,' I said.

'Anselm?' he said. 'Come and see me again.'

There was something significant in the way he said it that made it into more than a careless invitation. 'No,' I said. 'No, I don't think I can.'

'Why not?'

'I can't tell you. I just don't think I can.'

'But that is absurd,' he said.

'Maybe. I'm sorry, but I can't.'

I turned and walked away before I could lose my resolution.

As I drew close to our shop, someone shone a lamp into my face. 'Where are you going?' he said. There were two police officers in front of me, pistols in their hands. I had not even seen them approach, and for a second I had thought it was the Imperial Order.

'Home,' I said, stepping back against the window.

'Where have you been?'

'Nowhere. Just walking in the city.'

'Please raise your hands.'

I did it. My heart thumped sickly in my throat. The officers proceeded to search me, taking everything out of my pockets. Scraps of paper from school; a broken dial from an oil lamp, which they studied for several seconds; two or three coins. 'Can I go on?' I said.

'Yes,' one of them said as though granting a great favour. 'Yes, very well.'

I went round checking the bolts several times once I was inside the shop. The city outside seemed against us, and the few locks on the doors were no protection at all. I went up the stairs and closed the living-room door and locked that too. I was still breathing fast from the encounter with the police. I could not help connecting them with Dr Keller or the Imperial Order. After I went to bed, my bones ached with cold. I lay staring up at the ceiling, and dismal thoughts came to me, and I could not stop them. My tooth was still throbbing. It had already become part of my life, as if it had always been broken. I could not stop thinking, so I got up and spread out those papers Leo had left, then lit the lamp. I did not believe they would solve anything, but it was something to draw my mind away from the real world. When I was a young boy and real life was hard to fathom, I always used to turn to England. I surrendered to it now.

Ashley fell asleep on the underground on the way home. He woke as the train shuddered, drawing up at a station, and met the eyes of an old man. He was very thin, with a face like a skull, sitting in the last seat at the end of the carriage. His grey eyes trapped the passing lights. Ashley did not know where he was going, and his head ached. He stood up and made out the name of the station; it was far beyond the one where he had meant to change. He would have to get out at the next stop and walk.

Two women in suits left the carriage, and as the train drew away, they vanished down a lighted tunnel. Ashley sat down and rested his sketchbook against his knees. The carriage was almost empty now.

'It is quiet this evening,' remarked the old man.

Ashley nodded. It was the first time anyone had spoken to him on the underground in the nine years of his life here.

'I am going to the end of the line,' said the old man. 'Can you tell me, please, how much longer it will take?'

'About half an hour.'

'Thank you,' said the old man, and gave a gruff nod.

Ashley lowered his eyes and studied the man's face, pretending all the time to read the cover of his sketchbook. The old man reminded him of the Rolls-Royce Anna had sold, and their old life in the country, and an age that was already gone. The silence drew out. A cold voice announced another station. 'Are you an artist?' said the old man, nodding towards the sketchbook.

'Not really.'

'I wonder,' he said, 'may I possibly see that book?'

Ashley grinned suddenly; he could not help it. It was the way the man had asked. 'Here,' he said, and handed the book to him. The man turned over the pages carefully.

'This one is very good,' he said, pausing on a portrait of Anna.

'I got the light wrong,' said Ashley. 'It looks like she's in the dark, and you can't see her face.'

'It's a problem of tone,' said the old man. 'Not enough contrast in the work.'

Ashley did not know what to say. A wild thought drifted through his head that perhaps this man was a great artist and would take him away from everything and teach him to draw like a master. It was a childhood wish that he had tried to forget. But the old man only closed the book. 'I know nothing about these things,' he said. 'But I have a good friend who draws. Tell me, do you ever sell your work?'

'I draw portraits for tourists sometimes, in Covent Garden.' The man's accent made him add, 'If you know it?'

'Oh yes,' said the old man. 'Yes, I know Covent Garden. Such strange names your places have.'

'I think so too,' said Ashley. 'I mean, I've always thought so.'

But there had been nothing significant about the remark.

The old man was already thinking of something else. He laid the sketchbook down on the seat beside Ashley. 'Do you make much money from it?' he said. 'Drawing tourists' portraits?'

'I make some.'

'And what do you do with it?'

'I'm saving it.'

'For what?'

Ashley hesitated, then gave him the truthful answer. 'To go to Australia. To see my father.'

'Your father is Australian?' said the old man. 'You must miss him, if he is so far away.'

'No, he's a bastard. I'm going to Australia to tell him so.'

The train gained speed with a low metallic whine. And Ashley, for no reason he could explain, began to feel frightened. The old man was watching him as if he was reading his soul. Ashley hoped he would say something else, but he didn't. He held out for two stations, then got up and stepped down onto the platform.

'Wait,' said the old man. But the doors were already closing. Through the glass, the old man was mouthing something, like a fish in a jar, but the train was moving now. Then, when Ashley looked back, the man was no longer there.

He was at a different station to the one he expected, and the clock stood at a different time. Ashley did not know what had happened. Fear gripped him, and he turned and walked faster and faster, along the lighted tunnels, up through the hot draughts of the escalator, and out into the night. The train was far gone now, and Ashley listened for the next one to tremble under the paving stones. But no more came. It was late, and that had probably been the last.

Ashley ran his hands over his face and tried to come back to the real world. A light rain had fallen, and the pavement glistened blackly. He was stranded in some high-class area he did not recognize. The white houses stood in a stupor around fenced gardens. He climbed over one of the fences and crossed the immaculate grass, for no reason at all, then swung around a lamppost and decided he was going in the wrong direction. That strange dream had set his heart out of joint, and he wished he was back home. He thought that he would ask someone where he was at the next shop he came to. But there were no shops here.

For a while, he pretended to navigate by the stars. It was a kind of game he played. He stopped on each street corner and looked upwards for a moment, then turned left or right. Eventually he decided he was lost. He sat down on the steps of a white house and considered the situation.

A silvery clock somewhere chimed eleven. Ashley stared around at the unfamiliar square. It was while he was looking round that he remembered the old maps he used to draw. Somewhere in his memory, this square must exist. He frowned and tried to fix his mind on it, and after a while, the lines of the streets became clear. He knew the accuracy of his memory was not natural, and sometimes it still startled him. He could recall anything, once he remembered that he knew it. The plan of the streets came into his mind now. Right, and then left. He got up and went on.

Ashley had been walking for several minutes when a car parked ahead made him slow his pace. It was a Rolls-Royce, gleaming with polish, an old model that looked out of date in this high-class street. The same model that Anna used to drive. Ashley stepped down into the road and walked around the car, then reached out and touched the passenger door. His fingers remembered opening it a thousand times, when they were still too small to grip the handle. It was the same car. He was certain of it. The number-plate was different, but the car was the same. He ran his fingers over the roof and found the trace of the dent that had once been there.

Ashley glanced up at the house, but the building was in darkness. No lights showed around the curtains, and though a burglar alarm flashed on the front wall, it was clear there was no one inside. He turned back to the car again and looked in through the windows. He had never known who Anna sold the Rolls-Royce to; he had been too young. But he was certain this was the same car. It was like a miracle – that strange dream, and then getting off at the wrong stop, and now here was the old car in front of him.

'Excuse me,' said someone quietly from the shadows. 'Is that your car?'

Ashley looked up, but it was too dark to make out the figure. A man dressed in black. 'I'm just looking at it,' said Ashley, and made to go on.

'Stay where you are,' said the man, and came out of the shadows.

Richard woke suddenly to find Aldebaran sitting in the corner of the room. He was not a ghost; there was nothing ghostlike about him. He was sitting on the chair with the worn-through foam seat, watching a train go past. 'Teacher!' said Richard, fear and sleep constricting his voice.

'Rigel,' said Aldebaran. 'I have been waiting for you.'

'I thought . . .' said Richard. 'I thought . . .'

Aldebaran came forward and extended his hand. Richard took it. It was as solid as his own. 'Aldebaran,' he said.

'We had an agreement once,' said Aldebaran. 'You were going to come here and find the people with powers. You were going to send me word.'

'I know,' said Richard. 'I know.'

'Don't look so sad,' said Aldebaran. 'I thought I would never hear from you again when I watched you go away from me that night. I think I always knew.'

'It was for Juliette,' said Richard. 'I thought I would die if anything happened to her. Teacher, maybe I've been stupid, but it was always for her.'

'Your daughter is a remarkable girl,' said Aldebaran.

'Yes,' said Richard.

He let Aldebaran's hand go. His old teacher had aged in the ten years that had passed. The moonlight rested in every line in his face. 'Teacher,' said Richard. 'Are you—'

'I am not going back home,' said Aldebaran. 'No.'

Richard had been going to ask something else. 'Why are you here?' he said instead.

'I need your help,' said Aldebaran. 'You won't refuse it.'

Richard hesitated, then shook his head.

'Magic is dying,' said Aldebaran. 'But there are still those with powers. Still a few of them. You are the first, Rigel. The second is Anna Devere. The third is your daughter, and the fourth is the king's son.'

'The king's son?' said Richard. 'What king's son?'

'No one knows about him,' said Aldebaran. 'Only Ryan and I know.'

'So why are you telling me?'

'The fact is, Ryan may not have long either, because

there are people who dislike him. Someone else has to know. His name is Ashley Devere, and he is here in England.'

'The king's son?' said Richard again.

'Yes. And there is one more person with powers left – at least, the only one who will ever be a true great one.'

'Who is that?' said Richard, still half certain he was dreaming.

'The only one still in the old country. My successor.'

Richard reached out towards Aldebaran, because he seemed to be growing fainter. 'Help him,' said Aldebaran. 'Help my successor. That's what I want you to do now.'

Richard woke up, and the window was open, blowing a gale into the room. People were arguing in the room next door, and a train was rattling past. And Aldebaran was nowhere. 'Juliette?' he said, a strange kind of fear gripping his heart. 'Juliette.'

He got up and went to the next room and tapped on the door. There was no answer, but the door was open when he tried it. Juliette was not there.

Juliette knew nothing of Aldebaran or her father's dream. She was sick of the hotel with its grey walls and of her father's silences, and she was sick of being followed everywhere she went by James Salmon. So she opened the window of her room and climbed out.

It was three floors to the ground, and Juliette climbed down by willpower alone. Every time she felt herself slipping, she fixed her eyes on the stars above and refused to fall. She reached the ground without injury, pulled her coat tighter around her, and started walking back to the old house. She had no fixed plan in her mind, only to get away.

It was a longer walk than she had thought, and by the

time she reached the square, the clocks were chiming eleven. She stopped on the corner and leaned against the railings of a house to catch her breath. While she was doing that, she heard voices. A man in black clothes was talking to a boy beside her father's Rolls-Royce. Juliette edged closer and listened.

'I'm just looking at it,' the boy was saying.

'Tell me who this car belongs to.'

'I don't know.'

'Tell me—'

'Honestly, I don't know!'

The boy's voice had risen. The stranger had pulled out a gun. 'Where have you been tonight?' he demanded.

'In Covent Garden.'

'Why?'

'Drawing portraits for money. It's where I always go. Put that gun down, please. I don't see what I've done wrong.'

Juliette hesitated, then stepped forward. Both of them turned to her. The man regarded her for several seconds, then turned and marched away. The boy was standing with his hands raised and a mutinous expression on his face. He had black hair cut short, a jewel in his left ear, and very black eyes. 'Are you all right?' said Juliette, breathing fast because of the long walk and the gun.

The boy made no answer. He just turned and walked away along a side street. Once he was halfway down the street, he broke into a run and did not stop when she called after him. As he turned the corner, something fell from under his arm. It was some kind of book. Juliette started after him, but already he was gone, leaving the book behind him.

Juliette went to the corner and picked it up. The pages fell open. Sketches came to life in front of her eyes: perfect portraits and detailed buildings and rain-blackened London parks with the lights of cars passing. But there was more than that within these pages, Juliette thought. She studied the portrait of a restless man in a shiny black suit and knew about him suddenly. She knew that he had a wife and a small child and lived in a tower somewhere and that he wanted more than anything to be a musician and leave the city.

On the book's cover was a name and address. 'Ashley Devere, 12C Forest Park Mansions'. Juliette hesitated, then put the book inside her jacket to keep it out of the rain. It had come down suddenly while she was studying those pictures. Now she came back to the real world, and fear of the night gripped her. She turned and ran.

Anna was mopping the floor of the hotel entrance hall when a man brushed lightly past her. She turned and looked. He was thin, with a face like a skull, and it made the blood stand still in her veins. She was sure she knew him. 'Arthur?' she said. 'Arthur Field, is it you?'

The man did not hear. He went on past her, out into the rain. And when she went after him, he was just a stranger, an old man who must have come to enquire about a room. He was not Arthur Field at all.

'Excuse me?' someone was calling urgently when she returned to the hotel. 'Excuse me.'

It was the man staying on the third floor. He was standing at the reception desk, looking about anxiously.

'Yes, can I help you?' she said.

'Have you seen my daughter? The blonde girl, about so tall. She's gone out without telling me.'

'She didn't pass this way,' said Anna. 'I've been here more than an hour.'

He was a tall man, with a scar across his cheek and an expensive suit. He marched about the entrance hall, then picked up the pen from the reception desk and set it down again with an exasperated sigh. Anna went on mopping the floor. The man's daughter returned not long after, wet through and out of breath from running, and an argument broke out between them. When Anna thought of Arthur Field again, after the man and his daughter had gone back upstairs and left the entrance hall in silence, she thought she had been stupid to mistake that man for him. Her great-uncle could not be still living, in that country he came from. He must be long gone by now. And yet things changed for her after that night. Things changed for all of them.

In the nights that followed, I began to dream about my real father. Sometimes I was kneeling at his grave, and I tried to make out the letters on the stone, but they shrank as I studied them or became a different language or were lost in the dark. Sometimes he was standing over my shoulder, and I could feel his breath cold on my neck. I would turn, too late to see him as he vanished, the breath becoming no more than a draught around the window. I went on dreaming even after my mother recovered. The midwife would not let her go back to work, but she sat in the shop instead. None of us could stop her. My grandmother cooked richer and richer meals every evening, adding expensive cream and lard to the stews in an effort to fatten up the baby. It only succeeded in taking away my mother's appetite altogether.

Then, in the last week of November, a letter arrived in Michael's writing. Jasmine came running up the stairs and shoved it into my hand, saying, 'Open it, Anselm! Open it!'

I did not know, until I had that letter in my hand, how heavily the anxiety had been weighing on my heart. I could not open it. I just stood and stared at the envelope until Jasmine snatched it from me. 'Hey, Jasmine!' I said, and took the letter back and opened it. 'Anselm,' it read. 'My parents are in the south of the country. I have gone north. I can't say anything else. I'll try to send word to you. Michael.'

'What does that mean?' said Jasmine.

I did not know. But at least it was something. I checked the postmark – he had sent it four days ago. I read it several times and put it in the inside pocket of my jacket. Four days ago, Michael had been safe. All through school, the corner of the envelope rested against my chest, along with those papers of Leo's that were in my jacket pocket. It was a good sign, in spite of everything. In spite of the fact that Dr Keller had ordered us to leave the shop by today, and we did not have the rent he had demanded. I still had not told the others about his letter. I was praying that some chance would come to save me, though I didn't know how.

'Anselm?' said Jasmine that evening. 'People sometimes die, don't they, when they have a baby?'

'Not often,' I said. 'Jasmine, what has brought this on?'

She wandered away across the room. I watched her go. We were down in the shop. I was trying to sort through the mess in an attempt to find something that might sell in the markets. I had thought about parting with one of the things Aldebaran had given us, after Jared Wright talked about it. I had even taken my medallion to the pawnbroker's to ask. But the woman there flatly refused to believe it was his. And so far, our searches in the shop had unearthed nothing of any value.

'Not often,' I said again. 'Hey, Jas? Don't worry.'

She gave me a weak smile.

'Mother is better from her fever,' I said. 'And the mid-wife says the baby is still all right.'

'How often do they die?'

'Hardly ever.'

'If a hundred women had a baby, how many would die?'

'I don't know. Less than one.'

'Less than one is one,' said Jasmine.

'No, it's not. It's not the same. It means if two hundred women—'

'Oh, shut your mouth, Anselm!' she said. 'There's still a chance, isn't there?'

I could not blame her. We were all worried, and my own replies sounded heartless and inadequate.

'What if Mama dies?' said Jasmine, half crying now. 'Papa has already gone. Then we'd just be left here, us two and Grandmama.'

'It's not going to happen,' I said. 'She's better, and the midwife is looking after her now.'

'If we don't have enough money, will the midwife stop coming? Grandmama said—'

'Don't listen to Grandmama.'

But I could not help asking, in the silence that followed, 'What did she say?'

Jasmine brushed away a tear and sniffed. 'She said she didn't know how we would find the money to pay for the midwife, and if we didn't, she would stop coming, without any doubt.'

'It will be all right,' I said. 'She won't give up on us just like that.'

'And Mama said we hadn't paid the rent,' said Jasmine. 'She was worried about it.'

'We'll pay the rent,' I told Jasmine. 'You'll see.'

'How?'

'I have a plan.'

'What is it?' said Jasmine.

'It's a very good plan, only I can't tell you about it, because I haven't completely worked it out yet. Not completely. But you'll see.'

'Really?'

'Yes.'

Jasmine watched me for a moment. Then she sighed and raised her eyes to heaven before trailing upstairs, leaving me alone in the shop. There was no point in lying to her, though we all still tried it. She always knew.

'Jasmine,' said my mother that Sunday evening. 'Get out the Advent lantern.'

Jasmine ran to the cupboard to get out the lantern we had been saving, then set it carefully on the table in the back room and lit it with Leo's matches. Last year came back to me clearly as she did it. Jasmine had climbed onto a chair to light the lantern, and Leo had put his arms around my mother's waist and kissed her hair, in one of his fits of light-heartedness. I saw that moment as clearly as if I had fallen back into the past to stand there again.

'Anselm?' said Jasmine. She was leaning with her head on the table, watching the flame. 'Anselm, by the time the candle burns down, what will happen to us all?'

'The baby will be nearly born,' I said. 'Or maybe born already.'

'And Papa will be back?'

'Come on, Jasmine,' said my mother. 'Five minutes and then it's time for bed.'

My mother slept early, but Jasmine was pacing about her room all evening; I could hear her light footsteps on the floorboards and her quick impatient sighs. She came trailing into my room at ten o'clock, demanding a story.

'Where is Mother?' I said.

'Asleep. And Grandmama is doing some important sewing and doesn't want to be disturbed.'

'A quick story, then,' I said. She climbed onto the end of my bed and pulled the covers over her. I had been studying the words Leo wrote, but I set the pages aside now and turned to her. 'What story shall I tell you?'

'One about us.'

'You mean our family?'

'Yes. Tell me about Mama and Papa and you and the places where you used to live, and about when I was born.'

'All right, I'll try.'

I made it into a fairy tale. There were all kinds of stories I could tell her about her own life, made fascinating by the fact that she no longer remembered them. Like how when she was four years old, she used to dream about Aldebaran, and the next day he would confirm every detail, the colour of the ink he had written in or the time he had lit the fire. And then I told her about the night that she called us to the window to look at angels over Malonia. Though they were just bedraggled geese flying south, we all saw them transfigured by her powers. 'I was silly then,' she said, laughing at that.

'It was only a few years ago. And you weren't silly.'

'I was small, so I didn't know any better. When you're small, having powers makes you see things differently.'

'How?' I said.

'Well, you see an old dead leaf, but you think it's maybe a bird. Or you see clouds, and you can read words in them. It's like' – she formed the word carefully – 'like imagination.'

'Well, that's the best part of the story,' I said. 'The part about you.'

'How does it end?' she said.

'The king wins the war,' I said. 'And the baby is born. And we are all back together again, on Holy Island.'

'Tell me about what it's like there,' she said.

I had only the few stories Aldebaran had told me. 'It never snows,' I said. 'And there are mountains, and cliffs, and long beaches running along the coast, where you can walk for miles. And no fighting.'

'I wish we were with Papa. Will we ever see him again?'

'Yes. Of course we will.'

'Anselm?' she said. 'Do you miss your real father? I mean, not Papa but the other man?' In the lamplight, her grey eyes were just like Leo's. 'Well?' she said. 'Do you?'

'How do you know about my real father?'

'Mama told me, ages ago. Anselm, do you miss him?'

'It's different. I never even met him.'

'But don't you ever think about him?'

'He never did anything for me. Not like Leo.'

'What is so good about Papa?' she said. 'He's gone away and left us.'

'It was not his fault. Jasmine, don't talk like that about him when . . .'

'When what?'

'Nothing.' I had been going to say, when anything might have happened to him. Because still he had not sent word.

'Tell me about your real father,' she said. 'Tell me the story.'

I started to say that I did not know it. But that was not true. I had the tale that I had made up when I was a little boy. 'All right,' I said. 'Listen carefully. This might not be exactly true, but it's a story.'

'No stories are exactly true,' she said.

'All right, so long as you remember that.'

She leaned on one arm, gazing up at me intently. 'Once there was a young man,' I said, 'who fell in love with a beautiful girl, Maria Andros. She was the daughter of the richest man in the country.'

'Is that part true?' Jasmine demanded. 'Our grandfather was the richest man in the country?'

'Yes,' I said. 'One of them anyway.'

'That man in the picture in Grandmama's house?'

'Yes. Julian Andros, the owner of Andros Associates, which was the main bank in the square before I was born.'

'What is it now?'

It was the question we always asked about this city; every building seemed to change hands so fast. 'Now?' I said. 'A pawnbroker's and a restaurant and a theatre that closed down. But it was a grand place back then. And Julian Andros was a man of some importance. He had two hundred people working for him. He had a white marble office in the heart of the building, where people came to talk to him about borrowing and lending money and putting all their fortunes into the vaults there. And he had a paperweight made out of melted-down gold coins, so heavy you could hardly lift it.'

'How do you know?' she said.

'Mother told me when I was a little boy.'

'Go on.'

The story was making my heart ache less badly – the story and Michael's letter in my pocket. 'Well, my real father was a soldier and a reckless man,' I said. 'He met Mother at a ball.'

'What was a soldier doing at a ball? That doesn't sound right.'

Jasmine was an expert on matters of court; I always forgot that when I made up stories for her. 'He had been given a lot of medals for bravery,' I said, and the story invented itself now without any effort. 'So he was invited because of that. But it is true – he felt out of place there. He did not know who to talk to. And then one girl, the beautiful Maria Andros, came over and spoke to him. He fell in love with her straight away; he did not even think about it. She loved him, too, and they used to meet often. At those balls, there were always people watching, so they used to pass notes to each other as they sat eating dinner or stood out on the terraces of the big houses. Then Maria learned that the soldier was going to be sent away.'

'What was the soldier's name?' asked Jasmine.

'Raphael,' I said.

'That's your middle name.'

'Yes.'

'So what happened?' she said, tracing the worn-out pattern in the blanket. 'Was he really sent away? Just like that, when they were in love?'

'He had to go. And what was worse, on the day before he left, they had a bad argument. Afterwards, Maria wanted to set things right. But she could not leave the house because . . .' I frowned. 'Because . . .'

'Was Grandmama stopping her?' Jasmine asked. 'I bet that was it.'

'Yes,' I said. 'That's right. Grandmama secretly didn't want them to be together, so she kept Maria inside until she knew the regiment had set off for the border. But what the soldier did not know was that Maria was going to have a baby.'

'Baby Anselm,' said Jasmine. 'You.'

The lamp guttered in invisible draughts. Jasmine drew the blanket closer around her.

'Maria kept trying to send word to the soldier,' I said. 'But Grandmama stopped her and took away the letters she wrote.'

'So did he ever get them?'

'Only after the baby was born. That was just before the revolution, and the soldiers could not leave the border. It meant desertion, and that was a very serious crime. But Raphael wanted to make amends and see his child. He put on his overcoat and boots and began to walk back to the city.'

'How far?' said Jasmine.

'Two hundred miles,' I said, though it was barely fifty.

'Did he walk all that way?'

I nodded. 'He got within sight of the city. He could even see the lights of Cliff House, where the beautiful Maria lived. Maybe he saw her crossing the window with the baby in her arms. But then fighting broke out close by. The soldier did not know what to do. A band of rebels had attacked a group of villagers, and if he did not go to help them, they might be badly hurt. He had to choose between saving them and going to see his child.'

'What did he do?' asked Jasmine in a whisper. The snow rattled the glass of the window and hissed in the dying fire in the living room. It was always snow these days. I was sick of the heavy sound of it as it threw itself against the walls.

'He went back,' I said. 'He helped the villagers. And he was shot, with a bullet through his heart. He never reached the city.'

Jasmine looked so downhearted that I wished I had made the story less melancholy. 'What did Maria do?' she asked.

'She mourned for him for a while,' I said. 'The soldier had left a great fortune for his son, buried out in the trenches at the Alcyrian border, and people went to search for it. But it was never discovered. And when Mr Andros suddenly lost his money a few weeks later, the family had to move to Citadel Street and forget about their rich life. But Maria never forgot that soldier. She gave the baby Raphael as his middle name. And moving to Citadel Street was not all bad, because there she met Leo. He took the baby as his own son and helped to bring him up. So neither of them lost everything.'

'Is that really what you believe?' said someone, and we both started. I turned round. My grandmother was standing in the doorway. 'Is that really what you believe about your real father?' she said again. And I saw suddenly that she was trembling with anger.

'It was just a story,' I said.

'Anselm, someone needs to put you right.'

She advanced towards us. Jasmine sat up and reached for my hand.

'I didn't mean anything by it,' I said.

'Oh, I don't suppose you did! Let me tell you, Maria was more than half to blame in the whole affair. Do you really think that was why we lost our money – by chance?'

'People rise and fall,' I said.

'Market traders rise and fall. Secondhand dealers rise and fall. Not bankers with millions of crowns to their name.' She stood there glaring and waited for me to say something.

'No,' I said. 'All right.'

'And you were not born in Cliff House,' she continued. 'You never saw it. You were born in a temporary apartment in Paradise Way with cockroaches running up and down the walls. Your father knew full well that you existed. If he hadn't, we might still be rich now.'

'I don't understand what I have to do with—'

'Why do you think we lost our money? Because Maria had the nerve to get involved with a powerful man and then refuse to marry him. Because you were born. He was Lucien's right-hand man, and we lost everything. Our house was seized, Anselm. Can you imagine? Soldiers marching in and taking everything we owned. I was a rich woman. Your grandfather was a man of importance. What do we have now? He was sent to the border, and he fell very sick, and now he's dead. His chest was never right after that spell out in the trenches. And I'm an old woman working at a market stall, and we can't afford a midwife for your mother's baby, and Leo has gone and left you all, as I always said he would—'

'Don't talk like that about him,' I said, rising to my feet. Jasmine did the same.

'Leo didn't think much of your real father either,' retorted my grandmother.

'What do you mean?' I said. 'They never met.' My grand-mother was nearly laughing now, or nearly crying, with a kind of wild fury. 'Who was he?' I said. 'Tell me his name.'

'De Fiore,' she said. 'Jean-Cristophe Ahira de Fiore.'

'I have never heard of—'

'Yes, you have,' she said shrilly. 'Yes, you have, Anselm. You know him as Ahira.'

We stared at each other. I could see her nostrils flare as she breathed and the tears of fury shining in her eyes.

'Who?' I said. She did not repeat it. 'You're lying,' I said.

'I am not lying. Why would I lie? She was a stupid, stupid girl, and she didn't know what she was doing. I wanted her to marry him, of course, but no one listened. Not even your grandfather. And here we are, Anselm. Here is what we have to show for it.' She gestured around the room. 'When you fall in the world, you never rise again. Never. Sixteen years of struggles – that's all I've had. Struggles and poverty and Julian dead and Maria lost to me. And look at you, Anselm. You are so like him. So much like him.'

'You're lying,' I said again.

'Ask your mother. Ask anyone who was in our circle at the time. They all knew – the Marlazzi family and the Wrights and the St John daughters, who were so close with Maria. No one said anything, but they all knew. I could tell by their glances and the gossip that went round. Is there any shame worse? I always said you should have been told, Anselm. Well, there!' She was still breathing fast. 'There! Now you have been. What do you think of that?'

I turned and started down the stairs. My hands were shaking, and I could not unlock the side door. 'No,' Jasmine said, starting to cry. 'Anselm, don't go away too.'

'I'm not going away,' I said.

'Don't leave! Please!'

I wrenched the door open and started across the frozen

yard. Halfway across, I collided with the remains of Jasmine's snow statue.

'Fine,' said my grandmother, a black figure in the doorway. 'Go running off as you always do. Anselm Andros, I sometimes think you know nothing about real life!'

'Don't go away, Anselm!' cried Jasmine.

I had not even taken my jacket. I ran anyway, out into the snow.

Jasmine tried to follow me at first, sniffing and stumbling after me across the yard. 'Go back!' I told her then, so fiercely that she obeyed. Ahira's face was everywhere, on the side of every shop, with his fist raised in defiance. How had I not realized it? A red-haired man with determined features. A man who looked like me.

Jared Wright's shop was in darkness, but he appeared at the door the third time I rang the bell, his shirt collar undone and his hair tousled. 'Anselm,' he said. 'It is past eleven.'

I said something that I can't remember now. He raised one eyebrow and stepped back to let me in. A woman was standing halfway down the stairs, drawing a shawl around her. 'Tomorrow, Estelle,' he said, and their hands closed on a few crown notes. She nodded and left. 'Well,' said Jared. He lit a cigarette and frowned at the smoke rising. 'What can I do for you?'

I stood there and could not say it.

'Well?' said Jared then.

I found my voice again, what was left of it. 'Was my real father Ahira?' I said. 'You know.'

Jared dropped his cigarette. It burned a black hole in the varnish of the table. 'My God,' he said. 'I thought you had been told.' He looked up when I did not answer. 'Everyone suspected it,' he said. 'At least, when your mother and I were young. It was the gossip of the whole city. How did she keep that from you? How the hell did she manage not to tell you . . .'

I walked to the table and back again. Then I opened my mouth to speak, but I could not do it.

'Sit down,' he said. 'Don't get so agitated.'

I sat, then stood up again. Jared's cigarette was burning deeper into the table; he rubbed at it distractedly.

'There aren't many people who know for sure,' he went on. 'Maria. Your stepfather, I would assume. Maria's parents. And me. I was Maria's closest friend at the time, or had been. I was working with Ahira in the government. I was his apprentice, I suppose – or would have been, if he had lived long enough. But we used to talk. My father was a great friend of his. Ahira confided in me.'

'Ahira,' I whispered, as if saying his name would make sense out of it.

'Yes,' said Jared. 'He was no prince; it is true.'

'I want to see his grave,' I said.

Jared breathed in carefully. 'He doesn't have a grave,' he said. 'Not a real one. They set up a memorial stone with the other war criminals.'

'But he must be somewhere,' I said. I felt suddenly that if I could find where he was, it might still be all right. There might be some kind of mistake.

'Some of his supporters fled north,' said Jared, 'and took Ahira's ashes with them. I think they were fleeing to the town where he was born. It's a few hundred miles; they were probably caught on the road.' He spread his hands helplessly. 'I'll take you to his memorial stone.'

I waited at the door while he fetched his overcoat and

boots. In the darkness, everything in the shop looked altered. The dark pictures towered oppressively from the ceiling.

'Haven't you even brought a coat?' he demanded, as if we were out on a day's excursion. He threw me a jacket of his own. 'We have a long way to go. The war criminals' graves were exhumed and taken beyond the graveyard.'

'Why?' I said.

'Why what? God, it's cold.' As he opened the door, a current of ice drove in at our faces. He lit another cigarette and led me out into the dark. 'Why were they taken away from the graveyard? Because it was a mistake to bury them alongside the dead resistance members. Everyone saw that as soon as they did it. There were incidents. Vandalisms and . . . robberies. Bones were taken.' He caught my glance. 'Ahira's stone is still intact. To a certain point. To tell the truth, I think no one dared.'

Jared went on talking as we set out through the dark city. I walked in silence beside him. Once, we glimpsed two police officers on the road ahead, and he pulled me into an alleyway. A few Imperial Order men ran past, but they ignored us. Eventually he fell into silence too, lighting and relighting his cigarette.

'He was misunderstood,' said Jared abruptly as we crossed the new bridge. 'You have to know that. He was uncompromising, and the government used him as a symbol. A symbol of fear – that's what he was. But, towards the end, he was very unhappy with the way things were going. Very unhappy. He was an idealist, you know. At least at the start.'

'My family lost everything,' I said. 'Because of him. Because of me. Is that the truth?'

'He wanted to make amends for it. He was shot before he could make things right.'

'But it was because of that, wasn't it?'

'Anselm, in his will, he left everything he owned to you – his house, his estate, the money he had, everything. A small fortune. He regretted what he did. Under a proper government, he would never have had the power to do it.'

A cat leaped from behind a grave and shot between us, its mangy fur on end against the cold. 'A small fortune he left to you,' said Jared, 'but the king came back, and the last wishes of a notorious war criminal were not respected. Those things were seized and redistributed. You know all this from your history books, don't you?'

I had read about it, but that was a story that had nothing to do with my own life. I had thought the re-distribution highly justified.

'He wrote you a letter,' said Jared. 'He asked me to give it to your mother.'

I could not ask the question, but my mouth formed the words. 'Did you?'

Jared ran his hands over his oiled hair. 'I feel guilty about this, to tell you the truth,' he said. 'I had to get out of the country. He wrote to you the day he was shot, the after-noon before he died. Naturally, that night was the start of the revolution, and things fell out hard for the rest of us directly after that.'

'But the letter—'

'I still have it,' he said. 'I will give it to you as soon as we get back. Anselm, it's been weighing on my mind these sixteen years. I should have passed it on years ago.'

We had left the graveyard now and were crossing the waste ground that edged the eastern hills. The king had begun some building project here and had given it up when it was still half finished. The lights of the Alcyrian army

burned along the horizon. 'We have a way to go yet,' said
Jared. 'Can you see?'

'Yes.'

'Your teeth are chattering.'

'I'm all right.'

Jared stopped to light another cigarette. 'This is not too
much?' he said.

I shook my head. He gave a strange kind of humourless
laugh. 'Anselm, I have wanted to speak about this for so
long,' he said. 'I can't tell you how long. So many years I
have kept silent. I wanted to find you again – it's half the
reason I came back. He haunts me, you know. I promised
him that I would give you the letter. And then for you to
come walking into the shop like that . . .' He shook his
head. 'I knew I had seen you before. It's your father. That's
who I've seen. It was like a sign. I'm not a superstitious
man, but that's how it was. I know Maria has probably not
told you the half of this. I want you to know the truth about
him.'

The wind blew cold over the eastern hills, driving the
snow at us like grit. 'What is the truth?' I said dully.

'He was misunderstood,' said Jared. 'He was part of the
de Fiore family, but there was some disagreement, and he
fell out with them when he was still a boy. He came here
with nothing, completely homeless. The king's government
failed him. The Kalitz family took him in. That was why his
allegiance fell where it did. And he was a brilliant man,
Anselm. Absolutely brilliant. He taught himself completely;
he was never at school. I think he genuinely believed in
change, you know. I was in it for the money – I won't deny
it. My father was a rich man and set me up in Lucien's
government, because it was a way of staying rich. But Ahira

had ideals. His family disowned him completely when he joined Lucien's government; he lost an absolute fortune in inheritance. I am not denying he grew unbalanced towards the end, but he had ideals.'

We had stopped walking now and stood there at the end of everything with the wind driving around us. I could tell by the tones of the darkness that we were between two hills. Jared lit a match, and a fence rose in front of us; then the dark snatched the light away. He stumbled through the snow along the side of it, cursing, and after a long search found the gate. 'Come on,' he said.

I followed him. We were surrounded by graves. Stones dug into the soles of my boots under the snow. 'Where are we?' I said.

'Devil's Cross,' said Jared. 'It's just a crossroads in the middle of nowhere. Go that way and you'll drown in marshes; over that way, the soil is so bad it poisons every plant that tries to grow. Even the cattle sicken and die.' With the snow and the dark, I could not see where he was pointing. 'It's where the notorious were always buried,' he said. 'In true archaic fashion. Come here.' He was kneeling in front of a grave, brushing the snow from the weathered stone. 'There,' he said. 'You can just make it out.' I saw him trace something, pronouncing the name as he did it. 'Jean-Cristophe Ahira de Fiore. It's just a marker – there is no one buried here.'

The wind wailed like a lost child, the way Jasmine cried when she dreamed of terrors in her sleep.

'He had his full name on his grave,' said Jared. 'He asked me to tell them to put that. Perhaps he had a change of heart towards his family, at the end. Perhaps he had a change of heart towards Ahira and all that name stood for. Because he did change, Anselm. No one knows what was in his mind that last night of his life, but he did change. He was the one—'

'The one who shot Lucien,' I said.

Jared looked up at me sharply. 'How do you know that?' he demanded.

I could not recall at first. Then I remembered it. Years ago, when I was still a young boy and my history books were full of bitterness directed against that man, Aldebaran had told me.

I fell to my knees in the snow. I could not read the letters, so I reached out and touched the stone instead. It was a plain cross, smashed in several places so that the letters were disconnected. Someone had scrawled words on it in black. 'What does that say?' I whispered. My voice came out hoarse.

'Here,' said Jared, lighting a match and shielding it in his cupped hands. It burned just long enough to let me read: I HOPE ALL YOUR DESCENDANTS FOLLOW YOU TO HELL was on one side and MARTYRED FOR HIS BELIEF IN FREEDOM was on the other. And between them were the carved words JEAN-CRISTOPHE AHIRA DE FIORE and the dates.

'He was a very clever man,' said Jared. 'The clever are often misunderstood. The clever are often very unhappy. I was never an intelligent man, and I thank God for it. They destroy themselves from the inside, those people, and no one ever really knows what they are thinking; no one can ever really make them out. I don't think he believed in Lucien's government any more. When he wrote to you, I don't think he believed in it.'

'But he was the worst of them all.'

'Was he? He was cleverer than the others. Does that make him worse?'

I brushed the falling snow from the grave but more fell. 'Ahira believed that you had to compromise to get anywhere,' said Jared. 'I am not denying that some of his measures seemed extreme. But I think he was constrained by a system that had lost all its ideals. Does that make sense to you?'

I got to my feet. I did not know the way out, but I turned anyway and began struggling through the snow. I collided with the fence, and then I was throwing myself against it, like I was in prison and trying to break free. Every time I did it, the whole world lost its bearings.

'Hey, hey,' said Jared then, catching hold of my arms. I broke away from him and set out into the darkness. 'Anselm!' he said. 'Stop. Careful, for God's sake. The city is that way.'

I turned and saw the lights.

'All right,' he said. 'It is bound to be a shock. All right.'

He steered me out of the gate, then made me sit down in the snow at the side of the road and took out a flask of spirits. 'Here,' he said, tipping some into my mouth. He thumped my shoulder and made me cough. 'Come on, Anselm,' he said. 'At least he was not no one at all. He was an important man. He came from a noble family. He has been misunderstood, it's true, but . . .'

He went on, but I did not hear him. I felt the burning cold of the snow around me without caring. It was as if my life had stopped being real any more, as if its connection to the world was shaken and might drift free altogether. The dark was more than infinity around us. I had not understood until then what it was like to feel nothing. Here it was, the truth that I had wanted ever since I realized my grandmother half hated me. And now I didn't know what to do with it.

★ ★ ★

Jared must have taken me back to his shop, but I remember nothing of the journey. The next thing I knew, we were in the back room, and he was pushing a cup of hot tea towards me, because I was still shivering with cold. I glanced into the gilded mirror that was propped against the wall. My face looked back, so altered in this knowledge that I would hardly have recognized it. I had Ahira's red hair and his definite eyebrows; even the bones under my skin were set out the same as his, on some invisible pattern that ran in my blood. Whatever I had expected to find out about my real father, it was not this.

'Listen,' said Jared. 'I was the one he confided in, and I know he was not a bad man. Not at heart. He had been discontented with Lucien's government for a long time. He was looking for a way to get out. He visited the Alcyrian border and saw the terrible conditions there, and he began trying to find a way of getting out of that war. But you can't break free of a prison like that without leaving damage behind you. The fact is, he acted one way and thought another for a long time before he found his chance.'

I tried to remember the dates on his grave. 'How old was he?' I said eventually.

'Thirty-five when he died. About.'

It was older than my mother was now. Jared got up and began polishing the mirror, avoiding my glance.

'That letter . . .' I said.

He disappeared up the stairs. I wandered about the shop in the darkness. My thoughts could not settle, and walking about was better, because I did not have to listen to the silence.

'Here,' said Jared then, putting an envelope into my

hand. It was fastened with a blue seal, and the paper was brittle and lifeless with age. 'I have not read it,' he said. 'I have been carrying it about the continent with me for sixteen years. I wanted to give it to you when I first realized who you were. It was why I came to your house. I wanted to ask Maria first, but I kept losing my courage. I know you think I am a man without scruples. But there, I have kept my word, and I hope it helps you.'

I took it from him.

'You know,' he said quietly as I turned to leave. 'I wish I could tell you better. I wish I could explain those days, just after the Liberation, when families like mine were the kings of the world. We thought everything was going to change for the better. We thought we could make it change. You know?' He broke off and ground his cigarette on the side of the door frame.

I turned and walked away into the snow.

They were all awake when I got back, even my mother. 'Where have you been?' demanded my grandmother, marching over. 'You have kept us all awake with worrying. Have you been drinking, Anselm? I can smell the spirits on you. For heaven's sake, you are as bad as Leo.'

'Anselm?' said Jasmine, reaching up to take my hand. 'Anselm, what's the matter?'

My mother watched me in silence. I could not meet her eyes, and it seemed the longest journey to my bedroom door. I shut it behind me, bolted it, and lit the lamp. My hands looked strange in that light, like someone else's. They were arguing, my grandmother and my mother. I made out phrases through the door: 'completely out of control' and 'just stop lecturing' and 'needs a firm talking-to.'

I took out the envelope. The words were written in a scrawling hand: 'Anselm Raphael Andros'.

He had known my middle name. Hardly anyone knew it, but my father had taken the trouble to find it out. I broke the seal carefully and opened it. There was a single sheet inside, the writing so scrawled and shaking that I could hardly read it. I stood in the lamplight and held the letter out in front of me. It was my last hope of redemption, this letter. I didn't know how, but I prayed it would somehow make everything all right.

My son.

> *I see such visions. In the dark outside the window, I can hear them accusing me, & I do not have much time. I want you to know that I am sorry. For the actions I have done in the name of this government & for the wrongs I did your mother. I will be dead by the time you read these words. Anselm, I would have loved you, if I had seen you. I would have tried to make amends. For all it is worth, I loved her. She was so beautiful & so kind and young, Anselm, & I was sick with everything & had no one I could trust. I had just come back from the Alcyrian border that night. My God, if you had seen it. I was supposed to be holding a party. I came in covered in mud and sweat, & the guests were already arriving. My heart was so sick with everything. I cannot explain it. Anselm, my life was burned out far too young. I had done so many bad things that I was already damned. I drank very heavily in those days, & perhaps my judgement was not what it could have been. In my defence, I thought she loved me or that perhaps she would come to. I see such visions. I am afraid for your safety. I am most heartily sorry for what I did. I want you to grow up in peace. I want you to be a better man than*

me. I ask one thing of you. It is my only request. Anselm, never forgive me. I want to die condemned, and stand condemned for ever.

Two more lines followed, written so shakily that I could not make them out. He had not even signed his name. I dropped the letter and sank to my knees on the floor, biting my fist to stop myself from crying. Something about that paper brought the man back to me the way none of Jared's stories could. I could tell they were all in the living room listening. I closed my eyes and tried to breathe in and then out again, but my chest was aching so badly that I could not. I picked up the letter instead and stared at the words again. And I realized suddenly that my life was not a story that I could somehow make all right. This was the truth, however strange and tragic, and it would never go away. This was all I had, this yellowing scrap of paper with a few sentences that were nothing like an explanation.

I don't know what I had expected. But not this rushed note, with almost every *and* written with a sign, as though he was sending me his week's news. It read as though he was not sane. Or had too little time to explain anything. And suddenly what he had done came over me like a storm. I had told and retold his story, and my mother's and Leo's and my own. I had told them as if the telling made them somehow true. But the truth exists of its own accord, whether you know it or not.

I could see my mother, a fourteen-year-old who knew too little about love, dancing at some party in new heeled shoes. And this man, thirty-four years old, who was captivated by her beauty because he had seen too much of death and violence and felt suddenly too old. Perhaps he felt contaminated by his life, and he was looking for purity. Perhaps he was just drunk and used to getting his own way. I did not want to think about it.

Jasmine was saying something tearfully in the next room. I covered my face with my hands and tried to breathe. The alcohol and the cold and the shock were clouding my brain so that I felt nothing properly.

My mother was terrified of this man and had refused to marry him. And this man, who had power over heaven and earth, had the whole Andros family brought down to nothing.

'You wanted an epic story,' said my own voice in my head. 'You wanted to be at the heart of a clash between noble dynasties. This was what you always wanted. To be the son of a famous man.'

My mother left her great house, and my grandfather was sent to the border. I could see the two of them – my mother and my grandmother – arguing mutedly as they packed up their few belongings. It was the way they would argue for the rest of their lives, never saying what had to be said and always divided from each other. And months passed, and I could see my mother in some apartment with cockroaches and peeling walls, fifteen years old with a baby she never asked for, and that baby, that mistake in all their lives, was me.

I read the letter over and over until the words no longer made sense to me, until every sentence was cut into my memory. Then I lay down and stared up at the ceiling and tried to forget. But I did not. Instead, I thought of Leo. He had shot a man, he had told me. And Ahira had died outside our old front door, and no one knew who had killed him. And the price on Leo's head was the price of a resistance leader. It was thousands and thousands of crowns.

If there was anything that could make the truth about Ahira worse, it was this. It was suspecting that the one I loved, the one who was my true father, had fired the shot that killed the man whose face was mine.

'Anselm,' Jasmine whispered. It was past two o'clock. The whole building was in darkness. My own lamp had gone out. I went to the door and unbolted it. She was standing there wrapped in a blanket. 'Anselm, I was worried about you,' she whispered. 'Grandmama made me go to bed, but I couldn't sleep.'

It was only when she reached up to brush the tears from my face that I realized I was crying. 'Don't be sad, Anselm,' she whispered. 'It's going to be all right.'

I went on crying.

'Shh, Anselm,' she said. 'It's all right; it's all right. Papa is going to come back, and then we'll all go to Holy Island and have a good life there. And be happy. Honestly, we will. So don't cry. It seems bad now, but there will be a happy ending. You know that.'

She probably had no idea what I was crying about, but she was young enough to have the wisdom not to question it. We sat there side by side, alone in the dark and the cold, and I cried and she tried to comfort me. I felt far away from everything. It was too difficult to understand, so I just drifted away from the world. It was still going on – my mother was still sick, Leo was still gone, my grandmother nagged, and Jasmine marched about pretending to be a great actress. But I had fallen out of it, like a drowning man going under, and no one had noticed me surrender.

'Jasmine,' I whispered. 'I am so afraid that I will turn out to be a bad man.'

'No,' she said. 'You are a very good man, Anselm. Just like Papa.'

I turned to her. Through my tears, her face swam insubstantially. I could make out Leo and my mother in it. 'Jasmine,' I said. 'What would you do if you found out something about the past and afterwards you didn't know if you could go on the same way?'

'What would I do?' Jasmine frowned and put her thumb in her mouth. 'The past is the past,' she said eventually. 'It's gone away.'

But that was not true. The past is what makes everything else, like the foundations of a city. And I felt like they had all deceived me. My whole life had been constructed on lies and deceit, and when all of them told me they cared for me, no one really meant what it looked like they meant. 'Jasmine, all this is so confused,' I said.

'No,' she said. 'You'll see. Mama will be all right; everything will be all right.' She took the tears from my cheeks and put them on my ears like jewels. It was something my mother used to do whenever Jasmine cried. I remembered myself at six years old and a phase I had of drawing Mama, Papa, and Anselm all grinning in front of our house, as though nothing could divide us three. I wondered if I would ever see my childhood as I had seen it, whether on looking back it would for ever stand contaminated. Jasmine put her arms around my neck, and I let her. And we waited for the night to end.

THE NIGHT OF
THE SIXTH OF JANUARY

As we drove into an isolated village on a cliff, just as night fell, a strange miracle rose before us. In the tiny square in front of the church, someone had laid out an Epiphany scene. Plaster figures of the Virgin Mary and St Joseph and the baby Jesus stood on a matting of straw, with lanterns shining around them and the statues of the kneeling kings and the animals grouped around. We all stood before it for a long time, in spite of the bitter cold. 'Look at the fat donkey!' the little boy, Matthew, was saying, jumping from one foot to the other and laughing delightedly. He reminded me of Jasmine.

From the inn windows, we could still see that scene, a few streets away and shining through the dark. In this village, the invasion was still a distant rumour. There were no Imperial Order flags or boys in the streets with guns. Mr Hardy and I sat up talking, and I told him what was nearly the worst part of the story, the part about Ahira and that desolate night, when I suddenly saw all my childhood altered for ever, and nothing could make it right again.

Afterwards, he got up and walked to the window. He was twisting his hands together as he had that other night. He doubled over coughing and wiped his streaming eyes. Then he stood and looked at me and shook his head. He went on shaking his head so long that I could tell it was not just pity. There was something else. 'Anselm,' he said eventually. His voice was very hoarse. 'I am dying. I have been very ill. That was why I decided to go west and find my family. I have a few more weeks or months left. Or a year or two, God willing.'

I listened in silence. It was just past two o'clock, but this night was not desolate, and the sea in the distance was silvery and kind. 'Listen,' he said. 'Do you think they would want to see me after all this time? Do you think it would only make things worse for them?'

'No,' I said.

'But' – he twisted his hands again – 'but surely, after all this time—'

'I think you should go,' I said. 'I think most people want to know the truth. Not knowing it destroys you as much as knowing it. I mean, in the end.'

He opened his mouth as if to speak. Then he closed it again. It was true; he could say nothing. It was true even about Ahira, no matter the pain it caused me. I could never not have found out. There would have come a point when I could not go on in ignorance any longer.

'Anselm, if you knew,' he said, and looked at me tenderly, like Leo would have done. Then he sat for several minutes, unable to say a word. Afterwards, he asked me to tell him something else, but no more words came to me, so I took out Leo's papers and read to him. He did not seem to be listening. His eyes were wandering from corner to corner of the room, as though he was in prison.

After he found the old car again and after he lost his sketches, Ashley went home and got out his old maps and ripped them into pieces. First, he found the square where the Rolls-Royce was. It was in the heart of Belgravia. He thought, I must have been stupid to think that these places were magic because of their romantic names.

His father's necklace was lying on the bedside table, between a drawing of the pigeons on the roof and a worn-out radio. Ashley picked up the necklace and held it to the light. It had been years since he had worn this necklace, but when he slept, he kept his hand closed around it, and then he dreamed. In his dreams, he found that other city, the place he had been searching for when he was a little boy.

Tonight, he was walking through a town where gunfire troubled the streets, and people kept telling him to take cover. But he went on walking, up a steep road to a castle on a rock surrounded by machine guns. No one stopped him at the gate, and he knew where to go, up the steps and across a marble hall and into a narrow room at the end of a corridor.

A man with dark hair was sitting at a desk, looking out into the night. As Ashley went in, he turned and shut the door. The man had a lined face, and his clothes were crumpled. And there was something strange about this castle. Every room had old wooden furniture, and the walls were bare.

The man was moving papers about on the desk and studying a map. Every few minutes, he let out a quick sigh. Then he swept the papers onto the floor and rested his head against his arms. Ashley watched him for a long time. Then he went up to him and put his hand on his shoulder. The man shivered slightly and sat up, but he did not see Ashley. He went to a cupboard in the corner and took down paper and a pen.

Dear Ashley [he wrote] I dreamed about you, that you were almost grown up now and standing in front of me. Ashley, you will never read this, but you were my son. I would have been your father. This was all a mistake.

I thought I would stop loving her, but I never did, and now I have nothing. I will not be the ruler of this country much longer. Ashley, where are you?

Ashley did not read any more. He watched until the man laid his head on the desk again in exhaustion. As he did it, the dream faded, leaving Ashley alone, with the orange streetlamps outside and the soft London rain falling against the glass. But when he woke, a strange thought came to him. He had dreamed about his father because his father was dreaming about him.

Whatever else grew distant as he sat up and turned on the light, one thing was certain: that castle had been in a real country, a country that was not Australia, and wherever it was, that was where he had to go to set his heart at rest. Ashley no longer had his sketchbook, so he got out a scrap of paper instead. On it, before he forgot, he drew two faces. One was the old man from the train, and the other was the man in the castle. Then he lay down and listened to the rain falling and knew that he had to get away from here.

It was several days before Richard would let Juliette out of his sight. He kept her home from school, and they sat and played cards on the floor of her hotel room while the rain fell outside. 'Father,' she said one afternoon after a long time had passed in silence. 'Have you ever met a boy called Ashley Devere?'

Richard dropped the cards in his hand. 'What?' he said.

'Ashley Devere.'

Richard looked at her for several long seconds. Then he gathered up the cards and said, 'Tell me what you know about that boy.'

'Nothing.'

'You must have heard the name somewhere.'

'Nowhere. I mean, I can't remember.'

'Juliette, tell me.'

She hesitated. 'He's a friend of a friend of mine,' she said. 'That's all.'

'He lives in this city?'

'Yes.'

'And why do you think I would know him?'

'I don't know, Father. I just wondered.'

Richard put the cards back into their box, went to the window, and glanced down into the street. He did this several times a day, to check that James was still out there on guard. 'Listen to me,' he said. 'You are never to speak to that boy, do you hear? You are not to go looking for him, and you are not to speak to him. Ever. Do you hear?'

'No,' said Juliette. 'I don't hear. Because that's stupid.'

Richard stared at her as though she had hit him. Then he pushed his glasses up and tried to reach his hand out to her. 'I'm sorry, Juliette,' he said. 'I've been on edge lately; I know. It was only this dream.'

'What dream?'

'I dreamed about an old acquaintance of mine. It was so real. He was sitting there in the room, talking to me. And ever since then, I can't help worrying.'

'You've hardly slept in a week,' said Juliette. 'Maybe it would do you good, Father.'

'No,' said Richard. 'Not in the middle of all this.'

Juliette knew better than to argue. But that night, sleep got the better of him anyway. He fell asleep over a worn-out book some other guest had left, The Return of the Native, with the pages falling out. He did it suddenly, without ceremony. His head slumped onto the table, and the book hit the ground with a low thud.

Juliette hesitated for several minutes. Then she whispered, 'Sorry, Father,' and opened the window and climbed out. Richard did not wake. Once she was down in the street, she took Ashley Devere's sketchbook out from her coat and examined it. But she did not know where Forest Park Mansions were, and she had never walked about the city by herself – except for that other night, she had always been with someone else. She remembered a play in Covent Garden, when England was still new to her. She knew how to get there at least, and that was where the boy drew.

Without thinking much about it, she set out that way instead.

On the evenings when there were no tourists, now that autumn was closing in, Ashley sat in the park next to the old church and sketched other things. The park was paved with flat stones, and benches stood by the fence, and a few wind-ruffled pigeons hopped around the benches. He threw them a handful of crisps and bent his head over the sketchbook. He was drawing a ruined house today. He had been drawing for several minutes uninterrupted when someone stopped in front of him. She was a girl his own age, with blonde ringlets and a haughty kind of look. 'Yes?' he said.

She held out his sketchbook.

'What's that?' said Ashley, then recognized it.

'It's yours,' she said. 'So I brought it back.'

Ashley turned over the pages without breathing. He had fully believed that he would never see these pictures again. He glanced up to thank her, but she was already halfway to leaving. 'Wait,' he said. 'Listen, thank you. You're the girl who was there that night, aren't you? The girl who asked me if I was all right.'

'Yes.'

'What's your name?'

'Juliette.'

Juliette was how she said it. Ashley could hear the last two letters in the way she pronounced it, like it was the most important name in the world. 'Right,' he said. 'And I'm Ashley.'

The girl sat down and twisted the sleeve of her coat in her hands, first one way, then the other. 'How did you know where I would be?' said Ashley. 'How did you find me to give the book back?'

'I heard you say you drew portraits here.' She hesitated. 'Who was that man with the gun?'

'I've never met him before in my life,' said Ashley. 'I was only looking at the car. I don't know what that was about.'

The girl went on twisting her coat sleeve. Then she said, 'I think he was looking for my father.'

'Why?' said Ashley. 'Is your father the man who owns the car?'

'Yes.'

'So why do they want to find him?'

Juliette hesitated, and when she spoke, he heard her voice shaking. 'I don't know. But it means nothing good.'

'No,' said Ashley. 'Bloody hell.'

Luckily, the girl did not think this inadequate. She gave a half-smile and said, 'How much for a portrait?'

'Nothing,' he said. 'To you. If you really want one?'

'Yes.'

It was a strange thing to ask, but he turned over a new

page anyway and studied her face, then tapped the pencil against the spine of the sketchbook, trying to think.

'I always thought this should have been a garden,' said the girl after a few minutes had passed.

'What should?'

'Covent Garden.'

Ashley smiled at that. 'You aren't from round here?'

'Not originally, but I've been here ever since I can remember.'

'How long?'

'Since I was five years old.'

Ashley looked up. 'Can't you remember before you were five years old?' he said.

The girl considered it, then shook her head. It seemed to trouble her, not remembering. 'I'm not from here either,' said Ashley. 'And nothing in this city is like its name. I couldn't understand it when I first came. Half the places sound like magical lands out of some story.'

'White City,' said the girl. 'I've never been there, but I always imagined the buildings all made out of white marble, like a palace.'

Ashley shook his head and won a faint smile. The first lines of his sketch were emerging now under his right hand. Half the time his drawings came easier if he did not concentrate. He fixed the girl's spirit in his mind instead. She was rich enough to have the glossy look of someone who had always been well fed, and she was rich enough to wear impractical shoes and a white coat. She was twisting her sleeve again and rearranging each strand of her hair. Ashley thought if he could make her stop doing that, he might stand a chance of getting this portrait accurate. 'There are places in America with better names,' he said.

'Really?'

'Some of them,' said Ashley. 'Like Rifle or Telescope. Eureka. Bumble Bee.'

'Are those real towns?'

'What about Truth or Consequences?'

'There isn't actually a place called Truth or Consequences?' He nodded. 'That's a poetic name,' she said. 'As if you have to tell the truth or suffer the consequences.'

'I think it means the game. Like Truth or Dare.'

A chill wind troubled the pages of the sketchbook. From her expression, Ashley could tell the girl had never heard of that game. He drew on, glancing up at her face every few seconds.

'Can I ask you a question?' she said.

'Of course.'

'Those pictures in your book. How did you capture the people's spirits?'

Ashley looked up, and when he did, he realized that she had been studying his face too. 'Their spirits?' he said, and set down his pencil.

'Yes. That man in the black suit – who is he?'

'Show me.'

She took the sketchbook and turned over the pages. She had very white fingers, as though she had never washed a plate or swept a floor in all her life. 'Here,' she said.

Ashley looked. 'He's the man on the door of a club somewhere. I was waiting in the queue, so I drew him.'

'What's his name?'

'I don't know. I never spoke to him.'

'But I know things about him just from looking at it,' said Juliette.

'Like what?'

'He wants to be a musician. He has a wife and a child.' Ashley looked up at her. 'What is it?' she said.

'Nothing. Only that's what I thought about him too.'

'How is that possible?'

'Maybe this sounds strange,' said Ashley, 'but I understand about people when I start drawing them.'

Juliette held his gaze for a moment, then looked at her clasped hands. 'It's not strange,' she said. And then: 'So what do you know about me?'

'You have a lot of money,' he said.

'Not a lot . . .'

'No? Then I made a mistake.'

She looked down at her hands. 'Maybe. But I don't want that to be the first thing you think about me.'

'It's not. It's just the first thing I see. It's on the surface, you know?'

'Tell me what else.'

'You want to be liked,' he said, abandoning tact in favour of the truth. 'You look like you don't feel safe in this city, which is strange, because you must have been here a long time. You are on your own too much. And something else.'

He looked up at her and frowned, and this time she did not look away. And suddenly he knew what it was. She was like him. In this whole city, with its millions of inhabitants and millions of visitors, someone like him had come up and asked him to draw her portrait, and he could see her soul and he knew.

'What is it?' she said. 'What else?'

'Nothing,' he said. 'That's all. I should go home.'

The girl took hold of his arm. She did it lightly, as

though afraid of hurting him. 'Listen,' she said. 'Can I tell you what I see about you?'

Ashley wanted to say no, but his voice had constricted to a whisper. 'You don't feel safe in this city either,' she said, 'because you don't feel safe anywhere. You don't know where you belong. It's a kind of restlessness. You probably drink and smoke and think you're very old. I've seen other people like you; they come and ask my father for work. He says they are lost people. At first I thought they were just eccentric, but it's not exactly that. I'm like them, I think, and you are too. You walk about the streets drawing pictures, and that's your way of searching for another world.'

'Another world,' said Ashley. And there in the cheerless dusk, he felt his whole life alter. He had never considered that there might be anyone else like him.

Anna went home to the wrong flat after work. She had done this twice before, and each time she had the same sinking sense like missing a step and then had laughed at herself for being stupid. But as she went back down to the Underground, she thought, I have never been fixed in one place. Sometimes I forget where I am when I wake up in the morning, and when I leave work, I have to think about where to go, because I have never belonged anywhere. She and Ashley were back at Bradley's now, because they were looking for another flat. In truth, his old house in Forest Park Mansions was the place she thought of as home more than anywhere.

A merciless tiredness came over her on the Underground, but the crowds of people kept her standing. On the escalator, she closed her eyes. She walked the last few streets in a stupor and went up the stairs of the building one at a time.

When she got back, past nine o'clock, Ashley was sitting at the table. 'What are you doing here?' she said.

'Just sitting.'

'I know. I thought you would be out late as usual.'

'I'm finished with that.'

She gave him a quick smile, threw her keys on the table, and went to the sink to fill the kettle. But she was too tired to lift it, so she just stood there and watched the pigeons fighting on the wet glass of the roof. 'Mam?' said Ashley.

She turned. He looked unlike himself, like he used to look when he was a young boy. 'Tell me about my father,' he said.

For the first time in months, Anna considered her son properly, the way she sometimes studied his face when he was sleeping. His features were almost settled now, black eyes like his father's and a mouth that seemed permanently fixed in defiance.

'There are things I don't understand,' said Ashley. 'Like why I can make things happen that aren't possible. And why I believe that this isn't the real world. Mam, sometimes things come to me out of nowhere. Once I heard music, but it was the middle of the night and everywhere was locked up. And another time I thought I saw . . .' He shook his head. 'I thought I saw people moving out of sight. You know why, don't you? There's some reason.'

'I used to tell you stories,' she said. 'You thought they were fairy tales, and you asked me to stop.'

'Maybe I would believe them now,' he said quietly.

She turned back to the sink. Rain was falling outside. Whenever it rained, the glass roof beyond the kitchen window thundered and drowned all conversation. Lightning flared in the small square of sky. Anna thought that made it easier, to speak with her back to him and her voice half covered by the storm.

'Tell me,' said Ashley again. And Anna, as well as she knew, told him. In the years of silence, she had perfected the story as she knew it, and that made it easier than it had been before. She told him everything.

'Are there other people who know about this?' said Ashley when she had finished.

'I don't know,' said Anna. 'I used to think there would be. I thought there must be people. But I don't know any more. It's just us, isn't it? It always has been.'

'Do you still love him?' said Ashley.

She had refused to answer this question nine years ago. But what was the use any more? 'Yes,' she said. 'I think so. As much as I loved anyone.'

'But then couldn't you find some way—'

Anna shook her head. Ashley watched her. He was turning Bradley's expensive saltcellar around in his hand. The salt covered the table and half the floor, but Ashley had not noticed. 'Can I go back there?' he said. 'Not for ever. I just want to see it.'

'No,' said Anna. 'No, you can't.'

'Couldn't I go and look for him?'

'No, Ash.'

'I want to see him,' he said. 'I have to see him. Otherwise I think it might be too late.'

'Too late?' said Anna, real fear in her heart now. But Ashley did not continue. He just got up and went to his room and closed the door.

Lying awake that night, things became clear to him. He would find some way to go back to Lowcastle, to the house on the banks of the lake where his first memories were. He would travel backwards, on the road to the north, and somehow by doing that, all the years between would be cancelled out. And somehow by doing that, he would find his father.

Maybe Juliette had been misled by the title, but to her, Forest Park Mansions looked unimpressive and bleak when she found it at last. A broken tree stood in a small square of dirt; in front of it, a bicycle lay stranded without its wheels. She checked the address several times. While she was still checking it, Ashley crossed the window of the flat and stopped and recognized her.

She waited for him to come down. While she waited, she heard her heart take up a steady rhythm and beat faster and faster, as though it was trying to choke her. Then the door opened, and he looked out at her. 'Ashley,' she said. 'I want to talk to you.'

She saw him tap one finger against the door, and he seemed to be considering. 'I'll get a coat,' he said finally.

She waited. Then he appeared again, and they started out together. They walked for several streets without talking. Then Ashley sat down on a low wall and said, 'What do you want to talk to me about?'

Juliette did not know how to begin. 'After I saw you last time,' she said, 'things changed to me. It was that and other things. My father's old life. He used to work for a man called Mr Aldebaran. I've remembered it now. And we used to live in a house in a city with a castle on a rock. I do have memories from before I was five years old; I just didn't know, but you made me remember them.'

Ashley studied her face for several seconds. Then he said, 'That's where I want to go. That city with the castle. That's where my father is.'

337

Juliette had felt, with something like dread but softer, that there was some connection between them. She could not work it out, but she had known. 'Can I ask you a question?' she said. 'Have you ever been able to do impossible things?'

'Impossible things?'

Juliette hesitated. Then she picked up a dry leaf from the pavement and held it in the air in front of them, and let it go. It did not fall. Ashley stared at it for several seconds. Then he snatched it out of the air and said, 'Did you really just—'

'That was what I meant by impossible things.'

Ashley did not answer for a long time. Then he nodded and said, 'I can do that.'

'My father writes all the time now,' she said, 'and I broke the lock on his door and read what he was writing. It was an explanation about these impossible things. It's willpower. And people have been born with it in all generations. There are other people, even here in England. It lets you see other worlds and manipulate forces. In my own country, people train in willpower. And that's where I want to go. Because my father is going to take my whole life away if I stay here. He doesn't let me out any more. He thinks something is going to happen to me, and he's sworn never to go back home to our old country; I know he has. But I won't be happy — I won't know what the real world is — unless I can go back there.'

Ashley stared at a burned-out car on the corner of the street. He stared at it so fixedly that he might have been somewhere else altogether in his thoughts. They sat like that for a long time, saying nothing. Juliette was breathing fast because of the cold and because of telling him all these things so suddenly.

'I know about that place you call the old country,' Ashley said eventually. 'I think it's the same place I'm talking about.'

'Where is it?'

'North,' said Ashley.

'North, and then what?'

'And then I think I'll know the way. Once I get there.'

A question was forming itself in her mind, and she did not dare to ask it. But after he fell silent, there was nothing else to say. The wind cut like knives, and a cold rain started. Juliette thought, This rain and this wind are not part of my real life, and if I stay here a hundred years, I will never get used to them. 'Ashley,' she said. 'I hardly know you, but you're the only person I've ever met who understands this.'

'So what are you saying?'

'Let's go together.'

An engine broke the silence, and they both turned. The Rolls-Royce was cruising through the empty streets, with Richard glancing about anxiously from behind the wheel. 'Quick!' said Juliette. 'If my father knows I was talking to you—'

She pushed Ashley down behind the burned-out car.

'What is it?' he said.

'My father told me I could never speak to you.'

'I don't even know your father.'

'I have to go.'

'Wait—'

Juliette turned and ran towards Richard, with no thought except to stop him before he came any further along the road.

He saw her and shut off the engine and came out to meet her. 'What on earth—' he began. 'Juliette, where have you been all this time?'

'I'm sorry,' she said.

'I was worried about you. I had to get the car and come looking for you, I was so anxious. Where have you been?'

'I just wanted a walk.'

'Get in. Come on. We'll have to leave the car somewhere and walk; it is much too recognizable.'

Richard opened the car door to let her in, then got in and started up the engine again. They passed the burned car where Ashley was hiding, but Richard did not even glance at it. As they drove off, Juliette could see it receding in the rearview mirror. She directed her thoughts at it, as though the glass was a concentrating lens. Wait for me and we can go together, she thought. You are the only person who knows the truth.

'Are you all right, Juliette?' said Richard, but she did not answer. It was like finding your balance or listening for a true note. Anything could set it off-key. As they gained speed across a roundabout and into the traffic of the main road, she found Ashley's answer in the low hum of the engine. Yes. I'll wait for you. Tell me when.

JUST BEFORE DAWN ON
THE SEVENTH OF JANUARY

Mr Hardy stretched out his legs, and I heard the joints crack like an old tree in winter. A strange kind of calm seemed to have come over him. He took out a metal flask and poured us spirits, and we both drank. 'The coach will be moving on soon,' he said. I glanced to the window. But the coach was not there; the night drew out a while longer. I did not want to go on with my own story, not yet. The hardest part was still to come, I thought, like the last miles of this journey.

I knew him well enough by now to wait for his verdict without asking him for it. He rubbed his hands together, and I heard the joints crack again. Then he poured out another glass of spirits. I swear his blood must have been pure alcohol. He sipped the spirits thoughtfully, then said, 'All this makes sense, you know.' Then he was silent for so long that I was sure he was thinking of something else.

He was still racked with coughing. 'Are you sick?' I asked him.

'Not so bad,' he said, wiping his eyes. 'No, not so bad – thank you.'

I waited for him to stop coughing.

'Can I ask you a question?' he said when he had finished. 'Do you think Leonard started to write these things after he read the book?'

'What book?' I said.

'The Darkness Has a Thousand Voices.'

I frowned. I was not certain if it was that or Aldebaran dying or both. 'Maybe,' I said. 'It was only after he read the book that I saw him writing again. That book haunted him. I think he always had a faint hope that Harold North might still be alive.'

'You read it too,' he said.

'Yes,' I said.

'And what did you think?'

'It's very like Harold North.'

'Do you remember that night when we talked about love?' he asked me.

Sometimes I could not keep up with the drift of his thoughts. 'When you told me about the girl you fell in love with?' I said.

'Yes.'

'I remember.'

He set down his glass of spirits. 'I was dishonest,' he said. 'I made it sound as though I had always acted properly, when in reality I am not such a good man at all.'

I wondered if he was a criminal. But that thought passed. He was too honest; it ran through his whole being, and it was impossible that he had committed any shameful act.

'We're almost at the harbour,' he said. 'It will only be a day or two more. And, Anselm, there is something I've been meaning to tell you before I lose my courage. And before I hear the end of what happened. I've been meaning to tell you for days.'

'All right,' I said, misgivings rising in my heart in spite of my attempts to dismiss them. 'What is it?'

'After I married the girl with the angel's voice,' he said. 'After I married Amelie—'

'Amelie?' I said, making us both start. 'Did you say Amelie?'

'Yes.'

I stared at him, and he coughed violently again. 'Go on,' I said.

'Well, after that, our luck turned,' he said, speaking quickly

now. 'She became a famous singer and dancer, and I became a famous writer. At one time, I was said to have been the best of my generation. Probably just the fashion of the times. Anyway, the times changed. We had to get out; people no longer liked what I said, and there was a price on my head. There was no way we could take our children without endangering them too. It was like with your father; just the same. I could hardly credit it when you told me. And I did a very bad thing, Anselm. I told my eldest son that I would send word for him to come after us.'

Mr Hardy shook his head at that and went on shaking it. 'My wife passed away while we were in exile in Alcyria. I heard that my son, my younger son . . .' His voice choked. 'A boy I had left at two years old . . . my God. He died, too, in one of the silent fever epidemics.' He studied the surface of the table and breathed in and out again several times before he could continue. 'It was a year after when I heard what had happened. How could I go back to my other son then? How could we speak to each other, after I had betrayed him like that, after the others were both gone from us for ever? So I stayed in Alcyria, and I pretended I had no family. I told you I was half mad. I think that's true; it was no exaggeration. I had once been so great and so famous.' He took a shaking breath. 'No one reads my work now. But there was one other book I wrote, after I finally came back to the city to try and make amends.'

The spirits were dripping from the glass in my hand and falling heavily onto the floorboards. It took me several seconds to realize what the sound was, and I did nothing to stop it. I just stared at him while he twisted his hands.

'The Darkness Has a Thousand Voices,' he said, and his voice shook and quavered out of control. 'That was mine. I wrote it because I was too scared to go back and find my family. I thought that perhaps if I wrote something else, it would be like a sign . . .' He shook his head. 'I am not the same man I was. How could I go back and see my son again? But I wanted there to be some message out there for him. I wanted him to have hope.'

'Are you saying . . . ?' I began.

'Yes,' he said. 'Yes.' He doubled over coughing, and when he spoke again, it was in a faint whisper. 'I am just Mr Hardy now. Before that, I was Harlan Smith. And longer – a very long time ago – I was Harold North.'

'No,' I said. It was too strange to believe it like that, in one sudden blow. I felt as I would if a saint stood before me or a figure from some history book. I went on staring at him while the spirits dripped onto my boots. Then he stumbled forward, and I caught his hands. The glass smashed on the floor; neither of us heeded it.

'Shall I go on west?' he asked me. 'Tell me, will it be all right? Heaven knows I should have come back sooner. I thought I was too late, but I always had powers in my blood, and I think I was lucky to find you. I think I was more than lucky. Anselm, will he want to see me – even now, after all this time?'

I had to think about it. I could not answer him at once. I knew Leo's happiness or despair depended upon it. He had spent nearly all his life not knowing where his father and mother were, and to learn that one was dead now and one a broken old man . . . was that better than not knowing at all? 'Yes,' I said at last, and I knew with certainty. 'Of course he would want to see you. Of course he would.'

It was a long time before Mr Hardy grew calm. Then he wiped his eyes and said, 'I have to know what happened next. I have to know the end of the story. Do you see why now?'

'Yes,' I said. 'I see why.'

DECEMBER

After I found out the truth about my father, my heart was always elsewhere. I went about as normal, but I felt strange and distant, as if my soul had left my body and I had not gone with it.

'What is wrong with you, Anselm?' Sister Theresa demanded one morning. She had been asking me about the Bible, and I had not heard a thing. I came back to the real world.

'Nothing, Sister,' I said.

The air of the classroom was dismal. The Alcyrian army had advanced ten miles, and the flag at the front of the room was raised as a mark of respect for the casualties. We had all gone to stand in the streets at the king's most recent speech. Even my mother came to the window to watch the procession go past. But the Imperial Order was there, and people left early, even while the king was still talking. Every night, men stood in queues waiting to enlist for the army, the last stragglers rounded up for National Service. They had an old weariness that said they had seen all this before.

'David and Jonathan,' said Sister Theresa. 'Tell me about David and Jonathan.'

'"David made a covenant with Jonathan, because he loved him as himself,"' I said, the first thing that came into my head.

John Keller sniggered at that.

'What?' demanded Sister Theresa, rounding on him. 'What is so funny?'

'Nothing,' said John Keller, throwing me a glance. 'Nothing at all.'

I did not look at him. I opened the textbook in front of me and bent my head over it. I had been going through all the old history books, looking for Ahira's name. I had the town of his birth now, a place called Arkavitz, in the north. He had grown up there as a rich boy and had left his family at fourteen to come to the city. He enlisted for military service; he was involved with gangs in the city, then broke with them. He ended up homeless because there was no work. He only met the Kalitz family when Mr Kalitz took pity on him and invited him into an inn, where he was struck with his politics. I had written all this down again and again in the backs of my exercise books; then I had torn the pages out and burned them. It was what I did on the nights when I could not sleep. I had taken to stopping at the stalls we didn't usually go near, dredging through the relics of Lucien's regime for Ahira's portrait or his biography in an out-of-date history book. I knew it was half crazy, but I couldn't help it.

'I know it was you,' said John Keller loudly, making everyone glance up. He was talking to me. 'Someone has been stealing things, and I know it was you. And you haven't paid your rent.'

'Quiet,' said Sister Theresa. 'This class is not the place to conduct your personal conversations.'

I did not look up, but I could feel my face burning. 'I heard your friend Michael has taken up with some resistance men,' said John Keller. 'Apparently he's getting quite a reputation. He's a mad bastard; I always said. He'll get shot if he is not careful.'

That was enough, and Sister Theresa sent John Keller out. But I could not concentrate. My hands were shaking too badly to hold the pen. I kept my head down and waited for the class to end. I wondered if there was any truth at all in what John said.

Jasmine and I walked home in a dismal silence that afternoon. Every time I passed Ahira's picture on a wall, my stomach twisted, and I had to hurry past it. I kept thinking people saw his face when they met me in the markets, as though they would suddenly turn and accuse me. I could not help it. I was dreaming about him now, worse than ever. I would wake up sweating, convinced a red-haired man with a patch across his eye had been standing in the corner of the room seconds before I woke.

'Why aren't you talking any more, Anselm?' Jasmine asked as we walked home.

'I am,' I said.

'You aren't. And you look different, and you don't come with us to Mass even though Mama wants you to, but the thing I mind is that you don't talk to me.'

'So what do you want me to say?'

'You used to ask me questions about school,' said Jasmine.

'Tell me about school,' I said.

'No, not like that! Anselm, what's the matter?'

'Nothing.'

'Is it the same thing you were sad about the other night?'

'No.'

'You can't be like this!' she said. 'You can't just hide away and pretend to disappear.'

Her hand on my wrist was suddenly ironlike in its grip. 'Hey, Jasmine!' I said.

'I didn't mean to!' She released my wrist and stared at her own hand. She did this sometimes, and it always startled me. 'It's getting worse,' she said sadly. 'If Uncle was here, he would tell me how to practise, and then I wouldn't keep getting angry.'

'Yes,' I said. 'If Uncle was here.'

'Anselm?' said Jasmine as we walked on, her voice halfway to tears. 'Is Harold North dead?'

'Harold North?' I said.

'I mean Papa's father.'

'Yes.'

'Is he dead for sure?'

I shrugged my coat up higher. 'I don't know. I think so. He disappeared years ago. There's not much chance that he is still alive.'

'Oh,' said Jasmine. She studied the snow in front of her. Then she said in a rush, 'The newspaper said he might still be alive. It said he might be in the city.'

'I read it,' I said. 'But, Jas, this is what happens when there is a war – people start claiming the ghosts of famous people for their side.'

'Is that all?' said Jasmine.

'I don't know.'

'Is there a chance he might still be alive?'

I could not make myself care much, one way or the other. The snow lay hard on the ground, and my heart felt as desolate and lifeless.

'He might help us,' Jasmine persisted. 'If we found him.'

'Leo tried to find him,' I said.

'*Papa*,' said Jasmine. 'Don't call him Leo.'

'I'm sorry.'

We crossed the new square in silence. The stalls were covered in Christmas candles and Nativity pictures and were edged with lanterns, because it grew dark so early, but all the stallholders had a gloom about them that the lights could not dispel. 'Anselm?' said Jasmine. 'Take me to Mass tonight. Mama sometimes used to, before she was tired all the time.'

She was gazing up at me. 'Is this a test?' I said. 'Is this some kind of challenge of my faith, because if it is—'

'I just want to pray for the baby.'

'Can you not pray for the baby at home?'

'No.'

'Jasmine, listen—'

'We'll go to confession first and everything, and we'll pray for the baby and Papa and Michael.'

'Fine,' I said, giving up. 'All right.'

Father Dunstan always held half an hour of confessions before the service. Jasmine and I set out together just as the lines of candles on the windowsills were brightening along Trader's Row. Ice was creeping across the fountain in the square now; it hung in frozen drops from the horse's mouth. Over the silence, the explosives on the border coughed ceaselessly. Jasmine pulled me firmly across the square and into the church, and we joined the queue of people outside the confession box.

The people in line all had the same edginess. An old woman stood with her basket of shopping on her arm, sorting through the vegetables she had bought. A thin man about Leo's age was turning his hat around in his hand. We stood and waited while they filed in and murmured to

Father Dunstan, then took their places in the church. I sent Jasmine in before me. I could hear her confession clearly through the curtain: 'I said a bad word to Mr Victoire, and I was cross with Mama, and I wished bad things would happen to my grandmama, because she smacks me and scolds me, and . . . that's all.'

I could not help smiling at that. Jasmine emerged with a grin and took my hand. I wished I could just take my place beside her in the church, but I had promised her I would go to confession, and I had to do it. 'Find a pew near the back,' I told her. 'I will only be a minute.'

That sounded ridiculous when I said it. As though a minute was all it would take to set my heart to rights. Through the latticed window of the confessional, Father Dunstan's face appeared only dimly. 'Bless me, Father, for I have sinned,' I said, and did not go on. I had nothing to say. My voice felt strangled and I could not speak. Father Dunstan waited, watching me kindly. Eventually I muttered something about fighting and swearing, acts that I knew I was not sorry for, and Father Dunstan absolved me of them.

'Anselm?' he said then. He pushed aside the window of the confessional and turned over the pages of the Bible, then handed it to me. 'Here,' he said, pointing to the page. ' "The Lord is compassionate and gracious," ' he said, speaking the words by heart as I read them, ' "slow to anger and abounding in love. He will not always accuse, nor will he harbour his anger for ever; he does not treat us as our sins deserve or repay us according to our iniquities. For as high as the heavens are above the earth, so great is his love for those who fear him; as far as the east is from the west, so far has he removed our transgressions from us." '

I had thought he would give me a penance, four Hail

Marys or the Lord's Prayer. He watched me read the words, then took the Bible back and closed it. The people in the church were moving restlessly now, waiting for Mass to begin. 'If you ever need help or guidance . . .' Father Dunstan said quietly.

'Father,' I said. 'I found out something, about the past. About my history. And there's something else that I suspect, about someone close to me. A bad thing that he did. If it's true, I can't forgive him for it.'

I could tell the priest did not know what to make of that. I could not blame him. The service was about to start, but his thoughts were still running over what I had just said. 'It doesn't matter,' I said. I turned and went to the pew beside Jasmine, with all the worst guilt still lying on my chest unresolved.

Snow was falling in the square again as we left the church, coming down grudgingly out of a dirty sky. 'What did you confess about, Anselm?' Jasmine asked me.

'I didn't,' I said. 'Not really. I asked him about something.'

'Did he tell you?'

'No.'

She put her hand in mine. Sometimes now, when Jasmine took my hand, she did not feel like my sister any more.

'Anselm,' she said. 'I'm not going to give you anything for Christmas. I'm sorry.' I glanced down at her. 'I wanted to give you oranges and a gold-coloured notebook and a pen like Uncle's and a new overcoat,' she went on, all in a rush. 'And Papa coming home, and Mama being well, and lots of money and maybe a shop of your own, but . . .'

'But what, Jas?' I said, squeezing her hand.

'But I only have two pennies.'

I tried to remain serious, but I could not do it. I held out for several seconds. Then I burst out laughing, startling myself as much as her.

'It's not funny at all,' said Jasmine tragically. 'It's a terrible disappointment.'

I swung her up into my arms, and the sadness of the moment passed, and she was my sister again. 'Listen, I don't need anything,' I said. 'I'm coming to see your play, aren't I?'

'Then I'll make sure I act well,' said Jasmine.

That evening, I went out to the yard and stepped into the freezing shower and stood there until the cold clouded my brain and washed all traces of warmth from my skin. Then I carried the coal up for the living-room fire. I pretended that this was a penance for my sins, however far they extended, and every lump was an act of contrition. It was a crazy thing to do, but I did it anyway. My mother lay on the sofa watching me. Every time I caught her eyes, she smiled, then let the smile fall again, like she was too weak to hold it there. 'Anselm,' she said. 'Your friend John Keller was here, with a note from his father.' I looked up. 'Apparently we owe him three thousand crowns.'

Her voice broke on the word *thousand*, and she could not look at me. I put down the coal bucket and stood helplessly in front of the fire. 'Why didn't you tell me?' she said. 'Why didn't you say something? You must have known.'

'I didn't want to worry you.'

'Worry me? Anselm, you didn't want to *worry me*?'

'It was the day you took ill, and I didn't know what to do.'

'There isn't anything,' she said. 'There is nothing we can do.'

'Go to Grandmama's,' I said. 'I suppose that's all now, isn't it?'

She shook her head. 'Anselm, the landlords in the city are losing a lot of money fast,' she said. 'The debt collectors are busy. Do you really think he will let us leave and make that an end of it?'

'We'll find the money,' I said. 'Somehow. If he just gives us time.'

'Tell me how.'

'We'll think of something.'

She looked at me for a while, then forced her face into a smile and squeezed my hand. 'You're right,' she said. 'We will.'

On the coldest night of that winter, all the cups that Jasmine had fixed cracked into pieces. They did it without ceremony on the shelves of the back room, and it was only the next morning that we found them. That was the night the Alcyrian troops advanced as far as Ositha. They were clear on the horizon now, a grey line with fires burning between them. The tension of the city rose almost to breaking point. Carts piled with possessions rattled past the school windows all day.

When I came in from the markets that night, my fingers motionless with cold, Jasmine was studying the broken cups. The cracks had appeared where they had once been, as though they had never been mended. 'You said so,' she told me. 'You said I couldn't mend what was broken.'

'They held out for a while,' I said.

'What use is that?' She glared at me. 'What use is a

while? What use is anything? Why doesn't stupid Papa come home? Doesn't he know we need him?'

I did not know what to say. After that outburst, Jasmine fell very silent. My grandmother was kept late at the markets. I cooked the last remains of a stew, and we began eating without her. My mother kept glancing at me as she sat in front of her untouched food.

'Try to eat something,' I said at last.

'I am trying.'

'Mama, you're looking all white,' said Jasmine, creeping onto her lap.

'All right,' said my mother, her voice rising. 'I'm trying. Don't you both start.'

There was a silence. She raised a hand to her forehead and breathed shakily. 'I'm sorry,' she said.

'Why can't the midwife do something?' I said.

'Anselm, shh. You're making my head ache. There's nothing she can do. It's just the winter fever, like Father Dunstan said.'

'Please, just try and have a few vegetables. I can't sit here and see you eating nothing.'

She tried, but it did no good. She pushed the plate aside and retreated to her bedroom, without troubling even to take off her shoes as she got awkwardly into bed. Jasmine brought a tin bowl for her, because she was already looking sick, and I brushed out her limp hair. She still kept trying to smile weakly as I looked at her. I did not understand how this had happened. With no ceremony about it, and while we were all looking the other way, she had faded and fallen very sick. And it only made me feel more guilty, because I could not help thinking now of the other time. I saw her at fourteen years old, and myself the baby, and I felt responsible for all her sickness and all the trials of our family since. I had always known it, really. Even when I was a young boy. I had always thought I was the reason that everyone's lives altered sixteen years ago. It was never just coincidence.

That night, I dreamed about Michael again. He came out of the dark and spoke to me. He had some revolutionary medal on his chest. When he raised it to show me, I could see a bullet hole dark with blood under where the medal had been. He did not notice it at first. Then the blood began to run out of it. 'Michael,' I was saying. 'Michael.' But he could not hear. Then at last he saw. He tried to stop the blood, but it was no good, and I could do nothing either, and all the time the blood was running and he was growing paler.

I came back from a long way off. I was lying on the hard floorboards with the bedcovers twisted around me and one hand gripped around the head of the bed like a sailor clinging to some piece of wreckage. And downstairs, someone was hammering on the door.

In the second before I was properly awake, I thought it was Michael home again, or Leo. I stood up and pressed my face against the window, but it was too dark to see out. The hammering came again. I ran across the living room and down the stairs and stood irresolute in the middle of the shop. Then I went forward and unbolted the door.

There was no one there. The street was deserted. Terror came over me suddenly, and I slammed the door shut and locked it. I was certain it was the Imperial Order. Jasmine was behind me, hopping up and down in the doorway with fear. 'Jasmine, go back upstairs,' I said.

Outside, someone sniggered. We both started. Then the

thumping came again. This time I saw them through the grilles on the shop's front window. Just a gang of boys, no older than me, with bottles of spirits in their hands, laughing stupidly.

'Anselm?' my mother called from upstairs. 'What is it?'

'Nothing,' I said. 'Go to sleep.'

We went back upstairs. The lamp was burning in her room, and she was leaning over the side of the bed, retching, her beautiful hair tangled and matted.

'Make them stop,' Jasmine said.

'All right.' I handed her the tin bowl. 'Hold this for Mama. I'll go and tell them to leave. And get Grandmother to wake up and do something.'

The thumping came again. I was ready this time. I opened the door and was in the snow and running. Two or three people were ahead of me, laughing and waving the bottles in their hands. I recognized John Keller among them. 'What are you doing?' I shouted. 'Bastards like you should be arrested – do you know that? Stupid bastards!' I shouted a lot of other things that only made them crow louder with laughter and double over in the snow. I could not see them properly. I thought there was blood in my eyes, because my vision had turned red.

'You always owe my father money,' said John Keller when he had recovered himself. 'He is being too lenient with you, so I thought we would come and teach you a lesson.'

Even in my rage, I despised that high-class sentence: 'Teach you a lesson.' I started forward and pushed him to the ground. Hitting him was the release of everything that had turned my heart black over the past weeks. And then his friends were no longer laughing, only shouting and trying drunkenly to pull me off him. Police officers appeared round the corner and shone lanterns in our faces.

John Keller was lying motionless in the snow. I turned my face to the wall of the pharmacist's shop and leaned there, shaking with fear. Even when John got dazedly to his feet, I still believed he was dead. I believed it because just for a second, I had fully intended to do it. Leo had killed someone, and Ahira had. It was no more than my destiny.

The police officers marched me back into the shop and took names and addresses and details. My grandmother could hardly speak with outrage, and all I could do was ask, 'Is John Keller all right? Is he all right?' over and over again.

'Yes,' said the kindest of the officers. 'He'll have a concussion if he is unfortunate, but beyond that he will be fine.'

John was shouting curses over his shoulder as the police ushered him and his friends away. His blood lay darkly on the snow; I could see it even from the shop. I rested my head against my hands. 'We don't have time to sort out personal grievances,' the officer told me after he had attempted to unravel the story. 'You owe his father three thousand crowns, as it seems. If you pay the money, the law is on your side. If you don't, it is on his. Now fight it out between you.'

'Listen,' I said. 'That boy's father is our landlord. He will do something – I know he will.'

'He can hardly throw you out in the snow,' said the officer.

'You don't know what he is like—'

The other officer raised his hands, then let them fall again. 'There is nothing we can do any more,' he said. 'I'm sorry.'

The house was very quiet after they left us. I listened to my grandmother's scolding without complaint, then sat alone and watched the last coal burn on the fire. The next morning at school, John Keller pushed past me so hard that I almost fell, and he whispered, 'We are sending in the debt collectors. We are sending them in tomorrow, so watch out.'

'We'll have to go to your grandmother's,' my mother told us.

Jasmine and I stood sullenly side by side and could not argue. My grandmother came back after work with her barrow, and we began piling our belongings onto it and dismantling our life while my mother watched helplessly, tears rolling down her cheeks. Her despair at leaving the shop made each box feel as heavy as stone.

We hardly took anything. Even with ten journeys between Trader's Row and Old College Lane, we had to leave most of it. The furniture was not ours anyway. I gave the contents of the shop to Mr Pascal, under the agreement that he would pay me fifty per cent of what he made as the goods sold. I knew he was profiting more than we were, but I was too weary to fight the point. On the second day, Jared Wright saw us clearing out our belongings and stood watching with an air of faint puzzlement. Neither my grandmother nor Jasmine noticed him. They went ahead of me across the snow, the barrow pitching and sliding between them, piled perilously with our saucepans and half of Leo's books. I felt ashamed to have everything we owned exposed to the street like this. I had a box clutched to my chest that contained Leo's battered collection of Harold North books.

'What's all this?' said Jared, sauntering towards me and eyeing the box.

'We are leaving,' I said.

'Leaving Trader's Row? Can it be?'

'Our landlord issued a notice.'

'Who is your landlord?'

'Doctor Keller.'

'I know Doctor Keller, and I could put in a word. Do you want me to? It might do some good.'

I shook my head. I wanted to leave the shop. I would rather struggle with the ridiculous barrow through the snow, taking apart our old life, than stay here and fight any longer. 'It's all right,' I said. 'It was time to move on anyway. There's no point in trying to stay when he wants us to leave; we won't win.'

'Anselm,' he said, half exasperated. 'If you would just let me help you—'

'No,' I said. 'We don't need anyone's help.'

It was nearly impossible to be in the same two rooms as my grandmother. Even just arranging our things in the corners and listening to her as she tutted and threw shawls over them made me want to turn round and walk away into the snow. Our shop looked strangely empty now. The last few nights we slept in it were just out of habit. By the end of the week, we had cleared out everything we could take and had abandoned the rest. Most of the furniture was Dr Keller's. My grandmother and I closed the door carefully, refusing to look at each other. 'Come on,' she said then. And we had to leave. This was the end of it, our life on Trader's Row. A few barrow loads of worthless belongings and a key that was no longer ours.

'I'm just going to check one last time,' I said. 'I'll catch up with you.'

I went back inside, but I did not know what I was looking for. I ran back up the stairs. The place was the same five rooms, except that the shelves and tables, usually piled precariously with books and papers and Jasmine's toys, were deserted now. The living room was empty, the last embers of the fire fading in the grate. I straightened the chairs at the table out of habit and closed the curtains in Jasmine's room to stop the snow from coming in. That window always leaked unless you wedged it shut with a book, and all the books were gone. As I turned, the curtains flailed in the draught; that was the only movement in our silent house.

Everything was still lying about in the shop, waiting for Mr Pascal to take it away. A newspaper from last week, a broken teacup, and an old chair I had been halfway through sanding stood on the table of the back room. I checked the drawers of the counter, but they were full of rubbish. As I straightened up, Leo's presence was there suddenly. I remembered him writing our name on the sign, precariously balanced on that old ladder in his soldier's boots. I wandered through the shop, trying to fix our old life in my mind for ever, but it was already the past. Then I ran back up the stairs. I wrapped my jacket around my fist and smashed all the windows and let the snow howl through our empty house. After that, it was easier to turn and leave.

But the want of money never lets you go. The next day, the midwife took me to one side and recommended the government hospital for my mother. She would be in danger if she did not go there for the baby's birth, and it would cost us two thousand crowns.

That night, I went back to the abandoned house beside the Royal Gardens. I was trying to think, and it seemed as good a place as any. I had not been there since Michael had left. The snow was drifted so high against the barbed wire that I had to dig a space underneath it to crawl through. The house was more black and majestic in the snow; every tangle of dead plants and each broken carriage wheel was frosted over and glittering under the stars.

At the far side of the grounds was a frozen pool and what had once been an artificial waterfall but was now a mass of icicles and tangled grass. Michael and I used to throw a coin in and wish; Aldebaran had told me it was an English custom. Our traders' upbringing decreed that we always took the coins out again. I tried to break the ice to see if there were any we might have forgotten, but it was too solid. There was a statue of an angel beside the water-fall, his mildewed face giving him a black and dismal look. I leaned forward and tried to brush the snow from the angel's forehead, but it was fixed there and would not let go.

The angel reminded me of my father's grave. I had been back to Devil's Cross once and had stood before the memorial stone. I had sat on the steps of the de Fiore tomb in the snow, waiting for some trace of his spirit to speak to me. But I could not find it. Maybe it was superstition, but I thought his spirit must be where his ashes were buried, if they were buried at all. Somewhere in the north. I was certain it was Arkavitz. Perhaps that was where I would find what I was searching for.

I went back to the abandoned carriage, but the snow had drifted against the door, and I could not get it open. I made the circle of the house instead. Beyond the far wall, where the weeds and brambles rose so high that I had to struggle waist-deep through them, I came upon a light. It was burning behind a ragged curtain in the cellar of the house. I hesitated, then went down the steps.

Cold had misted the window, but I could make out two people inside – a boy and a girl no older than me. The boy was adding coal to the grate. The firelight made his eyes shine very black. The girl was watching him. Every few minutes, she would reach up to push a strand of hair across her forehead. Their belongings were wrapped in a battered tarpaulin and piled beside them. Apart from the square of floor where they knelt, the room was dingy with cobwebs and filth. What looked like an old oil painting hung above the fireplace, some relic left there by the rich owner of this house more than sixteen years ago.

The boy stood up and rubbed his hands together. There were streaks of dirt across his face. A jewel glittered in his left ear, and it looked like something too good for his life, the way Jasmine looked in her new school boots at the start of every year. Then the girl put her hands around his, and he glanced up quickly and said something. Even through the glass, I could read the three words of her reply.

I turned and climbed the steps again and went on. A grudging snow was falling again, freezing my skin where it touched. I went back to the hole under the barbed wire and scrambled through. As I walked along the outside wall, I passed a long section that had crumbled and fallen. Perhaps the cold had cracked the cement that held it together. That must be how the boy and the girl had got in. As I went on, a streak of red caught my glance. It was an old slogan, daubed on the wall years ago and covered with ivy; but now the wall had fallen and taken the ivy down with it.

I made out HERE and CRIMINAL. Night was falling fast, but I struck a match and raised it and began scraping the frost off the wall to try and make out the letters. The words emerged slowly: HERE DWELLS AHIRA, CRIMINAL AND MURDERER.

I glanced around – I could not help it. My heart was thumping, and I expected to see some sign of his presence in the dark street or the grimy snow. Then I realized it meant the house. This house had stood empty and half ruined all my life, and this was the reason for it. No one wanted to touch it, because it had been his. And it seemed a cruel kind of joke, that the place Michael and I had thought haunted had been haunted all the time – by my real father's ghost.

'Anselm?' Jasmine hissed that night, just after the clock struck two.

'What is it?'

'Can't you sleep?'

I shook my head. We were lying on makeshift beds in my grandmother's living room, on either side of the narrow space between the sofa and the fire. I had been watching the flames and trying to think what to do.

'I can't sleep either,' Jasmine whispered. 'Can I light the candle?'

'All right.'

She sat up and lit it, shielding the flame carefully with one hand. 'Anselm?' she whispered. 'Can you hear them shooting out there in the east?'

'Not now; the wind is too strong.'

'I can.'

That must be her powers. The wind was howling and lamenting in the chimney so loudly that it drowned all other sounds.

'Anselm?' she said. 'What's going to happen when they get to the city?'

'I don't know.'

'Will it be all right?'

'I don't know, Jas.'

'Robert at school said they want to lock up people who have powers.'

I turned to her. She was sitting with the blanket wrapped around her, staring into the flames. 'Robert doesn't know,' I said. 'He hasn't been to Alcyria, has he?'

She did not answer.

'Well?' I said. 'Has he?'

'He has an uncle there.'

'But this uncle wouldn't write and tell Robert what was happening. They would lock him up if he said things like that in a letter. The police there search your post.'

'Are you sure?'

'Yes.'

'But it still might be true. Even if Robert doesn't know, it might be.'

I tried to find an answer, but none came to me.

'Anselm,' she said while I was still struggling to think of something. 'Sometimes I wish I'd never been born with powers at all.'

'I know, Jas,' I said. I knew what it was costing her to keep her powers unseen in this house. Sometimes paper curled in her hands or her hair crackled as she combed it out, as though a lightning charge ran through it.

'It was all right when Uncle was here,' she said. 'But now it's just me on my own. I used to wish the baby would have powers, but I don't now. Not any more.'

'Can you tell whether it will or not?'

She shook her head and would not answer. She got up instead and reached under the sofa for something. It was

Aldebaran's box, the one he had left to her. She traced the patterns in the wood. 'Why didn't he leave me something proper?' she said.

'He probably thought you'd like that box. He might have picked it up on one of his journeys – and it has a beautiful pattern, after all.'

'Stupid Uncle!' she said crossly, and threw the box down on the floor.

'Shh, Jas, you'll wake Grandmama!' I picked the box up before it could roll further. When I did, something rattled inside.

'What's that sound?' said Jasmine.

'I don't know. Maybe you broke one of the hinges.'

I opened the box. The fall had split two sides of it, so they were half an inch apart now. The base was loose. 'Fix it, Anselm,' she said, halfway to crying suddenly.

I was exasperated; I could not help it. 'Jasmine, if you hadn't broken it in the first place—'

'Please, fix it.'

'I'd have to get out Papa's old tools and do it properly. Can't it wait until the morning?'

'Please, Anselm.'

She was crying in earnest now. 'I didn't mean to break it,' she said. 'Please, Anselm!'

I got up, making much of it, and went to our pile of crates in the corner and found the old woodworking tools from the shop. Jasmine clutched the box to her and kept a close watch on it all the time it was in my hands. 'Be careful,' she said at intervals while I tried to force it back together.

'Shh,' I said. 'You'll wake Grandmama.'

'Is it going to be all right?' she said. 'Anselm, don't break it!'

'I'm not breaking it!' My irritation got the better of me. I had been fighting it for several minutes without success. 'Jasmine, you were the one who broke it,' I said. 'Stop complaining and let me work.' She put her thumb in her mouth and regarded me in silence. 'There's something wrong with this – it won't go together. Sit back and let me have the light.'

Jasmine shuffled back a few inches, without taking her thumb out of her mouth.

'I have enough to worry about already,' I said. 'Jasmine, we have no money, and if someone doesn't do something about it, I don't know what's going to happen, and now you ask me to fix this bloody—'

'Don't do it after all,' said Jasmine, taking it back. 'It doesn't matter.'

That only infuriated me more. I threw myself back down on the bed and stared at the ceiling. Jasmine was still studying the box, trying to push it back together herself. I let her. 'Anselm?' she said when several minutes had passed. 'Anselm . . . ?'

'Yes, what?'

'What's this?'

She put the box down on my chest and pointed to something in the base of it. I picked it up and looked. 'What?' I said. 'I can't see anything.'

She gave an impatient sigh and said, 'Feel there.'

I traced the line she was pointing to and felt a small dent in the wood, like a fingerprint. 'Give me the candle,' I said. I got the file and edged it under the base of the box. The mechanism had broken since Jasmine had dropped it, but it was a hidden compartment. The base creaked and came loose. Inside was a folded sheet of paper.

We stared at each other for several long seconds. We should have known, I thought suddenly. That story Aldebaran had told Jasmine about the smugglers and the fact that this box looked like it was from somewhere else. And yet I had never expected him to resort to a trick out of a story to pass his secrets on to us.

'Shall I open it?' said Jasmine.

'Go on,' I said.

She took out the paper and unfolded it. Aldebaran's familiar writing wrenched my heart now that he was gone. The date on the top was more than a year ago.

Dearest Jas [the letter read]. *If you are reading this, I am already gone from you. I have been worried for some time that I am in danger. I want you to know that I was only cross with you because it made you a better student. Also, that time when you stamped on my foot, you were quite justified. If you decide to give up your powers, I will always understand. Yours with great affection, Uncle.*

Jasmine laughed and then started to cry. 'Let me see,' I said. It was Aldebaran's writing for sure, the firm down-strokes and the letters that sloped as though they were on an arduous journey. 'What's this?' I said. There was another sheet. It was only a few lines, and I read them in a minute:

Magic is dying, and a time will come when no one remembers the old ways. I name my last descendant as your hope in times of trouble, a very certain help in the darkness of the road. But there are those who will not return, those who will go forward into another place. Have courage.

'What does that mean?' I said. 'I don't understand.'

Jasmine's face had turned very serious. 'It's a vision of the future, Anselm,' she said. 'I think it is.'

I tried to take the letter from her, but she was studying it in the light of the candle. 'It is,' she whispered. 'And he meant us to find it and no one else, so he put it in this box.'

'His last descendant,' I said. 'Who is that?' Jasmine read the page again, then folded it and put it back into the compartment and closed it. 'Hey, Jas,' I said. 'I wanted to read that.'

'I'm tired,' she said, and blew out the candle.

I could not tell if she slept that night, but I could not. I was thinking about what Jared Wright had said. That he would pay a good deal of money, thousands of crowns perhaps, for Aldebaran's last prophecy. And so would any political man. And here it was, in that box of Jasmine's, and I could not help seeing it as the answer to all our troubles. I knew it was dishonest of me, but I could not help seeing it like that. For the first time, I thought I could see a way out.

My mother was worse in the week that followed, and the thought of that prophecy haunted me. Father Dunstan called one evening; he came back with my grandmother after Mass. 'How are you, Maria?' he said, taking her hand and sitting carefully on the side of the bed.

'Not so bad,' she said.

'And when is the baby due?'

'Not for another few days. Or weeks perhaps.'

The door fell closed at that point. Jasmine and I were in front of the fire, pretending to do homework that we had not looked at for weeks. My grandmother was making tea and laying out biscuits on a plate.

'Grandmother,' I said, looking at the ornate china. 'How much is all this worth?'

'What?' she said.

'This furniture. How much is it worth?'

I had not spoken to her properly for days. She looked up at me, stirring the tea without noticing it. 'What on earth do you mean?' she said.

It was something I had been thinking about for a long time. 'How much are the contents of this house worth?' I said. 'I just wondered, because of the hospital—'

She shook her head. 'Anselm, do you think I haven't thought of it already? When your grandpa Julian died, he was in that hospital for three weeks. Everything of value went. My little sewing table and the silver, and all my jewellery. Look at what is here. It wouldn't fetch above a hundred crowns in an auction.'

I must have looked unconvinced, because she raised her voice. 'Look at it. Do you hear me? Get up and look at it!'

I got up and examined the furniture properly. It was true. What wasn't worn out was worthless, and the few things that might have had some value were chipped and broken and stained with use. Life can be deceptive – that was what I thought, looking at it. You can give yourself airs and a high-class accent and really have nothing at all. The care with which my grandmother dusted this old furniture had always made me believe that it was worth something.

In the bedroom, Father Dunstan murmured a question, and there was a pause. Then my mother burst into tears. We listened without looking at each other. My mother's voice went on like a river, speaking and crying at the same time, and I knew she was telling him about the hospital and the two thousand crowns we did not have.

I sat there and watched the fire, but I could not really see it.

Eventually Father Dunstan came back out. 'I am sorry for your trouble,' he said. 'I would have asked the congregation to contribute to a small fund. You are all such respected members of the church that I'm sure they would be willing. But we won't raise two thousand crowns. Not in a year.'

'Thank you,' said my grandmother. 'It's a kind thought anyway.'

'I would advise you to borrow the money somehow,' he said. 'I will underwrite the loan, if you wish. It's all I can think of to do.'

It was a brave offer. All the moneylenders were controlled by gangs, and if we could not pay, they would come down on him instead. But he was only a priest. His cell beside the church had a table and a bed and a narrow kitchen with no window; that was all. His word against a loan was worthless. 'Father,' I said. 'Do you think she really needs to go to the hospital when the baby is born?'

'Yes,' he said. 'I think so. My knowledge is limited, but I think it would be safest.' I rested my head against the side of the fireplace and stared into the flames. 'If there is any way you can afford it,' he said.

'I think I can get the money,' I said.

There was a pause while they both looked at me.

'How?' said my grandmother then. 'How will you get it? Honestly, Anselm! You live in a world of dreams.'

I did not reply. We sat with the priest, drinking tea, and he left soon after. Jasmine fell to sleep early, with Aldebaran's box beside her. My grandmother went down to fetch water, and I took my chance. I knelt beside Jasmine, levered open the secret compartment, and took out the paper.

I set out not long after that. I put on my Sunday clothes and my overcoat and that old hat of Leo's because it made me look older. I felt like I was preparing myself for a great ceremony – a marriage or a funeral – or like a soldier going to war. I glanced at myself in the hall mirror as I passed, but it did not make me feel any better. I looked like Ahira. I tried to forget that picture of my face and started towards our old part of the city.

I went to Citadel Street first. I knew it was a faint hope, but no one had lived in that apartment since us, and a few nights ago, I had remembered a high cupboard in which my mother kept everything of value. I had worked it up into a whole story, this cupboard, in my efforts to find some other way of raising two thousand crowns. There might be something left in it. Had any of us checked before we left? Perhaps it was a strange kind of morality, but if I went to Jared Wright, I wanted it to be my last resort.

I struggled with the rusted lock on the side door of our old building. Leo and I had got in once, I remembered, a long time ago. I had the file from the shop in my pocket, and with some leverage, the door opened. The blackness inside was like drowning. I lit a match and went up the stairs as quickly as I could. I wanted to run, but I concentrated on keeping the match steady in the freezing air. I had a candle, but I was saving it until I got inside our old apartment.

I reached the third door and walked a few steps forward before I lit the candle. The flame steadied uneasily. I made out old packing cases, and a pile of fallen ash in the fire-place, and broken glass glinting in front of the nearest window. Dust and frost sparkled on the floorboards, and spiderwebs hung as thick as wedding garlands in the corners. Over the mantelpiece, a scrap of paper fluttered in the breeze from the doorway. I crossed the room and took it down, then recognized it. I had drawn this at school, when I was a little boy; we must have forgotten it when we left. Three grinning figures stood in front of a tall black building. I had printed words underneath it: *Mama, Papa, Anselm.*

I checked each of the rooms. The kitchen window was broken, and birds must have got in, because the floorboards were strewn with dirty feathers. A patch of damp had spread on the wall of the smaller bedroom. The other was completely bare. I stacked up two packing cases and raised the candle, flooding the cupboard on the wall with light. It was empty. My courage failed me at that point, and I turned and ran.

As I was leaving the alleyway, I saw the words on the front of the building, faded now because of the frost that obscured everything. THIS IS THE PLACE. This was where he had died. And I could not help thinking again of Leo and the man he had shot. Had that man and Ahira been the same person? How could they have been? I fell to my knees in the dust and thought of Ahira falling there while I was a baby sleeping in the house above him. I wondered if I had woken and begun to cry. I wondered if he had known it was our house.

I did not want to think about it, not now, when I had to talk to Jared Wright. I knew suddenly that I was losing my way. But knowing it doesn't help you when you are already lost. I got up and made myself set one foot in front of the other. On the way, to put Ahira out of my mind, I worked out my price. It was what Leo had always told me to do. It was dishonest to cheat people, he said, like Mr

Pascal did, but there was no shame in knowing how much money you needed to make. There was no shame in deciding how much money you needed to come home with, in order to survive.

I wondered what we needed. Two thousand for the hospital. A thousand for Dr Keller – it was two months' rent that we owed him, plus the price of the windows. He had backed down over the three thousand crowns but not over the rest. A hundred or two, I thought before I could stop myself, to get out of this city. A few hundred crowns for the journey west. Because if the invasion really did come, what else could we do? Really we needed five hundred, I decided, in case we had to stop at inns on the way, and to buy clothes and things for the baby, and to transport our belongings with a shipping firm. And Christmas presents, I thought, because Jasmine expected something. Another twenty crowns would cover that. But then what about Michael? How would I ever go and find him again, without money saved now to go and do it?

By the time I reached Jared's shop, the figures were reaching dizzying heights, and I knew it. I stopped outside the door and brushed the cobwebs off my jacket and straightened out my hair. There were no lights in our old shop, but the windows of J. W. Fortune, Esq., were lighted. I could see Jared behind the glass. He was sitting with his feet on the counter, smoking. One thing I had decided on the journey to his shop: I would ask him to lend me the money first. And only when he said no would I resort to the other plan.

Jared got up and came to the door at last. 'Anselm,' he said. 'How long are you going to stand outside my shop before you come in?'

'I was about to come in.'

He gestured me through the door and closed it again behind me. I did not know what to say. 'Well?' he asked me at last. 'What can I do to help you?'

I hesitated, then gave up altogether and said it. 'Lend me five thousand crowns.'

To his credit, he did not laugh. He sat down heavily behind his counter and said, 'Five thousand? You are serious?'

I could not swallow – my throat was dry. I nodded.

'Come here,' he said quietly. 'It is a lot of money. A hell of a lot.' I nodded again. 'What's your security?'

I had not thought of that. 'I have a watch that belonged to my grandfather,' I said. 'It's at home, but I could go and get it.'

'How much is it worth?' said Jared.

'One hundred and thirty,' I said.

Jared did not laugh as I had expected him to. He just watched me, his eyes narrowed, then sat down at the counter. 'I'm a rich man,' he said. 'I did not become so by giving out loans, but that is of no consequence for Maria Andros's son. Who wants your money?'

'It's for the hospital for my mother's baby.'

He gave a twisted smile at that and ran his hand over his oiled hair. 'She needs a hospital?' he said.

'The midwife thinks there may be complications.' He glanced up. 'I would pay it back,' I said, playing quickly on his concern. 'I swear I would.'

'Not this year, though, surely? Not for a long time.'

'As soon as I could.'

'And what would you do in between? To prove that you were no liar?' I stood there helplessly. 'As far as I can see, you have no income,' he said. 'You are at school. This country is about to fall altogether, and there are a lot of people who are borrowing far beyond their means, because they think they can get away with it.'

There was a silence.

'I will be honest with you,' he said. 'Five thousand crowns would not bankrupt me. But I would need more than a hundred-pound watch as security.'

'All right,' I said.

'All right what?'

I caught sight of my reflection in the gold-framed mirror and glanced away again. 'Nothing,' I said. 'I was only thinking; I have things I can sell instead.'

'Do you? I'm glad to hear it.'

I wanted to mention the prophecy then, but I could not do it. My initial courage had passed. I stood stupidly halfway across the shop with my hat and coat still on.

'Come in,' said Jared. 'Will you have a drink, and we'll talk about it?'

I nodded. He poured out two glasses of spirits and carried them into the back room. I followed him. Jared motioned me to a chair and set a glass down in front of me. He raised his own, and the crystal glittered. 'To better times,' he said. 'No – to freedom. Why not drink to that?'

'To freedom,' I said, though I didn't know what he meant by it.

He drained his glass in one swallow and lit a cigarette. 'More doom and destruction,' he said, pushing today's newspaper towards me. According to its account, the Alcyrians had taken the villages surrounding Ositha and had started north to cut the city off. 'The government is growing desperate,' he said. 'Have you heard its latest story?

Apparently the king has a secret child somewhere, the son of a former lover. I suppose the suggestion is that this boy can somehow be brought forward to rule the country if King Cassius is assassinated. Do you know what I think it is? I think the king knows that he is in danger of his life, and he's trying to make himself look immortal.'

'Can I ask you a question?' I said. 'Who is your allegiance with?'

'Who is my allegiance with?' He frowned. 'No one. I thought you would know that by now. But I am a close acquaintance of several members of Joseph Marcus Sawyer's government. I knew them in the old days. I have some influence.'

'You support the king?' I said.

'I support the king's government . . . and the king, I suppose, until a strong leader comes to take his place.'

'But you have nothing to do with the Imperial Order?'

'Good heavens, no.' He leaned forward on the table and grinned. 'Apart from anything, there is no money in it. Not yet anyway.'

'They think they are going to be rewarded,' I said. 'When the Alcyrians come.'

'Anselm,' he said. 'Let me tell you something. With those regimes, no one is rewarded. No one wins in the end. It might take twenty, or thirty, or a hundred years, but in the end, the cards are all down and everyone loses. Everyone is deceived.'

I was not certain he was right. 'There isn't justice,' I said. 'Not like you say there is.'

He gave a faint smile. 'Look at you, Anselm. Your whole life is before you. What is there to be so bitter about?'

'Yes, I suppose so,' I said, because he wanted me to.

He picked up the empty glasses. 'Another drink?'

'No,' I said. The alcohol was clouding my brain, and I wanted to think. 'Do you remember when we talked about Aldebaran's last prophecy?' I said before I could lose my resolve.

Jared set down the glasses very carefully and looked at me. 'Yes,' he said.

'And you said you would pay money for it and so would any political man?'

'Yes. I remember.'

'Why would you?'

He sat down. 'Why? Because it would be the most powerful weapon. There are people who dislike the king. Sawyer as the new chief adviser is not well liked at all. But everyone loved Aldebaran. They loved him to the point of stupidity. And I would pay money for it because other people would pay me more. I am, first and foremost, a trader.'

'Who would pay you more for it?'

'Well' – he shrugged – 'other political men.'

My words were following each other now, though I hardly knew where they would lead. It was like setting out on a road in the dark; I did it with blind faith. 'How much would you pay?' I said.

'Whatever it was in my best interests to pay. The thing is worthless, but not to other people – and that, Anselm, is the first principle of trading.'

'Why is it worthless?' I said. 'I mean to say, if it was a real prophecy.'

'Good Lord,' he said. 'You are not suggesting there is any truth in these old stories? No, it is only worth something while the superstition of the general public is enough to make it so.'

'Don't you believe in powers?' I said.

'I doubt,' he said. 'Because people say they are dying out, and I can't help thinking that what is dying out is the super-stition necessary to believe in them at all.'

'But if there was a prophecy, people would believe it. You still think so?'

'I'll tell you what I think,' he said. 'I think it would save this country. I really do. I think it would give people the will to fight back.'

'Sir,' I said. 'Aldebaran was my uncle by adoption. My great-great-uncle, that is. He left us a few things in his will.'

'Yes,' said Jared.

'He left a prophecy to my sister, Jasmine.'

Our eyes held each other for a moment. Then he set down the glasses and lit a cigarette, but I was certain that it was just an attempt to seem nonchalant. He exhaled slowly and said, 'Are you lying to me?'

'No.'

'Because if you are . . .'

'I'm not.'

'Do I trust you?' I did not answer. 'I'm not so sure,' he said. 'How do I know you are telling the truth?'

'I can take it to someone else if you don't want the risk.'

I had learned this trick from Mr Pascal; it was an old and hackneyed method. 'Five thousand crowns is no risk to me,' said Jared. 'It's not about the risk.'

I shrugged as though it mattered nothing at all to me.

'I am going to tell you a fact,' he said. 'I will say this once only. I work with people who make the Imperial Order look like a brotherhood of monks. I know the gang leaders, the debt collectors, the criminals, all right?'

'All right,' I said. Already the plan was starting to taste

bitter, and I half wished I had never started it. 'But you aren't going to sell it to them,' I said. 'You aren't going to do that, are you? Because if you were—'

'Lord, Anselm, who do you think I am?'

'I'm sorry; it's just—'

'Right,' he said. 'Enough of this. Five thousand crowns.'

I had fixed my face carefully before he named the price, and I did not even blink. 'What would you do with this prophecy?' I said. 'I mean to say, I'm willing to help the king and the government. It's better than the Imperial Order taking over. But it isn't really mine to give you, so—'

'You trust me, don't you? I have always dealt fairly with you?'

I did not answer.

'Here,' he said. 'I am being generous. Take my hand and make this a bargain before I lose my patience.'

I could have turned and left. But the five thousand crowns already held me like a prisoner's chains. 'Go on,' he said. 'Just take it.' I took his hand.

I put the paper on the table. It was strange to see Aldebaran's writing here in the back room of Jared's shop; it felt like selling a family member to a gang of thieves. Jared bent his head over it, fixing his expression so that I could make nothing of it. Then he nodded. He went on nodding as he crossed to a safe in the wall and began counting out notes. 'Go on, take it,' he said. Our bargain hung in the air for a moment, while the wind and the snow howled around the walls of the shop. Then my fingers took hold of the notes, and the deal was closed.

'Can I go?' I said. 'It's getting late, and I should get back.'

'As you wish.' I turned to leave. 'Wait,' he said as I started towards the door. 'Are you going to walk through the city like that?'

'Like what?'

'With that money in your pocket. Here.' He went to the counter, reached up, and took a pistol down from the rack. 'Have this.'

'It's all right,' I said.

'But you must. I insist.' He took a box of ammunition from under the counter and began loading it.

'I can't take it,' I said. 'We had a no-guns policy in the shop. I don't want to go against—'

'Oh, don't act so sanctimonious. Look, you can leave the safety catch on if you want to; just take it out if anyone gives you trouble on the way back.'

'No,' I said. 'I really don't want a gun. I don't even have a licence.'

'No one does any more. The police cannot control it. Anselm, it is dangerous to walk about the city without a gun in these days.'

'People do,' I said.

'Listen,' he said. 'How far away are the Alcyrian army? Answer me.'

'Ositha,' I said.

'Twenty-five miles. And when they are here, those who can fight will have a better chance. I worry about you – all of you. Maria has no one to look after her.'

'She doesn't need looking after.'

'I have seen invasions,' he said. 'I've traveled, and I've seen them. Every war-torn city on this continent. There will be fighting in the streets. People will raid the houses. You might not want to accept the situation, but it's here, whether or not you choose to look at it straight. It's a few miles away, with machine guns and armoured vehicles. All right?'

He held my gaze so that I had to nod. 'So take the gun,' he said, and put it into my hand. 'It's a Delmar Philippi .45. A good gun. You have heard of that one?'

People sold them at the market for a hundred crowns. I made an attempt to push it back into his hands. 'I am not letting you walk home with that money unless you take this gun,' he said.

'Are you armed?' I said.

He opened his jacket wearily, as though submitting to a search. He had two pistols and a rusty knife that looked like it could kill. I think it was then that I realized properly I had made a mistake. 'Listen,' I said. 'Maybe this was all a bad idea.'

'What was?' said Jared. 'Our bargain? But I'm afraid it's made now, and sealed.' He let his jacket fall again and put the paper with Aldebaran's writing into the safe. 'It's getting late. Just go on home, and we can talk about it another day.'

'What are you going to do with it?' I said. 'I just want to know.'

'Listen,' he said. 'You can trust me. All right?'

I put the gun into my pocket. There was nothing else to do. 'Good lad,' he said, as though I was six years old. Then he raised his hand in dismissal, and I was in the road and running, the pistol thumping against my ribs and five thousand crowns in my pocket. I had known that Jared Wright was dishonest from the start. But I had not thought him dangerous. And now I was not sure. Anyone is dangerous who has no restraint, Leo told me once, when I was a little boy and too small to think him wise. Standing there with those guns in his pockets, Jared had looked like a man who was capable of anything. He had been in Lucien's government, after all. And Aldebaran's words were lying there on the table waiting for him to do whatever he chose with them.

I could not hold out beyond the end of Trader's Row. I turned and ran back to Jared's shop. The light was still burning. I hammered on the door. But Jared did not answer, and I could not see him through the glass. I only succeeded in waking half the street. The snow was falling harder now. I had no choice but to give up and go home.

I dreamed about Leo that night. He was sleeping on a bunk somewhere in a dark building, among strangers. I could see every detail of his face, the lines that had crossed his skin too early and the grey strands in his hair. I could even make out the letters on the ring on his finger: M.V.A., my mother's initials. He was turning the ring around as he slept, and I was willing him to wake up. I was willing him, in spite of everything, to come home. I was calling his name when I woke. 'Leo,' I was crying. 'Papa, come back.' It was like when I lay awake as a small boy and wished and wished he would sense it somehow and wake and come to my side. I knew what I suspected him of, but my heart could not shake him off so cheaply.

I got up and dressed and walked back to Trader's Row, though it was barely six o'clock and still night over the city. Jared's shop was in darkness. I sat on the step, wrapped in my overcoat, and watched the birds cling to the skeletons of the trees, waking out of a cold sleep with their feathers ruffled. I was determined to get those papers back. But though I hammered on the door at intervals, and though I sat there over an hour, Jared did not come to the door. I got up and went round the side of the shop and looked in at the window. The shop was in darkness, and the back room stood deserted. Eventually I turned round and went home.

The money weighed heavily on my chest all through that day and the next. On the third, my grandmother said, 'We really must pay this midwife's bill.'

I held out for a long time without speaking. We were sitting round the table – Jasmine and my grandmother and me – while she sewed and we pretended to do our homework. 'How much is it?' I said eventually.

'Two hundred crowns.'

I took a few notes out of my jacket pocket, as though that was all I had. 'Here,' I said.

My grandmother held the money away from her suspiciously. 'Where did you get this?' she demanded.

I had this plan worked out. It had to be something dishonest, because no one ever earned five thousand crowns entirely honestly – and they would know before long that five thousand crowns was what I had, even if I handed it over by degrees. 'I won this money,' I said. 'Playing cards with some of the old traders.'

'You did what?' said my grandmother.

'Won it playing cards.'

'Gambling, Anselm!'

'Who has been gambling?' said my mother from the next room.

'Your son has, Maria. Honestly!' My grandmother stormed into my mother's bedroom. 'He gave me this money and told me quite boldly that he had won it playing cards.'

'How much is it?'

'Two hundred crowns,' I said. 'It's for the midwife's bill.'

My mother took the notes and studied them. 'Oh, Anselm,' she said, and looked at me so tenderly that I had to turn away. My grandmother tutted and marched back into the living room. 'I suppose I should be scolding you,' my mother said. 'But I can't. I really can't.' And she agreed to take the money.

Two days before Christmas Eve, something happened to drive the prophecy and Jared Wright out of my mind. The Alcyrians gave up Ositha and retreated two miles.

The atmosphere in school that day was like a national holiday. Sister Theresa let us leave early, and nearly all the class joined in the national anthem. A weak sun was shining over the city, making the snow glitter in crystals of lilac and blue. I could not remember when we had last seen the sun. 'Two days until my school play,' said Jasmine as we crossed the new square. 'Is Mama coming?'

'She is still very sick. But she will if she can.'

'Do you think Papa will come back for it?'

I hesitated. I was uncertain how to answer that.

'It might happen,' said Jasmine. 'Mightn't it?'

And then my heart stopped. I was certain that I had seen Leo. People were crowding around us on every side, and I caught his cigarette smoke on the air and saw a gold-haired man turn for a second, then vanish among the stalls. I began struggling through the people towards him, dragging Jasmine by the hand. 'What is it?' she said. 'Anselm, I'm getting squashed! Don't run so fast.'

'Come on,' I said. 'Stay with me. Jasmine, come on!'

The man was walking faster now, towards the edge of the market. We followed him. Jasmine ran beside me, her shawl trailing and her thumb in her mouth. He was several yards ahead, and carts were surging between us.

'Leo?' I said. He did not turn. I broke into a jog, trying to keep pace with him. He was almost running now, taking a watch out of his pocket every few steps to check the time. I did not recognize that watch. 'Leo?' I said, louder.

The man turned, and his face was wrong. 'What is it?' he said. 'Are you two following me?'

He had an accent like my mother's employer, a high-class accent. 'No,' I said. I could hardly speak for disappointment.

'You were. I saw you. What are you playing at?'

'We aren't playing at anything.' I took Jasmine's hand. 'I thought you were someone else.'

'Anselm?' said Jasmine timidly as I turned and pulled her back towards the square. 'Why did you think he was Papa?'

'I don't know.'

'He didn't even look the same.'

'I don't know what I was thinking,' I said.

The sun vanished behind a new bank of snow clouds. People hurried towards their houses, and the city grew empty and bitterly cold. The gunfire was clear again, if you stood still and listened. I wondered how long we would keep that meagre two miles of land. When we got home, the answer was in the newspapers. It was already lost.

Jasmine could not sleep that night. I heard her turning over and sighing, a quick impatient sigh like Leo's. 'Anselm?' she said eventually.

'Yes,' I said.

'Will you light the candle?'

I did it. 'Can't you sleep?' I asked her. The clock in the square was chiming twelve.

She shook her head. 'I've done a bad thing, Anselm.'

'What have *you* done, Jasmine?' I said, startled.

She looked at the ground, opening her mouth and closing it again. I could tell she was working up to tell me. Eventually she said, 'I've lost the prophecy Aldebaran gave me.'

My heart turned over. I had been waiting for her to realize that someone had stolen it, but I had never thought she would blame herself.

'I've lost it,' she said in desperation. 'I can't find it anywhere.'

'How?' I said.

'I don't know. I thought it was in the box, but it isn't. I must have forgotten to put it back in.'

'You can't have forgotten,' I said.

'But it's not there.'

'Maybe someone took it.'

'Mama wouldn't. You wouldn't.' She paused, then said, 'Grandmama?' I did not answer. 'But Grandmama wouldn't know about secret compartments,' said Jasmine. 'Unless . . .' She frowned. 'Those Imperial men might have done it. They're always standing around here, aren't they?'

'Are they?'

'Yes. At night when everyone else is asleep, I get up and sometimes I see them.'

My heart gave a strange jump. 'When, Jasmine?'

'Just sometimes.'

'Yesterday? Or the day before?'

'Maybe.' She sighed. 'Anselm, I shouldn't have lost that prophecy. I think it was important.'

'Can you still remember it?' I said.

'Yes, of course, but—'

'That is what matters,' I said. 'Uncle wouldn't have cared

about you losing a scrap of paper. The words are what count with prophecies.'

'Are you sure?'

'Yes. We studied it at school, when I was at Sacred Heart.' Before magic grew unpopular and all the great ones vanished. That was when we studied it.

'Thank you, Anselm,' she said, as though a burden had suddenly been lifted from her. 'I'm glad about that.'

I felt like the worst brother in the world. Jasmine got out of bed and went to our box of books in the corner, throwing aside the old shawl my grandmother had laid fastidiously over it. 'Will you read to me?' she said.

'What shall I read?'

'A story out of the Bible. It's nearly Christmas, and I want to hear one.'

'The story of Mary and Joseph going to Bethlehem?' I said.

She shook her head. She returned with my mother's old Sunday school Bible, but she did not open it. 'Anselm, I'm sick and tired,' she said.

'What of?'

'Everything. Everything is going wrong.'

'Everyone has to go through troubles,' I said, though I felt the same. 'And it doesn't look like it now, but when they are finished again, we will forget about them. When the baby is three or four years old, we will tell him about how he was born in a country at war, and we'll make it into a story.'

'Anselm,' she said. 'Why hasn't Papa sent us a letter?'

'He will.'

'Mama said yesterday that once the baby is born, we are going to Holy Island. Is that true?'

I did not know. Since that night Jared Wright had taken me to Devil's Cross, I had hardly spoken to my mother. Jasmine got back into bed, drew the blanket up to her chin, and watched me. With only her grey eyes showing, she looked very like Leo. 'I keep dreaming that we go to find him but we can't,' she said, 'so we just keep walking until we come to the sea. A horrible black sea, with ice all over it, and we can't find Papa. Then Mama says, "Quick, the baby is going to be born. Where shall we go?" But men with guns come, and they start pushing us into the sea, and—'

I handed her the Bible. 'Read us both a story, Jas. Choose one. Like when you were little.'

'That was when I couldn't even read properly,' said Jasmine, wrinkling her nose. My mother had taught her to read on three pages of the Bible every night.

'Still, you read better than me. You have more expression.'

'What's expression?'

'Acting. Here, I'll find you something to read.'

I turned over the pages, searching for a chapter. December was Isaiah, I remembered. I found the passage from Mass the week before. 'There,' I said.

Jasmine pulled the blanket up over her face so that I could not even see her eyes, and she read to me like that, but at least the dream was temporarily forgotten. ' "Comfort, comfort my people, says your God," ' she read. She went on reading, in the same voice Father Dunstan had used, a ringing voice like a real prophet. I knew where the chapter finished when Jasmine came to it; this part was why I had chosen it. ' "Even youths grow tired and weary, and young men stumble and fall; but those who hope in the Lord will renew their strength. They will soar on wings like eagles; they will run and not grow weary; they will walk and not be faint." ' Jasmine looked up then. 'But what about the people who don't hope in the Lord? What about them?'

'Everyone hopes,' I said. 'I mean, everyone has faith in something. Everyone has something that makes them want to go on. I think that's all it means.'

'You sound like Michael. He always made the Bible into something else.'

'Yes,' I said. 'I suppose he always did.'

'Was it because he didn't believe in it?'

'I don't know, Jas. I think everyone makes the Bible into something else. If that's the only way it can help you, is there any harm?'

'Do you miss him?' she said. 'Do you miss Michael?'

'Well . . .' I said. 'It's not so bad. I might see him again.'

I didn't know how we had got onto this so abruptly. I took the Bible from her and made as if to study it. 'I wonder who Isaiah was,' I said. 'He was a very great poet. When I was a little boy, I always imagined him like Aldebaran.'

She watched me. 'Anselm,' she said. 'If you miss Michael, just say yes.'

I didn't know what to answer to that. Jasmine lay down and pulled the blanket up to her chin. We watched the last coals dying on the fire. My grandmother never built it up in the evenings; by the first light, the windows were always frosted. I turned it over to make it burn hotter.

Jasmine reached out and shielded the candle with her hand. She looked very solemn in that light, with her hair falling loose across the pillow and her face still young, like hardly more than a baby.

'Jasmine,' I said. 'I am a very bad person. If you knew, I don't know what you would say.'

'Is it because you gambled?' she said, gazing up at me. 'And because you fought with John Keller and smashed the windows of our old shop?'

I could not tell her the truth. I hesitated, then nodded.

'I'm glad you did all those things,' she said fiercely. 'Stupid Doctor Keller. If it wasn't for him, we would still be in our shop.'

'Yes,' I said.

'And I don't think gambling is a very bad sin,' she said. 'Not like killing someone, or hurting a little baby, or being in the Imperial Order.'

I almost smiled at her earnestness. She was halfway to sleep now.

'Anselm?' she said. 'Do you think it will be all right, acting a real play in front of important people? I keep thinking about it.'

'Of course,' I said. 'You'll forget about being nervous at all when you are acting.'

'This will be the start of my career as an actress.'

'That's right.'

'It's in the Royal Gardens, isn't it?' she said. 'Billy says he saw them putting up the stage.'

I nodded. She was lying with one eye open, as if to check I was still watching over her. 'You know that prophecy?' she said.

'Yes.'

'You know the last-descendant part?'

'Yes.' I had to whisper, 'What, Jasmine?' several times before she heard me. She rolled over and murmured the answer, already halfway to sleep. By the time I deciphered it, she was gone. She had whispered, 'It means the baby.'

★ ★ ★

We did not mention that conversation the next day, but it weighed heavier and heavier on my mind. Jasmine was in a state of high excitement about her play; even the troops marching through the city could not crush it. But when we were down in the yard, shovelling snow from the door on my grandmother's orders, she kept breaking off to stare at the gap between the houses. 'What are you doing?' I asked her at last.

'Trying to make Papa come home.'

I paused, halfway to lifting a shovelful of gritty snow into the barrow. For a moment, I was certain he would appear there, dragging his battered suitcase with the belt around it, a cigarette jammed in his mouth. But no one came. The street was in darkness. Christmas lanterns were hanging along the washing line of the middle apartment. They swung in the wind, and the line sang mournfully, almost too low to hear.

'I think he will,' she said. 'I really do. I think I can make him come back.'

'Maybe you can,' I said.

'He has to see my play.'

We had walked home past the Royal Gardens and had seen the stage and the barriers where the thousands of people would stand to watch the play and the king's speech. The whole city would be there.

'I wish I could go to see Jasmine acting,' said my mother that evening, sipping tea and shivering. My grandmother had dragged Jasmine off to Mass to stop her from running about the living room reciting her part.

'She will tell you all about it,' I said.

'Yes.' She was sitting up in bed, watching a few snowflakes fall past the narrow back window. They were too large to look real, very bright against the grimy stone of the buildings. 'Anselm?' she said then. 'Is something wrong? I hardly seem to see you any more.'

I was halfway to the door. 'No,' I said. 'Nothing is wrong.'

'Don't go. Come and sit with me a while.'

I went back reluctantly and sat on the edge of the bed. She was studying my face, but I could not look at her. I watched the steam rising from the surface of the tea instead. 'There is something,' she said.

'No.'

'You don't even look at me any more.'

'I do,' I said. But I was not looking at her even when I said it.

'Anselm?' she said, and touched the side of my face so that I had to meet her eyes. They were awash with tears.

'What is it?' I said, startled.

'Listen,' she said. 'Anselm, listen.'

'What is it?'

She handed me something. It had been in the pocket of her dressing gown. A folded scrap of paper in an envelope. I opened it and held it to the light of the lamp. It was a warrant, with the Imperial Order's sign at the top, for Leo's arrest.

'Who brought this?' I asked.

'It was slipped under the door. Someone had re-addressed it from our shop – Mr Pascal probably.' Her voice became hardly comprehensible on the last words. The tears fell from her eyes, and she shuddered with grief. 'Is this why he left?' she said. 'Is that why he went away? Because the Imperial Order want to kill him?'

I tried to touch her arm. She fought me away suddenly.

'You knew! Why didn't you tell me? You knew, Anselm!'

'I didn't . . . I couldn't tell you – I didn't want to worry you. Please, don't cry.'

'Worry me?' she said. 'Do you think I was not worried? Believing Leo had left us for ever? Thinking he didn't send an address because he didn't want to see us ever again?'

'How could you think that?'

'I don't know!' she said with a trace of anger. 'I don't know, Anselm, how I could be stupid enough—'

'I didn't mean that you were stupid, but, Mother, listen . . .'

She surrendered to tears. They racked her whole body. I did not know what to say, and I looked at the warrant instead. The final words hit me coldly in the stomach: *Wanted for his conspiracy in the murder of Ahira.*

'Anselm, there is something else,' she said. 'It's what it says he did.'

' "His conspiracy in the murder of Ahira," ' I said.

At the name Ahira, she shivered. 'Anselm, it's not just that it makes him a murderer. If you had any idea . . .' She trailed off and shivered again. I hesitated. I knew what she was talking about, but I did not know if I had the courage to say it.

'Mother,' I said eventually. 'I know about him. Ahira. I know all about it.'

Her crying froze as she looked at me. The tears rolled down her face and came to rest in the corners of her mouth.

'I know about my real father,' I said. 'And I thought Leo might have had something to do with him dying, right from the start. I don't know how. The two stories seemed to make sense like that.' I was startled by my own voice. It held very steady, and it was easier to go on now than turn back. 'But why didn't you tell me any of this?' I said. 'I don't understand why you let me grow up without knowing.'

She shook her head. She went on shaking it, looking at me as if she had never really seen me before. 'How could I tell you?' she said eventually. She tried to brush the tears from her face, but more fell. 'Anselm, if Leo did shoot him, what are we going to do? What on earth are we going to do? How are we going to carry on living?'

'We can't pretend everything is still all right,' I said. 'Mama, don't you have any idea if he did or didn't?'

'I don't know the truth,' she said. 'I don't know if he did or didn't do it. But I think . . .' She shuddered again. 'I think he did. Anselm, he talks in his sleep – he has for years. He confesses things that he never would say in real life.'

'Then I don't know how things can ever be the same,' I said.

She went on crying. She reached for my hand, and I let her take it, though I felt nothing. I felt like we had all divided from each other weeks ago, when things started to go wrong, and I could not close the distance between us now. 'What are we going to do?' she said. 'Anselm, what on earth are we going to do?'

'I don't know,' I said.

'Ahira was a hated man,' she said. 'Someone else would have done it. Anyone would. That's what I always told myself when I first suspected Leo . . .'

My hands were trembling slightly, like an old man's. 'What I don't understand,' I said, 'is why you don't hate me too.' She glanced up with a quick breath, as though she was in pain. 'I look like him,' I said, and now my voice lost its composure. 'Everyone thinks so. Didn't you hate me? Didn't you wish I'd never been born?'

'Anselm, don't say that.'

'But why not? I look like him – I have his same features and his red hair. And maybe I'm even like him. I don't know.'

'You are nothing like him!'

'The whole thing is such a cheap story.'

'Anselm, it sounds so terrible in theory. I sound like such a slut and a stupid, worthless girl, and your father sounds nothing but evil. And, yes, I should have hated you, in theory. But listen to me. Life isn't a theory like that.'

'Isn't it?' I said.

'No! Of course it isn't.'

She touched the side of my face. I closed my eyes and let her go on; I did not have the heart to stop her. 'I thought I was dying when you were born,' she said. 'I was only fifteen – the worst pain I had lived through was a sprain in my ankle when I fell off riding.' She half laughed and half sobbed. 'And then suddenly it was all over, and they put you in my arms, this tiny baby not even crying, and I loved you. And you were the best thing that happened to me, Anselm, when he was the worst, and he was the reason I thought I'd lost everything, but you were the reason I had to get up and start again. I couldn't have seen it like that until it happened, but that was how it was.'

'And what?' I said. I sounded like a sulky child, which was not fair, because my heart was breaking.

'Of course it's complicated,' she said. 'I used to pray that it was not true; I used to pray that I would wake up and everything would be like it was before I met him. But after you were born, I started praying the opposite. I started to pray that nothing would happen to take you away from me. Anselm, I loved you more, I think, because I never expected to. You are the one thing that redeems him for me. You are everything he would have been if he had been a good man. I even find I'm less afraid of him now, because I know you. All that was stupid, that superstitious fear I had of him. He was just a man.'

'I'm not good,' I said. 'I've done bad things too. If you knew . . .' I could not go on; tears were obscuring my voice.

'Shh,' she said. 'Hey, Anselm. Anselm. Don't cry like that. Please. It is not so terrible. It will be all right.'

It reminded me of when I cried when I was a little boy, and she would try to comfort me with any old words that came into her head. 'Listen,' she said. 'Everyone is just a person who makes mistakes and does things wrong, some-times in the full knowledge that they are evil, yes, and sometimes for no reason. But no one is the devil incarnate. Not even him.'

'But Ahira—'

'No,' she said firmly. 'Not even him.'

'Didn't you hate me?' I said. 'Ever?'

'I expected to,' she said quietly. 'But everything works out differently from what you first intend.'

I still could not look at her. But she reached out to take my hand again, and I let her. 'Leo loves you like his own son,' she said. 'He always has. You saved him, Anselm. You really did. You were the only one who could bring him back to life after Stirling died. I don't believe everything happens for a reason, but sometimes I've come close to it. And even now, even with this' – she nodded towards the warrant resting on my knees – 'I still wish we could go back to how things used to be. Is that stupid?'

I could not speak. She gripped my hand tighter. 'What shall we do?' she said. 'Tell me what to do, Anselm.'

I picked up the warrant. It stood there in black letters: *his conspiracy in the murder of Ahira.* Somewhere out there, the truth existed, the heartless fact of who had fired the shot. I hesitated. Then I threw the warrant into the fire. I did not know I had decided to do it until it was already done. And I knew it was for the better not to know. The past is the past, like Jasmine said. Things were bad enough already.

We watched the page curl and vanish. My mother raised a hand to brush my hair back from my forehead, then stopped with a strange expression.

'What is it?' I said. 'Are you in pain?'

'No,' she said. 'No, it's all right. Just the baby kicking.'

And in spite of everything, we could not help taking it as a sign.

NIGHTFALL
THE EIGHTH OF JANUARY

'So that was what you did,' said Mr Hardy after a long silence. 'You never mentioned it again?'

I shook my head.

'And what about the prophecy?' he said. 'And what about Jasmine's play? And what about Leo? Were they all right?'

'There isn't much more to tell,' I said. 'I'll finish it now.'

CHRISTMAS

'Mama isn't coming to my play, is she?' Jasmine asked me on Christmas Eve. She had crept across the living room before it was yet light and woken me. I turned over. I had not been dreaming, and the absence of dreams surprised me. Usually I had to drag myself back into reality from a thick fog of nightmares. But today, nothing. Just the white snow light beyond the curtains and Jasmine's face leaning over me.

'No,' I said, and sat up. 'Sorry, Jasmine. She is too sick to go and stand with all those crowds.'

'Will Papa come back for it?'

'I don't think so.'

'No,' she said seriously. 'Neither do I.' She went to the hearth and dressed there in the faint heat of the fire, braiding her hair carefully in the ornate mirror. My grandmother was bustling about, setting pans on the stove with a loud clattering.

'I will be there,' I told Jasmine. 'Whatever else happens.' She gave me a quick smile.

My mother was trying not to cry as she said goodbye to Jasmine; I could tell by the brightness of her smile. Jasmine would go with the rest of her class straight to the Royal Gardens, and we would not see her until the evening. I missed her as I walked home from school. My grandmother and I left early, in our Sunday clothes. Father Dunstan was going to call in on my mother on his way past. I could tell as we descended the four flights of stairs that the rest of the building was empty. It made my heart ache, to leave my mother here while the rest of the city hurried past her towards the Royal Gardens.

The place was already packed; we had to stand at the back of the crowd. There were soldiers everywhere, lined up against the fences with rifles on their shoulders. Overhead, the snow clouds were drifting fast. People stood close to coal braziers and pulled their shawls and scarves up over their faces.

'Where will Jasmine be?' my grandmother asked anxiously, standing on her toes to try and see through the crowd.

'I didn't know there would be so many people,' I said. 'I hope she isn't nervous.'

'Would Jasmine ever be nervous?'

I almost smiled. My grandmother and I had not made our peace, but the atmosphere united us. When the snow clouds parted, I could see a few stars. The crowds stretched in every direction, more solemn and motionless than they were on any national holiday. I pulled Leo's old jacket tighter around me. Over the dark and overgrown far wall, I could see the top of Ahira's house. I wondered if that boy and girl were still there beside their fire. I hoped they were far from here, already on some journey.

A long way off, on the stage, I could see Mr Victoire. I recognized him from my own days at Sacred Heart. He was a very thin man with a glaring expression, marching about ordering the children into their positions. Another teacher was standing there too. 'Let's go further forward,' I said. 'I want to see Jasmine.'

We began struggling through the crowd, but it was solid and we had to give up. 'We'll see her well enough from here,' said my grandmother.

Lanterns were coming out around the fences. With the snow swept away, and the fires burning, and the temporary stage there under the shadow of the castle rock, I imagined we were still living in the days when Malonia prospered, the days Harold North wrote about. A makeshift band was playing patriotic songs on the other side of the gardens, a violin and an accordion and an old four-stringed guitar. A few people joined in.

'I hope Mother is all right,' I said.

'She will be. The baby is not due for another week or more.'

I leaned forward, trying to see. In front of us, a group of rowdy boys were throwing a glass bottle about, almost knocking the surrounding people over every time they tried to catch it. 'Stop it, William,' said a girl beside them sternly, and one of the boys made a feeble attempt to look sober. The girl was jogging a baby in her arms. It was wrapped so tightly in shawls that I could not make out its face, but from among the shawls issued an angry wail.

'Where is Jasmine?' my grandmother kept asking.

'She comes in from the left,' I whispered. And at that moment, people began muttering. My grandmother started and put a hand on my arm, but it was only the beginning of the play.

A small figure crossed the stage in a shawl and cloak and with an old-fashioned alms cup around her neck.

'There she is,' my grandmother whispered to me.

I nodded, but I could hardly believe Jasmine was real from this distance. She looked like an imaginary child or like a real storyteller, one of the wandering minstrels in those noble days that were gone. She walked to the middle of the stage and stood there, waiting for the other character, the soldier, to come on from the other side. He was dressed in red, like the modern guards, a boy a year or two older than her.

Jasmine waited while he sat down wearily at the edge of the stage. Then she knelt beside him and began: 'Good friend, draw close and hearken to my tale . . .' And in that whole crowd, in the thousands upon thousands of people, no one made a sound.

My grandmother clapped harder than anyone when the play finished. She clapped until her hair fell down out of its neat scarf. The atmosphere had unfrozen suddenly; the silence had held us all united, but now the crowd drew apart again. Jasmine and the other children dragged each other by the hands to the front of the stage and bent into an uneven bow. Then two soldiers escorted them down to where the teachers were waiting. I could not see Jasmine unless I stood on tiptoes. Her eyes were moving over the crowd, trying to find us. I waved but she did not see it.

A few snowflakes fell. I could taste their chill in the air.

'Will she be all right?' said my grandmother, still clapping.

'I suppose we can go and fetch her after the speech.'

'She was the best one in it,' said my grandmother. 'She was the star, wasn't she?'

People were still clapping. My grandmother glanced about with pride, as if to tell the rest of the city that the girl with the red shawl was her granddaughter. 'Anselm,' she said then, pointing. 'I declare I know that man.'

'Who?' I said.

'There. Over there, by the fence.'

I followed her glance. 'It's Jared Wright,' I said, startled. 'Isn't it?'

'Do you know him?'

'Only a bit.'

'I haven't seen him since before you were born. Someone told me he was back in the city. How do you know of him?'

'He took the Barones' shop after they left. He was living next door. I'm surprised you never met him.'

'Heavens, no. I never thought I would see him again in my life.' My grandmother took a final look, then turned back to me. 'They say he has two hundred million crowns,' she said into my ear. 'I don't know what he is doing keeping a shop.'

'Nobody has two hundred million crowns.'

'I spoke to Lady Marlazzi in the square; she often stops to see me. The rumour goes that he made his fortune running guns into Alcyria.'

'No,' I said. 'I never heard that.' And yet I could not help glancing back over at Jared. I told myself it was just my grandmother's gossip. But I could not quite believe it.

The king came up the steps, and the crowd began murmuring. I could see him more clearly than I had in my life as he emerged onto the platform. A tall man, with greying hair and a strange look that came from growing old too young. He was dressed in ordinary clothes, surrounded by four men in black suits. People bowed and knelt down around us. I knew it was only superstition, but I did the same. He looked so exhausted that he could hardly acknowledge the crowd's applause. People were reaching up onto the stage to grasp his hands or the hem of his cloak. He took the hands of the people who reached out to him, but the bodyguards closed around him almost at once. They ushered him back into the middle of the stage, where soldiers were setting up a lectern. Before the speech began, there was a long silence in which the snow still did not fall.

'People of Malonia,' he said at last, leaning heavily on the lectern. 'On this Christmas night, I greet you. I thank you for your sixteen years of good faith. But tonight I also ask you to keep this faith a while longer. I ask you to keep it no matter what trials lie ahead. I ask you to stand united, no matter how many of us fall behind in the struggle. Because there will always be another generation to carry on the faith, as long as you do not let it go out.'

I stood on tiptoes again and made out Jasmine among the crowds. She was watching the king with her thumb in her mouth. I had heard all his speeches but never one that began like this. These were the most impassioned words that I had ever heard him speak. Then, as he raised his head to continue, there was a burst of explosions. They sounded less than ten miles off. Scattered gunfire echoed on the breeze. And I realized then why he was speaking differently. This was his last speech to us. The rest of the city realized it at the same moment and panicked.

As soon as the crowd began surging, Jasmine started towards us at a run, breaking away from Mr Victoire and vanishing as the people closed over her head. I lost sight of her altogether. I struggled towards the stage, not caring who I knocked aside. Jasmine and I met close to the fence, crushed between two groups of boys. Then someone elbowed me hard in the head, and we both went down. We were on the ground, among the cigarette butts and the grimy snow, and the crowd was trampling around us now in terror. I struggled to stand up and fell again. A boot collided with my ribs. 'Jasmine!' I said, trying to protect her from their blows.

Then someone caught my collar and Jasmine's wrist and dragged us to our feet. I turned to thank him and met Jared's eyes. 'Come on,' he said. He took out a pistol and the crowd parted. He threw his arm roughly over my shoulders, picked up Jasmine, and battled towards the gates. My grandmother was waiting, wringing her shawl in her hands. Jared delivered us to her, then turned to leave. 'Get out,' he said. 'I have a bad feeling about this.'

'Wait,' I said, catching hold of his arm. 'Jared, why have you been avoiding me? I wanted to talk to you about that paper—'

He shook his head. 'It's too late.'

'How is it too late?'

He looked at me for a moment, then turned away. 'I have to go,' he said. 'I will see you . . .' He did not finish the sentence.

'Did you make your fortune selling guns?' I said. I don't know why I asked it, but suddenly I had to know. I knew I would not see him again before this was over. Jared shook his head, but I could tell it meant nothing. He went on shaking it as he turned and vanished into the night.

'Come on, come on,' said my grandmother, pulling us after her.

'I wanted to hear the speech,' said Jasmine, dragging on her hand.

'It was almost over anyway. Let's go back and see your mother.'

They went on arguing, but I did not listen. I had noticed

the newspaper sellers. They were setting up their stands on the street corners, in spite of the late hour. The commotion in the Royal Gardens had died down again.

'Look at that,' I said into the silence. Neither my grandmother nor Jasmine looked; they were too intent on their argument.

I could only remember the newspaper sellers doing this ten or twenty times in my life; usually it was not worth selling the next day's paper when the city was already closing down for the night. They had done it last year when there was a series of murders and the whole city was in uproar. And they had done it the day Aldebaran was assassinated. I stopped at the nearest stand and tried to see the headline. But the girl unloading the papers kept them covered and did not seem inclined to speak to me. I wondered if it was the Alcyrian army, if the newspapers would proclaim that they had reached the city.

'Come along, Anselm!' my grandmother called. 'Let's get back home.'

As we walked through the city, the newspaper sellers began shouting in chorus. At first I could not make out what they said. Then, as we came round a corner, I heard it clearly. 'Aldebaran's Last Prophecy!'

I stopped, horror fixing me to the spot. Jasmine had stopped too, and she turned and looked at me. In that second, she understood; I could tell by the fierceness of her eyes. Then she ran away, her shawl trailing behind her.

'Jasmine, come back this instant!' my grandmother shouted. 'What on earth are you doing?'

I could not call Jasmine's name, but I ran after her. She was too fast for me. As she rounded the corner of Old College Lane, she collided with someone. He caught hold of her arms to stop her from falling. 'Hey, Jasmine,' he said. It was Father Dunstan.

'Let me go!' said Jasmine. She was angrier than I had ever seen her. 'Let me go now!'

'Shh, shh,' said the priest. 'Is your grandmother with you?'

'She is just behind,' I said. 'Jasmine, listen. I swear—'

Father Dunstan caught my arm. 'Don't go any further. I need to talk to you.'

My ears had been pounding, but now I heard a clamour coming from the street ahead. Jasmine broke free, and I followed her round the side of the building. A hundred people were standing outside my grandmother's house. Men with notebooks and shabby suits, what looked like half the police, and several members of the Imperial Order.

'What are they all doing there?' said Jasmine.

'Where is Mother?' I said.

Father Dunstan caught my arm again to stop me from advancing any further. 'She's not there,' he said.

'Where is she?'

'I was on my way to find you.' He picked Jasmine up to stop her from running away again, despite the fact that she kicked and struggled. 'You can't go back there,' he said. 'They are looking for you. Maria is already at the hospital, but when I came back, I saw all this commotion.'

'At the hospital?' I said.

'Yes.' He set Jasmine down; her struggles had died abruptly. 'She was taken very badly, but they are looking after her. She sent me back to find you. When I saw this crowd, I knew you must still be at the Royal Gardens. I knocked, but there was no one in the building, so I started back to look for you.'

My grandmother came running up at that point, her heeled shoes slipping on the icy street. 'What is all this?' she said.

'Come away,' said Father Dunstan, explaining again as he ushered us back along the street. At the next crossroads, we were separated by the crowds coming from the Royal Gardens. Jasmine would not push through, and on the other side of the road, my grandmother was shifting from foot to foot with anxiety. 'You two catch us up,' she shouted, when the flow of people showed no sign of dwindling. 'Don't lose Jasmine, whatever you do.' And she and the priest went on ahead of us.

As soon as they rounded the corner, Jasmine caught my arm and said, 'We have to go back.'

'Where?' I said.

'Grandmama's house.'

'What? Why, Jasmine?'

She was running again before I could catch her, back the way we had come. I had no choice but to follow. I stopped her at the corner of the street. The building was still surrounded; a few journalists were trying to break in at the window. 'Jasmine, come on,' I said. 'We have to go to the hospital.'

'Wait,' she said. 'Oh, Anselm!'

'What is it?' I said, alarmed now.

As we watched, something began, so faintly that I was not certain of it. A drift of smoke started to rise from the building. We watched it curl into the still air. It steadied, then began billowing blackly. 'My God,' I said. 'The house is on fire.'

The police noticed at the same moment. They began blowing their whistles and running around the street.

Someone filled his jacket with snow and threw it at the smoke-filled window.

'What shall we do?' I said. And as I said it, the whole house went up in flames. It did it suddenly and completely. The fire-service carts were already approaching from the distance, but I knew it was too late. The heat forced us back against the wall. We stood there in hopeless terror and watched the house burn to the ground.

I don't know how long we stood there staring at it. By the time either of us moved, the crowd had vanished altogether and only the police and the firefighters were there, putting out the last smouldering remains of the building. The neighbours were standing about in the street, shaking their heads or crying mutely as they returned from the Royal Gardens to find everything gone.

'Come on,' I told Jasmine. 'We were supposed to go to the hospital. We can't stay here; let's just go.'

She took my hand when I held it out, and followed me. What we had seen had taken both our voices. 'Listen,' I said eventually. 'Don't tell Mama or Grandmama yet.'

'Anselm,' she said. 'Let's run. I have bad feelings about everything.'

That was enough, and we broke into an uneven run, hand in hand across the hard snow. The newspaper sellers were still shouting about the prophecy. The Imperial Order were out on the streets. The city was in chaos now. People were running in every direction, dragging their children and the old people after them in an attempt to reach their houses and get out. We could hear gunfire, quite distinctly, but the snow distorted every sound, and I could not tell if it was in the city or outside it. We struggled up the hospital steps, Jasmine holding up her long costume so as not to trip. The entrance hall was eerily silent. An abandoned wheelchair stood near the doors; two lines of hard benches lined the walls, with only three or four people on them.

'Anselm!' said my grandmother, appearing at a door. 'We have been waiting nearly an hour. We didn't know what to think – come on!' She dragged us down a dark corridor and up a flight of stairs. Jasmine kept tripping on her long dress, so I picked her up and carried her as we ran.

'Is Mother all right?' I said.

'She is holding out.'

'But is she all right?'

My grandmother did not answer. As we passed a narrow window, I thought I saw fire along the horizon. 'Come on,' said my grandmother, and pulled me away before I could see properly. We hurried up more steps and along a room with curtains at the sides that were patterned in grimy leaves, then into another entrance hall. 'We have to wait here,' said my grandmother. 'Father Dunstan has gone to check how things are going.'

We sat down on the nearest bench. We were all breathing fast now. Jasmine's shawl had come unfastened and was trailing from one shoulder. My grandmother had lost her headscarf entirely. She looked younger and less certain without it.

'Anselm?' said someone then. 'Mrs Andros?' It was Father Dunstan; he had appeared again through a swinging door at the end of a corridor.

'How is she?' said my grandmother.

'Doing as well as can be expected, I think. They say these two women are very good doctors.'

'Father?' said Jasmine. 'Can we wait outside the door where Mama is?'

'The nurse said no . . .' began my grandmother.

'I don't think there would be any harm in it,' said Father Dunstan. 'That nurse has left now. Come with me.'

We got up and followed him. My mother was behind a door at the farthest end of the corridor, where a dingy staircase wound out of sight. There were two battered chairs outside. My grandmother sank onto one and Father Dunstan onto the other, beside her. Jasmine and I sat on the bottom step. She had her thumb in her mouth, and she would not let go of my sleeve. She kept clutching at it as though she was afraid I would leave her. We waited without speaking.

'Is the baby going to be all right?' said Jasmine after a long while had passed.

'Yes,' said my grandmother. 'Of course.'

'He has to be,' murmured Jasmine.

We lapsed into silence again.

'Father?' said Jasmine. 'Will you say a prayer?'

Father Dunstan nodded and took his prayer book from his pocket. It made me think suddenly of Aldebaran's funeral. ' "Lighten our darkness, we beseech thee, O Lord," ' he read, ' "and in thy mercy defend us from all perils and dangers of this night . . ." '

Jasmine went and stood beside him, one hand on his arm. I remained where I was. I could not listen. He started the Lord's Prayer, and my grandmother and Jasmine spoke the words with him, and then he read the psalm that begins, 'God is our refuge and strength, an ever-present help in trouble.' He read very quietly, with the book open across his knees. We could hear the fighting in the city clearly over his voice. Someone was shouting on the ground floor of the hospital, yelling something that we could not make out. Then after a while it went quiet. ' "He makes wars cease to the ends of the earth," ' Father Dunstan read. ' "He breaks the bow and shatters the spear; he burns the shields with fire." '

I got up and walked once to the door, then back to the stairs again. It was better to walk than to stand still, and I went on. As I walked, I counted. When I had paced fifty-seven times to the door and back again, there was a cry inside the room. We all froze. Then someone opened the door. I caught sight of my mother, her face pale and covered in sweat, behind some kind of curtain.

'What are you doing here?' said the nurse, closing the door behind her.

'This is the family of Maria Andros,' said Father Dunstan. 'They want to wait outside the room for any news.' He said it so firmly that the nurse could not argue.

'Mrs Andros is holding out well,' she told us, and turned and marched away down the corridor.

'What does that mean?' said Jasmine.

'It's good news,' said my grandmother, but it wasn't. Father Dunstan forgot his prayers and sat there staring at the low barred window at the end of the corridor. 'You are going to have a little brother or sister,' said my grandmother. 'You should be excited about it, not scared, Jasmine.' Jasmine started to cry.

'Shh,' I said. 'It's all right.' But Leo was the one who knew how to calm her down. She was wailing loudly, her face pale and trembling.

'Shh,' said my grandmother. 'They will send us away if you don't stop crying.'

But fear and exhaustion had got the better of Jasmine. She lay on the floor and wailed. My grandmother glanced at me, and I picked Jasmine up and carried her back along the corridor to the entrance hall. She was struggling so hard that I had to set her down there. 'Stop it, Jasmine,' I said. 'Stop crying.' But she would not stop. So I let her lie there and cry. There was no one about anyway. I sat down on the nearest bench and rested my arms on my knees. I could hear all the church bells chiming. I wondered if they were ringing for Christmas Mass or if it was the invasion warning. I wondered how long we would be shut away here, cut to pieces in this uncertain world between hope and despair. Two nurses with a stretcher ran past us, throwing disapproving frowns at Jasmine as they vanished down another corridor.

'Come on, Jas,' I said, trying to pull her to her feet. 'They will throw us out if you don't stop that crying.'

'No.'

'Stop it. Come on. Mama is being brave – why can't you?'

Jasmine turned over and murmured something into her hair.

'What?' I said.

'Mama is going to die, isn't she?'

'No,' I said. 'It is probably going well. It was just like this when you were born.'

But it hadn't been like this. My mother and Leo had been together. I had waited out on the apartment steps, and every few minutes, Leo had come out and told me that things were going well, with a strange glitter in his eyes. Everyone had known then that it would be all right; no one had doubted it. I wondered if the best times lay behind us already. That thought made me feel old and tired, and I didn't want to consider it any longer. 'Hush,' I said. 'Stop crying now. Come on, Jas. You're making my head hurt.'

'I'm not just crying because of Mama,' she said.

'Then what?'

'Anselm, all our things have burned up, haven't they?'

I did not know what to say. I hardly believed that we had seen what we had seen. I began to doubt that we had really witnessed it. 'It might still be all right,' I said.

'No,' said Jasmine. 'No, Anselm. I was the one who did it.'

'What?'

'I made the house burn down.'

I knelt down and looked into her face. It was streaked with tears and red blotches, and her hair lay plastered over it. I pushed it away. 'Listen to me, Jasmine,' I said. 'It was not you.'

There were footsteps behind us, and we both looked up. Father Dunstan was hurrying down the corridor towards us.

'What is it?' I said.

'The midwife came out and told us things are going better.'

'Is she out of danger? And what about the baby?'

'I don't know. But that's what the midwife said.'

Jasmine tried to brush the tears off her face with the ends of her shawl.

'How much longer?' I asked.

'A while,' said Father Dunstan. 'A good while.'

I did not know what time it was. The night seemed to have stopped altogether.

'I've got a pain in my stomach,' said Jasmine, sniffing. No

one answered her. We went back to the door and waited. From behind it came urgent voices, and my mother's cries pierced the silence. I fixed my eyes on the cracked tiles on the wall in front of us. The cracks made a chart like roads or a branching river. I tried to follow the lines from the top of the wall to the ground, rather than have to think. Jasmine was turning her christening bracelet around in her hand, whispering, 'Please come back, Papa. Please come back, Papa.' I remembered dimly, from somewhere beyond my fear, where she had got that from. It was what Leo used to do after his own parents went away.

Time passed, and nothing changed. And eventually the night drew out so long that I slept, with my head against the hard tiles and Leo's old jacket pulled up over me, because there was nothing else to do.

When I woke, Father Dunstan was standing at the window. My grandmother was sitting with her shawl in her lap, twisting it fiercely, first one way and then the other.

'What was that sound?' Jasmine was asking, shaking me by the shoulder.

'I don't know,' I said.

A burst of gunfire came from somewhere nearby. I got to my feet without knowing what I was doing. Then my mother screamed in the room across the corridor, and I came back to the real world. I sat down again and glanced about the corridor, trying to stop my heart from beating so fast.

'I wish Papa was here,' said Jasmine.

'Listen to the city,' said my grandmother. 'It sounds like a real war.'

People were shouting out there, the way they might

shout in a play, and I could hear gunshots and footsteps running up and down in the alleys. I did not go to the window. I did not want to see. None of that seemed real; our world was these two chairs and the cracked tiles and the door behind which my mother screamed again. We stared at each other, and the horror held us and would not let us go. And then there was a weak and strange cry, very feeble, and we all started to our feet.

The nurse pushed open the door and said, 'The priest? She wants the priest.'

Father Dunstan was there in a moment. My mother was lying very still in the bed; the doctor was holding something bloodstained that moved feebly.

'Is that the baby?' said Jasmine, crying. 'And what's wrong with Mama?'

'Does anyone have a cup?' said Father Dunstan quietly. 'Does anyone have something—'

'Here,' said Jasmine, and held out the alms cup from her costume.

Father Dunstan took it, and filled it with water from the metal sink in the corner. 'What name?' he said.

'Is it a boy?' said my grandmother.

The doctor nodded.

'Leo,' said my grandmother. 'Name him for Leo.'

'Leo,' said Father Dunstan. 'I baptize you in the name of the Father, and of the Son, and of the Holy Spirit.'

As soon as that sentence was over, the doctor carried the baby behind a curtain. The nurse pushed us back towards the door and closed it firmly. We stood there and listened to the silence. My grandmother was grey-faced and shaking, her perfect make-up smudged and her hair dishevelled and tears tracking courses down her face. 'I was always too hard on Maria,' she said suddenly. 'I was always too strict with her. I wish . . . Anselm, I only wish . . .' She trailed off.

People were shouting in the hospital, I realized suddenly, and running to and fro below us. With a strange kind of calm, I went at last to the window. There were soldiers in blue in the streets, marching and shouting. At the door of the hospital, a line of stretchers was moving slowly in. Some of the people on them twisted and cried out; others lay there in silence. Some of the casualties walked in of their own accord, clutching a bleeding arm or a bandaged head.

A nurse came past briskly and glanced at us. 'What are you doing here?' she said. 'There's a war on out there – we need the space. Give me those chairs. And you.' She was looking at me. 'Shouldn't you be fighting?'

My grandmother and Father Dunstan stood up, and she whisked the chairs away along the corridor and vanished. Dimly, I realized I should be. Weeks ago, I had registered my willingness. But what did that signify now?

We waited through what felt like a year more of silence and darkness. I did not know how we stood it from one minute to the next. Then, after the dawn had risen, a nurse opened the door. 'You can come in now,' she said.

My grandmother was the bravest of us. She stepped over the threshold. Then she was running across the room to my mother's bed, and we ran after her. My mother was very pale, her beautiful hair clinging to her face in wet strands. The baby lay in the nurse's arms, clenching its fists feebly. Jasmine stopped in front of the bed and would not go any closer.

'I'm all right,' said my mother weakly. 'Why are you cry-ing? We are both all right.' But she was crying too. Then the doctor was telling us that they were out of danger, and my grandmother and Jasmine made such a clamour that the baby woke and raised his thin voice and cried as well. Anyone watching that scene from outside would have thought it a sad occasion. And if tears signified anything, my brother was baptized a thousand times.

When my brother was five days old, the Imperial Order put up posters calling for the arrest of Aldebaran's last descendant. When he was eight days old, we decided to set out west. We would cross the city under cover of darkness, with the baby wrapped in all our extra clothes. We had a few belongings now, purchased hastily from the one shop in the district that had stayed open. It flew an Imperial Order flag over its door, but we were past caring about that.

Father Dunstan brought us a box with food, soap, matches, a coat for Jasmine, and other things the remaining members of the congregation had collected between them. He was leaving the city too, but not yet, he said. Not until his work here was done. 'Go to Holy Island,' he told us. 'Ask at the munitions factory for Leo. It is on Harbour Street, in Valacia. They will be able to tell you where he is living, if he is there.'

He wrote all this down, and the name of the priest, on a scrap of paper for my mother. He had sent word to people he knew there to get the information for us. Holy Island was across the border, unoccupied territory. If Leo was not there, at least we could find out where he was.

'Will you be all right, Father?' my mother asked as the priest left.

'Of course,' he said. 'God go with you on the journey. And for ever, Maria, I hope.'

★ ★ ★

After he had gone, when we had all lain down to sleep for a few hours, Jasmine asked, 'Will we see Father Dunstan again?'

'I don't know,' said my mother. 'I hope so.'

The baby let out a faint murmur. 'Shh, baby,' said Jasmine, and got up and went to the side of the cot. Under his hospital blanket, his face was pink and untroubled, as though he had been born in the greatest palace.

'Will he have another name?' said Jasmine.

'Yes,' said my mother. 'When we get to Holy Island, we'll christen him again, and he'll have another name.'

I got up and went to the window. We were all living in my mother's small hospital room; we had been ever since the night the baby was born. They had found out about the house, in the end, my mother and my grandmother. Jasmine had told them in a fit of crying. We could not go back. Every last thing we owned had gone up in smoke. My grandmother was bearing it as well as she could, but every few hours, she would fall silent and a tear would slide down her cheek, for the lost furniture from Cliff House that she would never see again. But the hospital was full of people like us, sleeping on the floors of their relatives' wards or in the corridors, because there was nowhere else to go.

'Anselm,' said my mother. 'Do you want to hold the baby?'

'Maybe,' I said. 'Later on.'

'You have hardly looked at him yet,' she said.

'I have,' I said. 'He's almost asleep. I don't want to disturb him.'

But the truth was, I could not look at him. I had sold that prophecy to Jared Wright, and he had sold it to the newspapers. The last descendant of Aldebaran on the wanted posters – that was the baby. And the Imperial Order was the government now. Their posters were the law. If the king was still in the country at all, he had gone into hiding so effectively that no one could tell us whether he was alive or dead.

The air bit sharply as we reached the coachyard. We had to go west by coach; the river had frozen solid, and no ships passed in or out of the harbour any more. There were already people waiting, but they let my mother go first because of the baby, with tired smiles that forbade our thanks. The coachman was impatient to leave. The people already inside shuffled up reluctantly on the seats.

'All right,' said the coachman. 'All right, two more. Come along now. Women and children first. You two ladies – you with the baby and the woman with the scarf.' He meant my mother and my grandmother. The other people waiting were all young men and did not protest.

'We can't go without my children,' my mother said.

'There's no space,' said the coachman. 'The little girl can sit on the floor, but there's no space for the lad.'

'When is the next coach?' I said.

'First thing tomorrow.'

My mother glanced from me to the coachman. The baby started to wail; he had been out in the cold too long. 'You go without me,' I said. 'I'll catch you up.'

'Anselm, no!'

'Just do it. I will be all right. I'll get that coach first thing tomorrow and meet you at Holy Island.'

'No. Absolutely not.'

'Mother, we can't wait another night. The hospital won't let us stay again – there will be no space.'

'But where will you go tonight?'

'Here.' I took a hundred crowns out of my pocket, then gave her the envelope with the rest of the money folded in it. 'I'll take this and go to an inn,' I said. 'Have the rest.'

'Anselm, I really don't like this.'

'Come on, let's go now,' said the coachman. He was preparing to leave, strapping someone's case to the rack and checking the harnesses.

'Go,' I said. 'I will be all right. The baby can't come with us if we have to wander about in the cold here looking for an inn, but I'll be fine. Just go.'

They agreed at last, though none of them wanted to, and got up into the coach. My mother reached out and gripped my hand. Jasmine called, 'Anselm, promise you'll come straight away!' Then the coachman swung up onto the driver's seat and shook the whip. The coach moved off, sliding on the icy road. They were all crying as they rode away, even my grandmother.

After they left me, I wandered about the city for a while. Most of the houses were locked and barred. Once or twice I passed soldiers in blue uniforms, but they did not trouble me. No one seemed to know what was going on. There were no flags flying on the castle, and the printers and the newspaper offices stood darkened. I went back to my grandmother's old building, a skeleton now, but there was nothing there, so I went to the old shop instead. The windows were smashed again. I climbed in and slept on our old sofa, wrapped in Leo's leather jacket. My only belongings were what I had with me – the clothes I stood up in,

Aldebaran's medallion, the papers Leo wrote, and a hundred crowns. Sometime in the night, heavy snow fell and covered everything. When I woke, a strange hush lay over the city.

I got up long before dawn and went out into the street. Mr Pascal's shop was locked up, and so was the pharmacist's. Jared Wright's was abandoned too. People had smashed the unbarred windows and looted all its contents. I climbed through the window and pushed aside a gold table with a missing leg. Glass and crystal were lying smashed all over the floor. I thought that the castle Ahira had once owned must be somewhere among the dust. I found a stub of candle and lit it and began searching for the prophecy. I knew it was a small hope that Jared had left the original copy here, but if he had, I wanted to find it. Jasmine had lost her letter from Aldebaran – it had gone up in flames with the wooden box – and I had sold the only other thing she had.

It was light outside by the time I found it. It was neatly folded, in the back of the broken safe on the wall, with a seal that must have come from one of Jared's rings. At first I thought it must be something else, just a useless list or a page of calculations, but like a miracle it was still there – Aldebaran's words, finger-marked at the edges but un-damaged. I put it into my pocket with Leo's papers. I took a few things from Jared's shop. I knew he was gone now and would not need them, and they were worthless things anyway – a pencil, a stack of paper burned at the edges, a box of matches, and a candle. I think I did it more to pre-tend that I had a few belongings than anything else. When I closed his safe, I remembered our own. It was still there on the wall, and in our hurry to leave, we had never emptied it.

I went back into our shop for the last time and unlocked

the safe. The things inside were just as we had left them weeks ago. But I could not take them with me. Only the parcel from Aldebaran, marked *To the baby*. I put that carefully into my jacket pocket. The sun was coming up, and I glanced back as I left our old shop. If you looked closely at the window, you could still see L. NORTH & SON faintly in the glass.

EVENING
THE TENTH OF JANUARY

We came to Holy Springs late on the night of the tenth of January, and across the water glittered Holy Island. It looked very close; I could make out its cliffs and a mountain and even the lights of the city. A strange coldness came over me and made my heart ache, and I wanted to go with Mr Hardy across the water and find my family again. They might even be with Leo now. Things might still be all right. But I had already decided, in the cold nights of the journey. I was going on alone.

The last ships left at midnight. The woman and the boy, Esther and Matthew, gripped our hands politely, then turned and walked away. I watched them, our companions on the road, already becoming strangers, until they were lost to us altogether.

Then Mr Hardy turned to me. 'Are you sure you will not come with me?' he said. 'It may be your last chance for some time. They say the army are closing every state boundary.'

I hesitated. I had studied the notices with the listings of the ships, and still I did not know where else I would go. And then it had appeared clearly to me, out of the dark. A new sign, in green, pasted up over the rest. 'Workers required for factory,' it read. 'Board and lodging paid. Arkavitz, Northern Passes.'

The first ship the next morning left at six for Arkavitz, according to the notice. And it was enough of a sign, so I decided. 'No,' I said. 'No, go on without me. I will come as soon as I can, but I have other things to do first.'

'Finding your father's grave?' he said. 'And finding Michael?'
I shrugged. 'I suppose so.'

'Can I take them some message?' he said. 'Can I bring them
news at least? Perhaps it will make them gladder to see me, if I
have news of you.' He gave a dry laugh that became a cough. He
had been twisting his hands together nervously all the way along
this last stretch of the coast road, his eyes never leaving Holy
Island. I wondered how it must be for him, to think of seeing Leo
again after so many years without hope.

'Tell them I'm sorry,' I said. 'And that I promise I'll come
back. And will you please write to me when you know their
address?'

'Where will you be?'

'That factory on that board.'

'Anselm, I don't know if the post is still running.'

He lowered his voice as he said it. There were guards about the
harbour, but we did not know which side they belonged to.
The place seemed ominously subdued, and no one stood about for
long if they could help it. 'If it is,' I said, 'send me a letter.'

'All right. Very well.'

'I will come back soon,' I said. 'Tell them that. And give Leo
these.'

'Of course.' He took the papers and gripped my hand very
tightly. I kept the story I had been writing for my brother, but the
parcel for the baby went with him. 'Are you certain . . .' said Mr
Hardy.

'Yes.'

'Let me tell you something,' he said. 'It is one of the only things
of worth I feel I wrote: "We see condemnation everywhere when
condemnation is in our own hearts." '

'How do you mean?' I said.

He was growing weary now, with the long journey or with

something more serious. He coughed for a long time before he answered. 'I betrayed my family, a long time ago,' he said. 'No, don't look at me like that – it's true. I betrayed them. I left my two young sons and vanished, and they didn't know where I had gone. Let me tell you, from that day forward, every street had only young boys in it. Every marketplace, every crowded theatre, was full of fathers and their sons. When I opened the Bible, it was Saul and Jonathan, David and Solomon, St Joseph and Jesus. Do you understand what I am saying?'

I nodded, because he wanted me to.

'I don't think you are a bad person, Anselm,' he said. 'I've heard your story, and I don't think you have done half as much wrong as you think you have. Why condemn yourself to exile out of this misplaced sense of guilt?'

'I've decided,' I told him. 'I want to go north.'

He gave up protesting then. The ship to Holy Island was not leaving for another hour, and we went to an inn and sat watching the lights of the harbour. 'But that isn't all,' he said. 'You never told me the last part. You never told me how you ended up on this journey.'

There was really nothing left to tell. By the time I got to the coachyard, that morning I left the shop behind for ever, it was too late to travel west. The Alcyrians had started to surround the city with roadblocks. The driver shook his head and talked about going south and along the coast and the bad state the roads would be in. We set out anyway. There were four of us – an old man, a woman, a boy, and me. On the first stretch of the journey, I took out the pencil and paper and began trying to write, and Mr Hardy asked me about my troubles. 'That's all,' I said. 'And now we're here.'

Mr Hardy thought for a long time. 'Yes,' he said at last, stirring and taking out the papers I had given him. 'And I might as well know how this story finishes too.'

He handed them to me, and I read to him. It was a familiar ritual with us now, and it made a kind of farewell.

Once, Richard and Juliette had crossed the Channel to Europe. Richard had imagined it would be something like his homeland. One night he dreamed about that journey again. But this time Aldebaran was with him, not Juliette. It was a rough ferry crossing, and when the stars came out and the wind finally died, they stood at the rail and watched the horizon rise and fall, the lights of the ship reflected in the smooth water beneath the waves. The deep driving roar of the engine held them captive. As far around as Richard could see, there was nothing else but the ferry and the dark. The stars looked strangely bright, as bright as the stars had been once in his homeland.

'Before I go away,' said Aldebaran, 'I am going to record my life's work. All that I know about magic. Or at least, all that is important.'

He sighed. Richard thought that it was a strange and terrible sound, like a prayer for help.

'I am going to write a final prophecy,' said Aldebaran. 'To pass my work on to others. And it is only fair to give them some instruction.'

'How do you mean, instruction?'

'I want to set out my theory about what magic really is.'

'That does not sound like you,' said Richard. 'Explaining things that do not have to be explained.'

'I will not exactly explain. Only leave a few ideas, in case my successors find themselves without inspiration.'

'Tell me,' said Richard, 'how bad is the situation going to become?'

431

'It might be salvageable,' said Aldebaran. 'But there are so many things wrong. Even magic is dying.'

'How can magic die out? It is a force of nature.'

'Not exactly,' said Aldebaran. 'It is nothing mysterious at all. The generation that came after yours was so persecuted under the old regime that they nearly all refused to develop their powers. I have a nephew, a very talented boy, who let his skill fade and die away, because he did not have the heart for it. Surely you know what I am talking about.'

Richard realized faintly, from outside the dream, that this was a conversation he and Aldebaran had had years ago. His mind had reordered it somehow and put it onto the ship and dredged it up again in every detail. 'I was the only one from my school who went on to be initiated as a great one,' said Richard, just as he had said back then. 'The others, the younger ones, all burned their books and left before their final year. Even I had doubts. Look.' He rolled up his sleeve and showed Aldebaran the rusted metal band that had been there since his days in a secure unit for children with powers. 'But I always assumed,' said Richard, 'that people had the talent but not the will to act.'

'The will to act,' said Aldebaran, 'is the talent. Lose one and the other vanishes.'

Richard hardly understood this, so he fell silent and stared into the black ocean pitching under them. He had not understood it at the time, and he didn't now. But when he woke, it was with a strange thought. That account Aldebaran had written, the record of his life's work, must be out there somewhere.

On the day agreed, at six in the morning, Juliette began

packing. She did not have a suitcase – she had never travelled with Richard on his journeys – but she filled up several plastic bags and her leather school satchel with all the belongings she had taken with her to the hotel. Sleet was driving down the window. Juliette put on several jumpers and her school coat, a drab grey duffel coat that clashed with the rest of the uniform. As she shut the rickety wardrobe, her green hat fell from the top of it and landed on the floor. She set it back with care. It already looked like the relic of some former existence. She saw her life in this country like another person's, the life of some younger sister who she would always look on tenderly. 'Farewell,' she said to the room.

She was at the hotel's front door when Richard called out to her from above. He was at his window upstairs, still half asleep. 'Where are you going?' he said.

'Just for a walk.'

'With all those bags?'

'I'm visiting a friend.'

'Come back inside,' he said.

'I won't be long.'

Richard hesitated. In that second, Juliette ran down the steps, put her hand out for a taxi, and in a wash of grey sleet, was gone. She cried bitterly all the way to the station. But she did not go back.

On the first train, she and Ashley could think of nothing to say. He had a battered holdall and no overcoat. She could tell they were both wishing they could turn back. But if there was any chance of it, they would have decided to already. 'I wonder,' began Juliette, and stopped. She had been thinking that perhaps her father would come after them.

When they changed trains, the hills were so strange to

them that talking came more easily. The sun shone very cold and clear, and there was snow on the mountains. 'I remember that place!' Ashley kept saying, until she laughed at him. The wind cut bitterly when they got off the train.

'It's getting dark,' said Juliette. 'Let's find somewhere to stay.'

They ended up at a bed-and-breakfast on the outskirts of the town. At the end of the garden, chilled sheep huddled against the fence. Their bleating made Juliette's heart cold, but at the same time, something in her chest was loosening its grip. She realized she had grown too used to the greyness and the smoke of the city. The sheep knew and cared nothing about Belgravia.

Juliette went to Ashley's room and sat on the bed and said, 'Talk to me.' Ashley was studying maps and did not want to be distracted, but eventually he closed them and came and sat beside her.

'My aunt used to run a hotel like this,' he said. 'But bigger. It was the best place in the whole valley. My mam worked there, and I went to the school in Lowcastle. I think I was happy then. I think that was the time when my life made the most sense. And one time I saw my father.'

'How?' she said.

'I don't know. He was just there one night, on the hill with the stone circle. You can see it from here.' He guided her to the window and drew the curtain aside. Through the darkness, she could make out the outline of the stones against the sky. 'I'd forgotten,' he said. 'Afterwards, I couldn't remember it properly. But it happened. Like the story you told me, about the boat and the river when you were five years old.'

'Do you think it's because it's too unbelievable?' said Juliette. 'So you just forget?'

'Maybe.' He sat back down and turned over the maps. 'Tell me about your own life.'

'Mine?' said Juliette. 'I can't remember much before I came here. I remember the castle on the rock. It was red – the stone was red. And our house had railings and red and green windows.'

'Red and green windows?' said Ashley. 'Why?'

'I don't know. I think it was an idea of my mother's.'

They talked for a long time, until Juliette's head began to nod with exhaustion and she fell asleep. He covered her with the quilt and slept in the armchair. His last thought as he drifted away was that this girl's father would probably come after them and kill him. Then he thought of nothing else except the lake and the mountains. And the sheep bleating, the one sound he had forgotten, ran like a familiar song through all his dreams.

When Richard came running down the stairs, there was some kind of commotion going on at the reception desk. He registered it only dimly. He pulled up his coat collar and went out into the sleet. Juliette had already gone; the taxi was rounding the corner. He shouted her name anyway, then ran back up the steps. In the shelter of the doorway, he tried to think. But he could not concentrate with all the noise behind him.

'I'm sorry,' one of the hotel employees was saying, brushing sleet out of her hair. 'I would have been here on time, but my son—'

'It's not good enough,' the manager was saying. 'You've been unreliable from the beginning.'

Richard turned to go back up the stairs. He didn't want to be here when this woman was fired. He would ask James to fetch the car and he would go out and look for Juliette.

The woman was close to tears as he edged past. 'It's my son,' she said. 'He said he was going to meet a friend and left without telling me where he was going, and he had half his belongings with him. I have to go after him.'

'You can do that later.'

'No,' said the woman. 'No, I have to go now. I promise I'll be back by the afternoon.'

The hotel manager shook his head. He went on shaking it, and the woman said, 'All right,' and took off her badge and laid it down on the counter. 'Then I'll have to resign,' she said, and left.

Richard turned and ran back down the steps. At the bottom he almost collided with the woman. She was sitting there in the sleet, swiping angrily at the tears on her face. 'Excuse me,' said Richard. 'I could not help overhearing.'

The woman looked up at him. 'Yes?' she said.

'Your son,' he said. 'Is he Ashley Devere? Are you Anna?'

Richard knew it was too late even as he and the boy's mother were driving north, not speaking to each other. They stopped in cold white service stations, like the one where he had bought chips that first night, and five-year-old Juliette had fallen asleep in his arms. Sometimes in the silences, he felt that weight still, like a terrible burden. He could still feel the way his arms closed around his only child. Anna Devere drank tea with several sugars; Richard, the black English coffee that he had never acquired a taste for. They drove all day and half the night, because the minor roads were treacherous with black ice, and they had to go slowly. It was one o'clock when they came to Lakebank and parked the old Rolls-Royce close up to the gates.

They crossed the grounds in silence. The inhabitants of the house, whoever they were, were all asleep. Richard and Anna went carefully across the gravel and up into the woods behind the house. The path was already trampled, but the chapel was empty.

Anna said, 'He's gone,' and sat down on the broken wall, resting her head on her hand. Snow was falling now, and it seemed like a sign, this rare English snow obscuring the night and covering her shoulders.

Richard's mind was clearer the colder it grew. 'Take the car,' he said eventually. 'Here are the keys. Drive home and wait, and I will send you word. I promise. I'll go after them. I am Aldebaran's disciple; I'm a relative of his. I won't let either of them come to any harm.'

'No,' said Anna. 'No, I'm staying here. I'm a relative of his too.'

'Trust me. I promise I will send you word. I promise.'

It took a good deal more arguing before she would be persuaded. Then she turned and shrugged her jacket over her shoulders and went away from him. He saw the car's lights come on below the trees. She sat there for a long time without moving. Then she pulled out slowly and drove off along the lake road, and the snow obscured her tracks. Richard was shivering now. He wrapped his overcoat around him and sat down in the shelter of the wall of the old chapel. He thought that this was how he would find his way home. As he grew steadily colder, he wondered if this had been Aldebaran's plan all along. His daughter was the last in one branch of the family, and Anna's son was the last in another, and he, Richard, was willing to die to protect them. It was like one of those English plays. To keep himself warm, Richard repeated lines to himself in the darkness. 'When sorrows come, they come not single spies, but in battalions!' 'Oh, now be gone! More light and light it grows. More light and light – more dark and dark our woes.'

He knew there were cheerful lines, but they never spoke to him. His was a bleak and melancholy land, and his heart wished to be back there now.

Out of the dark, Aldebaran's voice came to him, telling him that old story of the magician and his daughter, just as he had when Richard was his pupil. He had read the play since, and he knew it. The part that struck him was the ending, where the magician stood at the front of the stage and lifted up his hands and asked the audience to forgive his mistakes. And asked them to let him go.

Richard decided that he was dying of cold, but he did not have the will to get up and move. And then, out of the dark, a gas lamp emerged. It shone very brightly, and others came out, the silent lights of a city already prepared for war. The last lines of the play came to him, very clear and certain. 'As you from crimes would pardoned be, let your indulgence set me free.'

In a minute, he would get up and start out into his old city. In a minute, but not yet. Into the darkness, with a faint surprise, Richard felt his powers drifting away from him. He thought, Is this the effect of my own country? Or is it something else? Then he made himself get up slowly and go into the church. He was no longer the great one, the lord Rigel. He would go on foot and unaided by magic, and he would find them both and find Aldebaran's last descendant. He would go as the boy who dreamed of magic once, as Richard Delmar.

★ ★ ★

Anna threw her keys on the table without turning on the lights. She stood and looked out at the sleet-washed darkness. It was almost Christmas. A few lights flashed gaudily at the window of the house opposite, a plastic silhouette of Father Christmas and his sleigh taking off into the stars.

Anna had stopped on the way back and gone into a public phone box and thought about calling the police. Her fingers moved from key to key for what felt like several hours. Ashley was missing, and this man, this friend of her great-uncle's, seemed no hope at all. But what could she say? How could she start to say it? Because if people don't believe you, you can't tell them, she thought. That is the loneliest thing in the world. Not to be understood.

Bradley came in and put his arm about her shoulders and said, 'Anna, any news?'

'There will be,' she said.

She found a book and wrote in it, trying to concentrate her mind. It was something Ryan had told her about, in passing, years ago. 'Any news?' she wrote, over and over again. Eventually she heard on the still night air, 'It will be all right.' Then it vanished, and she thought perhaps it was a mistake. But its stillness stayed with her. That night, things became clear. If there were other people like her, her heart would not be at rest until she found them. She had left it too long.

When Anna slept, she dreamed about her grandmother and thought she was a child again. And then she saw Ashley, in an empty house with a blonde-haired girl, sitting close to the fire. She woke up and thought about the man called Richard, and Ryan, and her son. Maybe there was a silence constraining everyone, but those with powers understood each other. Their hearts were connected, and their *minds reached out across the miles, across the years. And if you listened and had the willpower, you could hear them speak to you.*

JUST BEFORE MIDNIGHT
THE TENTH OF JANUARY

After I finished that story, the bells of the last ships were already clanging. 'You had better go,' I told Mr Hardy. 'If you miss it, you will be waiting until tomorrow evening.'

'Yes,' he said. 'Yes, I suppose I had.'

I walked with him to the harbour. He gripped my hands and went, with his few belongings in his hand. I watched him go slowly along the gangplank. People who passed him did not glance up; no one knew that he once had been a famous man. I thought that perhaps no one would ever know, except our family. He did not have many years left. At the lighted door of the ship, he turned and waved. He looked like a saint already, on the path to some better place. I raised my hand to him. Then he disappeared from view, and the ship was moving out across the harbour. I watched its lights until they began to fade. Then I turned and walked away. I slept in the front room of a charitable innkeeper, and when it grew light, I went out and boarded the ship to Arkavitz. On the way, to pass the silent hours, I finished the story for my brother.

NIGHTFALL,
THE LAST DAY OF MARCH
ARKAVITZ

Arkavitz, Northern Passes, is a drab, grey place. It is just a few streets in the shelter of a church, the final outpost before the first pass north. The Alcyrian army took hold of it long before I arrived. And I did not find my real father's grave. There is a graveyard, but no Jean-Cristophe Ahira de Fiore lies buried there.

The factory makes tin plates and saucepans. I work all the hours of daylight, and then I sit awake and think. Sometimes in my sleep, my arms move by themselves and try to carry on working, rearranging something on a production line or checking the rivets on a saucepan over and over, until I wake up confused and uncertain of where I am. It is the kind of work that dulls your mind. Already things are changing. Two months ago, the gleaming machines of the factory made me wonder, and its noise was deafening. Now I am used to it all.

Nearly all communications are severed. But in the old newspapers that reach this place, the king's disappearance is reported again and again. KING CASSIUS FEARED DEAD, say some, or KING CASSIUS IN HIDING, or NO NEWS OF THE KING. I study all those newspapers without hope of finding out the truth. Sometimes I dream that I am my father. It probably sounds strange to you, but it is true. I can feel the scar across the right-hand side of my face and the emptiness of the socket where my eye once was. My skin feels older, as if it has been eighteen years longer in the world. And the strangest thing about this is that my soul is different. A different man, older and tougher and less sure of the rights and wrongs of life. I cannot explain it. But when I wake, just for a moment, I cannot separate myself from him. My father's letter was lost in the fire, but I know it anyway. Sentences repeat themselves in my mind. 'My Son. I see such visions. I want to die condemned, and stand condemned for ever.' In spite of the absence of any gravestone, I have found his spirit here.

Just after I arrived, I went to the graveyard and laid down a sprig of holly, the closest thing to flowers I could find. I laid it on the corner of the wall, where no graves were. Then I stood there a long time thinking of him, when he was a boy like me in this town, before he ever knew Malonia City. I disobeyed his last wish and forgave him. Because I can't live here in this grey abandoned town for ever. I can't live without all that my life used to be. Love never lets you go, my brother. It never lets you lie down and rest. But someday I will come back and find you all. Just not yet.

Parts of the story come back to me, and they are a kind of consolation. 'He does not treat us as our sins deserve or repay us according to our iniquities.' I suppose too many of us would stand condemned for ever.

At the inn in the town, the Prince and Beggar, people talk about the gangs of revolutionaries who are hiding in the hills. They are forming a resistance movement already. They come down to the farms and demand food, and people give it to them. I asked if anyone had seen a boy with untidy black hair and grey eyes and a hat with a feather. Someone said, 'Maybe,' someone else shook their head. I can send word with one of them when they next come down into the village. It is a faint hope. They all know of each other, and I believe Michael is with them somewhere. He never wanted to keep his head down. If I can't find him, I don't know what I will do next.

Sometimes I think about everyone back in the city, Father Dunstan and Sister Theresa and Mr Pascal. I wonder where they are and whether our paths will cross again. I understand that it will be a difficult task, and exhausting, to rebuild what we have lost. But what else can we do? I am too young to lie down and give up the fight.

I was trying to explain this story to you, my brother. I have written the rest of it now. Between telling it to Mr Hardy and travelling north on my own, the pages are completed. But in truth, I don't think it is right. In telling it to Mr Hardy, I have lost it. I will never write it as truthfully again. Maybe it is better not to give this to you, my brother. Your life will be hard enough already without other people's guilt to bear.

Just after I arrived, Harold North sent me a letter. It reached me yesterday. 'All is well,' it said. 'Baby is well. He is christened Harlan.'